MW00585943

Praise for The Rossetti Diaries

"Kathleen Renk takes us beyond Charlotte Perkins Gilman's "The Yellow Wallpaper," to Victorian England and into the imagined lives of women on the periphery of artistic greatness by association with the Pre-Raphaelite Brotherhood whose careers eclipsed their own. The lover and the sister of Dante Gabriel Rossetti, Lizzie Siddall and Christina Rossetti, reveal in diary entries over a century after their death their profound commitment to their own painting and poetry, respectively, along with the immense challenges in being taken seriously as artists and independent thinkers. When the women eventually meet, the passionate bond they form as friends serves as a brief respite from the society they must move among as girls/women experiencing injustices around mental health, health care, sexual abuse and artistic achievement readers will recognize today. At the same time, the novel illuminates the era through memorable historical detail such as the story behind the painting of John Everett Millais's *Ophelia*, séance societies, and abortion practices. But one of the most distinct pleasures of the novel was encountering familiar poems of Christina Rossetti resonating with the author's biographical interpretation, which renders them newly, heart-achingly, accessible. Siddall and Rossetti paid a steep price for daring to live on their own terms as artists and friends; but despite the inevitable tragedy, these are women we should see more of in narrative, women who defined themselves not through men but through their art." — Carol Spaulding-Kruse, author of *Helen Button, A novel*

"Poet Christina Rossetti and artist/enigma Elizabeth Siddal step right out of the mid-19th century and into the 21st as Maggie, a historian with artistic longings of her own, finds and reads their diaries, which have been locked away in a dusty chest in the crypts beneath St. Clement's Church. The heartfelt pages of the diaries—imagined into being by Kathleen Renk in her latest novel—bring Rossetti and Siddal to vivid life, recreating their voices to give readers a "behind-the-scenes" experience of the art created by two extraordinary women and the struggles they faced as artists and as women in the Victorian age. Though based on the works of both women and tracing the paths of their lives, Renk's novel takes us beyond the history she knows so well to tantalize the reader with what might have been." — Mary Helen Stefaniak, award-winning author of *The World of Pondside* and *The Cailiffs of Baghdad, Georgia*

"While gradually revealing the lives and love of Pre-Raphaelite poets and painters Christina Rossetti and Elizabeth Siddal, this engaging dual-time novel raises timeless questions about money, talent, inequality, and the power of sisterhood. It's a mystery, a romance, and a window onto a little-known sector of Victorian society, all in one." — C. P. Lesley, host of New Books in Historical Fiction

"The Rossetti Diaries explores the indomitable artistic aspirations and achievements of the poet Christina Rossetti and the artist Elizabeth Siddal, her brother, Dante Gabriel Rossetti's, model and eventual wife. At the engaging heart of the novel lies the tormented relationship of Siddal with Gabriel Rossetti and her struggle to realize her creative gifts." — Mary Martin Devlin, author of *The La Motte Woman*

Other Books by Kathleen Williams Renk

FICTION
Vindicated: A Novel of Mary Shelley

Orphan Annie's Sister

CRITICISM
Caribbean Shadows and Victorian Ghosts:
Women's Writing and Decolonization

Magic, Science, and Empire in Postcolonial Literature:
The Alchemical Imagination

Women Writing the Neo-Victorian Novel: Erotic "Victorians"

The
Rossetti
DIARIES

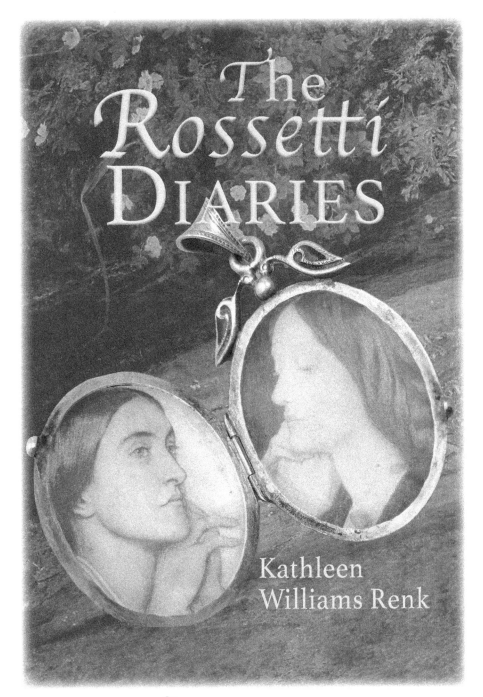

The Rossetti Diaries

Kathleen Williams Renk

Bink Books

Bedazzled Ink Publishing Company • Fairfield, California

978-1-960373-15-1 paperback

Cover artwork
by
Dante Gabriel Rossetti
"Portrait of Elizabeth Siddal" 1854
"Christina Rossetti"

Cover Design
by

Sapling Studio

"John Everett Millais (1829-1896). Ophelia (1851-2), Tate Britain, Apr 2016" by
ketrin1407. Licensed under CC BY 2.0.

Bink Books
a division of
Bedazzled Ink Publishing Company
Fairfield, California
http://www.bedazzledink.com

For Kevon, who loved poetry and a good story

Author's note: This novel employs British spelling.

"Lizzie, Lizzie, have you tasted
For my sake the fruit forbidden?
Must your light like mine be hidden?
Your young life like mine be wasted,
Undone in mine undoing
And ruined in my ruin,
Thirsty, cankered, goblin-ridden?"

She clung about her sister,
Kissed and kissed and kissed her:
Tears once again
Refreshed her shrunken eyes,
Dropping like rain
After long sultry drouth;
Shaking with aguish fear, and pain,
She kissed and kissed her with a hungry mouth.

From Christina Rossetti's "Goblin Market"

Part I

Beata Beatrix by Dante Gabriel Rossetti and Ford Maddox Brown, 1877 (Birmingham Museum and Art Gallery)

1870, London
Lizzie

As I cross the threshold, I am haunted by those who've passed through this doorway, particularly the artists, like me, who seek truth and beauty. As a woman, I was never admitted into the Royal Academy of Art, but that is no longer my goal. I've entered the National Portrait Gallery searching for Dante Rossetti's final portrait of me as Beatrice, which he painted after he murdered me.

Like his mediaeval namesake, who worshipped *his* Beatrice, Dante always idolised *and* idealised me. Until the point where he loathed me and I him. I search through the galleries but can't find the painting that he claims transfigures me from sinner to saint. I tried to destroy his rendering of me as Beatrice but failed to keep him from transforming me into her. In the portrait, he poses me with the dove, one of his patronising pet names for me, but also with the yellow poppies that I loved and which, ultimately, led to my death. Ironically and rather cruelly, he even placed poppies in my coffin to imply that poppies effected my death, and that he had no hand in my demise, but I know differently.

All I see in the galleries are the usual portraits of our monarchs. Our queen, who recently lost her Albert, appears ubiquitous, although not as omnipresent as Charles I, who left his mark despite his beheading. He's intact in all his heroic grandeur, often atop his horse, even though in real life, like me, he was humiliated and rejected. When I view these paintings, I can almost smell the paint and feel the chaos of creation, both of which I relished during my solitary moments with my paints and watercolours.

I hear the murmurs, the whispers of the elite as they gaze at the paintings of the monarchs and as they feel my chilling presence as I glide by. Someone brushes against me, and I feel the scratchy wool of his coat. Briefly, I think that I recognize the person—he looks like Dante's friend, William Holman Hunt, but I think that this can't be because Hunt has likely travelled once more to the Holy Land in his quest to find *his* version of Beatrice, his lodestone, his Holy Grail.

I will not be found here, because I am not a queen, even though Dante painted me, when he finally married me, as Regina Cordium, the Queen of Hearts. I am not a monarch; I am a myth.

Portraits of writers are exhibited on the second floor—Mr. Dickens, who disparaged and mocked Dante and his friends in the all-boys club, the Pre-Raphaelite Brotherhood; the utopian Sir Thomas More, who lost favour with Henry VIII and then lost his head. I spot the painting of that alluring cad, George Gordon, Lord Byron, dressed in Albanian garb. I study the portrait and note the vibrant colours, the crimson and saffron; I admire the way that the artist captured Lord Byron's icy, audacious stare, as if he challenged anyone to confront him; he looks both virtuous and evil as he plays the hero and for a second, I see how he eerily resembles my Dante.

Alone in the writers' gallery, I search for portraits of Dante or his sister Christina, but neither have been captured as important enough as poets to be remembered in our national consciousness. He should be remembered though, not for his poetry and his paintings, but for his treachery, because he is as deceitful and merciless as perfidious Albion. Instead of being ignored, *she* should be remembered, not for being poet laureate, as she desired, but for creating an artist's studio and a woman's world with me.

I soon realise there's no hope of locating my portrait unless they fashioned a room for mythic creatures, such as myself and the Sphinx, the Minotaur, Medusa, and Beatrice leading Dante through hell.

28 September 2019
Hastings

"I'm sorry, but you should come back tomorrow," the old woman said perturbed, as she locked the church's door and began to walk away. "My Reginald is waiting for his tea."

"Might you reconsider? I'll be ever so swift," Maggie replied. "Please, I only set aside a short time for this research."

Although Hastings is famous for being the place where in 1066 William the Bastard, better known as the Duke of Normandy, put an arrow through King Harold's eye and afterwards ruled England as William the Conqueror, the historian Maggie Winegarden had never been to Hastings until now. Instead, rather than studying the Norman invasion, she specialised in the history of World War II. She'd read that after bombing London and northern industrial cities, including Manchester and her home, Sheffield, Nazi pilots, in an effort to lighten their load, dropped the remainder of their payload on Hastings. Maggie wished to investigate the Norman church, St. Clement's, which sat atop a hill overlooking the sea in Old Town Hastings, which had been frequently bombed in 1943. Following her visit, she hoped to write an article for publication about the German attack on Hastings and the decimation of countless Norman and Anglo-Saxon buildings. Such scholarship would help advance her career, for she needed to publish more articles in order to apply for a senior lectureship at the university where she taught.

But, while in Hastings, she also wished to gaze at the sea to soothe her spirit. She and her partner Bethany had had a falling out, for Bethany, a Victorian literary scholar and professor, disliked the fact that Maggie, who had studied art before turning to history, had recently started painting again after visiting the David Hockney exhibit in Saltaire Village near Bradford. Of late, she spent most of her free time mixing colours while trying to capture the shades of green that saturated the landscape of the Northern fells in Yorkshire. Bent on achieving international fame for herself, Bethany thought painting a whimsical, foolish occupation that would never help Maggie achieve the teaching rank that Bethany desired for her. But painting was Maggie's first love above all else.

When Bethany tried to dissuade Maggie from heading out once more to try to capture on canvas what she saw in and on the fells, Maggie announced, as she grabbed her easel and paints, "You don't understand. I'm an artist. I need to create. It's who I am. If I don't paint or draw, I don't feel fully alive. I've neglected part of myself for too long." But then Bethany snidely reminded Maggie that Maggie's art teachers insisted that she was no Vanessa Bell, Dora Carrington, *or* David Hockney; her art was inferior to the works of these British artists. As she walked out the door, Maggie couldn't hide her hurt feelings and she angrily replied, "Beth, how could you? That was low. You claim to love me, but what you just said was belittling and contemptuous. And you've no right to dictate how I spend my time. I'll work on my scholarship when I wish to, not when you think I should. You're not in charge of my life." That evening, after Maggie returned, she and Bethany did not speak and for the first time in their seven-year relationship, they slept in separate beds. In the morning, Maggie boarded the train to Hastings.

But, for now, Maggie tried not to think about that row and the rift between her and her lover. She'd visit the church to gather facts for her research and then she'd descend to the shore to study the sea. She would put off thinking about Bethany's offensive remark, her orders about how to live and thrive. Instead, Maggie would observe the way the sunlight danced on the waves. She would try to mimic nature and paint what she saw before the sun hid its face for the night. There would be time later to sort out her relationship with Bethany.

"If you promise to be quick, I'll let you in; my Reginald is not a patient man," the caretaker replied gruffly, as she turned back toward the church.

"Oh, thank you so much. I promise I'll be brief."

As she pointed her cane toward an exterior wall, the old woman spoke in a more congenial but authoritative manner. "You might be interested to note that there's still a cannonball left in the building from one of the countless French attacks over the centuries."

"Indeed. I'll be sure to take a look after I see the interior. Why *was* the cannonball left in place?"

"I'm sure the town fathers wished to remember our troubled history with the French who live straight across the channel," the caretaker remarked as she placed a large skeleton key in the lock. "Who knows when they'll return to try to decimate us once more."

The heavy oak door groaned as the caretaker struggled to open it. Maggie immediately saw that St. Clement's resembled countless Anglican churches in England. The baptismal font in the back, the choral pews perpendicular to the altar, the magnificent and elaborate arched stained glass behind it that depicted the crucified Christ.

As they walked down the right aisle, the caretaker related the church's history. "The original church washed away, for it was foolishly constructed too close to the sea. This edifice was built in 1286; even so the French ransacked the town and destroyed the church in 1339 and 1377, so the townspeople rebuilt it in 1380." Maggie thought about this woman's particular disdain for the French, which was not unusual for people of her generation. Youngsters during World War II, they were influenced by their parents, who often considered the French cowards and enemies, even though they were allies at the time.

Maggie nodded to acknowledge the caretaker's words, but then looked up at the ceiling and was overcome by the beauty above her. The dome resembled the sky itself. Painted a robin's egg blue and dotted with wispy white clouds, in each corner the virtues of Faith, Hope, Charity, and Fortitude were allegorically depicted as graceful maidens holding flowers; "Fortitude" grasped yellow poppies. No doubt the architect placed those figures there to remind parishioners over the centuries which virtues were most important, if one sought heavenly salvation from the perpetual miseries of earthly life. Then Maggie turned toward the wall and glanced at the unadorned, clear glass that graced each arched window.

The caretaker noticed that Maggie's gaze had shifted and said, "You're probably wondering about the clear glass. In 1943, when the German devils mercilessly bombed this area, all of the stained glass shattered from the blasts that destroyed the building next door, the Old Swan Inn. Afterwards, the congregation thought it prudent to install plain glass in the windows, but they did commission the artist Philip Cole to design and create the glass behind the altar."

"Oh, I see. That makes perfect sense," Maggie remarked as she turned toward the altar. "The altar glass is extraordinary. I like how the artist used bold colours, reds and yellows, to depict the disciples and onlookers, but Christ is dressed in pure white, as if He were already resurrected."

"True enough," the caretaker said and then paused. "You seem attracted to art. Perhaps you'll wish to look in this direction." She pointed toward a painting Maggie instantly recognized. It was one of the earliest of the Pre-Raphaelite paintings, painted by Dante Rossetti. It was his *The Annunciation*, later called *Ecce Ancilla Domini* (Behold the handmaiden of the Lord), where Rossetti posed his prepubescent sister Christina as the Virgin, and his brother William as Angel Gabriel. Christina seems surprised and fearful, nearly cowering in the presence of the angel. She appears hesitant to accept her role as a handmaiden of the Lord, much like Jesus's reluctance to do God's will. Maggie recalled from her Art History course that some Victorian art critics denounced the painting for being too earthy and sensual. The child Mary is in her bed, perhaps awakened from sleep by a male angel who has snuck into her bed chamber. The wingless angel has flames at his feet, and he's handing a lily to Mary, but she is not reaching out to accept it. The angel is also rather scandalous, for his bare skin can be easily seen through his gossamer clothing.

"Oh, my! Why does the church own a Rossetti painting? Were the Rossettis parishioners here? Did they live here at any time?"

"Heavens no. But Christina Rossetti and Elizabeth Siddal frequently sojourned in Hastings, and Elizabeth often painted in Old Town. Most importantly, I suppose, is the fact that Dante Rossetti and Miss Siddal were married here in 1860. In fact, last May 23rd they were married here one hundred and fifty-nine years ago," she proudly replied. "We've been told that the painting, which is a copy, was a gift from the family in 1928 on the centenary of Dante's birth. During that time, the church community created a memorial to the Rossettis, including, of course, Dante's wife, Elizabeth. Did you know that she was also an artist?"

Maggie had no idea that this old church exhibited a famous Rossetti painting, well, a copy of one. And she wondered why this particular painting was given to the church and not one of Lizzie Siddal, who Maggie knew was Dante's favourite subject who mysteriously died of a laudanum overdose. Whether a suicide or an accident no one really knew. "How unexpected it is to have this painting of Christina as the Virgin adorning the wall of this church," she said as she gazed into Christina's frightened eyes. "Yes, I've heard that Elizabeth drew and painted, but I've never studied any of her work. By any chance, do you know why this painting was bestowed on the church and not another, perhaps one of Elizabeth Siddal, who was Dante's almost exclusive subject. He frequently painted her as the Italian Beatrice, the mediaeval Dante Alighieri's 'beloved.'"

"Yes, I'm aware of Dante's preference for Elizabeth as his subject and his obsession with Dante Alighieri. It seems Rossetti somehow thought that he was the new Dante, the Victorian one, I suppose. I can't say why the family gave the church this painting of Christina," the caretaker replied. "But I suppose it's because Christina was a devout Anglican who attended this church when she visited Hastings."

"I see." Maggie turned away from Christina's fearful face. "I wonder what Christina was thinking as her brother posed her as the girl that God impregnated."

The caretaker blushed. "You're a bold one. I'm sure Christina considered it an honour, after all she was devoted to God."

"Did the Rossetti family leave any documents that relate to the gift? Perhaps they'd explain Dante's interest in this subject, this Annunciation, this announcement that Mary will give birth to God. If so, I'd love to see them."

The caretaker hesitated. "Are you a literary critic? We don't allow such people to study our archives. The vicar thinks they perhaps misconstrue such papers."

"No, certainly not. I'm not a whimsical person. I'm Dr. Maggie Winegarden, an historian in Sheffield, but I study painting as my avocation. I've seen the Pre-Raphaelites' paintings at the Tate. Unfortunately, my Victorian Art History course only focused on the Pre-Raphaelite male painters." Maggie not only thought about her own attraction to these painters but also about Bethany's interest in and knowledge of the Pre-Raphaelite Brotherhood, the painters and writers who referred to themselves as the PRB and who shook up the Victorian art world when they challenged the style of the time. Instead of painting, as the Royal Academy painters did, banal portraits of Queen Victoria's spaniels and ponies or a herd of cows grazing in a bucolic pasture, the PRB painted stunning portraits of long-haired, lithesome women, often portrayed as mediaeval maidens. The most famous painting and the one most reproduced was John Everett Millais's *Ophelia*, a painting that Lizzie Siddal modelled for in a cold bath that was supposed to mimic the stream that Ophelia floated down and drowned in after Hamlet rejected her. Maggie recalled that Lizzie herself nearly died from lying in that bath after the candles resting below the bath blew out with a gust of wind. Bethany wasn't as fascinated as Maggie was by the paintings, for Bethany claimed she couldn't comprehend art; she had no head for it, but she had written numerous articles about the poetry, especially Dante Rossetti's "The Blessed Damozel" about a dead lover looking down from heaven with longing for her living partner.

The caretaker nodded and seemed reassured. "Well, in that case, we do have a large chest full of papers that the Rossetti family buried in our catacomb for safekeeping. I don't think anyone has glanced at the papers in years. According to the vicar, Reverend Mr. Carson, they're rather a jumble, if you know what I mean, and quite old and delicate. If you come back tomorrow, you may look at them, if you assure me that you'll take care as you handle them. You'll need to wear gloves. She placed her finger on her chin as if considering something. "The vicar's on holiday, but I think he'd allow you to take a peep at them, since you're no literary sleuth. You may look around a bit more, but I must lock up soon. I must get my Reginald his tea or he'll be beside himself, wondering where I am. He'll think that I stumbled and fell down the hill and may try to come find me."

"Oh, dear. I hope your Reginald stays put. I'm sorry, I didn't catch your name."

"I'm Mrs. Reginald Highclere."

"Yes, thank you kindly, Mrs. Highclere. I've seen enough for today," Maggie replied. "I don't need to look around, but I would like to return in the morning if it isn't too much trouble. What time is best?"

"Be here at eight sharp. I'll have fed my Reginald by then."

"Oh, I'll be here early," Maggie said, as the caretaker locked the door and ambled down the path, gingerly placing her cane on each stone step.

Maggie didn't pause to observe the cannonball left behind by the French. She knew that her research plans had changed. She would not travel to London tomorrow nor return to Sheffield the day after. She felt exhilarated at the thought that there might be a treasure trove of Rossetti writings that no one had perused. Perhaps they'd provide a hint about Christina's attitude toward being cast as the Virgin or about Lizzie Siddal's sudden death, something Maggie had long wondered about. She considered what Bethany would think of such a literary cache; surely, if genuine, such a find might change all that we know about Dante Rossetti, his art, and the women associated with him. And Maggie speculated about what Bethany would do with it if she got her hands on such treasure. Surely, such a find would give Bethany fame and fortune, the two aspirations she most desired.

Maggie stood on the hill and felt the sun warm her face. She looked down the path toward the sea, watching the sunlight sparkling on the water. She felt excited as she started to descend the path, recalling that the Pre-Raphaelites painted from nature. So, today she would work like a Pre-Raphaelite artist. She would study the light on the sea and paint until the sun sank in the sky, and then in the evening she would spend time on her laptop learning more about Elizabeth Siddal. She hoped that the inn she was staying at had a strong Wi-Fi connection; otherwise, the evening's research would be futile, and she would have to try to imagine what it was like to be Lizzie Siddal.

29 September 2019
Hastings

Mrs. Highclere was waiting for Maggie in the church vestibule.

"Please forgive my tardiness, Mrs. Highclere. I set my alarm for half seven, but it failed to ring," Maggie said. "Perhaps I accidently turned it off because I was tired. I painted near the sea for several hours last night. I do hope you haven't waited long."

"You'd best get yourself an old-fashioned, windup timepiece if you wish to be punctual. And perhaps you shouldn't spend so much time painting by the sea," Mrs. Highclere said. "Well, never mind. I've been folding altar cloths and trimming the candles. I had things to do. If you'll follow me, I'll take you to where the chest is buried. It's rather dark down there; we'd best tote a candle," she said as she lit an altar candle.

"Might I carry a candle also, Mrs. Highclere? It's also rather dark on these steps. I don't wish to stumble and fall on you."

"I don't wish to have that happen either. I don't have time to go to hospital. Who would take care of my Reginald? You're welcome to fetch a candle from the altar, Dr. Winegarden. Or there's a torchlight in the office if you prefer. I'm not sure whether the batteries work though."

"A candle will be fine. Seems more fitting as we descend into the crypt," Maggie said with a little chuckle, as she grabbed a second candle and lit it. Even so, she now wished that she had brought along the smart mobile phone that Bethany had given her on her birthday, instead of the old flip phone she mostly used for emergencies. A bit of a Luddite in terms of technology, she didn't think she needed a bells-and-whistles type of phone, and she fretted about privacy issues associated with these gadgets, but at this moment she could have used the torchlight on the smartphone, especially when examining whatever was contained in the chest.

The stone steps were steep and narrow, and Mrs. Highclere proceeded gingerly with cane and candle in hand. As Maggie descended, she smelled the mustiness of the damp stones and felt the coolness of the catacombs, which sent a shiver through her. She wondered what or who else might be buried in the crypt along with the Rossetti treasure.

"Mind your head here," Mrs. Highclere instructed as she bent to go under a low-hanging lintel. "I suppose those who built this catacomb were far shorter than us."

"Either that or they never wanted anyone to descend into its depths," Maggie replied. "It's rather grave-like, isn't it?"

"I wouldn't know. I've never been in a grave. Have you?"

"Well, no. But this is how I imagine it. Cold, dark, damp, silent."

Mrs. Highclere reached the bottom step and then held her candle over a large chest. "This is the trunk that someone in the Rossetti family placed here. As I said, it's a jumble of writings. I believe some have been read but not all. Did you bring gloves?"

Covered with dust, dirt, and mould, the trunk looked as though it had once actually been buried. Mrs. Highclere dusted the top of the chest with a handkerchief, sweeping the grime onto the stone floor.

"Yes, of course. I'll put them on right now." Maggie placed her candle on one of the sarcophagi, removed her white gloves from her trousers' pocket, and pulled the gloves onto her hands.

Mrs. Highclere fetched a large key out of her jacket and unlocked the chest.

"I wonder why it's locked. Has it always been so?" Maggie asked, as she crouched near the chest.

"Yes, this is the way we received it many decades ago, locked up tight. And for the longest time we had no key that fit the lock. I suppose it was lost in the transfer from the Rossetti estate to the church. So, we had one made to fit the lock to ensure that the contents were not destroyed after the catacomb flooded a few years ago. At that time, the vicar opened the chest and found the documents unharmed, and then he read some of the contents. I believe the vicar is the only one who's done so. He told me that he found nothing of great interest, but the vicar isn't much of a scholar. He possesses no literary acumen or historical curiosity whatsoever. I often wonder how he graduated from university. He spends much of his time in the pub drinking ale and playing darts or billiards with other lackadaisical fellows. Well, I'll leave you to it. The dampness makes my old bones ache."

"You're leaving me here? You don't wish to see what's inside?"

"Certainly not. I have no wish to read the contents. Never have. The vicar told me the documents are Dante Rossetti's musings about his rather lacklustre artistic career before he fulfilled his destiny and painted his masterpiece, *Beata Beatrix*, his famous painting of his dead wife. You know some say that he posed Elizabeth while she was dead so he could sketch her. I don't know if I believe it but based on what I know of the dastardly fellow, it could be true.

"I'm not in the least bit interested in Dante Rossetti's thoughts. But I'd be interested if the writings were Christina's or Elizabeth's. I so love Christina's poetry. We often sing 'The Bleak Mid-Winter' at this church on Solstice. Do you know it?"

"Of course. It's a beautiful poem and a comforting hymn. We sang it at school just like everyone else."

Mrs. Highclere nodded. "You know that Elizabeth Siddal also wrote poetry? I haven't read any, but I would like to. Don't think it's available anywhere. Strangely, some writers now label her Britain's first supermodel. That seems an odd and rather degrading term for a Victorian female artist and poet, don't you think? It reduces her to a mere body. She was more than that I suspect. I'm intrigued by *her* paintings and poetry, not the portraits men painted of her, even though the portraits are quite stunning.

"Well, I'll leave you to it. You'll have a time making sense of the papers and putting them in some sort of order. I think the vicar tried but gave up. I do know, according to the vicar, that there are some incredibly old journal entries from the mid-Victorian era. Why they're buried here no one knows."

"Perhaps a family member wished them to remain secret?"

"Could be. Or perhaps they just wished to dispose of them. And now, at this point, I doubt the descendants know the trunk exists. So, if you read some of its contents, maybe you'll be able to add to the historical record about what we know about Dante Rossetti. You said you're a sort of muse of history, a Clio, correct?"

"Indeed, I am."

"Well, then, here's your chance to make history, I suppose," Mrs. Highclere said as she slowly ascended the steps. Maggie briefly listened to the sound of Mrs. Highclere's cane as it hit the stone steps; the sound reverberated throughout the crypt.

Without Mrs. Highclere's additional candle to illuminate the darkness, the catacomb felt more like an actual graveyard, which of course it was. The almost total darkness and the knowledge that she dwelled among the dead made Maggie shudder. To try to calm her fear, she reached for her candle. She placed it on the floor and carefully opened the chest. The lid was heavy, and she had to use both hands to hoist it. Even before the chest was fully open, the acrid scent of mildew hit her nose. She picked up the candle again and held it over the open chest and then carefully removed a handful of yellowed paper on top that crinkled as she lifted it out of the chest. Oddly, the contents were not chaotic but were neatly stacked documents arranged in rows. Maggie noted that, even though the papers smelled musty, the writing was completely legible, as if someone had written them yesterday and not over a century ago.

As she handled the papers, she heard a scurrying in the corner. Must be a mouse or a rat. She trembled a little but told herself that, although such vermin are filthy creatures, they would not harm her. Besides, she was intruding on their habitat.

Even though she hesitated to sit where rodents had likely walked and lain, she spread her jacket on the cold stone floor and sat down. She began to read, trying to ignore the scratching she heard in the corner of the catacomb. As she concentrated her attention, she soon discovered that the entries, which appeared to have been removed from diaries, were not a jumble as Mrs. Highclere claimed. Oddly, they were in perfect chronological order beginning in 1845 and each was labelled by the same elegant hand as to who the writer was. She wondered if the vicar had placed them in order or if they actually arrived that way, that one of the Rossettis or their descendants had read and organised the entries as if they could be compiled into a book. And, as she rifled through the contents, she quickly realised that the writings were not Dante's but surprisingly were his wife's and sister's. Why in the world had the vicar lied to Mrs. Highclere? What was he trying to hide? Why were these diaries buried in this old church? Why weren't they published?

While she read the first entry dated 1845, labelled as Lizzie Siddal's concerning a notorious murderer that Lizzie knew as a child, Maggie felt as if someone was watching her. Had Mrs. Highclere trundled down the stairs? No, Maggie would have heard her. She peered into the darkness and saw no dark shadow or amorphous form, no living being or real or imagined ghost, what locals up North in Yorkshire where she came from called a barghest. So, she told herself she was being silly. No one's here. I can't let my imagination run wild and stop reading because of fear. There's no bogeyman or woman haunting this place. I must be sensible, rational, not given to whimsy. These diaries are too important. They could change what we know of Lizzie Siddal and Christina Rossetti. They could reveal whether Lizzie committed suicide or was accidentally overdosed. They could shed light on Christina's poetry and her cloistered life. She never married, Maggie recalled, even though Christina was engaged at least once. These diaries could even change what we understand about the Victorian art world. I must continue.

So, Maggie read until the candle burned down to a nub. She ignored the sense that someone or something nearby watched her discover this treasure. She hated to shut the chest, because as she read, she heard Lizzie's and Christina's voices. Closing the chest, she had stifled them once more. Even though the crypt was cold and eerie, she decided that she would descend into its grave-like depths as often as necessary to hear Lizzie's and Christina's voices and she would embrace whatever or whomever she encountered there. And next time she would bring a camera to photograph the entries to prove that the diaries exist.

2 February 1845
Lizzie

We now live next to the Deaf and Dumb Asylum and the Glue Factory. In both cases they parade their charges, the mute and deaf children, and the condemned horses around, putting them on display. Fortunately, the children are not disposed of as the horses are; the horses are sacrificed so that we may bind objects together.

I am now sixteen, but when I was a child of eight, we lived below Mr. James Greenacre, our greengrocer, who in 1837, was hanged for beheading and dismembering his intended. He seemed like such a nice, genteel man, for a grocer turned murderer. My mother bought all of our fruit from him— our apples, quinces, lemons, oranges, pomegranates, and figs, and, in fact, he was our landlord. He offered me a quince or an apple whenever I visited his store, and he once gave me a rag doll, telling me I was a pretty girl, a little queen. He was a giant of a man; like Atlas, he once carried me across the filthy street so I wouldn't muck up my new pinafore.

His affianced, Hannah Brown, was a young woman who he believed possessed immense wealth. He courted her and paraded her around our neighbourhood near Hyde Park like she was the Queen of Sheba, and he was some grand sheikh. He wanted his neighbours to know how high-class he would become when he married his young woman who defied convention. She refused to wear a corset and wore the latest Parisian fashions. Unfortunately, when he discovered that she possessed absolutely nothing, other than her fancy bonnets and gowns, he cut off his beloved's head, cut out her heart, sliced her body into pieces, and then, with the help of Sarah Gale his mistress, threw Miss Brown's body parts into various tributaries of the Thames and elsewhere. Shortly after Christmas, the police found Miss Brown's head, wrapped in a crimson handkerchief, in Regent's Canal and they discovered her torso in a sodden bag near Edgware Road. They found other parts and body organs in the tanning yard nearby and a bobby found Hannah's left hand, still sporting her gaudy rhinestone engagement ring, behind my da's ironmongery shop. The detective from Scotland Yard interrogated Da to see if he was involved in the notorious crime, wondering whether Da had sold Mr. Greenacre his butchering equipment. Da had but, like all of us, did not know that Mr. Greenacre would defy God's fifth commandment. He assumed that Mr. Greenacre would just use the knives in his grocery to slice up the goods that he sold, not cleave his intended to pieces.

For months afterward, I couldn't sleep; sometimes I lay awake until dawn; often I talked to and cuddled with my sister Lydia. On the night that Mr. Greenacre was hanged at Newgate Prison, I begged that we keep a candle burning, even though Mam said that it was dangerous and wasteful.

"Lydie," I whispered, "Mr. Greenacre might have snuck downstairs and slaughtered each of us in our beds. He was like a goblin. He cut out his beloved's heart. He could have done the same to us, and then he might have eaten us. Please, may I get in bed with you?"

"Come, don't be frightened," she said as she threw her counterpane back and made room for me.

As I climbed into her bed, I asked, "Do you suppose his ghost walked home and is upstairs? I thought I heard footsteps." My heart was pounding so hard I thought it would burst right through my chest. I snuggled closer to Lydie.

"Oh, Lizzie, Da said that Mr. Greenacre was buried at St. Mary's in Battersea. His ghost would have a long walk to get back here. Besides, I'll protect you if I have to." She put her arms around me and soon my heart stopped hammering.

Lydie, who is three years older than me and far wiser, always makes me feel better. Even so, I thought that the worst part of this was that Mr. Greenacre didn't look or act like a murderer. He was comely; handsome even; he had a broad forehead that indicated intelligence. He gave me gifts; besides the apple or quince that he bestowed on me, he once gave me Lord Tennyson's poem, "The Lady of Shalott," which he'd cut out of *The Times*. He knew that I was fond of drawing, so he gave me drawing pencils and a sketchbook. I trusted him and even looked up to him.

When I told Mam that I was still frightened, especially of men who looked to be good men, but were in fact goblins, she laughed. But then, when she saw that I was genuinely afeared, she advised me to be careful and always be on my guard, because all men are not what they seem, and you can't always tell from someone's looks or actions if they have a murderous, treacherous heart.

4 June 1845
Christina

I've lost myself. I'm not sure who or what I am anymore. Mother says that I cut my arm with a pair of scissors, harmed myself, but I don't recall doing that, even though my arm is sliced and bandaged. And I can't comprehend why I might have done it except that Mother reprimanded me for failing to take proper care of my ailing father. I'm confined at home, often caring for him by myself because my sister and mother must now work as governesses since Father is too ill and distressed to earn a proper living. Father spits blood and claims he's going blind. (I know that he is not losing his sight. I have seen him reading his poetry on the sly—he can see every word. He feigns blindness to try to elicit our sympathy, but I do not pity him.) Moreover, he sometimes falsely believes that his political enemies are at the door waiting to murder him. I must calm his nerves. To do that, he insists I read to him from the books he's written about the poet Dante Alighieri. When I read, Father often comes into my bedroom and forces me to sit on his lap so he can hear better and snuggle my neck when he's so moved.

The first time he coaxed me onto his lap, he seemed playful, and when I pulled away, he laughed and allowed me to return to my own chair. But more recently, whenever I try to stand, he holds me firmly on his lap and tugs me even closer.

Once when he was pulling me toward him, I struggled and asked, "Father, please may I just sit next to you?"

"Don't you love your papa, Christina?"

"Of course. But sitting on your lap is what children do. I'm no longer a child."

"No, you're not but you are still my *bambina*, and this is how Italian papas show love and affection for their daughters," he whispered into my ear. He then told me to proceed with the reading and I reluctantly complied. Father's words about Dante Alighieri tasted bitter in my mouth.

As his sole companion during the day, I am tethered to him. I am not free to grow and explore the world as my brothers William and Gabriel are.

My brothers, sister, and I have received similar educations through our mother at home until recently, but Maria and I have suffered because as girls we are prevented from furthering our education by attending a proper school as William and Gabriel are allowed; we are unable to escape our family and its expectations for us. Even so, Maria, the eldest of the four of us, has always wanted to keep up with our brothers. She has taught herself Greek; she can even read and translate it and has taught me the beginning of the *Iliad:* "Rage—Goddess, sing the rage of Peleus' son Achilles, murderous, doomed, that cost the Achaeans countless losses, hurling down to the House of Death so many sturdy souls . . ." Our maternal grandfather, Gaetano Polidori, believes that Maria is intellectually superior to my brothers, as does Father, who calls Maria the daughter of Clio, the muse of history. Maria even reads Euripides in translation. After Father learned that Maria taught herself Greek, he quizzed her daily. Father finds it disappointing that his sons, who are educated in the classics, care little about what they are free to learn.

In fact, Gabriel frequently argues with Father. One time, Gabriel became frustrated with reading Latin and threw down his copy of the *Aeneid.* He then picked up a slim leather-bound book and challenged Father.

"Papa, instead of always reading classics, you must read this poem by John Keats, who lived nearby in Hampstead; it's about Truth and Beauty."

"Bah, what would an Englishman know of Truth and Beauty? Englishmen have shuttered minds and cold, calloused hearts."

"What? You've read Shakespeare and Milton. You would discount their work?"

"Their poetry does not equal Dante Alighieri's."

"Ah, Dante's also brilliant," Gabriel replied. "I greatly admire him and naturally take his name as my own, but there are others. Poets in our time who have open, expansive minds, and hearts afire. Here, let me read a poem to you." And he began with great dramatic flair to read. "'Thou still unravish'd bride of quietness, Thou foster-child of silence and slow time . . .'"

Father listened, then raised his arm as if to swat not just Gabriel but Keats himself away. Father shook his head, then shuffled toward his study.

Not dissuaded, Gabriel laughed and continued to read, raising his voice even louder. "'Sylvan historian, who canst thus express a flowery tale more sweetly than our rhyme . . .' Can you hear me, Papa? Aren't these sibilant tones?"

Father ignored Gabriel and slammed the door to his study. Gabriel laughed louder at Father's antics, and then read the rest of the poem to me, finishing with "Beauty is truth, truth beauty—that is all Ye know on earth, and all ye need to know." Gabriel mentioned that Keats was a Neoplatonist, but I didn't care, for I'm not at all certain what Neoplatonism or Platonism, for that matter, entails. I just liked the sound of the poet's words and the grand ideas. I asked Gabriel to lend me the book and for once he did as I asked. I stayed up all night reading Keats's poems and thinking about the unravish'd bride frozen in time, unable or unwilling to kiss her lover on the Grecian urn.

In addition to Keats, my brothers prefer to read bowdlerised Shakespeare, Waverley novels, and even that blaspheming atheist Percy Shelley. Unlike Gabriel, William does not argue with Father, but he quietly and covertly reads what he wants. Even so, when Gabriel is angry or quarrelsome, Father always forgives him his outbursts and his lack of interest in becoming a scholar; he coddles Gabriel because he is so much like him in looks and temperament— proud, clever, and charming; witty and provocative, a dashing Byronic hero as Father once was.

Dante, as he actually calls himself now—not his given name—Gabriel Charles Dante Rossetti, was expected to financially support our family, because he is the eldest boy. Father sent him to work at the telegraph office, but Gabriel soon quit; he claimed that he "cannot do what he ought to do."

He may be clever and talented, but he lacks self-discipline and is not learned. He is no real Dante. And even though he disappoints the family, our parents pardon him, because they consider him a genius. Thus, he's pampered and is not required to assume familial responsibility. Gabriel has been encouraged to flourish in his art because he exhibited profound artistic talent even as a young child. When he was seven, he was able to draw like an adult. He drew the Greek heroes, Agamemnon and Achilles, in their full battle gear with their delicately wrought shields.

"Look, Papa," Gabriel said as he handed him the sketch, "here are your favourite heroes."

"Did you draw this, Gabriel?"

"Yes, of course. I drew it for you."

Father puffed up his chest, picked Gabriel up, kissed him on both cheeks, and told him to continue drawing, for he had a great gift. He bought Gabriel a proper easel, artist's drawing paper, pencils, and paints, and hired an art tutor for him. Father framed that heroic drawing and placed it above his desk in his study.

Father was also delighted when Gabriel used his new pencils and paints to illustrate Father's poems and the Sicilian folk tales he told us each night. In addition, Gabriel painted the landscape of our grandpapa's farm near Holmer Green in Buckinghamshire, its orchard and pond, so accurately that you believed you could amble right into the sketch and smell the chamomile, honeysuckle, and roses.

I sometimes stare at that painting and pretend that I am at the farm with my Grandpapa Polidori sitting in his garden under an arbour of white roses where he reads me his poetry and teaches me to speak Italian.

Grandpapa hands me a rose and then says, "Christina, *annusare la rosa; è dolce comete.*"

I take the rose, inhale its fragrance, and then say, "*Nonno, voi annusare la rosa; sei dolce,*" (Grandpapa, you smell the rose; you are sweet.) He laughs, sweeps me into his arms, and bear hugs me. With Grandpapa, I feel safe and loved.

16 June 1845
Christina

As our parents' favourite, Gabriel attends an elite art school, Sass Academy. We can ill afford the fees now that Father has gone a bit mad and his Italian lessons for British men have fallen off because German is now the vogue language, ever since our queen, Victoria, married her German cousin Albert.

Gabriel has also studied painting in Bruges and Bologna, whereas I've not travelled or studied anywhere, although I long to do so.

Even though I often daydream about running away, I always tell visitors that I prefer London rather than other locations, that London suits me. I claim that I prefer London, but that is just a way to stop me from raging like a Greek goddess and losing my temper about my confinement. Mother and Maria say I must quell my temper lest I go mad, like Mother's brother John Polidori did, when he poisoned himself with cyanide and died.

Despite admonitions to stay calm, I have sometimes given into my anger. Once I reprimanded Gabriel when he boasted about his artistic talent. As he lounged on the settee and sketched, he proclaimed that he would one day be as great an artist as Titian, the brilliant Renaissance painter.

I looked up from my Bible, where I happened to be reading *Psalms* 119:37's warning about hubris. "Turn my eyes away from worthless things . . ." You know that you commit the deadly sin of vanity when you brag and claim that you'll be as great an artist as Titian."

"Christina, you pious little nun, I only speak the truth. You belong in a convent with other smug saints where you can read your Bible all day long," he said as he continued to sketch.

"Take that back, Gabriel."

"No, you know it's true. 'Get thee to a nunnery,' I say. You and Maria both belong in a cloister, the sooner the better. There's no place for you in this world."

At that point I lost my head; I became so angry that I did the unthinkable. I said words I'd heard Father shout regarding his enemies.

"*Dio ti maledica, vai all'inferno*, Gabriel!" (God Damn you, Go to Hell!)

Gabriel laughed at me and mocked my pronunciation, even though Grandpapa compliments it; instead, Gabriel told me that I'd never pass for an Italian as he does when he's in Italy. Then he tattled, telling Mother that I'd cursed. She told me to fetch a switch. While reminding me that good girls do not take the name of the Lord in vain or express anger, she humiliated me by whipping me in front of Gabriel, and then she sent me to my room without dinner. She told me to beg God for forgiveness for blaspheming and for acting and cursing like a man, for not behaving as a young lady should.

I knew that I had gone too far, saying forbidden words, and breaking the third commandment. Even so, I fumed all night, thinking about how as a male, Gabriel can do and say whatever he likes, while I must conform to what is expected of good girls. Life is certainly not fair for the fairer sex. Ruminating about this, I became so enraged that I broke a mirror and threw a chair across the room. Even though I knew it was wrong to express my feelings in this violent manner, it felt satisfying to release my pent-up rage. Finally, by morning, I had calmed myself sufficiently, after beseeching God's forgiveness and then I dissembled and acted the pious nun when I came down to breakfast, even though a storm continued to stir within me. (Later Gabriel mocked me by drawing me in a fit of frenzy—not only did I break a mirror thus bringing me bad luck, but in his drawing, I had smashed windows and a table. Like Father, Gabriel exaggerates so. His drawing enraged me once more and I tried to destroy it, but he held on to his sketch, ran out of the room, and squirrelled it away).

In contrast, as the eldest male and as an Italian, Father's permitted to curse and is even expected to show frequent emotion, rage, and passion and cry false crocodile tears. But we "mongrel" British girls must practise restraint and never cause a row or fly into a rage, especially if we endeavour to remain acceptable to our social class and exercise British decorum.

I wish that I could be Gabriel and have the freedom to do as I like and to study and travel. I would relish learning Greek and Latin, the new science and medicine, astronomy, the arts. I would sojourn in Italy, Egypt, Algeria, China . . . I would ride over mountains on a donkey, pilot a hot-air balloon, swim out to sea, traverse the Nile, safely flowing past the ravenous crocodiles.

I would then write poetry and stories about these subjects and not just about death and dying, which is all that surrounds me. Father struggles with life; he sometimes wishes that he were dead. He compares his walk from his bedroom to the privy to Christ's struggle on Calvary. He exaggerates so that I have a difficult time believing he is ill. His death is not imminent, but he acts as though it is. He acts so peculiarly that Mother no longer shares his bed.

Mother is healthy but she forces Maria and me to contemplate death and destruction. She only makes us girls, not the boys, attend church. We listen to the preaching of the Reverend Mr. Pusey, the disciple of the Reverend Mr. Dodsworth, the perpetual curate of Christ Church, St. Pancras, a High Anglican Church of the Oxford Movement. Mr. Pusey rants about the impending apocalypse, its inferno, and how Jesus will separate the sheep from the goats. (Unlike me, Maria trusts Mr. Pusey's prophecies and told me that she feared gazing for too long at the mummies in the British Museum, lest she miss the rapture into heaven!)

I know that I want to be among the sheep but why must we Christians incessantly envision a terrifying end? I would prefer a new beginning where I could gaze at the stars through my own telescope, loosen my hair out of the severe knot that I've had to adopt now that I'm fifteen and dream of a new Garden of Eden, where women take their rightful place beside not behind men.

Ever since I learned to scribble, writing has always been my salvation, my way to express my innermost thoughts, my secrets, my hidden rage. And thus, I have started to write a new poem, which I call "Hope in Grief."

> Tell me not that death of grief
> Is the only sure relief.
> Tell me not that hope when dead
> Leaves a void that naught can fill,
> Gnawings that may not be fed.
> Tell me not there is no skill
> That can bind the breaking heart,
> That can soothe the bitter smart,
> When we find *ourselves betrayed*,
> When we find ourselves forsaken,
> By those for whom we would have laid
> Our young lives down, nor wished to waken.
> Say not that life is to all
> But a gaily coloured pall,
> Hiding with its deceitful glow
> The hearts that break beneath it . . .

I try to be hopeful, but no one knows how deeply I have been injured and betrayed by one who is close to me, not even my dear sister. I do not deserve it and I know that *my* God has not preordained my suffering and injury, merely because I am female.

17 July 1845
Christina

Last Sunday, while we were in church listening to Reverend Pusey prophesy the end of the world by a great conflagration, the room started to spin, and I suddenly grew hot and felt nauseated. I called out, "Mother, help me." I felt faint and fell into Mother's arms. She placed me on the ground, turned me on my side and noticed a large red stain on the back of my gown.

She whispered discreetly, "We must get you home."

The next thing I knew I was in my own bed. Mother had changed my clothes and had placed menstrual rags between my legs and under my hips. I continued to bleed heavily and my stomach and back ached. Fortunately, Maria had warned me about how girls bleed when we become women and are able to conceive children, but she had not told me of the pain that accompanies it or the possibility of haemorrhage. All morning I worried that I might bleed to death. I did not want to die and prayed for God to spare me.

Mother tried to reassure me but because of my continued haemorrhaging, she sent a message to Queen Victoria's gynaecologist, Sir Charles. He arrived in the early afternoon and examined me in my bedroom with my mother attending. He first pressed on my abdomen and asked me if that caused me pain. I winced and nodded, for my womb was cramping. I felt a gush of blood escape from my womb, and I clenched my mother's hand. Then Sir Charles said, "I need to examine down below. I will need to have you breathe deeply and relax."

I looked at Mother and asked, "Mother, must I?"

She nodded, as Sir Charles used his elbows to spread my legs. I saw blood on my legs and was horrified. Then he quickly pulled down my drawers and touched me. I clutched my mother's hand harder and winced and pulled back. I hated the way that he touched my private parts; it felt dirty and sinful.

"Please stop!" I shouted. I shoved his hand away and closed my legs.

"All right, but I haven't done an internal examination," he said. "We can save that for another time," to which I thought, No, you will never touch me in that way again.

I sat up and pulled up my drawers, straightened my nightdress and tucked my legs up, wrapping my arms around them. Mother put her arm around my shoulders. I glared at Sir Charles, but he didn't seem to notice. I guess he was accustomed to molesting young girls.

After he wiped his hands on a towel, he asked Mother whether I indulge in too much mental activity. Mother said, "Not too much, not like her sister. Christina has always been a scribe though. She writes poetry and stories."

"Well, she must stop. Too much mental exertion engenders female problems. Her womb could wander."

Mother looked sceptical. Maria is highly intellectual, and she never had such issues, and Mother herself is quite learned. To combat my physical and "mental" affliction, Sir Charles advised that I be bled by leeches. He also prescribed iron filings steeped in beer to compensate for the loss of iron caused by my excessive bleeding.

"Is it absolutely necessary, Sir Charles, to bleed her since she's already lost a considerable amount of blood? Her menstrual rags have soaked through five times this morning," Mother said as a blush spread from her neck to her cheeks. "Couldn't she just cut back on her writing and perhaps visit the sea?" She knew I hated being bled. In the past, I had been bled with cupping and leeches for fevers and chilblains; bleeding seems the only remedy these doctors know.

"Absolutely not," Sir Charles said. "We must get her curses under control, otherwise her mental health will suffer. And she must not give into her unladylike temper as you've indicated she frequently does, for such choleric disposition also engenders female maladies and indicates a disordered mind, a type of madness."

I'm certain that Mother immediately thought of her favourite brother, John, and his tragic demise, which no one in the family talks about, and thus she relented and allowed Sir Charles to bleed me to keep me from going mad. I despised being bled and especially loathed the leeches that Sir Charles insisted on using. He tried to place some down below, but I kept my knees locked and he eventually gave up.

Oddly, I felt weaker than I felt prior to the treatment and my curse, and its associated pain continued unabated for days until it finally subsided. The only remedy that seemed to help with the pain was the hot water bottle that Mother placed on my abdomen.

Luckily, God has not chosen to take me to heaven at this time. But He has resolved to let me know that becoming a woman is a dangerous and painful undertaking.

18 July 1845
Lizzie

Even though it's been many years since Mr. Greenacre was hanged, I dreamt about him last night. In my dream, I was a small child, and I was back at our old home near Holborn as Mr. Greenacre was being marched to his death from the prison near our house. I stood in the crowd that had gathered to witness the execution. They were gleeful as they purchased mugs and flags to commemorate the death of the Edgware Road Murderer. When I saw Mr. Greenacre, I started to run away, but he recognized me and moved toward me, even though he was in handcuffs and leg irons. He rattled his chains and yelled, "Save me, Lizzie; you know I'm innocent." He lurched toward me, grabbing at my bosom, intending to pull my heart from my chest.

I cried out in my sleep, "No, I won't. Don't touch me. You cut out your beloved's heart!"

Lydie shook me awake and I wept in her arms. "How could he cut up his beloved? Had *he* no heart?"

Lydie didn't answer my question but reminded me that Mr. Greenacre cannot harm us. We are safe. He has been rightfully dead for years, and by now has certainly passed on to his judgement and eternal punishment. Even so, my dream felt so real that I felt his presence in our room, and it took me a long time to return to sleep, even though Lydie softly sang "Greensleeves" in the dark to quiet my rattled nerves.

30 August 1845
Christina

Gabriel and I are somewhat reconciled. At least we are not always at odds with each other, but I often feel alone because I miss Maria, who is working as a governess in distant Wolverhampton. I haven't seen her for months, although we frequently exchange long letters. She tells me to ignore Sir Charles and write my poetry, which has always helped me; it secures my survival and likely keeps me from going mad. Maria is the one who declared that I would be the family poet, way back when I was twelve and just starting to scribble. My poems then were immature and childish, as were the stories that I wrote about mermaids and mermen.

Today, I took Maria's advice and wrote my longest poem yet. It's about a naiad who lives under a waterfall. Each evening she travels to the ocean to find her sister, the Queen of the Ocean. She and her sister join hands and swim in the depths of the sea. No one comes between them. I liked the poem so much that I sent it to Maria with a simple sketch of the two of us perched on a rock as if we were mermaids. Here are my favourite stanzas:

> She dwells in a palace of coral
> Of diamond and pearl;
> And in each jewelled chamber the fishes
> Their scaly length unfurl;
> And the sun can dart no light
> On the depths beneath the sea;
> But the ruby there shines bright
> And sparkles brilliantly . . .
>
> The mermaids sing plaintively
> Beneath the deep blue ocean
> And to their song the green fishes dance
> With undulating motion
> And the cold bright moon looks down on us.

I imagine the two of us free to sing our songs and tell our tales without interruption or reprimand and that our song is so powerful the fishes joyfully dance in unison.

3 March 1846
Christina

After the snow melted and the daffodils sprang from the ground, it rained for three days, subsided, and then rained for seven more. Thankfully, not 40 days and nights. Of course, it often rains in London, but this rain was different—not Noah's Ark rain but just as ominous, filling the streets and gutters and lapping against the storefronts. By this time, I finally felt well enough to cope with my curses and return to church, but it had rained so much that we had trouble getting to church, even though it is around the corner from our home. *The Times* reported that the stinking Thames overflowed its banks near Battersea Park and the Tower, and the authorities advised denizens in those areas to seek higher ground. The entire Embankment was underwater. The royal gardens of Windsor Castle were inundated with filthy flood water, and parts of Eton College were submerged. The roads became rivers and carriages were replaced by punts and rowboats. Perhaps the Reverend Mr. Pusey is correct, and the world will end soon. I thought that the *Book of Revelations* predicts a "fire next time" though.

Maybe Mr. Pusey is wrong about his entire prediction. I hate contemplating and focusing on the end, the impending apocalypse. How many ministers, soothsayers, and charlatans over the centuries have convinced their minions that the end is near? Instilling fear is their way of controlling their people, their sheep. Mr. Pusey is expert at engendering fear, as are others who seek to dominate their followers.

I recently read in the newspaper about a woman in Scotland who persuaded her followers that they would bring about the Second Coming through a 40-day fast. They wasted away, became skeletons, the walking dead. Some rebelled against Mistress Luckie Buchan, who fancied herself the woman in St. John's end-times book, that final book of the Bible, when they learned that she herself did not fast but hid bacon under her cot while also eating in a carnal way with a man, one of her disciples. Her charade came to an end when her followers caught her with bacon drippings dribbling down her cheeks. Then she blamed the people for their insufficient fast; it was their fault, not hers, that Christ did not appear and rapture them into eternity.

Mr. Pusey asks us girls to fast, not to make Christ appear, but to fast as penance, sometimes for three days at a time, even when it's not Lent. We are told to eat nothing but may drink as much water as we want. We may taste and eat the communion wafer. Our mother approves of the fasting. I mostly abide by Reverend Pusey's edicts, even though I wonder about fasting's usefulness regarding sanctity and grace. And I often crave sweets and find it difficult to abstain from eating the custard tarts that our cook expertly makes. So, when meals are served, I cloister myself in my room and pray for the strength to starve myself. One night last week, I didn't possess fortitude. I was so hungry I snuck out of my room and rifled through the pantry. Famished, I ate six custard tarts in a row. Mother heard the ruckus and caught me in the act of gluttony, but she only said, "Christina, shame on you. You must not disobey Reverend Pusey who disciplines your body and tries to save your soul. I trust that you'll never do this again."

I wiped the custard tart from my face and lips and said as I swallowed, "Of course, Mother. I'm sorry that I was so weak." Afterwards, in my room, I stuck my finger down my throat and vomited to atone for my gluttony.

In church, Mr. Pusey tells us girls that we are sinful, that we resemble our mother Eve, and that we must resist temptation and starve our bodies to strengthen our souls. We must become spiritual, not carnal, beings. I think that he aims to make us invisible. He even beseeches our Lord to cut out our hearts, casting our dear Lord as a murderer: "Circumcise, yea, cut them, Lord, round and round, until none of the vanities or love of this world cling unto them; break and bruise them in pieces." Why would Mr. Pusey figure Our Lord as a murderer? And what if Mr. Pusey is as much a charlatan as the Scotswoman Buchan? Unlike Maria, who faithfully practises Mr. Pusey's rules, I would prefer to not be a heartless, fasting girl who starves herself to death, even if it is the only current means to become a saint. If it is, perhaps it's better and wiser to be a sinner.

Here's another poem that I've been working on, inspired by my nightmares brought on by my long fasts and Mr. Pusey's admonition for us to reject the world.

> By day she wooes me, soft, exceeding fair:
>   But all night as the moon so changeth she;
>   Loathsome and foul with hideous leprosy
> And subtle serpents gliding in her hair.
> By day she wooes me to the outer air,
>   Ripe fruits, sweet flowers, and full satiety:
>   But thro' the night, a beast she grins at me,
> A very monster void of love and prayer.
> By day she stands a lie: by night she stands

In all the naked horror of the truth
With pushing horns and clawed and clutching hands.
Is this a friend indeed: that I should sell
  My soul to her, give her my life and youth
Till my feet, cloven too, take hold on hell?

Would I lose my soul if I sinned and loved this world? What if the world is not a monster, a Medusa, devoid of love and prayer? What if the world contains goodness and beauty? What if it is the only paradise that we will ever experience? What would Mr. Pusey say? Do I dare ask? If I did, would he call me a heretic and cast me out as a devil?

17 June 1846
Lizzie

When I'm done with my chores, I often spend time near the Thames and watch the children, the Mudlarks, as they gather refuse, garbage that they can sell to keep their families from starving. I sit on the Embankment and study these children, so that later on I can attempt to draw them from memory. I have no formal training, but I seem to have what you might call a natural gift for sketching.

I have been drawing since I was quite young, and I even gave Mr. Greenacre, after he gave me pencils and paper and before he became a murderer, a drawing of the faeries that I believed lived under toadstools behind our flat. He pinned my drawing to the wall in his grocery and said, "Little Lizzie, you have a rare and precious talent. You are quite an artist, but you forgot to sign your drawing," he remarked as he handed me a pencil. Later, on my birthday, he gave me a small book about Titian and other painters so I could study the work of the Masters. Then he asked Da if he might pay for art lessons for me, and Da agreed; but then Mr. Greenacre killed his fiancée and was taken away to prison, so I never received the promised lessons. And I often feel badly that a murderer had pledged to help me create art. I do my best to banish him from my consciousness, but he still occasionally appears in my dreams and promises once again to help me with my art lessons.

In any case, it would be so satisfying to learn about shade and light, perhaps to draw in nature, but girls sketching alone are considered unnatural females, unladylike monsters, and are told to return home to mend their da's clothing or to make a meat pie for the family. This happened to me once as I sat drawing near the Embankment. A vicar stopped and told me that girls cannot be artists and that girls should not be involved in any way with the arts, especially if they are good Christian girls. The arts corrupt girls' souls. (What about men and boys? Does art not corrupt their souls? I dared not ask for fear that he would reprimand me further). He said that girls should pledge themselves to God, not to art. Of course, I believe him to be wrong, but I refrained from going back to draw what I saw on the Embankment. I did not enjoy being harassed or ridiculed for doing what I love, what I have an innate talent for. Instead, I intently study and try to memorise what I see and then at home in my room I fetch the memory of what I saw and try to capture the fleeting image on paper.

8 September 1846
Christina

In many of his sermons, the Reverend Mr. Dodsworth recounts stories of his favourite female saints, those he believes we should strive to emulate. The tales are fearsome for they are the tales of Lucy, Agnes, and Agatha, all of whom were persecuted and martyred by the Romans.

Often, he begins his sermon by stating, "Today, I address the young ladies in our congregation. You must become like the courageous Saints Lucy, Agnes, and Agatha. Lucy committed herself to Christ; she pledged to remain a virgin and endeavoured always to aid the poor by sewing clothing for them and giving them alms. Even before her harrowing trials began, she acted benevolently like Christ. But, because she committed herself to be the bride of Christ, not the bride of a man, a spurned suitor sought vengeance against her and denounced her to the Roman emperor, the diabolical Diocletian, who tortured countless of our brethren. This devilish ruler wished to sully Lucy's sanctity and sought to force her to prostitute herself. But God intervened and unsexed the men. He made the men who sought to defile her impotent, so Lucy remained pure! Later, the Romans tried to burn her at the stake, but God sent Archangel Gabriel to protect her! And even though flames surrounded her feet, she was not harmed." Reverend Mr. Dodsworth paused, fooling us into believing that Lucy was saved. But then he raised his voice and said, "Then the Romans tried stabbing her, but their wounds drew no blood. Finally, God put an end to her persecution and allowed these wretched men to cut sweet Lucy's eyes and heart out! She no longer had to look at this evil and condemned world or feel its pain in her heart and, at last, God lifted her up and into His loving arms in heaven!"

I saw sweat break out on his forehead, and he mopped it with his pocket handkerchief. He appeared excited, drew a deep breath, and continued, "Likewise, Agnes was denounced as a Christian, and the Romans dragged her naked through the streets, shaming her and taking her to a brothel, where she was ordered to satisfy male lust. But the men who tried to rend her virgin knot were struck blind! As they did with Lucy, the Romans attempted to burn Agnes at the stake, but this time the fire would not light. Finally, and thankfully, God permitted Agnes to be released from her trials by allowing the pagans to behead her. She no longer had to think about the cruelty of men."

At last, the Reverend Mr. Dodsworth completed his terrifying tale of his trinity of female saints. "Similar to her sister saints, Agatha too was tortured for her Christian faith. She was stretched on the rack, burned, whipped, and then her breasts were cut off and held up as objects of scorn! Thus, she would never have to bear the burden of Eve, who suckled Abel and his murderous brother Cain."

Each time the Reverend Mr. Dodsworth tells us these tales I hold tight to my budding breasts; I touch my chest to feel my beating heart, and then feel my face to see that my head is securely attached to my shoulders. All to preserve my womanliness, my rational mind, and my clear, artistic vision. I feel the horror and the pain that these female martyrs experienced. I pray that I am never tested in this way.

Maria tells me that she would willingly go to the stake to defend her faith, but I fear that my faith is frail and that I could not withstand such torture. I too wish to be a saint, but why must we females be brutalised in this carnal way or shrunk to nothing by starvation to achieve sainthood? I would like to ask the Reverend Mr. Dodsworth this question, but I fear that he would denounce me to the church and exile me as if I were the devil himself. Inside, I rage against his exhortation that we become Lucies, Agneses, and Agathas. There must be less violent and painful ways to ensure that we attain godliness and the right to live in paradise.

As I prayed about my doubts about martyrdom, this verse arose:

> Yet one pang searching and sore,
> And then Heaven for evermore;
> Yet one moment awful and dark.
> Then safety within the Veil and the Ark;
> Yet one effort by Christ His grace,
> Then Christ forever face to face.

Perhaps, if tested, I could withstand torture, but I would rather not be tried.

8 November 1846
Lizzie

Our da constantly reminds us that we are the descendants of noble people, the Eyres in Sheffield, and that we are the rightful heirs to their estate Hope Hall in Yorkshire. Because of this, he and Mam raise us to have proper manners, to sit up straight, to walk with our heads held high, to know when to speak, and when to stay silent. To faithfully bear all things with grace and fortitude. Despite the fact that we are somewhat impoverished, we are literate; we have learned to read and write, even though Lydie, my brother Charles, my little sister Annie, and I have never attended a proper school.

Da says that we need to prepare ourselves to take our rightful places at Hope Hall when the time comes for us to leave what he calls hellish London and live in the bucolic countryside among the other landowners, not among thieves and murderers. He often tells us this when we are hurried past the gay "ladies" that frequent Tottenham Court, who walk about with strange men in order to earn their bread and feed their children. Da says that we should not look at these loose, disrespectful women. He says that we are better than them and finer than all our poor neighbours. I try to remember this, but I see no difference between me and these women, only that my clothing is not as shabby and worn, and I speak with a more refined tone. I do feel sorry for these women for they have no other means by which to keep themselves and their offspring from starving. Even so, if I were famished, I would try to find another way to satisfy my hunger; I would not sacrifice myself or my honour or discredit my family by going about with unworthy men who only need to satisfy their craving for female flesh.

8 November 1846
Christina

Maria came home just in time to see Reverend Mr. Dodsworth's newly formed order of Anglican sisters who were presented at services. I found these nuns to be frightening, like devils, in their black habits, cloaks, and bonnets, but even though Gabriel mocked us and wanted to banish us to a convent, Maria feels drawn to the nuns' lifestyle and their vows of poverty, chastity, and obedience. She told me that when she is freed from her governess duties, she will join this convent and minister to poor, fallen women who populate Soho and Southwark. She says that she will help all the Magdalenes who are persecuted and throttled by men; she will be their saviour, but in a pious, not boastful, way. She will save the Magdalenes from themselves.

When she talks about the Magdalenes, I think about the men who frequent them and who use these women and sometimes take their "pound of flesh." Aren't they as guilty of carnal sin as the women?

16 November 1846
Lizzie

Today, I decided to be bold and practise my art by the Thames. I would challenge whoever accosted me. As I began to use charcoal to sketch the river, I noticed a man fishing along the shore in a rowboat. The water was placid but dark and murky, likely filled with refuse and slop from the street. Suddenly, I heard a scream and looked up to see a woman jumping from Putney Bridge, her gown billowing out like a great sail and her hands folded in prayer. I scrambled to my feet, dropped my sketch pad, and raced to the shore. I was ready to jump in and save her, for I am a hardy swimmer. Just then, the fisherman rowed quickly toward the woman and grabbed her arm as she bobbed up. She struggled against him, but he managed to hoist her into his boat. Then, she shouted at him, "Why didn't you let me be? My family has cast me out. I wish to go to God with my unborn child!"

Then, much to my astonishment, I heard the man ask the woman for two shillings for fishing her up out of the filthy Thames. She laughed at him and said, "I should be paying you to drown me!"

I felt so disheartened and sick to my stomach that I ran home, leaving my sketch pad near the river. I was deeply troubled and saddened by what I had witnessed. Why would a woman deliberately set out to die? What led her to take such a fateful step? Was she better off dead than to be alive and ostracised as she would be because of her unsanctioned pregnancy?

When I got home, Da asked me where I'd been, and I said that I'd been sketching by the river. Before I could tell him about what I'd seen and now what I couldn't forget, he told me to put away my pens and pencils, that I must find work to help support the family. He said that I was comely and skillful enough with my needle to make and model hats down the street at Mrs. Tozer's millinery shop. I must forget about creating any art other than women's hats.

I started to argue with him, but he told me to be silent. I then said, "But, Da, I must tell you about what I saw today."

After I told him about the fallen woman who attempted to end her life, he said that I should tend to my own business. Besides, suicides are common along the river, especially young girls who've been rejected by men who have had their way with them. "Mind yourself, Lizzie; don't become a tart like that girl likely is."

When I went to bed, I thought about the desperate woman who was willing to throw away her life and that of her child. I kept seeing the image of her sailing down into her filthy, watery grave. To settle my own soul and to commemorate her, I wrote this verse:

> Life and night are falling
> from me, Death are
> opening on me
> Where ever my footsteps
> come and go life is a
> stony way of woe
> Lord have I long to go
>
> Hollow hearts are ever
> near me soulless eyes have
> ceased to cheer me
> Lord may I come to Thee

I prayed that the woman and her unborn child would be able to return home to God. For they would never be accepted by society, even though the man who had impregnated her was free to pursue his needs and desires without punishment.

Perhaps, with luck, she will try again and there will be no greedy fisherman or myself to save her.

16 November 1846
Christina

I have never suffered as some unfortunate females have. I have never had a broken bone or even a bruise. I have never fallen. I have never been battered, although my mother continues to occasionally whip me for my fractious nature. Even so, she has tried to shield me from all obvious physical injury that would be incurred by any other human. We do not jump into or bathe in the river or ocean for fear of being indiscreet, even though the current rage is to be dropped from a swimming machine or a strong man's arms into the sea. We do not climb mountains or hike the fells when we visit the North, because that would not be lady or gentlemanly-like. We do not hoist heavy objects, brass kitchen kettles or pots, or bathing tubs, because that is what our servant is for. Besides, I am so weak from my fasts that I am now an invalid, which is why I am permitted to remain in bed and write poetry and stories.

You see, I have read about our great poet Elizabeth Barrett, who suffered a spinal injury as a child. She was confined to a spinal crib and later kept to her bed, even after her mother died. Miss Barrett feigned weakness, I believe, (as I often do, when I'm called upon to read to or assist my father to the privy), but this allowed her poetry to flourish because she did not, was not able to assume domestic duties—all of which were expected of her as the eldest daughter.

Mother expected me to take care of my father and to be a governess, but, like Gabriel, I could not do what I was obliged to do. One morning I arose with all good intentions to help Father with his bath, but when I started to walk to his bedroom, my knees buckled, and I had to sit down on the floor. I felt slightly nauseous, even though I hadn't eaten anything substantive for two days. When Mother found me, I could barely walk so she helped me back to my bed and told me to rest. Father would have to care for himself, she said. And, she added, I could wait to become a governess.

Fortunately, once I was in my bed, I felt instantly better and I possessed sufficient stamina to write lyrics and to muse about death, my own and others'. To hide the dirty secret that festers in my soul.

The Reverend Mr. Dodsworth now requires that we attend services daily, receive communion weekly, and, like the papists, attend confession prior to receiving communion. I have not felt worthy of communion, for Mr. Dodsworth always reminds us of our innate corruption and tells us that we must confess every single sin if we are to be worthy of receiving the body and blood of Jesus Christ. He claims that if we take communion and are unworthy, we eat and drink our own damnation. Because I feel undeserving and fear damnation, I sometimes refuse communion, which makes Mr. Dodsworth order me to seek atonement.

The confessional is a dreary coffin, dark and foreboding, and the Reverend Mr. Dodsworth listens like a silent shadow on the other side of the screen as I whisper my faults and sins. I tell him about my occasional blasphemy, my false pride, my fits of rage, and the ways in which I dishonour my father and mother. But I can't and won't tell him my secret.

Somehow, after my recitation of sins, he suspects that there is more to my sinfulness and asks, "Is that all that you need to confess, young lady? Are you telling the truth? Or are you committing another sin by withholding the truth? Have you relieved yourself of your burden?"

I lower my eyes and peer into the corners of my soul. I feel unworthy of God, Mr. Dodsworth, and his Saints Lucy, Agnes, and Agatha. I commit another sin and lie. I reply, "Yes, I have confessed all."

When I leave the confessional, I vow that I will never enter this church again, for I am certain that Mr. Dodsworth can see the stain on my soul.

4 December 1846
Lizzie

I have acquired a position at Mrs. Tozer's shop. I am learning how to adorn funeral bonnets and hats with black lace, feathers, and plumes. It seems odd to me that we attempt to make beautiful those who gaze at the dead. I do not care for this task, but Mrs. Tozer says that many bonnets are needed at this time because of the cholera, typhus, and typhoid outbreaks. And, today, the sister of a young woman purchased a veiled hat to wear to mourn her death. I asked what she died of, and she reluctantly said, "She fasted and died of starvation." I was shocked and didn't know how to reply as I boxed the hat for her.

Mrs. Tozer promises that soon she will reassign me to making wedding hats and veils, but, for now, I must continue with this morbid task until young girls don't die of starvation or wretched fevers.

4 December 1846
Christina

Lord Wicklow's daughter, sweet Isabella Howard, who befriended me at Christ Church, has become a saint. I saw her laid out, surrounded by garlands of sweet-smelling white roses. She was breathless and motionless, her midnight eyes forever closed. Her perfected body, ravished through fasting, horrified me. I had to turn away.

I have written a poem about her death to calm my anguished heart, which broke to see her body lifeless, and her spirit fled. I can't say that it placates my fear or sorrow, but it rests on Christian teaching, which I must believe lest I truly go mad.

Lady Isabella,
   Thou art gone away,
Leaving earth's darksome trouble,
   To rest until the Day.
From thy youth and beauty,
   From each loving friend,
Thou art gone to the land of sure repose,
   Where fears and sorrows end.

Thou wert pure whilst with us;
   Now, we trust, in Heaven,
All thy tears are wiped away,
   All thy sins forgiven.

Who would wish thee back again
   But to share our sorrow?
Who would grudge thine hour of rest,
   Ere the coming morrow?

Let us rejoice the rather
   That thou hast reached that shore,
Whilst yet thy soul was spotless,
   And thy young spirit pure.

And if thy crown be brighter
   By but one little ray,
Why wish to dim its lustre? . . .
   Oh! rather let us pray
That when we are most fitted
   We too may pass away.

Perhaps the horseman will pass by me and not yet call me to the next world. Perhaps Isabella's sacrifice is sufficient to satisfy our sometimes-greedy God.

30 September 2019
Hastings

Even though, while in the crypt, she continually felt as if someone was watching her, Maggie returned the next day to read the diaries. Whatever or whoever kept an eye on her just seemed curious, not the least bit threatening. It didn't surprise her that such an old crypt contained at least one wayward ghost, lost between worlds. Maggie even felt as though the presence was a bit of a comfort. She wasn't alone among the dead and one time she felt a hand grasping hers as she fetched documents from the chest, suggesting what she ought to read next. Although eerie, she had felt the presence of the dead before in Yorkshire when she hiked Pendle Hill where a coven of witches supposedly met. Ghosts, barghests, never frightened her. She often thought that the living were far more terrifying.

Maggie continued to pour through the diaries as she took photos of the entries. Sometimes she felt as if the ghostly presence looked over her shoulder and read along with her.

She was astounded by how Lizzie and Christina, in their need to express themselves through art, were living parallel lives but she wasn't in the least surprised by the ways in which they suffered because they were born female. And she was horrified by their encounters with and musings about death. Whenever Maggie finished reading for the afternoon and closed the trunk, she couldn't stop thinking about these two teenaged girls. She wondered when Christina and Lizzie would meet and what they would think of each other. Would they recognize their commonalities? Would they become friends? She pondered reading their biographies but then thought that these diaries, these primary sources, would reveal truths that no biographer would know of or reveal. She would exercise patience and wait for Lizzie and Christina to speak of their relationship or, God-forbid, their animosity toward one another. She hoped they would become friends, not just because of Dante, but because they were two sides of the same coin, for both longed to make art and both were frequently hindered from doing so.

Even though she decided against reading biographies, Maggie thought that she would like to read more of Christina's poetry and, if possible, to locate Lizzie's. After singing the beautiful and melancholic song "In the Bleak Mid-Winter" as a teen, Maggie had read the poem. When set to music the poem is lovely, she thought, even if the lyrics only speak of giving your heart to God, not bestowing your heart on another imperfect human. She wondered if most of Christina's poetry dwelled on the love of God alone or if, as suggested by the poems in her diary, she pondered other secular musings.

Maggie didn't tell Mrs. Highclere about the chest's contents or about the benign ghost. She wanted to keep this knowledge to herself, at least for now. And she often pondered who among the Rossetti family placed the unbound diaries in the chest and brought it here to reside rather than at their family home. She wondered if someone had actually buried the diaries before the Rossettis brought them to the church. If that were the case, did a family rebel dig up the chest and deposit it here so that someone would discover its contents? Or was it left here to ensure that no one read the contents?

That afternoon when Maggie arrived at the church, Mrs. Highclere said, "Back again, Miss? You can't get enough of that poet's words, I suspect."

"You're quite right, Mrs. Highclere. By the way, might you recommend a local bookstore where I could purchase a collection of Christina's poems? Dante speaks of his sister's poetic gift, and I wish to learn more."

"Well, I love mysteries and write them. So, I go to the WH Smith Bookstore to purchase my Dorothy Sayers and Ruth Rendell mystery novels, but some locals prefer the Hare and Hawthorne Bookstore on George St. I believe the proprietor is a poet."

"Thanks ever so much. May I have the key now?" Maggie asked as she started to pull out her white gloves.

"You know where it's hanging. Help yourself. You may take a candle if you wish."

"You'll be alone shortly; I must make my Reginald his lunch."

"That's quite all right," Maggie replied, as she descended into the catacombs once more. She wondered if her barghest would read along with her once again. She began to read and as she did so, she reflected again on Christina's meditations on death and Lizzie's anxieties about murderers, suicides, death, and family loss. She wondered what new information and feelings they would express in their diaries, and once again questioned why no one wished to resurrect Christina's and Lizzie's words from the crypt and hear the voices of these two Victorian artists. Were they silenced because they were females who set out to tell the truth of what it meant for a Victorian girl or woman to become an artist?

Later that day, Maggie thought about Lizzie and Christina as she carried her easel and paints along the shore. The sun had finally come out from behind the clouds. It had heavily rained that morning and Maggie's boots sunk into the sand as she headed to the spot on the beach where she liked to paint. For several hours, she painted the sea and its iridescent blues and greens with the golden sun sparkling on it. But then out of the corner of her eye, she saw a woman walking toward her on the beach. From a distance, Maggie saw that she was oddly dressed; she appeared to wear a heavy brocade gown, as if she had just walked out of a Pre-Raphaelite painting. Maggie saw that she wore her ginger hair long and flowing. She was barefoot.

Perhaps I've been out in the sun too long, but she resembles Lizzie Siddal. How could that be? Maggie turned toward the woman who walked closer. As the woman did so, she picked up something from the beach. Then, she stopped, and stood before the painting. She didn't say a word but turned her head quizzically as if she had a question. Maggie started to speak, but then the woman fetched Maggie's pencil from the easel and gracefully outlined a womanly figure, that seemed like herself, on the beach, with her long hair flowing down her back. Then, she handed the pencil to Maggie along with a small sand dollar, smiled, and walked on without saying a word.

Maggie stood there dumbfounded as the sea washed away the woman's footprints.

5 June 1847
Christina

Sir Charles now diagnoses my illness as "religious mania" (as if such a thing exists!) Mother rejected his claim and said that I am merely following Rev. Pusey's guidance concerning my soul. Sir Charles ignored her justification and then threatened additional leeches. But I begged Mother to refuse further treatment and she sent Sir Charles away. Instead, she agreed to send me to convalesce at the Folkestone seaside in Kent in the company of my aunt Polidori. I wish that Maria accompanied me, instead of my fussy, curmudgeonly aunt, who surveils my every move.

On occasion, I have sufficient energy to sneak away early in the morning when she falls asleep while reading her Bible. I walk along the shore, feeling energised as I hunt for precious jet stones, hermit crabs, sand dollars, and starfish. I sometimes search for selkies and mermen. Yesterday, I found a dead seahorse and I quickly buried it in the sand. I find the sea soothing during the day, but at night, as I fall asleep to the roar of the waves, I dream about ghosts who claim their lovers, and drowned girls and their fathers on the shore.

4 September 1847
Christina

My aunt and I have remained at Folkestone all summer and as the leaves begin to turn scarlet, we are ready to return home. Even so, my thoughts still dwell in darkness. "Will These Hands Ne'er Be Clean?" came to me and I scribbled these lines before we boarded the train to return to London.

And who is this lies prostrate at thy feet?
And is she dead, thou man of wrath and pride?
Yes, now thy vengeance is complete,
Thy hate is satisfied . . .

See where she grasped thy mantle as she fell,
Staining it with thy blood; how terrible
Must be the payment due for this in hell!

I fear returning home but know that I must. Will this shameful darkness always cloud my mind? I feel like the nun in Elizabeth Barrett Browning's poem, confined against her will. What if I never escape this prison?

When I arrived home, Grandpapa was there and he greeted me warmly, calling me *cara* Christina and then referred to me as Sappho, as he frequently does, for he has read many of my poems. Because he himself is a poet, he knows that writing eases my mind and heart. When I write, I put aside my self-loathing, my leprous soul, and feel at ease within myself.

While I write my poetry and stories alone in my room, Gabriel brags of his admittance to the Royal Academy of Art, where he learns among his fellow artists. I wish I had a fellow poet with whom I could study. Even though Gabriel and William also write poetry, they do not suffice as my fellow poets. I pray someday to meet a fellow female poet who would share my dreams and longings.

I yearn to run away like Elizabeth Barrett did last year when she secretly married and then fled to Italy with her love and fellow poet Robert Browning. I have no love though. I imagine that, if I could flee, I would perhaps find love and my poetry would flourish.

3 October 1847
Christina

I have started to lock away my writing; I greatly fear anyone reading a poem that is not yet perfect. To that end, I have also started to write a semi-autobiographical story, "Maude." Perhaps it is presumptuous to think that a sixteen-year-old girl has a story to tell, but I feel certain that the story of a young female writer or artist must be told. Like me, Maude hides her writing when anyone enters the room. I do not wish anyone to see an unfinished product, especially Mother, who has changed her mind and would rather that I not express all my secret thoughts and desires in writing. She frets that I will destroy myself in the process of trying to save myself. She reminds me that her brother John was also a writer, and he ended his own life. And she said, "Look at your father and his mad ramblings about Dante Alighieri. Do you wish to become like him?"

"Of course not," I replied. "But don't you understand that writing keeps me from a state of madness?"

Once I said that, she appeared to understand and then didn't outright forbid me to write, but stated, "I would prefer that if you must write, you only write religious poems. Those bring glory to God and do not vainly seek attention."

Unlike my situation, Maude's mother reprimands her for writing and punishes her by burning some of her poetry. To that end, Maude has begun, like me, to lock away her writing, burying it in an old chest that gathers dust in her room.

Because she must conceal her desires and thoughts, Maude succumbs to illness. Before she dies, she asks her sister to burn all of her writing so that misunderstanding hearts will not confound her words. The sister promises to fulfil Maude's request, but instead of burning her work, she places the locked box of poetry and stories in Maude's coffin. Thus, all of Maude's secrets go to the grave with her.

I have made Maria promise that, if I should die young and poetically unfulfilled, she will gather all my unfinished work and my diary and bury them with me so that prying and curious eyes will not read my most covert and secret thoughts. Maria suggested that I am being morose in thinking that I will die before I reach maturity, but I told her that I am just being cautious and prudent; the young do die.

"Don't forget that we just wore black bonnets and garb as we walked behind Isabella Howard's funeral cortege," I reminded her. "I'm certain that she hadn't planned to die. She wanted to live, as I do."

16 October 1847
Lizzie

Even though my da prohibits me from drawing, I often sketch in my bed by candlelight. I peer inside my mind's eye and see the Mudlark children scouring the Embankment and draw a girl finding what she considers treasure, a teacup lined with roses and poppies and figures of a woman and a man under an arbour. She holds it up for her brother to see, but he looks at it disdainfully for the cup is chipped. Yet she is joyful because she found beauty in the muck and rubbish. Sometimes I see them find wayward starfish and an occasional piece of precious jet or a sand dollar and they are amazed by natural beauty, for even the poor can find joy in nature.

To keep my da from finding my sketches, I have locked them away in my wardrobe, which I share with Lydie. She is a faithful sister and would never betray me to our da. She tells me to keep sketching because she knows that, in my heart, I am an artist and to live I must create art.

16 October 1847
Christina

Mother dismissed Sir Charles and has now secured a new physician to treat me. Unlike the Queen's physician, our new doctor, Dr. O'Hara, encourages my writing, even my secular musings. After he took my pulse and listened to my heart and lungs and pronounced them sound, Mother left the room and then he asked me how I spend my time. I confessed that I find the greatest pleasure in scribbling thoughts and verses that are the product of dreams and musings. My only fear is that my poems and stories seek vain attention.

"What is your aim in scribbling then? *Do* you truly seek vain attention?"

"No, I write to express my heart and the fears that lie within it," I replied.

"Then, young lady, you should continue. I myself scribble and find it the best way to discern what I think and feel. Scribbling can heal."

He told me what I already knew to be true, and so I have continued my scribbling and have most recently written my longest poem to date, "The Dead City."

In it, my persona has entered a seeming paradise filled with palaces and sumptuous feasts—fruits of every sort known on earth. In this paradise, people are allowed to taste and eat until full but then pay the ultimate price for their indulgence and gluttony. Here are three stanzas:

In green emerald baskets were
Sun-red apples, streaked and fair;
Here the nectarine and peach
And ripe plum lay, and on each
The bloom rested everywhere.

Grapes were hanging overhead,
Purple, pale, and ruby-red;
And in panniers all around
Yellow melons shone, fresh found,
With the dew upon them spread.

And the apricot and pear
And the pulpy fig were there;
Cherries and dark mulberries,
Bunchy currants, strawberries,
And the lemon wan and fair.

In this succulent world, all people, young and old, are dead, petrified, turned to stone, from having given into pleasure alone, from loving and desiring self-indulgence, from eating succulent, tempting fruits.

How does one love the world and its gifts, its fruits, without becoming a mere godless hedonist? How can we keep our thoughts on the greater prize, God's heaven, when we are tempted by the bounty and beauty of this world?

11 November 1847
Lizzie

From my earnings at Mrs. Tozer's, I purchased a portfolio. Then I opened the wardrobe where I hide my sketches and placed my sketches in the new conveyance. With my sketches in hand, I walked to the Royal Academy of Art. As I was about to enter, a porter barred the way and asked where I was going and for what reason. I said that I wished to see Mr. Archer Shee.

"You wish to see the President of the Academy? Whatever for?" he asked gruffly.

"I wish to show him my sketches, for I would like admittance to the Academy."

The porter laughed and smirked. "You ignorant girl. Don't you know that girls and women are not allowed to study here? You're wasting your time. Go where females are admitted, the Bedford Square Ladies College." He then turned me around and escorted me out of the building, practically shoving me out the door.

I felt humiliated to learn that females cannot learn from the masters, that because of the body I was born in, I am considered inferior and am presumed to be unable to learn what men and boys can.

I returned home and put my sketches back in my wardrobe and locked the door. I must think about how I can learn to improve my artistry. For now, I will not pick up my pencil, not until I see a way forward that does not receive help from a murderer or a stifled, untrained female artist at the Bedford Square Ladies College.

12 November 1847
Christina

When I have my curse, if I bleed heavily, I tell no one and wash out my own bloody rags to hide my haemorrhaging. And I must confess that I occasionally still harm myself as I did a few weeks ago after Father belittled me and mocked one of my poems. He called it trite, a pathetic attempt to gain attention. After he said this, I ran from Father's bedroom into the kitchen, where I grabbed a knife. I then fled to the garden, pulled back my bodice, and sliced the skin on my chest above one of my breasts and near my heart. I immediately thought of St. Agatha and wished that I hadn't harmed my womanhood. I staunched the blood with some poppy petals from our kitchen garden and covered my wound so that no one could see the mark.

These days, I refrain from excessive fasts and try to atone in other ways. I have completely forsaken devouring countless custard tarts and I have taken to sometimes wearing the hair shirt that Mr. Dodsworth gifted me, even though it scratches and itches so at night that I can hardly sleep. I suppose that is part of the penance.

I have returned to being my father's full-time caretaker. I still feel weak, but sometimes I feel well enough to walk around London on my own, even though it is considered unseemly and dangerous for a young girl to do so. While Father sleeps, I sneak out and amble through the Italian Quarter, the notorious quadrant in Soho where petty thieves and prostitutes thrive and where my father Gabriele, the exiled poet, lived when he first arrived in London. I trace his steps.

Sicilian by birth, Father, the founder of the revolutionary Carbonari, wrote poems that the monarch Ferdinand the First considered treasonous, a capital offence. So, Father fled to Malta. While in Malta, Father's friends were murdered for their belief in the right to have a parliament, not just a king. When the king declared that all dissidents must be rounded up, even in Malta, a British naval captain, Sir Graham Moore, dressed my father as a British naval lieutenant and smuggled him out of Malta. When Father arrived in London, he kissed the ground; he was now an Italian expatriate, an adopted Briton, now a stranger in a strange land.

Yet Father was also a stranger in his own land, because he was labelled a heretic for speaking out against the Pope and the Pope's political alignment with Ferdinand. I am not political, and I am not a Catholic as Father nominally is; I remain, like my mother and Maria, a strict High Church Anglican who follows the Oxford Movement, which tries to restore mystery to the Anglican Church. As members of the Movement, we are, according to Reverends Mr. Pusey and Mr. Dodsworth, the true descendants of the original church; *we* are St. Peter's Church.

Father scoffs at my mother, Maria, and me, for our beliefs. He tells us that we are inflexible, intransigent; he tells us we should open our minds and hearts more. We should read more widely as he does from pagan sources—the Cabala, Swedenborg, and Hindu Scriptures on Brahmanism. How odd and contradictory though that he thinks that we ought to be flexible, when his family motto is "Break, Not Bend." But regarding religious practice, he follows no church doctrine, but only follows his own mind and philosophy, which he claims God himself bestows upon him. His own politics are allied with the Freemasons, the Illuminati associated with revolution, whose alchemical and cabbalistic secrets will never be revealed, especially to women. Through the encouragement of his patron, the geologist Charles Lyell, Father studies and writes about Dante Alighieri's poetry, claiming that it contains secret codes that align the poetry with the Freemasons and the Knights Templar, even though the Freemasons did not yet exist in the Middle Ages.

I have learned all of this through reading Father's writings about Dante to him, so even though, as a female, I am forbidden to learn cabbalistic secrets, I've been privy to my father's ruminations on them.

3 December 1847
Christina

Because of Father's rather obsessive study, the mediaeval poet Dante haunts our home, or at least some of the family believe this is true. Gabriel claimed when we were young that Father's copy of Dante's book about courtly love and his obsession with Beatrice, *Vita Nuova*, glowed malevolently in the dark. One night, Gabriel's fear was so profound that he refused to climb the stairs to the second floor alone because he said he had seen the poet lurking around corners, probably seeking his elusive Beatrice.

Another time, Gabriel claimed he saw Dante Alighieri face to face. We heard Gabriel scream, and he ran into Mother's bedroom, where she was braiding my hair for bed.

"What is it, Gabriel?" she asked, as she continued to braid my hair. "What's wrong?"

"Mama, I saw the poet Dante in the hallway. He started chasing me."

"You've allowed your imagination to run away with you." She stopped braiding. "Let's go see. You'll find he's not there. No one's there. Come now." She took his hand.

"No, Mama, I can't. Please don't make me," he begged.

"Don't be a coward, child," she said, as she started to drag him towards the door.

Suddenly, Father entered the room and asked what was going on. After Mother told him that Gabriel had said that he'd seen Dante the poet in the hallway, Father laughed. "Nothing to worry about. I see him every night. He has chosen to live with us because I am his disciple." He told Mother to let go of Gabriel, and then he grabbed Gabriel's hand, and they walked out into the hall to search for the poet.

None of the rest of us saw the poet, and later William, Maria, and I surmised that Gabriel suffered from English "madness" and melancholy. Mother tried to believe that, unlike her husband, whom she deems rather mad, Gabriel was only afflicted by a far-reaching imagination that would, in the long run, bear fruit.

In the Italian Quarter though, where I pretend that I am truly in Italy, I feel freer to exercise my mind and imagination and open my heart, as I speak my father's tongue, which my Grandpapa Polidori sweetly taught me. In the Italian Quarter, I throw off decorum and try to pry open the hinges of my shuttered mind and cold heart. I imagine that I am a full-blooded and bodied Italian girl, not a watered down, partly English one. As I walk the streets among the flower sellers and the children begging for bread, I pretend that I'm from Tuscany. I ramble the streets of Firenze and stop outside the Uffizi Gallery to gaze at the statues of all the famous Italian artists, poets, inventors, scientists, and politicians—Da Vinci, Petrarch, Dante, Galileo, and even the malevolent Machiavelli. Some were exiles and heretics like my father, but as I gaze at the statuary in my imagination, I look, but find no women, Italian or otherwise, even though women have long inspired all the arts and even in secret painted, wrote, and invented. I see no Beatrice, or Diotima who taught Socrates. I see no Sappho or Artemisia Gentileschi. I wonder why no statues were sculpted of them and placed on this avenue of artists and natural philosophers.

In the Italian Quarter, I feel the sun warm my bare arms, as I let down my hair as do the painters' models whom Gabriel adores. As I do so, I reflect on women becoming more than art. I see them taking up their pens, their pencils, their charcoal, and their brushes, as they begin to envision their own worlds. You see, like my father, I am also a heretic, but only here in the Italian Quarter.

In the Italian Quarter, I contemplate Sappho. Madame de Stael considers her a genius in female form, "the tenth Muse." All we have are fragments of Sappho's poetry, but because she wrote of love, I try to imagine how she perceived that love is our greatest need and how devastated we are when a lover has forsaken or betrayed us. Like Sappho, I sometimes write in fragments. My poem begins thus:

> Love, Love, that having found a heart
> And left it, leav'st it desolate; —
> Love, Love, that art more strong than Hate,
> More lasting and more full of art; —
> O blessed Love, return, return,
> Brighten the flame that needs must burn.

Grandpapa Polidori read a sheaf of my poems, including "The Water Spirit's Song" and "The Dead City." He praised them, telling me that I am my father's daughter, at least in the poetic sense. Unbeknownst to me, Grandpapa somehow gathered all my poems, forty in number, even the ones that I had written as a child and bound them in an embossed book; on the cover my name, Christina Georgiana Rossetti, appears under the title *Verses*. Inside, Grandpapa placed a sketch that Gabriel made of me while I was scribbling, a sketch that makes me appear somewhat comely and serene. I am an author because of my grandpapa who helps me cure my malady. Because the verses come to me purely inspired, I take no credit for them. They emanate from the Beauty and Truth that surrounds us. To defuse a charge of author vanity, Grandpapa wrote in the preface that the book was published for *his* own pleasure, not for the pleasure of the authoress. He also included in the preface the following lines from the poet Pietro Metastasio:

> Why should I fear? My songs I know are inexperienced; but my mother will not therefore refuse this first homage; indeed the lowly simplicity of the gift will tell her all the better how grateful I am.

Grandpapa is my champion and advocate; he knows my heart, even though he cannot know all that is buried within it.

15 December 1847
Lizzie

Today I was looking through my keepsakes and found the Tennyson poem, "The Lady of Shalott," that Mr. Greenacre cut out of the newspaper for me once he knew that I liked poetry. Reading it again and realising that a treacherous man whom I trusted at the time, who acted like a dear uncle to me, and was my intended patron, was indeed a man who had murdered his beloved, made me shudder. Clearly, Mr. Greenacre was a man with two hearts, one wholesome, beneficent heart that perceived that poetry is an artful form that speaks to the soul, and one heart bound in darkness and evil. I wondered if all of us bear two hearts; if all of us perhaps contain some evil within. Perhaps this evil is the original sin that the church believes we all bear.

I would much rather believe that this isn't true. That as William Wordsworth believes we come "trailing clouds of glory" and are untainted from the beginning of life.

3 January 1848
Christina

Gabriel is displeased with the instruction that he receives at the prestigious Royal Academy of Art. He bemoans and disparages the techniques he is taught. The Masters are no Masters; they are incompetent imitators and paint banal subjects and scenes. Their techniques are lacklustre and trite. He tells me that he reads William Blake, who is highly critical of Sir "Sloshua's" contrived and false art and claims that "man is like a Garden ready Planted and Sown"; Gabriel argues that art should naturally express the truth and beauty of this garden; it should not focus on silly scenes of cows roaming the countryside or portraits of Queen Victoria's menagerie of pets: her spaniel Dash, her greyhound Nero, Lory the parrot, and her deerhound Hector. Gabriel is especially critical of Landseer's trite painting of them.

My brother plans to leave the academy and work and live with a fellow artist whom he met at the academy, William Holman Hunt, who also finds the academy stifling. They propose to form a secret society, a Brotherhood. I asked him if his Brotherhood will be political, like Father's former society, and he said no. Instead, they would be an artistic community that seeks beauty and truth. They will call themselves the Pre-Raphaelite Brotherhood, trying to emulate the visual art that preceded Raphael. He says that they aim to paint in bold colours, and they will replicate nature. Hunt often paints outdoors in all weather, day and night.

"Hunt sounds eccentric."

"He's a bloody genius, Christina. I can learn much from him."

"If he's a genius, why must your brotherhood remain secret?" I asked.

"Because we stand against the establishment—Joshua Reynolds, Sir Sloshua, as we call him, and others who hinder genuine artistic expression.

When we exhibit, we will revolutionise the artistic world. Our work will be far better than theirs. You'll see."

He continues to appear proud and arrogant to me. He certainly is no Titian or da Vinci. But I suppose arrogance is the prerogative of male artists.

They also speak of a literary club, which Gabriel has asked me to join. Even though in the past he mocked me, calling me a pious nun, he thinks that my solitude and contemplation have perhaps engendered worthy poems. Even so, I have declined his invitation because such intermingling of the sexes is forbidden in my church and because reading my poems to strangers, men in particular, would be the height of arrogance and vanity. Besides, what if they mocked or belittled my poetry, as Father did? I would never recover from the emotional injury.

5 February 1848
Christina

Gabriel has painted me as the young Virgin startled by the Angel Gabriel appearing to her to announce that she is to bear the Son of God, that by some miracle God has made me pregnant, that I will bear fruit from my virgin womb. I suppose that I should be honoured to stand in for Mary but as I posed, I couldn't help but feel her surprise and fright. Naturally, even though Angel Gabriel offers a lily of hope and tells me to have no fear, as Mary, I cower because a strange man who claims to be an angel has entered my bed chamber telling me that I shall give birth to the Son of God. Like Mary, I am shocked and incredulous. And why or how has God impregnated me?

Gabriel's painting has been criticised for the painting's earthiness. The virgin looks too human and sullied, but that's because the virgin is me.

12 February 1848
Lizzie

Today I spent some time in Mudie's Lending Library for I wished to read some poetry. As I was looking for a Tennyson collection, I came across a slim volume of poetry by Christina Georgiana Rossetti tucked next to a larger volume by Percy Bysshe Shelley. I was intrigued to see a Rossetti volume for I knew of the Rossettis, because their father is a scholar, teacher, and poet, but I was also fascinated because here was a volume of a young woman's poetry. The preface announces that the poetess is a mere twelve years old.

What would be in and on the mind of another young female poet like me?

I was stunned to these verses from "The Dead City":

> In green emerald baskets were
> Sun-red apples, streaked, and fair;
> Here the nectarine and peach
> And ripe plum lay, and on each
> The bloom rested every where.
>
> Grapes were hanging overhead,
> Purple, pale, and ruby-red;
> And in the panniers all around
> Yellow melons shone, fresh found,
> With the dew upon them spread.

Such images reminded me of Mr. Greenacre's store, where the murderer sold his luscious fruits. And, as in Miss Rossetti's poem, death prevailed where items for a sumptuous feast were gathered.

I read many more of her poems and marvelled at her talent, for she was only a child when she wrote such profound poems that deal with the marketing of death. Many of these poems reminded me of my own words and verses that lie buried in my journal but also in my heart.

14 February 1848
Christina

Mr. Pusey continues to predict that the end of the world is at hand. Revolutions are spreading across Europe; the English Chartists have demanded universal manhood suffrage and a secret ballot; cholera, typhoid, and typhus outbreaks are widespread throughout England, and the sun and moon have eclipsed each other. Across the Irish Sea, the Irish are starving because of a potato blight. Mr. Pusey asks us to fast for three days in memory of the starving and dead Irish. Out of obligation to the unfortunate Irish, I fast for two, not three days, because I am voraciously hungry. Instead, I do penance and atone by continuing to abstain from devouring custard tarts and by no longer attending the opera.

19 February 1848
Christina

I read Ellis Bell's *Wuthering Heights* with pleasure, even though the love between Cathy and Heathcliff is forbidden and tragic. The writer's voice is quite poetic. I would love to meet him, but I've heard that he is a bit of a hermit, living with his siblings in Yorkshire who are also writers. Even so, I believe it would be edifying to spend time with a fellow poet. Is it possible that Ellis Bell is actually a female? We know that women writers often hide their female identities behind male pseudonyms in order to be published. Not so for me or Elizabeth Barrett Browning, my idol, but true for Amantine Lucile Aurore Dupin, known as George Sand, whose *Indiana* I have secretly read, even though the Reverend Mr. Pusey would likely condemn and forbid it.

I continue to ponder Sappho and have written another poem in her voice, a poem that speaks of my solitary life, of my restlessness and how I am starved not only for food but for affection. Unlike Gabriel, I fear that I will leave no mark on the world, that no one will remember me, that no one will weep for me when I die, as no one wept for Indiana's maid Noun.

> Oh! It were better far to die
> Than thus for ever mourn and sigh,
> And in death's dreamless sleep to be
> Unconscious that none weep for me;
> Eased from my weight of heaviness,
> Forgetful of forgetfulness,
> Resting from pain and care and sorrow
> Thro' the long night that knows no morrow;
> Living unloved, to die unknown,
> Unwept, untended and alone.

Perhaps it *is* better to die than to never experience true companionship and love—the kind that, even though fraught with pain, the fictional Cathy and Heathcliff experienced.

2 January 1849
Lizzie

Is it Paul who speaks of a stranger in a strange land? I should know, since my father reads aloud from the Bible in the evening and hopes to become a deacon in the Congregational Church. I don't study the Bible, but I am a stranger or, at least I am strange to those who see me walk about London town. Once auburn, my hair has lightened to ginger, a shade which the other English consider suggestive of the Irish, who are loathed and demonised here. Throughout much of the world, except for Ireland, ginger hair is considered treasonous. Judas Iscariot is said to have had red hair, and the Egyptians burned women to death for having red hair, but our most illustrious Queen Elizabeth was born a ginger; surely that absolves all of us gingers from the sin of possessing flaming hair. And I hear that the literary and artistic family, the Rossettis, including the young poet Christina, are descendants of the red-haired Della Guardias; Rossetti even means red-haired. So, ginger hair may not necessarily denote evil. Plus, I am not a traitor or Irish, as far as I know, but we don't know our full family history.

My da continues to insist that we were once nobility, descendants of the Eyres who owned Hope Hall in Yorkshire and who traced their ancestors back to William the Conqueror and the Norman Conquest at Hastings, but you certainly can't see that in us now. We have fallen in stature. And it's said that until a Siddall family member returns and lives once again in Hope Hall, we shall continue to experience ill fortune. Even so, our mam has raised us to have genteel manners, to read literature, and to delight in art and the finer things. We may have fallen in stature, but if we are restored to our ancestral home, we will be ready to resume our dignified and rightful place and Lady Fortune will look favourably on us.

With that said, I can't say that I am either liked or even considered trustworthy—all because of my ginger hair, but I am now sought after by young artists who do not find me beautiful but do find me compelling.

Yesterday, a young man accompanied his mother into Mrs. Tozer's shop. Mrs. Deverell, for whom I had previously modelled a mourning hat, asked to see a colourful bonnet in the window. "Miss Siddall, if you would be so kind, I'd like to see the green hat in the window, the one with the plume and veil. I'm attending a wedding and think that it would be a perfect addition to my ensemble."

I fetched the hat and placed it on my head. I knew that I looked striking for the green hat complemented my red hair. Plus, it was one I'd fashioned, and I felt proud to wear it, for hats are the only work of art I am now allowed to make; I am grateful that I no longer fashion mourning bonnets. I wondered if I would ever have enough money to purchase a hat like this for myself. As I considered this, I looked up and saw the fellow standing next to Mrs. Deverell staring at me, and I wondered if something was amiss. I straightened the hat and veil, but he continued to stare. Perhaps he liked the colour combination, even so, I felt uncomfortable, for a man had never looked at me in that way, as if he wished to possess me.

After Mrs. Deverell purchased the hat and left, the young man came running back into the shop. He was breathless when he said, "I'm Walter Deverell. I was just here with my mother. I have a proposition for you."

"I remember you, sir," I said as I lowered my eyes and laughed. "A proposition sounds rather scandalous."

"No, it's not what you think. I'm a painter, you see," he said, as he handed me his card. "I think that you would be the perfect model for a painting I'm working on. May I inquire as to your address?"

"I live with my mam and da. I'm not sure that my da would permit me to sit as a model," I said as I arranged a hat on its stand. I knew that most models are considered loose, disreputable women, like the women who stroll on Tottenham Court, for they sometimes model in the nude and spend time alone with the male painter.

"It's completely aboveboard. I don't paint nudes or prostitutes," he quickly replied, as if he were privy to my thoughts. I saw his face redden slightly. "And, of course, you'll be chaperoned."

Once he said that, I hesitated for a minute, but then wrote my address on his card. I thought, what harm could come from him knowing where I live? Besides, he looked a gentleman and would surely act like one. Even so, I remembered my experience with Mr. Greenacre and then my mam's sage advice; I always knew to be on my guard with any strange man, even if he appeared a benign, docile gentleman.

I expected a visit from him, but later that afternoon his mother visited our home to ask my parents if I could sit as a model for her son. Luckily, my da was not home, because he would surely have forbidden me from modelling for any painter, even if the painter proved to be a gentleman.

As soon as I arrived home, Mam sat with me in the parlour and told me about Mrs. Deverell's visit. She seemed quite excited for, as she reminded me, she had never had a grand lady visit our home.

"I was a little ashamed of our furnishings, but Mrs. Deverell was most gracious. She kindly inquired about the old tapestry on the wall from Hope Hall, and I told her how your father is a descendant of the Eyre family. We had a lovely tea together."

"What did she say? What did she propose?" I asked, growing a little exasperated with Mam's storytelling, which was rarely direct.

"Well, she told me that her son is an aspiring artist who paints scenes from Shakespeare. She assured me that you would be properly chaperoned and suitably attired."

"Who will act as chaperone?" I asked. "Will she supervise the visits?"

"She said that her daughter Mary will serve as chaperone, and she insists that her son Walter is a gentleman. She even said, 'Your daughter will be safe with my Walter; he is a gentle soul.'"

We sat in silence for a minute. I wasn't sure if I wanted to model, for I would rather be the painter than the painted, but I did note that Mr. Deverell seemed a harmless, sincere fellow.

Mam nodded, even though she had not met Mr. Deverell. "Lizzie, if you agree to this proposal, we must keep your modelling a secret from your da. I know that he will not understand that some painters are true artists who do not profane their canvases with lurid images. He will think the worst, but I think that such a proposal may benefit you."

"What do you mean? How will it benefit me?" I asked. "It could ruin my reputation."

"Not necessarily. If you maintain your status as a proper lady, perhaps your association with Mr. Deverell will lead to a grander life for you, a proposal, a good marriage with an upper-class man, a marriage that would ensure that you have a life of ease, not one of drudgery," she replied as she looked despairingly around the room, around at the disappointment found in her own blessed association with my da. "Perhaps your Mr. Deverell will be smitten with you and your relationship with him will return our family to the prosperous life that we've been denied. Wouldn't that be grand?"

I agreed that this certainly would be grand, but I didn't tell her that I wasn't necessarily interested in marrying Mr. Deverell or any other painter. I didn't tell her that I would rather be the painter than the painted. However, I did tell Mam that I would sleep on Mr. Deverell's proposal and that if I gave my consent, I would directly contact Mr. Deverell.

As I climbed the stairs to bed, I realised that even though I had no wish to marry a painter or anyone for that matter, I did desire a different life from being a shop girl. And surely modelling would likely earn me a greater salary than being a fashioner of ladies' hats and then I could buy myself more watercolours and charcoal, perhaps even some oil paints, despite the fact that I don't know the first thing about painting in that medium. Perhaps Mr. Deverell or another painter would be willing to teach me to paint with oil?

So, this morning, I quickly jotted a note to Mr. Deverell and dropped it in the postal box as I walked to work. I asked when I should come to his studio. I am eager to start a new life.

Part II

1 October 2019
Hastings

Maggie tried not to think of the strange encounter with the oddly dressed woman on the beach. Was she real? Or was she another manifestation of the supernatural? Of course, she was real. I saw her footprints in the sand before they were washed away. She drew on my canvas. She left a mark. She handed me a sand dollar. Ghosts don't do that, do they?

Maggie decided that the woman herself must be an artist—Unlike myself, many artists are often eccentric in their dress. Yes, the woman was likely an artist who was merely trying to encourage her to paint reality in nature. She was still intrigued by the uncanny nature of the encounter though and the way the woman had inserted herself into Maggie's painting as if she wanted to enter a woman artist's painting. Maggie decided that it would behove her to learn more about Christina and Lizzie and their artistry and whether either of them were also bothered by hauntings, real or metaphoric. Did Lizzie write poems about ghostly figures or the dead as Christina had? When she married Dante, did Lizzie experience supernatural encounters? What was the nature of her poetry and how similar was it to Christina's? Did she and Christina ever exchange poems or help one another with a line or two?

So, Maggie took Mrs. Highclere's advice and visited the Hare and Hawthorne Bookstore to obtain a copy of Christina's poems and perhaps Lizzie's, which Mrs. Highclere had thought were not in print. After browsing in the poetry section and only seeing nineteenth- and twentieth-century male poets, such as Tennyson and Ted Hughes, she asked the clerk, "Do you have a copy of Christina Rossetti's *Complete Poems*?"

The young woman with spiky purple hair and a nose ring was covered with body art; one tattoo read, "Bugger off!" She didn't look up from her mobile. "Who?"

"Christina Rossetti, the Victorian poet."

"Was she Dante's sister?"

"That's correct," Maggie replied, but wondered why Christina was not well known for her verse while Dante was. Perhaps the clerk was too young to know of Christina's fame.

"Let me see. I'll check on the computer."

After a cursory examination, the clerk smacked the chewing gum in her mouth. "The computer says no. We do have Dante's poetry though. Would you like to see that?"

"No, I'm not interested in Dante. Might you order Christina's for me, and while you're at it look for poems by Elizabeth Siddal?"

"How do you spell that surname?" the clerk asked, as she glanced down at her mobile, which had dinged, alerting her to a text message.

"S-I-D-D-A-L," Maggie said.

The clerk picked up her mobile and read the message before she returned to typing on the computer's keyboard. "I see a small volume by an author spelled S-I-D-D-A-L-L."

"Yes, it's sometimes spelled that way. I'm not sure why." Mrs. Highclere had been wrong, and Maggie grew excited about being able to read Lizzie's poems. She wondered who had gathered and edited them.

"And the book I see for Dante's sister is a book of religious poems. Do you want that?" she asked as she once again smacked the chewing gum in her mouth.

"There are no complete verses? I believe that she wrote secular as well as religious poems."

"The computer says no," the clerk said as she tugged at her nose ring and once more stared blankly at her mobile.

"I suppose that will have to do until I return to London. I'm sure I can find the complete verses there."

"Whatever," the clerk replied without looking at Maggie. "The computer says if you come back in a week, the book should be here." Once again, she fiddled with her nose ring, which seemed to aggravate her.

Maggie was bothered that the young woman kept touching her nose and then the keyboard, spreading her germs to anyone else who used the keyboard after her. She wanted to ask whether this girl had ever heard of what Louis Pasteur and Joseph Lister called germ theory and how disease is spread. She thought that this young woman was oblivious, so she moved on to a different subject.

"One more thing, where might I find Art History books?'

"On the back wall at the bottom," the clerk said as she continued typing into her mobile, which had dinged once more.

Maggie walked to the back wall and immediately saw a large book on whose spine was stamped Pre-Raphaelite Paintings. When she opened the book, the first painting she saw was Deverell's painting of *Twelfth Night*, which she had not viewed in her Victorian Art class. She sat on the floor, studied the personages in the painting, and saw a ginger-haired woman dressed in swain's clothing. That must be Lizzie. She looks so fitting as she pleads as if in prayer. Maggie wondered what Lizzie was thinking as she posed as a man who was actually a girl in love with the Duke. Did Lizzie have any love experience on which she could draw as she acted her part? Did it bother her that her first modelling session demanded that she act the part of a man or did donning male clothing feel pleasurable? As she posed, did Lizzie study, and learn from Deverell's technique? Did he teach her to paint with oils?

Maggie didn't recognize the other two characters in the painting, so she read the description, and learned that one figure was Dante Rossetti, Lizzie's future husband, dressed as a fool, and the other was Deverell himself.

She thought about purchasing the book but hesitated to hand it to the distracted and unhygienic clerk for fear that the clerk would cover it with her germs. Perhaps she'd come back another time when this clerk was not working, or she'd wait until she visited London. In the meantime, she flipped through the pages to remind herself of the daring and extraordinary beauty of the Pre-Raphaelite paintings. She wondered why no women painters, like Elizabeth Siddal, were included in this volume. Were any of them considered Pre-Raphaelite artists? Of course, they couldn't be part of the Brotherhood, but were they somehow part of the movement?

Maggie was eager to return to the crypt at St. Clement's to open the hidden chest in order to hear Lizzie's and Christina's voices continue to tell their innermost thoughts uninterrupted. What would Lizzie reveal about Dante? What was Christina up to as Lizzie began her modelling career? Had Christina broken out of her melancholy and found a worthy love? Had she decided to share her writing with some worthy person? Had her prayers been answered?

Maggie spent the late afternoons on the beach. She fully sketched the woman who had inserted herself into her painting and her world, but decided it was more fitting to cast her in trousers rather than the strange mediaeval gown the woman had worn. She tried her best not to mimic Deverell's painting of Lizzie, but to make this figure her own, walking assuredly on the beach. She wondered if her figure on the canvas was lonely, so she added a second figure, a woman with dark braided hair that hung over her shoulder. She intertwined their arms and sketched them gazing at one another. And, as she continued to draw her figures, whom she saw as women artists, perhaps even Lizzie and Christina, Maggie considered whether she, like Lizzie and Christiana, could allow herself to try to become the artist she had always longed to be.

16 February 1849
Lizzie

Mr. Deverell paid my train fare, and his sister Mary met me at the station. She escorted me to their home in Kew, near the Royal Kew Gardens, but I was surprised when she didn't take me in through the front door but smuggled me around to the garden where Mr. Deverell's makeshift studio is located.

"Miss Siddall, we must keep you hidden," Mary said. "You see, our father does not relish my brother being a painter, even though he himself is a designer. He wants Walter to be a banker, of all things, but Walter has no interest in money or fortune. He decries Mammon. He was born an artist and, like every artist, must paint. Can you keep our secret?"

"Of course, Miss Deverell. Whom would I tell anyway?" I replied.

Naturally, I personally knew of the need to draw and paint, but the secretive nature of my modelling for a painter made me feel a bit on edge, as if what I was about to embark on was truly forbidden and unseemly, exactly the opposite of what Mr. Deverell had proposed. But once I was in the studio, he put me at ease. He told me of his plans for his painting based on *Twelfth Night*, which he hopes to show at the Royal Academy. I thought that he must be an exceptionally fine painter if he dares to try to exhibit at the RA. While he spoke, Mary sat in the corner of the room and quietly read from a volume of Tennyson's poetry. I wondered which poem she was reading. Perhaps she also adores and mourns for "The Lady of Shalott." I hoped to talk with her about poetry.

My senses were pleasantly overwhelmed in Mr. Deverell's studio. The small space smelled strongly of turpentine and varnish; Mr. Deverell held a palette of oil paints, an array of bright primary and mixed colours—orange, red, purple, blue, yellow, and green. As I waited for him to pose me, I looked around the room and saw pots of brushes of various sizes and a mortar and pestle. I saw blank canvases strewn about the room. The room was chaotic, but Mr. Deverell was quite precise as he prepared to paint me. I eagerly watched as he first prepared the canvas where my image would reside. He said that his technique is to paint the canvas white and then apply the colours. He said that this makes the colours more vibrant, truer to nature. I tucked that knowledge into my mind so that, if I ever were able to paint with oil, I would try this technique. I realised that I was already learning from Mr. Deverell.

He had already sketched out two male figures on the canvas, one resembled himself and the other was a fetching, swarthy man dressed in a court jester's garb. I asked who the second figure was, and he said, "My friend and colleague, Mr. Dante Rossetti." I thought he must be kin to the young poet Christina whose verses I had read.

"Is Mr. Rossetti the brother of the female poet?" I asked.

"Oh, do you know Miss Rossetti?"

"I've read her verse," I replied.

"I haven't had the pleasure. Miss Rossetti is a rather secretive poet," Mr. Deverell said as he continued to prepare the canvas.

I felt like he must think me pretentious, so I remained silent, studied Mr. Rossetti's pose, and realised that, like him, I would have to transform myself and become my character.

"Mr. Rossetti is the court jester. And who am I to be?" I asked.

"Well, Viola dressed as Cesario. Do you know the characters in *Twelfth Night*?"

"Of course. I may be a shop girl, but I'm not ignorant," I said curtly. I felt my cheeks burn.

He held his paintbrush in mid-air and turned toward me. "I apologise. I meant no offence. Please forgive me." He seemed embarrassed and quickly placed down his brush and put on his smock. Then he pointed toward a screen behind which I would find my costume. I ventured behind the screen and found the clothing I was to don as I assumed Cesario's identity. I stepped out of my dress and took off my corset, then pulled on the tights and tunic of a young swain. It was freeing. Even though the Bible's sumptuary laws about male and female dress forbid a woman from donning male garb, I thought that it would be far more comfortable to always dress like this. And as a male, I could walk alone, free from harassment.

Once I was dressed, Mr. Deverell asked me to sit and then lean forward with my hands clutched in front of my heart pining for the love of Duke Orsino. I had never been in love, but I had seen the way that Mam looked at the daguerreotype of Da before he became a surly, portly old man. I would try to mimic that look.

As I attempted to settle into my character, I began to understand that this new world of modelling offered me a new way of being.

Whenever I sit, it's like I enter a painting's landscape and inhabit that space for a brief time. It is rather exquisite to just sit and pose and think, to dream of a different life for myself, where I am not a milliner's assistant but rather a painter. But for now, as I continue to model for Mr. Deverell, who insisted that I call him Walter, which I can't bring myself to do, I try to imagine myself as a boy-girl in *Twelfth Night*. What would it mean to be a boy-girl? How would I feel? What would I think? Whom would I love?

Would I love a duke or a duchess? Would I love a court jester or a female version of one? Or, if I were asked to pose as Ophelia, how might I imagine myself as another sort of Ophelia? Why would I drown myself, just because Hamlet does not worship and desire me? Because he wants to banish me to a convent or worse a brothel? Hamlet claims that I am mad, but he is the one who is mad, and I have no desire to heed his disregard. I own myself, and if I wish to drift downstream to a freer world, that's my choice. I certainly don't need his approval or his love.

After my session, I spoke with Mary about Tennyson and asked her if she writes poetry.

"No, I merely read it," she said. "I'm afraid I haven't the talent or imagination to write it. Do you write poetry?"

"Yes, I do. I have since I was young. I'm also an artist," I replied, astonished that I had confessed to making art.

"Are you? How fascinating. I've never met a woman artist. Who taught you?"

"No one. I'm self-taught, but I hope to learn from others," I admitted. "Do you think that your brother would teach me?"

"I haven't the foggiest . . . I'll happily walk you to your train, Miss Siddall. I must go help mother with the sewing. I do hope that you enjoyed your session with my brother."

"I did, but I would rather be the painter than the painted," I replied, as I pulled on my cloak. "I can find my way to the station. You needn't bother, Miss Deverell."

3 March 1849
Christina

Gabriel tells me that he is deeply smitten with, in fact he has fallen in love with, the most exquisite woman—a woman named Elizabeth Siddall—whom he calls a stunner, an unusual woman with flaming ginger-red hair, his friend Walter Deverell's model and now one of his. He met her when Mr. Deverell bragged about the beauty he was painting; he called her a "wonder." Gabriel immediately dashed to Deverell's studio and was overcome by her looks.

Gabriel said, "Christina, she's unlike any woman I've ever seen. Her hair hangs loose, like a waterfall down her back; her neck is long and graceful, like that of a swan's; her eyes contain countless depths."

As he spoke, I could easily tell that Gabriel more than fancied her; he had started to idolise her.

"She's a most unusual woman; in Deverell's painting, Miss Siddall poses as Viola dressed as Cesario, a rather unconventional heroine. In real life, she is as exceptional as her character; she dresses without a corset and wears bohemian clothing. She's extraordinary; she truly is a wonder."

When Deverell had difficulty replicating Miss Siddall's ginger hair on the canvas and cursed because of his ineptitude, Gabriel claims that he heroically stepped in, grabbed Deverell's palette, mixed the colours, and painted her hair on the canvas himself; he studied the way the light fell on it, and reproduced the golden and red tones on canvas in a striking effect, or so he says. I have yet to see the painting.

Gabriel told me that ever since he first saw her, he has known that Miss Siddall is his destiny and that once, in another life, he was bound to her.

"Surely, you jest," I said.

"No, it's true, Christina. I knew her before. I cannot escape loving her," Gabriel soberly replied, as he rifled through his desk, looking for something. He pulled out a piece of paper. "Here." He handed me the sheet of paper. "I awoke from a dream and wrote this. It captures what I know is true."

I read the following aloud.

> You have been mine before,—
>   How long ago I may not know.
> But just when at that swallow's roar
>   Your neck turned so,
> Some veil did fall,—I knew it all of yore.

"Perhaps that's merely wishful, fanciful thinking, Gabriel," I said. I thought about how these days he often envisioned *himself* as Dante the poet. Now he likely believes that he *is* Dante and that he has found his Beatrice. After he showed me the poem, he unveiled the beginnings of a sketch for a portrait of the two of them that he calls *How They Met Themselves*, where he and his love encounter their past selves, their doppelgängers. His Miss Siddall swoons when she sees her doppelgänger, and Gabriel holds her in his arms to keep her from collapsing.

"Do you think that you're her saviour, Gabriel?"

"No, surely not. I dreamt this though and had to paint it," he replied, as he continued to admire his work.

"Do you think it wise to sketch one's doppelgänger?"

"What's the harm? It was just a dream."

"More like a nightmare," I said under my breath.

I am not superstitious, but I have heard that meeting one's doppelgänger, like breaking a mirror or walking under a ladder, portends disaster. Fortunately, at least for now, he has not shared his painting with Miss Siddall, nor the fact that he more than fancies her; he worships and adores her and knew her in the past as his lady. I fear, if he told her this, she would conclude he is mad.

On occasion, I do truly fear he is mad, like Father, for they both continue to claim to see the poet Dante in our home. And, like Father, Gabriel derides Christian theology and reads Eastern philosophy and religions, populated by a plethora of gods and goddesses, which also makes him a heretic. He believes that we are all re-incarnated, living life after countless life until we reach a higher consciousness. Perhaps this is better than a life of misery and hidden secrets and passion. At least he's pleased that he believes that he has met his old love from a former life again.

I have never been in love, but I have read Maturin's *Melmoth the Wanderer* and know that love may lead to "demonic" possession, a certain kind of madness caused by Eros. Even though love is a form of madness, I wish to love. I grow tired of being alone and having no one who would mourn me if I should die. But I fear losing myself in love and merging myself with another.

Of late, I have spent some quiet time talking with Gabriel's friend James Collinson, the painter and poet, one of the members of the Pre-Raphaelite Brotherhood. With Mother as our chaperone, we have sat in the parlour and chatted about poetry and art. When he learned that I play chess, he challenged me to a game. He plays chess frequently with his sister and considers himself a fair student of the game.

Mother overheard our conversation and said to him, "Are you quite sure that you wish to play chess with Christina, Mr. Collinson? She's an expert at strategy."

Mother had never spoken to me about my chess-playing skill. Even though it is better to feel humble, I felt rather proud that she had noticed. I am the best chess player in my family. I have beaten my father and both of my brothers. I've even beaten Maria, my intellectual superior. I love disabling the king with my queen, who moves freely about the board.

"Well, why not? Let's give it a go," he replied.

As we played, Mr. Collinson tried to chat with me, but I ignored him, for I don't care to converse as I play. I plan my attack. I protect my king with flanks of bishops, knights, and rooks. I think about how to move my queen to the best advantage.

We played for an hour or so, and I could easily discern Mr. Collinson's feeble strategy and turn it to my advantage. "Are you sure that you want to place your king in danger?"

"I don't see that he is in danger."

"In two moves he'll be mine," I warned him.

He hesitated but he continued and foolishly placed his king in jeopardy. "Check," I said.

He looked confused and moved his king to a place that he assumed offered sufficient protection.

"Mate," I declared.

Mr. Collinson grimaced, turned crimson. "Well, Miss Rossetti, you've beaten me. I was warned that you are skilled, but I'll certainly prevail the next time we play. You can be assured." Secretly, inside I smirked because I knew, based on this game, that he would never conquer me.

Just then, the clock struck nine, and Mother said that it was time to retire. She announced that we would be pleased to visit with Mr. Collinson another time. And perhaps I would give Mr. Collinson more warning that he was in danger the next time we played chess.

In the ensuing days, Mr. Collinson called on me daily. Each day, we read a little poetry, particularly Browning, Mr. Collinson's favourite poet, and we studied some of Mr. Collinson's sketches of the Holy Family, where the child Jesus wears a crown like a king. He never asked me to play chess again, and I didn't challenge him, even though I wished to prevail over him. I suppose that he doesn't like losing and I didn't truly wish to hurt his masculine pride, although I would have enjoyed beating him.

After a few weeks of visiting me, Gabriel told me that Mr. Collinson had a private conversation with Father and requested to court me. Father did not ask me if I wished to be courted. He seems not to care whether I'm courted or not. Even so, I sense that Father is perhaps jealous that we are young and have our entire lives ahead of us, and he is a withered old man whose life is waning.

I am not opposed to courtship, if Mr. Collinson proves to be a noble and pious man who will support my art and my deepest desires (even if he's a poor chess player).

Gabriel encouraged me to allow Mr. Collinson to woo and then wed me; Gabriel has given up his plan to banish me to a convent. "Wouldn't you rather marry one of my artist friends than be required to leave home and become a wretched governess?" He made a valid point. I would rather die than become a scorned and belittled governess.

Yet Gabriel didn't ask me if I was attracted to or felt like Mr. Collinson is *my* destiny. I guess that destiny in love is only Gabriel's to possess.

5 April 1849
Christina

I lay awake all night beseeching God to help me decide whether I should accept Mr. Collinson's marriage proposal, which arrived far sooner than I anticipated. I barely know him, but last evening, when he was visiting the family, he asked to speak to me privately, and as we sat next to the fire in the parlour, he knelt on one knee and quietly asked if I would be his wife. The candlelight flickered and his face was cast in shadow.

I didn't know what to say. "Mr. Collinson, we have only known one another for a few months."

"Miss Rossetti, I've thought about it considerably. You and I are so much alike. You are as God-fearing as I. It seems that we would make a good pair in harness," he said, as he took my hand and squeezed it.

I imagined the two of us in harness and nearly laughed, but this was certainly no laughing matter, and I was certain that Mr. Collinson would think that I was mocking him.

"Please, Mr. Collinson, do stand. Of course, I will consider your proposal. But I will need to pray on it."

His face turned ashen, and at first, he couldn't speak. "As you should. I think that when you beseech God, you'll find the same answer that I did when I prayed on the question," he replied as he stood upright, towering over me. "Take your time. There is no rush. I will await your reply. Good Evening, Miss Rossetti." He bowed and quickly retreated from the room.

Even though I am of age, I was quite surprised to have received the proposal. I am nineteen, and unlike my sister, who plans to acquiesce to Gabriel's mockery of our piety by intending to become an Anglican nun, I do desire to marry and to love and be loved. Plus, marriage will be a way to escape continuing to care for my father. And I wish to become my own woman and not my mother's and father's vassal. But I am unsure as to whether Mr. Collinson is my soulmate, my destiny, as Gabriel claims Miss Siddall is his. Would that I were like Gabriel, who declares that he knew Miss Siddall in a past life. If I had known Mr. Collinson in another time, I would have perhaps known him long enough to ascertain whether he is my fate, and whether I could entrust him with my soul and my body.

Mr. Collinson is a good man, but he recently foolishly converted from being a High Church Anglican, as I am, to become a Roman Catholic. He is popish. I am not. My father abhors the Catholic Church and the power of the Pope. So do I. In my religion, we have no head of church, unless, of course, you wish to call the monarch the Anglican Church's Head, following precedent from Henry VIII's reformation of the church. But our monarch, Victoria, does not issue papal bulls, rules, and regulations, but rather lets us exercise our own private consciences. And, of course, there is Mr. Pusey who forbids alliances with Catholics, who are not the descendants of the true Christian Church, as we are.

Even so, I find aspects of Mr. Collinson appealing. He believes in self-sacrifice, as I do. He always wears the hair shirt to atone for his failings. I cast off my hair shirt and now atone through merely denying myself pleasure. In addition to denying myself the pleasure of attending the opera and the indulgence of devouring numerous custard tarts, I also forgo the pleasure of playing chess with my brothers and Father. Even so, it remains difficult to deny myself the pleasure of winning.

Mr. Collinson is also a fine painter, and more than my own brother, paints worthy subjects, biblical scenes, and saints. Oddly though, he paints the child Jesus and His playmates as if they lived in England among English flowers, such as honeysuckle and moss rose. Still, his mind is perennially on God, unlike Gabriel, whose mind often strays these days to the illicit and carnal; his mind resides frequently in the gutter. He no longer focuses on godly scenes, as he did when he painted *The Annunciation*, where a human encounters a fearful and awe-inspiring divine messenger. Of late, he paints Magdalenes rather than Virgins.

I suppose Mr. Collinson is a proper role model for me. One should always contemplate God, but my foremost concern is whether Mr. Collinson would love me, not just in a duty-bound way, but as his equal, as a woman, as an artist, as I assume a fair and just God would want. Would Mr. Collinson share my quiet passion; would we learn to love each other in a carnal manner, or would he treat me in the way that the art critic Mr. Ruskin supposedly treats his wife Euphemia? It is rumoured that he denies his own wife affection, love, and tender intimacies. I know nothing of complete carnal embrace, unlike Gabriel, who no doubt has much experience. Even so, I do worry about such intimacy and would hope that Mr. Collinson would be gentle with me.

In any case, I shall need to inquire further about Mr. Collinson's true feelings about his God and about me. After all, although he professes that he loves God, he did not confess, "Miss Rossetti, I love you with all of my heart. You are my destiny. Please honour me by consenting to become my wife." Instead, he wishes for me to be his horse in harness.

9 April 1849
Christina

I agonised over Mr. Collinson's Catholicism for hours and concluded, after much prayer and contemplation, that I must decline his proposal. I wrote to him and explained that I would only accept his offer if he, Mr. Collinson (whom I must not call by his Christian name until we are married), would give up his misguided popery and revert to the High Anglican faith. I told him, "I cannot convert to the Church of Rome if that is your intention. I will not bow down to a pope, who tries to take the place of God in our hearts. And I cannot marry a man who will not fully love God in the proper way." And, although I did not explicitly state this, naturally I cannot marry a man who would not consider me his equal.

My letter must have been persuasive for, after a week's prayerful consideration, Mr. Collinson has agreed to give up his wayward and false beliefs and return to Christ Church and the Anglican faith. Of course, this pleases me, and I am ready to consider whether I can become his wife.

Of late, we have sat next to one another on the settee in my family's parlour with Mother continuing to chaperone. Even though I fear criticism, I decided that, if he is to become my husband, I must share some of my poems with him. I read some of my religious poems, and naturally he praised them, saying that they brought glory to Our Saviour. I wanted him to know more about me though so I asked if he would like to hear my latest poem. He said that he'd be delighted. I commenced to read him one of my Songs.

> I saw her; she was lovely.
>   And bright her eyes of blue,
> Whilst merrily her white hands
>   Over the harp-strings flew.
> I saw her and I loved her,
>   I loved her for my pain,
> For her heart was given to another
>   Not to return again.
>
> Again I saw her pacing
>   Down the cathedral aisle;
> The bridal wreath was in her hair,
>   And on her lips a smile;

A quiet smile and holy,
　　Meet for a holy place,
A smile of certain happiness
　　That lighted up her face.

And once more I saw her,
　　Kneeling beside a bed;
The bright sun's rays were shining there,
　　And shone upon the dead;
From the body of her husband
　　Earth's gloom they chased away,
And she gazed on him without a tear,
　　And hailed the coming day.

After I read the poem to him, he seemed stunned, and didn't speak but then said, "I am not a poet of your calibre of course, Miss Rossetti, but is that a proper attitude for a wife to have? Shouldn't she weep for her dead husband, at least out of respect for her master?"

I looked at my mother, who nodded as if she agreed with him, but then I turned back to Mr. Collinson and couldn't hide my own reaction. I was appalled to hear him claim that a husband is his wife's master. I didn't respond to that assertion but said, "Well, in fact, she loves another, the persona speaking in the poem; perhaps she did not wish to marry the man for whom she doesn't weep."

"Why would you write a poem like that?"

"It came to me. I don't really write the poems. They surround me and I just pull them from the air. I scribble them before they dissolve before my eyes."

"Well, perhaps you should shut your eyes and ignore such poems. They don't seem suitable for a young lady. You should stick with your religious poems. They are worthy because they praise the Almighty."

Now *I* was stunned, so stunned that I couldn't speak. I resented him trying to tell me what I should do, which poems I should commit to paper. I held my tongue and my rage though, as Mother has repeatedly advised. I could tell from her demeanour that she wished me to remain silent and likely did not approve of the poem that I chose to read to Mr. Collinson. But I couldn't help but think: Do I tell him what to paint? What to think? Does he believe me to be his equal as a human being and artist? Or, if I married him, would I be his underling? Would he dictate my life? Would I flourish in his household, or would I feel smothered and stifled? Would I be able to live if I were to be cut off from the only activity that truly sustains me?

I put aside his remarks about my poem and did not discuss with him the hurt they caused. I think that he sensed my displeasure though because a few days later he asked if we might collaborate on a project whereby he would paint some of my religious poems and we would exhibit our work together. I now feel somewhat satisfied. Perhaps he regretted his remarks to me about my "Song." This new offer suggests the potential promise of equality as artists. Of course, I must remember that Mr. Collinson is perhaps more religious than I am. His head and heart always dwell on God, while mine occasionally dwells on earthly matters. I suppose that I must grow to be more like him in this regard.

If we do collaborate, I feel as though we can learn enough about one another in order to grow close, as we should since I accepted his proposal after I prayed once more for guidance. We are now informally promised to one another but are not formally engaged yet. We will wait to announce our banns. We must grow closer, and we must have similar goals and beliefs, if we are to thrive as a married couple.

However, I do fret because I do not feel a great attraction to Mr. Collinson. Gabriel constantly tells me about his intense feelings about Miss Siddall, feelings that seem to have taken possession of his very soul. Although I wish to be attracted to Mr. Collinson, I do not wish to become as enraptured with him as Gabriel is with Miss Siddall. (She seems to have bewitched him). I fear that I could lose myself and that I would put man before God, which is not the natural order of things. God loves us though; I believe that he wishes for us to be happy in this life, on this earth, and not be constantly pondering and fearing the afterlife. He wishes for each of us to have a suitable and loving companion (not a fellow horse in harness) with whom we can journey through life. No one should be alone; no one should be a solitary traveller.

12 April 1849
Christina

As an informal engagement gift, Mr. Collinson painted a portrait of me. It makes me look rather severe and homely. Is that how he sees me? Is that the way I truly look? Do I not possess joy? When I sat for him, did I look harsh and scornful? Does my look betray my lack of attraction to him? He plans to show this portrait to his mother and sister when he next visits them and he intends to take a copy of my *Verses* with him, so that they can meet me on canvas and paper before they meet me in person. Perhaps they'll think me comely when they see the portrait that Gabriel sketched of me. When I meet them, I shall endeavour to contrive a happy countenance, like that countenance that Gabriel captured, which is included in the book, so that they think better of my demeanour and my interior life. I still think Mr. Collinson's portrait of me is not accurate. Perhaps he does not see or grasp my soul.

2 January 1850
Lizzie

Dante Rossetti asked to sketch me in his studio, not just in Mr. Deverell's; I readily consented. I certainly need money, now that I only work part-time for Mrs. Tozer, who has learned of my modelling. I told her that my modelling was completely innocent and that I was chaperoned the entire time; nevertheless, she told me she worries about my good name. I can continue to work for her for now, but I must not sully my reputation.

Like Mr. Deverell's, Mr. Rossetti's studio was rather unkempt; but that's to be expected. Chaos creates art, they say. Dionysian wildness leads to Apollonian order. Such irrational disorder stirs my senses. In the studio, paints and paintbrushes were cast about, and blank canvases were spread out on the floor. I had to practically hopscotch over them to find the seat that he wished me to pose on and I did so with delight and anticipation.

Before I sat, I looked around for a chaperone but saw no one. Mr. Deverell told me that Mr. Rossetti has two sisters so I asked, "Will one of your sisters, perhaps Christina, join us?"

"How do you know of my sister Christina?"

"I read her *Verses* and quite enjoyed them," I said.

"Did you?" He paused and then remarked, "Those poems were rather juvenile. She's a better poet now; I serve as her editor. But, back to your question, my sisters are busy; Maria is sequestered in a convent studying to be a pious nun, and Christina is likely dutifully caring for my papa or scribbling a verse. Besides, there's no need for a chaperone. You're safe with me. I shall not harm you. I am a gentleman."

Before I could object and tell him that without a chaperone watching over his work with me, my reputation may be sullied, he ordered, "Take a seat, Miss Siddall."

"Am I to be myself or should I assume a character, like Ophelia?"

"You, Miss Siddall, are to be Delia, Tibullus's lover," he replied, as he rifled around on his desk to choose a drawing pencil.

"Tibullus, the Roman poet?" I asked.

He stopped hunting for the pencil and looked up. He raised his eyebrows. "You know of him?"

"Yes, of course. I know that he was greatly admired in ancient Rome. Of course, I can't read Latin, but I've read about him. I love all poetry; I write poetry." Like Mr. Deverell, Mr. Rossetti seemed rather surprised that I, a shop girl, knew about, read, and wrote poetry.

"Then you perhaps also know of Delia, and how Tibullus asked her to remain chaste, to pledge her bed to Diana, while he was away. He always returned to her, even though he took other lovers."

"So I've read," I replied. At first, I thought it unjust that Tibullus could have many loves while Delia by his order should remain chaste. And then I blushed at the thought of pretending to be someone's lover, but then realised that I didn't need personal experience with love; I remembered the look I painted on my face as I took on Viola as Cesario's persona. I remembered that I must learn to be an actress to be a model. I would need to contrive a particular look in regard to loving Tibullus.

"How do you wish for me to pose?" I asked.

"I want you to look with longing, dreaming about Tibullus, who is returning to you and walking into your bed chamber. You are unaware that he is there. He is gazing at you, and you are desiring him," he said. "I want you to close your eyes. Now draw a lock of hair into your mouth. Think about how Tibullus adores your ginger hair."

I did as I was instructed, but thought, why does Mr. Rossetti want me to pose as a woman who wants a man to enter her bedchamber? Why did he wish for me to pose as a neglected lover, another version of Ophelia? Is this the way a woman must always be seen? As a lustful and abandoned lover? As I sat, I thought not about Tibullus gazing at me, but of Mr. Rossetti. I opened my eyes briefly and saw that he looked at me as if he could see me naked. I felt exposed, but quickly closed my eyes and tried to become Delia once more. Modelling is an act, and I would need to become a good actress. Still, I would be my own version of Delia; I would not be a scorned lover; I would be a noble, modestly dressed woman with thoughts and plans of my own.

4 January 1850
Christina

Mr. Collinson and I attend church together, and afterwards we walk in Regent's Park. Even though I swore never to return to Christ Church, I have once again resumed attending Mr. Dodsworth's services and find them less troubling, although he, like Mr. Pusey, speaks continuously of the end times and how we must prepare ourselves for them. In one of his sermons, he claimed that there is "but one way of preparing for the end, and that is by living nearer to God and farther from the world." Mr. Collinson and I discussed this in light of our impending marriage, and we agreed that God must be foremost for each of us; neither of us should put our spouse before God, for even Christ himself said that we must abandon our fathers and mothers, our wives and husbands and follow him.

Mr. Collinson is working on a painting of St. Elizabeth of Hungary. He tells me that he is having difficulty with the attitudes of the Pre-Raphaelite Brotherhood and with being a member, because of its secularity. Mr. Collinson says that he loves Jesus and God's Holy Saints, and he thinks that the Brotherhood belittles them. He and I viewed Mr. Millais's Holy Family portrait at the Royal Academy's latest exhibition, which depicts the young Jesus and his family in the carpenter's shop. I said to him, "I like that the family is portrayed as prosaic, not divine. They are ordinary people. Their ordinariness is quite beautiful and helps us see our Saviour's humanity, don't you agree?"

"On the contrary, Miss Rossetti, Millais's painting is a disgrace; it's blasphemous and scandalous. It degrades God." He claimed that it was too worldly, and he agreed with those critics who also condemned the secular trend in the Brotherhood. "I believe that art must elevate, transcend the ordinary, and manifest God's divinity. My St. Elizabeth of Hungary will not exhibit human traits; she will rise above the earthly and transient."

After this conversation, I wrote a poem about St. Elizabeth and shared it with him.

> When if ever life is sweet,
>   Save in heart in all a child,
>   A fair virgin undefiled
> Knelt she at her Saviour's feet;
> While she laid her royal crown,
>   Thinking it too mean a thing
>   For a solemn offering,
> Careless on the cushions down.
>
> Fair she was as any rose,
>   But more pale than lilies white,
> Her eyes full of deep repose
>   Seemed to see beyond our sight.
> Hush, she is a holy thing:
>   Hush, her soul is in her eyes
>   Seeking far in Paradise
> For her Light, her Love, her King.

Mr. Collinson read my poem but did not praise it. Perhaps he thinks it too earthly since my St. Elizabeth is compared to ordinary flowers. Perhaps the poem is too common, like my "Song." I wished for him to understand, as I am beginning to comprehend, that the earthly is holy and should not be disparaged.

10 January 1850
Christina

Perhaps Mr. Collinson's Catholicism is difficult for him to abandon. I will read to him from Mr. Pusey's Tracts, and all will be well. Surely, he still agrees with Mr. Pusey, who says, "All ways are indifferent to one who has heaven in his eye. He that does not practise the duty of self-denial, does not put himself into the way to receive the grace of God." I sometimes forget these words myself and do not practise self-denial as I should. On occasion, I have succumbed to devouring custard tarts, which *are* divine. But I shall endeavour to be more self-effacing, remembering that we shall not find our paradise here on this earth, even if the earth contains some goodness, beauty, and sweet delights.

3 March 1850
Christina

While Mr. Collinson was away painting on the Isle of Wight, I visited his mother and sister. I spent a month with them in their village of Pleasley Hill, but it seemed more like a life sentence. I found my experience there tedious; I don't know if I could ever live in their provincial town. His sister Mary was pleasant enough, but we often sat in silence. Sometimes we played bagatelle and then one day she asked if I played chess. Instead of denying myself this pleasure, I once again decided to indulge myself, and I did not deny myself the pleasure of winning. She took the loss better than her brother did, but interestingly, she also did not ask me to play again.

So rather than play chess and hurt her pride, I followed her and her mother's example and knitted lace and helped in the garden. We sometimes visited and prayed with the sick in their parish. I often wrote to Gabriel, telling him that we should write rhyming verses, as we formerly did, but when he sent his rhymes, I could not finish them. I could not write while I was in the Collinsons' company or in Pleasley Hill, which is ironically dull. It's not in the least bit pleasing. I shall inform Mr. Collinson that we must remain in London or go abroad to Italy after we are wed. I cannot live where my art would be stifled.

The only moment of potential interest was an excursion to Hardwick Hall, which Mary promised would be delightful. We would picnic there. We travelled by coach, and then foot, carrying our victuals, crossing through fields of heather and gorse. From a distance, I could see that the hall itself was partially ruined, a portion of it contained no roof. Along the way, Mary told me that the hall was commissioned by the second richest woman after the queen in the sixteenth century, the Countess of Shrewsbury, Bess of Hardwick. Once inside, Mary marvelled at the long hall and the stained glass as she led me to a roofless chamber covered with ivy, as if nature itself was overtaking human achievement. We lunched in the chamber amid squirrels, robins, and magpies that had made homes in the crannies of the room. Even though Mary had started to call me Sister, we had little to say to each other for we have nothing in common, other than our mutual interest in chess; yet her interest was obviously not as avid as mine. As we settled down to eat our victuals, I attempted to make conversation and asked her if she reads poetry.

"Have you read Mrs. Browning's *Sonnets from the Portuguese*?" I asked. "She's an exceptional poet, better than her husband, I think."

"No, I confess I care little for poetry. James tries to entice me to read some of his work, but it all seems so unnecessary. I'm sure that I haven't a head for it. I take it that you've read it though, and James said that you write poetry. He showed me some. I'm sure that it's exceptionally fine, but again I find poetry confusing, and I don't have time to read it," she said as she concentrated on pouring herself some tea. "As you know, I must help Mother knit lace for the Church, and we must, as good Christians, visit the sick. I ask myself what good does poetry do for the world, for the sick and poor." She lifted the teapot. "Would you care for more tea, Sister?"

I started to speak about the value of poetry, how its grace saves us on a daily basis, but then Miss Collinson poured my tea, and we munched on cucumber sandwiches, never saying another word. The tea left a sour taste in my mouth. Instead of feeling delight as promised, the excursion made me feel dismal and lonely for genuine companionship and affinity. I resented Mary calling me Sister. I missed my own sister. And I wished that I missed Mr. Collinson more.

I suppose that I am not good at sacrificing myself. Perhaps I should reconsider our engagement, if Mr. Collinson wishes for us to live in Pleasley Hill. Or if we marry, I shall have to pray for the strength to bear my cross. And then I must find a way to indulge my art, even if family members are not keen to read it or to realise the value of art.

5 April 1850
Christina

Since I've returned from Pleasley Hill, I have corresponded with Mary to try to keep in her good graces, which I feared had suffered from our journey to Hardwick Hall. I felt that I had displeased and disappointed her. Certainly, she had frustrated me with her provincial view, but I never said so outright. While with her, I tried to be on my best behaviour. Even so, perhaps she thought me vain and pompous because I write and enjoy poetry. I inquired about her church work and her mother's health and whether she had gone on any further excursions with friends. I wished her good health.

I was shocked when I received a curt reply in which she stated that Mr. Collinson's prospects as a painter and poet are bleak, and she wished to cease our correspondence. I wonder if she is speaking the truth about her brother or if she and her mother have decided that I am not a suitable mate for Mr. Collinson. Surely, I must have offended them. Perhaps they did think me boastful or as tedious as I often found them. Although I did not feel contrite, I wrote her a letter of apology but received no reply. I do wonder what offence turned them against me, but I am hesitant to ask Mr. Collinson.

Mr. Collinson and I continue to keep company on Sundays, and I have refrained from asking him about his sister's missive. I don't wish to acknowledge her disbelief in his promise as an artist nor acknowledge her rather abrupt disdain for me.

15 April 1850
Lizzie

Walter Deverell told me of an exhibit at the Old Portland Gallery on Regent Street. I wished to visit it because he said that some of his fellow artists, those in the Brotherhood were exhibiting there; their paintings will be signed PRB. When I entered, I found that I was alone, except for the gallery owner, who asked me if I was looking for any painting in particular.

"No, sir," I said. "I wish to see them all."

"Are you a collector?"

"No, I'm an artist," I replied, even though I have never had an exhibit or any formal training. Once again, I felt rather bold to have proclaimed that I am an artist and I tried to keep my voice from trembling as I did so. Perhaps if I say it often enough, I will become what I claim.

"Oh, really," he seemed to scoff. "I recognize you though. Haven't you sat as a model for Deverell and Rossetti?"

"Indeed, I have; but I also sketch, and I paint with watercolours. I am more than a model for other painters," I said as I ambled away.

Just then, Mr. Deverell walked in and beamed when he saw me. "Oh, Miss Siddall, Lizzie . . . I'm so pleased to see you."

"Good morning, Mr. Deverell. I'm delighted to see you as well."

"I insist that you call me Walter, please. We are good friends after all, and friends should not abide formalities."

"If you insist, I shall try," I replied.

"Good," he said as he grabbed my hand and gently kissed it. "How do you like the exhibit?"

"I haven't seen anything yet. I was just about to start."

"Well, then, allow me to escort you," he said as he took my hand again and entwined my arm through his.

We walked by some rather drab paintings of sea captains and noble people, also of dogs and their masters in the style of Sir Joshua Reynolds. Walter had nothing to say about any of them, nor did I.

But then, we stood in front of an extraordinary painting of a cowering girl sitting on her bed while a man wearing a gossamer gown stands before her holding a white lily. He stands on fire but is unharmed. I checked the title on the plaque and its title was *The Annunciation*. Ah, I thought, this is certainly a new interpretation of the moment that Mary, the Mother of God, accepted her role in God's plan for humanity. Yet it was clear that the artist believes this Mary, or Miriam of the ancient world, is shocked by the expectation for her; she is unsure of or is unhappy about what is being offered her. And Mary looks like a mere child.

"Who's the painter?"

"Why it's our clown-friend, Mr. Rossetti; the man who always seeks your attention," he said.

"He is certainly not the jester here. The painting is serious. It is quite humanising though. This virgin is not Titian's."

"Oh, do you know Titian's *Assumption of the Virgin*?"

"Yes, of course," I said. Once more, he seemed surprised that I, a shop girl-cum-model, would know the work of Italian painters. "This virgin seems so innocent and young, a child really. Who is the model?"

"It is Dante Rossetti's sister Christina," Walter replied.

I stood before the painting and studied it for the longest time. I was not ready to move on to view another work. So here is the poet as the virgin-mother of God. She will give birth to the saviour of humanity. I must meet her and learn why she is so fearful of and reluctant to undertake her task of saving the world. I must ask why she, Christina as Mary, nearly turns away from her handmaid's task.

5 May 1850
Christina

I've decided to contribute to the Brotherhood's literary journal, *The Germ*. I only did so after Gabriel finally agreed to allow me to use a pseudonym. He will attribute my poems to Evelyn Alleyn. With this name, no one will know if I'm female or male.

Here is one of my poems, which I rather like and is based on the feeling engendered at Hardwick Hall:

> We build our houses on the sand
> Comely withoutside and within;
> But when the wind and rains begin
> To beat on them, they cannot stand:
> They perish, quickly overthrown,
> Loose at the hidden basement stone . . .
>
> Why should we hasten to arise
> So early, and so late take rest?
> Our labour is not good; our best
> Hopes fade; our heart is stayed on lies.
> Verily we sow wind; and we
> Shall reap the whirlwind, verily.

I made sure that Mr. Collinson received a copy of the journal and let him know that, if he wishes, he may call me Evelyn Alleyn. I thought it amusing, but he didn't seem, as is usual, in the mood to jest.

Rather abruptly he said, "Miss Rossetti, I'm leaving tonight to visit my mother and sister. I must make haste to catch my train, which departs in an hour."

"Why are you going to visit? Is something amiss?"

"No, Mother has requested my presence so that I can meet her new vicar. She wants to learn my opinion of him."

"Then you'll be back soon, I hope. Mr. Millais has a new show and I thought that we could attend together."

"Certainly, I'll likely be back within the week; I'm not sure that I wish to see Mr. Millais's show, but I will consider it," he said as he kissed my hand.

I felt an odd little flutter inside my chest and then requested, "Write soon, Mr. Collinson, James . . . I'll miss you when you're gone."

He raised his eyebrows, seeming to note my familiarity. Because we planned to soon announce our banns, I felt at ease for the first time calling him by his Christian name.

"As I will you, Miss Rossetti," he replied.

19 May 1850
Christina

He has been gone for more than a week, a fortnight in fact, and has not corresponded with me, even though I've sent him several letters. I wonder if he is ill or if his mother and sister have spoken out against me. If they have, I wonder why. I did my best to make myself agreeable to their lives and activities, even if my heart and mind were elsewhere.

26 May 1850
Christina

After an additional week, Mr. Collinson, James, wrote to Gabriel, but not to me. He told Gabriel that he wishes to resign from the Brotherhood. In his letter to Gabriel, he confessed, "I feel that I can no longer allow myself to be called PRB. I love [God's] holy saints and I cannot dishonour them as you and the others do." It seems that some of his denouncement of the Brotherhood stems from Gabriel's criticism of my intended's painting of St. Elizabeth of Hungary, which James apparently heard about from Mr. Hunt. Gabriel finds the painting a wreck; the prostrate Elizabeth looks, according to him, like a pile of rags rather than a saint seeking God over man. Contrary to James's hope that his subjects transcend earthly life, his subject appears utterly degraded, at least according to Gabriel. Gabriel said there is no truth and beauty in the painting, and he is quite willing to release James from the Brotherhood. It seems he was never truly their brother at all.

5 June 1850
Christina

The news was somewhat shocking but not entirely unexpected. I wrote to Mr. Collinson again but received no reply. Finally, I received a short letter from him, announcing that he is returning to the Roman Catholic Church. He declared that he had prayed for many days and that he has decided to seek the vocation of the priesthood. He soon intends to enter the seminary. I momentarily felt my heart ache; I had become somewhat attached to Mr. Collinson. I actually had missed him during his absence for the first time; I was becoming somewhat fond of him. I thought that eventually we could become suitable mates. But I respect his faith and know that his choice places God above me as it should.

I have returned all his letters and the copy of *Sonnets from the Portuguese* that he gave me at Christmas, which I assume that he, like his sister, never read because he never asked, "How do I love thee?" I asked him to return my letters and the lock of hair that I bestowed on him. It is fortunate that we were never formally engaged, that our banns had not been read, because I could sue him for breach of promise. Of course, I never would because it appears that, after all, he was not my soulmate, as Miss Siddall seems to be Gabriel's, as Elizabeth Barrett is Robert Browning's. In some ways, I am relieved to know that he was not my destiny, and I am eternally grateful that I am not his horse in harness.

5 June 1850
Lizzie

I continue to model for Mr. Rossetti but also pose for Mr. Hunt and Walter Deverell. Mr. Hunt had me model for Christ's hair in his *Light of the World* once more suggesting that I am a boy-girl rather than solely female. I am no longer chaperoned when I sit for any of them, even for Walter. They seem to vie for me, and often Mr. Rossetti will just show up when I am modelling for Walter. He often asks Walter for a loan so he can buy paint. Then he distracts me as he sits and sketches me while Walter paints me. Like a jester, Mr. Rossetti tries to make me laugh and often succeeds, which breaks my pose. He is rather comic and somewhat endearing as he charms me with his need for my attention. I must then compose myself and apologise to Walter for failing to model properly.

Sometimes Mr. Rossetti talks to me about his poetry and occasionally reads it aloud to me. One day, he read "The Blessed Damozel," a rather eerie poem, which portrays a dead woman wishing that her earthly lover could join her in heaven. As I cast myself in the role of the dead woman, I felt her anguish and pain as she looked down with longing on her lover who continued to live on and thrive without her.

"Rossetti," Walter said, "Can or would you stop talking? Your incessant babble distracts me and Lizzie . . . Miss Siddall. Please go away and leave us alone."

"But Miss Siddall enjoys my poetry, Deverell. Why do you want to deprive her of listening to the next poet laureate?"

"You're mad, Rossetti," Walter replied, as he continued to paint.

"And you're jealous," claimed Mr. Rossetti.

I find their rivalry amusing. In truth, I think that Mr. Rossetti doesn't like me to be alone with Walter, who is quite fond of me and I of him. After I sit for him, he often asks to read my poems and he has even looked at my sketches, offering advice on form. Walter has insinuated on several occasions that he may in fact propose to me when the time is right. When we are alone, he sometimes holds my hand, and once, he nearly kissed me on the cheek, but then his sister walked in. I felt somewhat like the female figure on Keats's "Ode on a Grecian Urn," forever waiting for my lover to kiss me. Even so, I am cautious, as I should be, about romantic entanglement. I don't wish to be taken advantage of by any man, even a gentle soul like Walter.

15 December 1850
Christina

The PRB has had their first exhibition and the knives are out. One critic wrote of the artists, whom he called "juvenile": "We can extend no toleration to a mere servile imitation of the cramped style, false perspective and crude colours of remote antiquity. We do not want to see faces bloated into apoplexy or extenuated to skeletons." Contrary to their aim to revolutionise the art world, the PRB have been denounced as callow imitators. Members of the Academy have disparaged their work, and Charles Dickens has even weighed in, calling Mr. Millais's rendering of the child Jesus in his *Christ in the House of his Parents* appalling. He described Millais's Jesus as a "wry-necked, blubbering red-headed boy in a bed-gown, who appears to have received a poke . . . playing in an adjacent gutter." I think that Mr. Dickens may dislike the painting solely because the child Jesus is portrayed as having ginger hair like Judas.

I saw Mr. Collinson at the exhibit, but I did my best to ignore him. Although my knees felt a little weak, I composed myself and then managed to feel nothing. He was like a stranger to me. I felt as though I never knew him, and I knew then that his decision to return to popery was the correct one for both of us. I wondered if he still intends to enter the seminary. I did not speak to him, as there was no need. I know that he agrees with Mr. Dickens and thinks that Mr. Millais's Christ Child degrades Jesus. Unlike him, I continue to find it extraordinary and inspiring because of its earthly humanity. And I like Jesus's red hair.

1 January 1851
Christina

Gabriel tells me that the PRB now have their champion. Mr. John Ruskin, the celebrated art critic, has heroically come to their rescue. Gabriel showed me the two letters that Mr. Ruskin has written to *The Times* in praise of their mediaeval approach, their vibrant colours, and their revolutionary approach to painting. In one of the letters he stated, "Look around at our exhibitions and behold the cattle 'pieces,' the eternal brown cows in ditches, and the white sails in squalls . . . The Pre-Raphaelite Brotherhood imitate no pictures: they paint from nature only . . . . If they adhere to their principles and paint nature as it is around them, they will found a new and noble school of art nobler than the world has seen in 300 years." Mr. Ruskin also chastised Mr. Dickens for his criticism of their work, noting that Mr. Dickens may have expertise in writing common comical fiction, but he knows nothing about the art of painting or truth and beauty. He should leave painting criticism to those who have studied the subject and stick to writing his flat caricatures, suggesting that Mr. Thackeray is a better comic novelist. Obviously, Gabriel is thrilled that Mr. Ruskin celebrates their work. No one rises higher in the art world than him in terms of aesthetic prowess and knowledge, even if he knows little about human intimacy and love.

4 November 1851
Lizzie

Dante Rossetti has become increasingly jealous of the other painters who have me sit and model for their work. Ever since he first painted my hair and then sketched me as Delia and then showed up continually at Mr. Deverell's studio, Mr. Rossetti has become quite possessive of me. He asks me why I pose for the other painters, and I confess that I need the money. I need to continue to help support my family as Mrs. Tozer has let me go. I cannot return to the milliner shop because my work as a painter's model has damaged my good name. Somehow, Mrs. Tozer has learned that I am no longer chaperoned when I pose. And she's also somehow aware that Mr. Hunt and Mr. Millais often look for girls on Tottenham Court to serve as models. I would guess that Mrs. Tozer equates these girls with me, and even though I insist that I am not like those streetwalking women, *she* insists that she cannot have what she perceives to be a disreputable girl working in her shop.

"Well, you can just model for me, Miss Siddall. I will make you immortal," he said as he began to sketch me, as I sat on his settee.

"I don't wish to be immortal, and I can't just model for you. You haven't any funds with which you can pay me, have you? You told me that you needed to borrow tin from your brother, and I know you borrow money from Walter, I mean Mr. Deverell," I replied.

I already suspected that Dante Rossetti was a complete wastrel, but unfortunately, I was starting to fall in love with him. His great charm, his poetic and artistic prowess attract him to me, that and perhaps the fact that he could teach me to paint with oils, as I've always wanted to do. He could be my teacher and perhaps secondarily my suitor, even my husband someday. When he reads his poetry to me, I feel as though he has written the poems for me and that I am perhaps his muse as he repeatedly claims. Oh, and, through him I might meet his extraordinary sister who seems a better poet than Mr. Rossetti in my opinion.

"Oh, but I'll earn a fortune once I capture you on canvas." He moved closer to me. "And once I earn that fortune, I will make you mine. You will be my wife," he said matter-of-factly, as if I had no say in the matter.

He is as handsome as a Greek god; he is a brilliant artist, even though he is slow as a tortoise in producing his work. I have seen his sketches from his youth, which are far superior to my own. He often tells me of his ambition to be the next Titian. Perhaps I can help him become a prodigious painter and he will help me become one as well if I become his wife. But I didn't say any of this for fear that he wasn't serious. So, in a slightly mocking tone, I asked, "What are you saying, Mr. Rossetti? Is this a proposal?"

"Yes, I suppose it is, Miss Siddall . . . Lizzie." He hesitated and then said quite soberly as he gazed at me, "I know that we have been joined previously; you and I were once wed in another life. You have always been mine. You are my destiny."

I wanted to say that I don't believe in destiny or in previous lives, but I bit my tongue. Of course, I now realised that I wanted to and could be his wife in this life, even if he was being overly dramatic or irrational in his belief that he knew me in another life. So, I consented.

And with that Dante and I were engaged.

3 February 1852
Lizzie

What did the water feel like on my skin? That is difficult to describe because I was covered from neck to foot with an ornate, silver, mediaeval-style wedding gown that Mr. Millais had purchased to dress his Ophelia. The water did permeate the gown though, which grew sodden and heavy from the moisture. The water occasionally lapped against my skin and warmed and soothed me, like a gentle sensual bath, a pagan christening.

As Ophelia, I imagined that I was floating downstream on my own—not in a deliberate act of self-destruction but to escape my tormentor, Hamlet, who thought *me* mad. As I floated, I felt fish nibble at my toes and hands and leaves fall on me from weeping willows that lined the stream. I gazed at the sky and watched the puffy clouds drift by. I imagined riding one of those clouds, and looking down on the great, green earth. I did this every time Millais submerged me in his vat, telling me to think about my death. Each day, for four months as I lay in that warm bath, I thought my own Ophelia thoughts and pondered life, not death; I thought about the freedom to become myself. To become a true artist.

4 September 1852
Lizzie

I donned the heavy and still slightly sodden wedding gown for the last time this morning, as I lay in the warm tub that mimicked the flowing stream. Once again, I thought *my* Ophelia thoughts, not the ones that Millais assumed that I thought. I pondered drifting downstream on my own will, escaping Hamlet and *his* madness, his brutal treatment of me, his desire to send me away to be sequestered, imprisoned as a nun, or perhaps confined to a brothel. I felt the reeds lightly brush against my hands as I drifted. I could see the robin's-egg blue sky dotted with wispy clouds. I carried poppies, willow, and nettle, but they floated out of my hands as I became relaxed in the warm bath. I heard nightingales sing in the willows above me. I was so enraptured by my own Ophelia-world that I didn't notice when a gust of wind from the open window blew out the candles beneath my vat, extinguishing the heat that kept me from freezing in my stream.

While I was dreaming my Ophelia thoughts, I heard a loud noise, as if something crashed to the floor. I could feel my teeth chatter, but I didn't know why. Someone was shouting, but my ears were underwater, and I couldn't hear. I tried to raise my head but couldn't. I felt frozen as if I had been cast in ice. What were they shouting, and why? Then, I felt someone suddenly lift me from the tub. I gulped and sputtered water and couldn't catch my breath. My body was stiff, and I couldn't comprehend what was happening or where I was. Who was holding me? My vision was blurry, but once I was able to focus, I realised that Dante was carrying me in his arms, and he was shouting at Mr. Millais.

"What have you done, Millais?" he yelled. "She's nearly drowned like Ophelia herself. Were you trying to freeze her to death?"

He laid me on Mr. Millais's bed, wrapping me in a would-be shroud, while further chastising Mr. Millais for being obtuse, for treating me in the same way that Hamlet would, not as a real human, but as a pound of flesh to be used and discarded.

Later, after Mr. Millais ran out to consult an apothecary about my condition, I remained in bed under a heap of counterpanes to counteract the shivering fit that had overtaken me. After Dante stoked the fire to warm the room, he sat on the bed, wrapped me in his arms, and confessed once again that he loves and adores me, that I am his muse, his destiny, his soon-to-be bride. "How soon?" I wanted to ask but couldn't because a shivering fit overtook me once more.

Dante then ordained that I shall sit for no other painter than him. "Lizzie, I am the only one who will treat you with dignity and respect. I will love and protect you. Deverell, Millais, and Hunt merely feed on the light that shines from you. They vampirize your radiance. I will save you from the others. I am your Dante, and you are my Beatrice."

Knowing that Dante Alighieri never married his true love, that he was haunted by her, that he dreamt of her dying and becoming an angel, I concluded I would rather not be Dante's Beatrice; I merely desire to be Dante Rossetti's Lizzie.

17 September 1852
Lizzie

After my ordeal of posing for Mr. Millais's *Ophelia*, Da sent me to Hastings to convalesce by the sea. I told Da that I am not ill, but he insists that I am. I do lack appetite and get an occasional chill, but I doubt the cause of these issues was lying in a freezing bath. Of course, we are always wary of cold baths and the ensuing chilblains that they can cause. Often, we are bled to treat these conditions, but I hate being bled, so I sought rest along the sea. Even so, I do believe that Da wishes for me to be ill so that he can sue Mr. Millais for possibly harming my health.

Da should have been a lawyer. He loves filing lawsuits. For years, he sued the descendants of the Eyre family, saying that we are the rightful owners of Hope Hall, which we've been told is habitable. Because of his suits, he depleted our family funds so severely that we were forced to move to smaller accommodations. All of the lawsuits finally ended when my sister Lydia had enough of Da's nonsense and, much to his dismay, she threw all his petitions, claims, affidavits, and proofs of descendancy pertaining to the suits in the fire. Now he has no proof. Likewise, he has no proof that Mr. Millais permanently injured my health. Despite this, he insists that Mr. Millais pay the doctor's fee after my chilling immersion in the would-be stream.

10 November 1852
Lizzie

Mr. Millais's *Ophelia* is an enormous success. The Royal Academy exhibited it, but Dante scorns it. I have not asked why. Perhaps it reminds him that I nearly caught pneumonia and certainly acquired chilblains from being submerged in a cold bath for hours at a time. Fortunately, the bumps and redness have dissipated. Or perhaps Dante sees green because of his friend's accomplishment, an accomplishment that even the famous art critic, Mr. Ruskin, praises.

Dante fancies me his Beatrice, but I am not an Italian girl, and I certainly don't guide him through heaven and hell. And, unlike Beatrice, I do begin to worship, not merely love, my Dante. I adore his poems, the way he sometimes reads Tennyson to me in the evenings in his studio, the time he now takes to instruct me in the art of love. He continues to insist that he knew and loved me in another life. If he actually did love me then, wouldn't I remember the art of love?

I can't say that I share his belief, but I am satisfied and happy that he says he loves me in this one. Still, I wish that he spent more time teaching me the art of painting and less time teaching me the art of love.

10 November 1852
Christina

Per Gabriel's invitation, I attended the unveiling at the Royal Academy of Mr. Millais's *Ophelia*, an extraordinary painting that Gabriel's muse posed for. Ophelia looks as if she's dreaming of another world as she floats downstream. Weeping willow branches drift along with her, indicating Hamlet's betrayal of her. Her eyes are open; she appears awake, perhaps discovering for the first time how much Hamlet has deceived her. Her silver embroidered dress clings to her body somewhat like armour. Perhaps she has shielded herself from any further hurt by her beloved.

After my lengthy study of the painting, I turned around and I saw Gabriel's muse, Miss Siddall, standing in front of me. I was so stunned that I needed to turn away and compose myself. Gabriel is correct; she is a wonder to behold. She emanates light so strongly that I felt I might go blind from looking at her. I wished to speak to her but didn't have the nerve to approach such an exquisite woman, a goddess really. I quickly left the exhibition without saying goodbye to my brother, who was busy sulking in a corner, while crowds of admirers swirled around Mr. Millais and his model.

15 November 1852
Lizzie

I am Dante's disciple in all things. I watch as he sketches my face and ask why he makes so many portraits of me.

"Because there are many Lizzies hiding inside of you, all of them are noble and divine. I sketch to find and immortalise all of them."

I think that this is rather absurd. I am an ordinary girl, not divine; yet he does treat me like a holy thing.

I watch him as he sketches. I pay close attention to how he creates borders in his sketches, and what he calls the negative spaces. I note his use of colour and shade.

Last evening, as he once again sketched me in his studio, I snatched one of his drawing pencils from his hand and told him to hold still and pose for me. He made a mocking face, and I ordered him to please be serious.

"Dante, I pose for you, whenever you ask, now you can pose for me for at least a few minutes. You are my model."

He finally composed himself and struck a gallant pose. I quickly sketched his angular face and his wild locks that resemble Apollo's.

When I was done, he grabbed the sketch from my hand. "Lizzie, where did you learn to do that? Where did you learn to draw?"

"I watched you and it just came to me." Of course, I lied. I didn't want him to know that I was self-taught or that I once sketched for a murderer who was my would-be patron.

"You, my dove, my Sid, are a natural artist. You need proper training, but I can see that you defy Ruskin's belief that women are generally incapable of creating truth and beauty." He gushed. "Now, you are not only my only muse, my greatest love, but my fellow artist. But I have known this—as I told you, I knew you in another life."

"You flatter me, sir," I said sardonically. "I recall no past life with you. What do you want from me?"

"Nothing. Just a chance to know you more fully. Come, let's to bed so we can know each other better," he said, as he laid down the sketch pad and led me once again to his bed. At first, I struggled, for I wished to complete my sketch, but, when he placed his warm hands near my heart, I relented.

2 October 2019
Hastings

Maggie had fetched Lizzie's book of poetry from the Hare and Hawthorne Bookstore and purchased a copy of Christina's *Complete Poetry* from WH Smith Booksellers. She couldn't wait until she travelled to London to read Christina's verses. She eagerly read their poems by candlelight at night in the crypt, which she thought romantic and fitting for the Victorian time setting of the diaries. She found it fascinating that both poets were starved for affection and love. Both dwelled on death and disappointment. And they both seemed haunted by their pasts; Lizzie literally by Mr. Greenacre and Christina by her troubling relationship with her father. Maggie realised that, surely, if they had met and became acquainted through confessing their life stories to one another, they would understand their affinity and would be companions, intimate friends even. Perhaps such friendship would help them overcome the hopelessness they each seemed to have felt. She wondered if there were other diary entries that filled in the gaps in their reflections on their daily lives. Had some of them been destroyed by the vicar or some Rossetti descendant or perhaps by Lizzie or Christina themselves? She understood that sometimes before death people want to maintain their privacy and guard their intimate thoughts.

As Maggie pondered the likelihood of missing entries, she decided to look more thoroughly through the chest. She was eager to discover the moment when Lizzie and Christina met. So, she foraged around in the back of the chest and pulled out a random group of papers from 1858, wherein she began to understand why the diaries had been buried.

2 January 1858
Lizzie

Even though I believe that trying to find a golden age, a golden past, is futile and perhaps foolish, after much surreptitious preparation and planning, Christina and I headed north late one evening while Christina's mother slept, and Dante went to the pleasure gardens. We boarded the train toward Sheffield, where my ancestors lived. As we left the noise and stench of London behind, I began to feel excited, but I still felt nervous. I fretted about what we would find when we arrived at Hope Hall. Would Hope Hall be inhabited, intact, available to us? Would the estate provide us with a home where we could practise our art undisturbed? I also worried about what Dante would do when he found that both of us were gone. Would he suspect that we were together? Would anyone search for us? I felt like a runaway wife, even though Dante had no legitimate claim to me. His promises were never fulfilled, and now I had a chance to forge my own life with my new "sister in art," my friend, my confidant, my Christina. Perhaps Hope Hall would fulfil our deepest desires.

After we alighted from the train, we expressed exhaustion from the twelve-hour trip. Even so, I had sufficient energy to hire a carriage to take us to my family's ancestral home.

"Are you sure that you wish to go there, lass?" the driver asked. "Nowt is there. None have lived there for years, and it's said that the place is in shambles; and some even say that no tyke, no person, lives there. A barghest inhabits the place. A wretch supposedly killed one of the Eyre daughters there."

Being unfamiliar with the Yorkshire diction, I asked, "What's a barghest?"

"Why, a ghost, a spirit, as you Southerners say," he replied.

I hesitated momentarily and thought about Dante's vivid encounters as a child with Dante Alighieri's ghost, which he repeatedly told me about and how much he feared the ghostly poet who lived in their home, but then I screwed up my courage and said, "Yes, Hope Hall is our destination. It is my family's home. If it's haunted as you claim, the ghost is my ancestor. I'm not afeared; the barghest, the ghost, is family." Christina reached for my hand and gave it a squeeze.

He shrugged. "As you wish, lass."

From far away we could see that the driver was correct, at least about the condition of Hope Hall. The place looked partially in ruins. It was obvious that it had been abandoned by the Eyres. Perhaps it was haunted by this barghest, and no one wished to live there any longer. Or perhaps they decided, after all the lawsuits that my father levied and the costs incurred, that they would leave the estate to the creatures that live on the land. The house itself was covered with vines, even over the doorway. Some of the stones from the top floor had fallen off and lay in the yard. Even so, the house was still standing and looked rather grand. It had once been a very great house. It presided over a valley; behind it stood an ancient forest of oak, elm, and pine. Once we stepped from the carriage and the driver drove off, saying, "Ta'rra," the way they say Goodbye in the North, Christina and I first looked in through the windows and saw that the house was in disarray. It was clear that no one was living there.

"So, this is the Siddall home; it is ours now that the Eyres seem to have abandoned it. Of course, we would be squatters. Shall we go in?"

"We came all of this way, of course we shall," Christina replied. She began to yank the vines that covered the doorway, and I helped her. Together we struggled to pull open the door; the hinges squeaked from disuse. Once inside, we were enchanted by the rusticity, the broad wooden Tudor-style beams in the ceiling, the open hearth, and the vines and ivy that encroached on the house itself. It was as if the house and the natural environment were trying to become one. Blossoming orange trumpet vines, honeysuckle, and ivy had even grown inside the windows, finding their way through the crevices and cracks. We found a few creatures indoors, a mama raccoon and her babies, and some feral cats and kittens, but they became frightened and quickly found their way out of the house through the open door. The furniture left behind: a settee, a long pine table and chairs, were dusty but sturdy. The hearth was laden with wood, as if we'd been expected by some guardian servant or perhaps the barghest.

"This will suit me," I said. "Are you satisfied, Christina? Is it what you expected? Will you be happy here? Can we live with the barghest, my female ancestor murdered by a man?"

"I thought you weren't afraid of the ghost," she replied.

"I feigned courage in front of the driver. But I think that you and I together can withstand the ghost, especially if she is my ancestor. Perhaps she's lonely and would like company. Perhaps she wishes for us to release her from her confinement and unhappiness. I have sympathy for her."

Christina found an old broom perched next to the door and began sweeping. "Indeed, as do I. But just in case, I'll sweep out the old lives and perhaps the ghost that inhabits this place. She can go elsewhere with our blessings. We'll make Hope Hall ours. Our sisterhood and good fortune start here."

2 October 2019
Hastings

Before Maggie could process the fact that Lizzie and Christina had run away together to Hope Hall and had tried to sweep away the ghosts of the past, she heard footsteps on the staircase. She worried that it could be an intruder but then thought perhaps it was just the return of the crypt's rat searching for food, or maybe it was her silent reading partner, for she remembered that the church was locked. As she was taking a photo of the 1858 entry, she was shocked when she saw a man standing in front of her holding a torchlight and a bottle of whiskey. He swayed as he stood there; he seemed a bit tipsy.

"Who are you and what the devil are you doing here?" he asked.

"I'm a historian from Sheffield, Dr. Maggie Winegarden. I'm conducting research."

"And who gave you permission to open this chest?"

"I might ask who you are, sir." Maggie had trouble seeing the man's face because of the shadows falling on it.

"Reverend Mr. Carson, Miss," he replied as he continued to sway. "I'm the vicar here."

"Oh, I see. Well, Mrs. Highclere allowed me to review the contents of the chest," Maggie said as she stood up while still holding her camera. Reverend Carson was a short, rotund, red-faced man. Maggie towered over him.

"Well, she had no right. That stupid old woman. And historian or not, you have no licence to read these writings; and you certainly have no right to take photos. Close the chest immediately," he replied.

"Is there a reason that you don't wish for Christina Rossetti's and Lizzie Siddal's words to be read?"

"They are private musings, and the family does not want their contents revealed. That's more than enough for you to know," he said, slurring his words a bit. Then he reached over and grabbed Maggie's camera and threw it on the floor. Then he shut the chest and turned the key. Placing the key in his trousers' pocket, he told Maggie to leave.

"You broke my property. *You* had no right. I'll report you to the constable."

"And I'll tell them you were trespassing. Leave before you get arrested," the vicar replied.

She reluctantly did as she was told, but knew that she'd be back, for she needed to read Lizzie's and Christina's musings to learn more about their parallel lives and to learn how and why they decided to abandon their London lives, families, and real and potential lovers. She wanted to know why they set up house together and what became of their sisterhood. The slightly inebriated, rude, and violent vicar would not stop her.

3 October 2019
Hastings

Maggie fumed all morning about how the Reverend Mr. Carson banished her from the crypt and had broken her camera. Fortunately, the sim card had not been harmed. She would have to find a way to return to complete her reading of the manuscripts and to take more photos in case the diaries were destroyed. They were important. They revealed that Lizzie and Christina were not adversaries as previously thought; they were actually friends and sisters in art. And she was particularly disturbed to learn in Lizzie's last entry that she and Dante had become lovers and that Lizzie had fallen in love with the capricious artist. Maggie needed to know what happened next and why it took so long for them to eventually marry. Did Lizzie and Christina run away before or after Lizzie and Dante married? How did Christina factor into this relationship? Maggie wished that she knew more about Lizzie's life and regretted that art history courses slighted women painters at the expense of lauding male ones.

When her phone rang, she was sitting on the sea wall stewing over the angry, rude, sexist, ageist, and condescending vicar who knew there was something in the diaries that the Rossettis hoped to hide. Maggie looked at her phone and saw that Bethany was ringing her up. She dreaded answering the call but felt that she must.

"Hello, Beth," Maggie answered.

"When are you coming home, love?" Bethany asked. "I've missed you, Maggie, and I'm sorry about our row. Do you forgive me?"

Maggie hesitated. After being apart, she wasn't sure about their relationship anymore. Bethany was too controlling, and Maggie didn't always feel free to be herself. "I'm still in Hastings."

"Whatever for? I thought you were headed to London to work at the Imperial War Museum."

Maggie thought about not revealing what she had found in the crypt, for she didn't want Bethany to get her hands on the diaries. She feared what Bethany would want to do with them. But because of the magnitude of the discovery, and without fully thinking, she blurted out, "I stumbled on some writing . . . some diaries that belong to Christina Rossetti and Lizzie Siddal."

"You're certain they're real?"

"Yes, they're old and mildewed but perfectly legible. They're in a trunk that the Rossettis hid in St. Clement's Church, where Christina attended church and where the Rossettis bestowed Dante's painting of Christina as the Virgin. Unbelievably, the diaries reveal that Lizzie and Christina ran away to Yorkshire together, to be artists together. I was just about to read more when the exceedingly rude vicar interrupted and prohibited me from reading any more of the entries. He even broke the camera I was using to take photos of them."

"If he wants to hide them, they must be important. I'll be there tomorrow. I need to see them."

Maggie heard the phone disconnect.

Even though Maggie regretted telling Bethany about her discovery, she realised that Bethany could possibly help her with it, but they would also need to sort out their relationship in order to do so. She wasn't sure which of these situations was more important. She'd sleep on it after she painted by the sea this evening. At least no one could stop *her* from painting, as others had thwarted Lizzie. She could choose to paint by the sea and no one, not even Bethany, could stop her.

As Maggie set up her easel once more, she thought about how she and Bethany had become acquainted and eventually lovers. Even though at the time, they were both enrolled as graduate students in the Humanities at the University of Warwick, they met while attending a summer artists' retreat in Donegal. Bethany was a fine poet and Maggie was continuing to study painting, but now as her avocation. They both enjoyed each other's hobby and encouraged one another. They quickly became best friends, for they shared many common interests: theatre, film, hiking the fells, swimming in, and walking by the sea. They grew closer and eventually confessed to loving one another and then moved in together after only knowing each other for six months.

But after they became a couple, Bethany gave up her creative work and encouraged Maggie to do the same. They sought and secured academic careers at the University of Sheffield, which did not support or leave time for creativity, only the writing of scholarly monographs and articles written for other academics, a kind of narcissism and mental self-pleasuring that Maggie abhorred but Bethany enjoyed and said was necessary if they were to succeed. Now that Maggie had read about women artists, like Lizzie and Christina, who were often discouraged from practising their art, she felt a powerful desire and almost an obligation to make up for what they had been denied.

She was thinking about all of this as she started to paint the figures she had sketched onto her canvas. Like Walter Deverell, Maggie had difficulty mixing the correct colours to mimic the hair colour of the ginger-haired woman who had inserted herself into the painting. But Maggie patiently tried different combinations on her pallet and saw that one combination of magenta and light yellow worked brilliantly. She added the flowing ginger hair to the canvas and the figure began to live as she dipped her toes into the sea.

4 October 2019
Hastings

"I hear the vicar doesn't approve of your reading of Dante's musings. He scolded me for allowing you to read the documents," Mrs. Highclere said, as she placed a candle in its holder on the altar.

"Right, I'm sorry, Mrs. Highclere that he chided you for allowing me to read the documents. But you should know that the documents aren't Dante's musings. The writings are Lizzie's and Christina's diaries going all the way back to 1845," Maggie confessed.

Mrs. Highclere seemed shocked at first but then she smiled. "Never mind about the vicar. He's often unpleasant and condescending; sexist, as you youngsters say. And he's a bit of a dolt. The drink doesn't help; he's sometimes surly. Hmm, I suppose that I shouldn't have believed his description of the contents, but I was so put off by the idea they were Dante's writings. I wonder what the vicar is trying to hide."

"I'm not sure," Maggie responded. "They are absolutely intriguing though. Lizzie talks about her art and the need to express herself through it, and Christina does the same. Both seem to have been betrayed by those who care for them. Both seem quite lonely, solitary, both hunger for true companionship and love; both want to advance women's art. I keep wondering if they will end up as confidants and friends, sisters in art. And I wonder why their diaries are hidden from the public." She didn't mention how Lizzie and Christina ran off to Lizzie's ancestral home to form a sisterhood of sorts. Mrs. Highclere seemed the conservative sort. She might not understand.

Mrs. Highclere said that she liked all mysteries and longed to know more. "I always knew that the vicar was a bit duplicitous besides being an insufferable fool. Well, we'll have to find a way to read the rest of them. The Reverend Mr. Carson can't have the last word about whether the world learns what these women wrote about their art and their lives."

At that moment, Bethany breezed into the vestibule. She looked rather harried, but she still looked lovely. Her golden-red hair was piled atop her head and tied up with a scrunchy, and when she smiled at them, Maggie felt a little in awe of Bethany's grace even though she was still miffed about her treatment of her, and the way she didn't understand Maggie's need to make art.

Bethany approached them, grabbed Maggie's hand, and pecked her on the check. "Hello, love, I came as soon as I could. I'm eager to see what you found. And who do we have here?"

Maggie turned to Mrs. Highclere. "Mrs. Highclere, allow me to introduce my partner, Bethany Cross. She's also a scholar."

"What sort?"

"The kind the vicar doesn't care for. A literary sleuth."

Mrs. Highclere chuckled. "That's just what you need now, I suppose, since the vicar doesn't want a literary scholar to read the writings. You ladies follow me." She grabbed a candle from the vestibule and handed a second to Maggie.

"No need for that. I have my mobile," Bethany said as she turned on the torchlight on her phone.

"That's quite nice. Better than a candle. I should get one for my Reginald. He's always intrigued by new gadgets. Well, please mind your heads."

5 October 2019
Hastings

Bethany stood over the trunk, which Mrs. Highclere had opened after nicking the key from the vicar's pocket while he napped after imbibing his evening whiskey. "I'll put it back directly. He won't even know it was missing. He mentioned that he plans to move the chest, so we need to read quickly."

"If that's the case, we have to get the trunk out of here somehow," Bethany said.

"That's not possible," Maggie replied, "It's exceedingly heavy. I tried lifting it and it wouldn't budge. What's to stop us from copying the contents?"

"Mrs. Highclere, does the church own a copier?" Bethany asked.

"We don't need a copier. Miss Cross, don't you have one of those fancy mobile know-it-alls that can take photos, the one with the torchlight?" Mrs. Highclere asked.

Bethany and Maggie looked at each other and laughed, and then Bethany said, "I should have thought of this sooner; how silly of me." She pulled out her mobile and began to snap photos.

Mrs. Highclere stood like a sentinel holding her candle for hours over Bethany as she took photo after photo of the old diaries that attested to the need for women to make art. Maggie recognized the excitement on Bethany's face, for Bethany knew that what they would read could change Victorian literature, and perhaps this would finally establish her career as a premier Victorian scholar.

Later, that evening, after Mrs. Highclere had locked the chest and returned the key to the vicar's pocket, she followed Maggie and Bethany to Maggie's room in the inn, even though Reginald would wonder where she was.

"Let him fetch his own dinner," she said. "I've always loved Christina's verses. I want to know more about what she thought, and Elizabeth Siddal also deserves a fair hearing. Now that we're sisters in crime, I'm happy for you to call me by my Christian name."

"If you wish. What is your Christian name?" Maggie asked.

"Agatha. My parents named me after the martyred saint of course, but, as soon as I learned of the torture poor Agatha experienced, I decided there was no need to follow her example and become a saint like her. Instead, I'd rather be a sinner. Well, let's get on with it, shall we?" Maggie realised that she had completely misunderstood Agatha Highclere and was glad to know that the old woman was not at all as she had surmised.

"Did you tell Agatha that Lizzie and Christina ran away to Yorkshire, to Hope Hall?" Bethany asked.

"What?" Agatha said, as she followed them down the stairs into the crypt. "How clever of them. Men are often such trouble. Women belong together. Girls, let's proceed. Where did you leave off?"

"I was reading diaries from late 1852 but momentarily skipped ahead when I was rifling through the chest," Maggie said.

"Well, we must reconstruct how they ended up together—how their parallel lives took them down the same path. This is so exciting I can hardly contain myself," Agatha replied as she reached for Beth's mobile. Beth had to show her how to find the photos on the mobile and then expand them to make them easier to read, but Agatha quickly managed. She donned her trifocals and read until the clock struck midnight.

Then Bethany and Maggie took turns reading the diaries aloud until they were quite exhausted. Even though the diaries were frequently full of sorrow, the three women were absolutely overcome with joy at their discovery.

There would be time later, Maggie thought, for each of them to sort out their own troubles and sorrow. Perhaps Lizzie and Christina would reach out from the grave and show them how.

22 November 1852
Lizzie

I have written a poem in Dante's voice and wonder if Dante will understand its meaning and intention. I often feel frustrated, for I do not believe that Dante knows the real me; he only knows the one that he idealises and sometimes worships. I am flesh and blood, not some ethereal spirit. I will not always garner attention for my so-called stunning looks. Dante must love my body and my soul. He must love me, not the poet's elusive Beatrice. He must treat me with respect and advocate for my artistic goals.

"The Lust of the Eyes"

I care not for my Lady's soul
Though I worship before her smile;
I care not where be my Lady's goal
When her beauty shall lose its wile.

Low sit I down at my Lady's feet
Gazing through her wild eyes
Smiling to think how my love will fleet
When their starlike beauty dies.

I care not if my Lady pray
To our Father which is in Heaven
But for joy my heart's quick pulses play
For to me her love is given.

Then who shall close my Lady's eyes
And who shall fold her hands?
Will any hearken if she cries
Up to the unknown lands?

Will Dante love me after my comeliness fades? When I become commonplace? Does he care whether I have desires or goals? Does he love and care for my soul or just the body in which it resides? Does he truly promise himself to me? When I die, will he fold my hands over my chest; will he close my eyes and weep for me?

23 November 1852
Lizzie

This morning Dante said, "How can you not know where you are?"

"That's not what I meant, Dante. I meant that I don't know where I stand with you."

"What? What do you mean? You live with me—this place, my studio, is your home. You're my muse," he replied, as he pulled me towards him and started to unlace my gown.

"But I don't wish to be your muse or a piece of art. I wish to be your student and eventually your colleague," I said, as I pushed him away and tidied my dress. "It's not enough to be an object of art, a painting. I wish to escape the paintings, not enter them. I wish to be the painter."

"Lizzie, painting is not something that most women can do. Ruskin says so, and he's the authority. You should stick to your drawing, which is quite good; and you should be satisfied that your face will be memorialised forever."

"I'm not, and never will be," I said with finality, as I picked up one of his paintbrushes and began to outline his face on a fresh canvas.

1 December 1852
Lizzie

Over the past weeks, when Dante was visiting his friends, I have donned my painter's garb and painted my self-portrait, which is far different from any image Dante has captured of the countless Lizzies he believes reside within me. My eyes and mouth reveal my serious nature and rather than my hair flying loose, it's tied back into a tidy knot and swept away from my face, as it is ordinarily. I keep my mouth closed, not open, as Mr. Millais insisted, which begets a sense of the sensual to these Brotherhood painters, as if the female figure invites them into a carnal embrace. Here I truly am myself. Not a queen, not a mad and scorned Ophelia, not a boy-girl, not Dante's muse, past and present lover, and destiny, but an ordinary woman artist, who wishes to convey truth and beauty.

I looked from the painting to the mirror and believed that I captured my likeness, even though my real face and hands were smudged with paint, and the painter's smock I wore over my green gown was covered in green and red paint. I briefly thought about adding the smudges, the imperfections, to my self-portrait, but then decided that I wished to capture my essence, not produce a flawed and common daguerreotype for a carte-de-visite, which is all the rage.

Recently, I have felt more comfortable thinking of myself as a genuine artist because Dante introduced me to two women painters: Miss Anna Howitt and Miss Barbara Leigh Smith. They praised my efforts. Anna and Barbara have studied at art schools for women in London and in Munich. Barbara is a fierce advocate for women's rights, arguing that women want work, professions, and creative outlets. She is also an unusual woman; she is an adventuress who sometimes dresses, like Viola/Cesario, in men's breeches. Or on occasion, she shortens her skirt and wears blue spectacles. She talks about her love of nature and mountain climbing. She wears a scant swimming costume and swims in the sea. She is fearless, defying what is expected of her as a woman. Dante says she's a "jolly fellow." I don't think of her as a fellow, but I find her outlandishness quite fetching, and wish that I could completely throw off restraint as she does. And Miss Howitt is equally intriguing because she wants to form a Sisterhood in Art, a female painters' group akin to the PRB. She believes that such artistic companionship will save women from lunatic asylums, where we end up if we are not allowed to practise and freely develop our art. Miss Howitt even thinks that women should run their own colleges and art schools, alternatives to finishing schools that merely prepare women to be a man's helpmeet in the only profession available to us, the profession of marriage.

After they learned that I draw and paint, they asked to see my work and requested to visit our Chatham St. flat. At first, Dante told them I was feeling poorly, but then, I told him to inform them that I was much better, and that I wished to visit with them. Before they arrived, Dante left for the Cremorne Pleasure Gardens to meet Hunt, and the women artists reviewed my paintings and drawings.

"Lizzie, my dear, your paintings are astonishing," Anna said. "How long did you say that you've been painting?"

"I've sketched since I was a child. But I've only painted in oils for a few months."

"Only that short while? You are indeed gifted. Don't you agree, Barbara?"

"Yes, certainly. Who is teaching you?" Barbara asked, as she picked up my painting, *Pippa Passes*, an interpretation of Robert Browning's poem.

"Well, Dante gives me suggestions, but they aren't formal lessons."

"You must come to visit us in Hastings, where I have a private studio for women artists and poets at Scanland Gate," Barbara advised, as she placed the painting back on its easel. "Our friend the poet Bessie Parks writes there, and you could have a residency. You would be my guest. Do consider it. I would also gladly instruct you. And it would likely improve your health to get away from the smog, stench, and chaos of London." She waved her hand. "I can't comprehend how you and Dante can abide living and working in this wretched neighbourhood with the foetid air and all those poor mudlarks scouring the riverbank for broken crockery and coal. Where is Dante by the way?"

"He's gone to the pleasure gardens with Hunt," I replied.

"Hmm, Well, the countryside and sea would do you both vast amounts of good."

I wanted to say, but didn't, that I grew up around the impoverished mudlarks, the street children, who were among my first artistic subjects. I gave a pence or two to the poor children who roamed the riverbank to find treasures to sell to help their families. I wanted to say that my family lived near the filthy Thames, and people in Southwark, including some of our neighbours, suffered cholera from drinking the wretched water. I wanted to say that in my "past" life, I created and adorned funeral hats for those whose relatives died of cholera. Clearly, Miss Leigh Smith and I sprang from drastically different backgrounds, and I doubted that she would understand my affinity for those children and for my old neighbourhood, so I kept mum. Later Dante told me that Miss Leigh Smith is a philanthropist and that she provides for impoverished children, as did her father who lived with her mother out of wedlock and treated his five children as legitimate, even when they weren't legitimate by law. I felt ashamed for assuming that she didn't care for the poor or ostracised.

After they studied the paintings, I showed them my sketch of "The Lady of Shalott," who like Tennyson's Lady, refuses to look in the mirror to see the world's reflection. I cast her as the weaver that she is, but her weaving is chaotic; it does not lead to Apollonian order. Her thoughts are elsewhere; her spirit moves her to look out the window to find genuine love. I do not have her see Lancelot; perhaps she seeks a different human, one who satisfies her longing. I do not cast her into the river to float downstream to be gazed at and pitied by those who do not know or understand her. She is satisfied to look out on the glorious world that beckons her to venture out of her tower and make her art *within* the world. Anna and Barbara approve the sketch because, unlike Tennyson's Lady, this Lady is the product of a woman's imagination. As they studied my drawing, Barbara mused, "outflew the web and floated wide/the mirror crack'd from side to side." Then she said, "You must paint the Lady of Shalott; you should paint her abandoning her tower; you must immortalise her and her quest in oil."

2 December 1852
Christina

I have started taking drawing lessons from Ford Madox Brown, Gabriel's friend. Gabriel warns me that I must not "rival the Sid." He claims she is a genius, so I very much doubt that my rudimentary drawings of my mother and brother William will compete with hers. He has shown me a few of her drawings and, although they exhibit a primitive style, they certainly are compelling. Someday, he wants me to meet his "Sid," whom he also calls his "dove," even though I am terrified to do so, for I would be unable to converse with such a great beauty. I recalled how her light nearly blinded me; I felt I looked at a goddess straight out of Ovid. Perhaps, if I dare meet and look at her, this goddess can advise me on my sketches.

I often sketch my poems about drowned daughters and their blubbering fathers. Father is ill with chest congestion and heart palpitations, and Mother insists that I act as his nurse. I attend to his needs, but sometimes ignore his pleas for help. Like Gabriel, he's a bit of an actor; he always desires attention and sympathy. I have my work to achieve, my sketches and my poetry. When Father repeatedly rings his bell for me to take him to the privy, I make him wait, and then he is even more quarrelsome, and sometimes he has wet his trousers, which I then must change. God forgive me but I often wish that he would leave us and pass into the next world.

3 December 1852
Christina

My heart breaks. My darling Grandpapa Polidori, my champion, who knew my heart, has passed. Oh, how I will miss his love. To whom will I turn now when I need confidence and solace? Who will love my poetry?

3 December 1852
Lizzie

My new friends, Barbara and Anna, hold regular salons just for women. They do not meet to knit lace or sew baby booties, but rather to talk about a woman's right to be treated as a complete human being, to be properly educated and professionally employed. They even advocate for women's suffrage. The ladies and their friends are called "The Ladies of Langham Place," and I have attended several meetings while Dante cavorts with Hunt and others in the pleasure gardens.

Last evening, one of the ladies suggested that we hold a séance and call on the spirits. At first, I was hesitant because it seemed like sheer deviltry, but then Barbara said that many serious artists and thinkers, such as Elizabeth Barrett Browning, are believers in this new "religion," the only religion where women serve as leaders. Spiritualists, as they call themselves, say that because we women are more open and intuitive, we are far more receptive to the spirits that surround us in what is called the Fourth Dimension. I don't know that I agree that women are more open and intuitive than men. Perhaps we are thought more open because the church teaches that we are empty vessels, blank slates that can be easily manipulated. I find that contradictory though since we are thought to have brought evil into the world because of Eve's temptation of Adam. If one believes these myths, Adam should have possessed a stronger will. Despite these apparent contradictions, I was curious, so I joined the others and participated in the séance.

After we snuffed out the candelabras and lit only a single candle on the table around which we sat, Anna asked us who we wished to call forth. Someone laughingly said, "Sappho, of course."

But then another said, "It may be scandalous, but may we contact Mary Wollstonecraft? She is our foremother after all."

All agreed and we commenced with the séance, which proceeded more like a prayer meeting with the dead. I felt a cool presence in the room. When Anna requested Mary Wollstonecraft's presence, the candle blew out and we all held our breaths as Anna asked the spirit questions and the table rapped back the answers. General questions, such as, "Were you an ardent supporter of the French Revolution during the Reign of Terror?" Two raps for "No." And more personal ones: "Did you deliberately throw yourself off Putney Bridge when your lover betrayed you?" No answer, but an eerie silence. Right then, I recalled the horror of watching a woman attempt suicide and how helpless I felt and how hopeless she must have been.

Certainly, the dead do not really die, but surround us with what they leave behind—their writing and their art, and sometimes their presence when they have been ill-used.

7 December 1852
Lizzie

Once more, I have been feeling ill of late. I can't sleep unless I take the medicine that Dante bought for me at the greengrocer. It's called "Godfrey's Cordial," and it promises to cure sleeplessness, headaches, stomach ailments, rheumatism, cholera, depression, nervous tension, and women's menstrual maladies. It even claims to cure insanity. I am not insane, but I find that I have difficulty eating, not because I deliberately fast, but because I have little appetite. Dante is frequently away with friends, and I feel lonely and confined. I have only one female friend, Emma Hill, Dante's friend Ford Madox Brown's intended, but she is busy with her newborn child, Catty, and has little time to spend with me.

I only feel free and at ease when I am drawing or painting. When I paint, I feel centred and complete. I feel that I am becoming my true self. But I cannot pursue my art every second of the day. I must sleep and the cordial makes it possible. Besides the sleeplessness, Dante's recent neglect makes me furious, and I have told him so.

"I wish that you wouldn't go out so often to the gardens and leave me alone. You promised to cherish me, but instead you neglect me. You'd rather spend your time with the tarts that frequent the gardens," I complained.

"Don't be a shrew, Lizzie. It doesn't become you. What right do you have to tell me what I can or can't do?"

"None, for I am not your wife."

"Correct and acting in this manner won't make you my wife; you're acting like my mother. You're driving me away by your constant haranguing," he said as he slammed the door and left for the gardens once more.

What happened to his promise to love and respect me? To not treat me as other painters would? After each row, he promises to stay home in the evenings and read poetry to me as he used to, but then he forgets his promise and leaves when he receives a note from Hunt telling him about the acrobats, jesters, and magicians, who will be in the gardens, along with all the potential "stunners." Dante still insists that he loves and worships me, but that he needs to partake of the gardens because they provide him with ideas and inspiration for his paintings. I thought that I alone am his muse, but I am beginning to understand that my face no longer inspires his art. Perhaps he thinks that I no longer need him. Perhaps he is jealous of *my* art.

Because of my occasional malaise, Anna and Barbara insist that I visit their doctor in Oxford, a Swedenborgian spiritualist. Like Emanuel Swedenborg, Dr. Garth Wilkinson believes that he has visited the various heavens, which he describes as replicas of our verdant world. Because I value Anna and Barbara's counsel, I plan to travel to see him. I do not wish to visit his heaven, but perhaps he will locate the source of my illness and help me find a remedy for my suffering. I must find some genuine solace. Even though Dante sometimes scoffs at spiritualism, he agreed that travel will be good for me and that perhaps this physician will find the source of my sorrow and cure what ails me. Perhaps Dante will be happier when I am gone and then will be overjoyed to see me on my return.

3 March 1853
Lizzie

I journeyed to Oxford and was quite moved by the sight of the dreaming spires, the mediaeval walls, the golden meadows, and the River Thames, renamed Isis, which flows through the town. As I strolled and looked at the various colleges and their Gothic architecture and long histories, I wondered if women will ever be allowed to study at the university or if it will always remain the bastion of men. As I thought about this, I spent some time setting up my easel next to the river, and I sketched undisturbed for a half hour, until a gentleman wearing a scholar's robe told me that I must move off the grass, and that it's unseemly and unladylike for a woman to be alone painting by the river.

"Move on now," he said, "Or I shall call the constable."

I arose and pretended to pack up, but then waited for him to depart, and as soon as he walked away, I resumed my seat and kept sketching the punting boats moored by the river and one woman in particular who served as a punter while holding her skirts high. It made me happy to see a woman's athleticism and audacity. Fortunately, no one else harassed me, and the women who passed my easel smiled and nodded as if they approved. I felt happy and satisfied and stayed by the river until the sun drooped in the sky. I ambled through Christ Church Meadow enjoying the breeze off the river, and then attended Evening Song in Christ Church College. Even though

I am not a believer, the music felt like the perfect ending to a glorious day where I felt complete.

The next morning, I went to Mr. Wilkinson's office. I was eager to see if he could help me. Surely, my friends' physician would discover what ails me. While waiting, I saw a woman struggle to walk out of his examining room. She looked pale and she nearly fainted. I rushed to her side and asked if she was all right.

"You're kind. I just need air, luv," she said as she lifted my hand from her arm.

"Shall I escort you outdoors?"

"Don't trouble yourself; I'll be right as rain as soon as I get outside and catch my breath." I watched as she walked with slight difficulty out the door, which I held open for her.

When I returned to my seat, an assistant called my name and then escorted me into a cold room that smelled of alcohol and chloroform. She told me to disrobe.

"Is that necessary?" I asked.

"Yes, how else can he perform the internal examination?"

"What internal examination?"

"Why the one where he sees if your womb is wandering," she said smugly. I had never heard of a womb wandering and wondered what that even meant. I was about to ask, when she handed me a sheet with which to cover myself, and then she abruptly left the room.

When Dr. Wilkinson came in, he asked me to lie back and get comfortable. The room was so cold that I trembled, and I shook even more when he touched me in intimate places. I felt quite sullied by the whole affair. No one but Dante had ever touched me in this way, and he always touched me with tenderness. Mr. Wilkinson did not; he invaded my womanly privacy, my very being, and I felt both angry and ashamed.

When he finished probing me, he asked me to sit up and then he offered his diagnosis, after he asked me about my interests, hobbies, and pursuits. After I told him that I'm a painter and poet, he announced that I suffer not only from a curvature of the spine but also from a tilted and wandering womb due to my intellectual and artistic pursuits. His prescription to cure my malady is that I cease painting and discontinue my poetry writing! He claims that painting and poetry excite my faculties too much, such activity causes loss of appetite, sleeplessness, and anxious thoughts.

"You must rest and do absolutely nothing. No painting, no writing poetry, no mental or artistic effort whatsoever," he ordered.

"But if I did that, I would surely go mad," I replied.

"No, you'll be healed," he insisted. "You've exerted yourself too much, and your womb has wandered away from its natural place; it vacillates between your head and your heart."

Even though he is Anna's physician, someone she trusts, surely she would disagree with his absurd diagnosis. I will ignore his diagnosis and prescription. I will not abide by either.

Painting, drawing, and poetry writing give me strength and allow for my free expression. When I left Mr. Wilkinson's office, I diagnosed myself. I realised that I know the cause of my weakness and suffering but hesitate to acknowledge it. Even though Dante professes to love me when he touches me as his intended wife, it is he who feeds my sickness, and is the underlying cause of my malady. He wrecks my spirit when he refuses to legitimise our union after promising long ago to marry me. He puts off or outright avoids introducing me to his family. He plays at being my lover but does not genuinely love me. Perhaps he never loved me, even in a past life.

4 April 1853
Lizzie

Last evening, one of Dante's friends from Newcastle, Mr. Scott, visited him. When Mr. Scott arrived unannounced, I quickly saw that Dante seemed embarrassed to be found alone with me. Noting his shame, I arose and made haste to depart. Dante did not bother to introduce me, even though Mr. Scott bowed to me. I believe that he expected an introduction. I didn't acknowledge his bow, since Dante hadn't acknowledged me to his friend, even though I am Dante's intended.

Later Dante told me that Mr. Scott wrote to Brown that when he came upon us, we were "like Adam and Eve in Paradise, only [we] weren't naked, and Dante was reading Tennyson." Dante thought this amusing, but I didn't. Dante disrespected me that evening. I was not his love, and I was not his equal but his underling. He is ashamed of me.

3 January 1854
Lizzie

I suffer from loss of appetite and sleeplessness and continue to lose weight. Dante believes that the thinner I become the more stunning I am. I wonder if he wishes for me to become invisible. I should attempt to eat, but I find food unappealing.

On occasion, I gorge myself on custard tarts that I buy at the corner bakery, but then I feel sick and must force myself to vomit in order to feel less gluttonous.

4 January 1854
Lizzie

Dante and I have received the most wretched news. Poor Walter Deverell has died. He was only 26 years old. We knew that he suffered from kidney disease, but I had no idea that this chronic ailment would claim his life.

I feel even worse because Walter and I were close. He proposed to me but confessed that he feared that his family would not accept me because of my humble background, even though they personally like me. I turned down his proposal, although now I deeply regret not becoming Mrs. Walter Deverell. My mother was right when she said that I should try to marry him. He was a gentle soul, and I was exceedingly fond of him. He would have made a suitable husband, and perhaps, through my care, he would have grown stronger and would not have succumbed to his disease. But now he is gone, and I am despondent. I'll return to Hastings alone to see if nature and the sound of the sea's waves will cure my melancholy and my deep regret. Barbara has arranged for me a convalesce on High St.

24 January 1854
Lizzie

The sea provides no cure for what ails me. I am saddened by the loss of Walter and realise that I should have continued to model for him or should have at least visited him. He did love me, unlike the one that I love, Dante. But once again, now that I am away from him, I can't help but miss Dante. He is a magnetic force, and I am drawn to him, even though he causes me ceaseless suffering. I want to go home to him to see if he will eventually love me as he promised. Perhaps when I return, he will attend to me and not feel ashamed of me. Perhaps he has grown fonder of me due to my absence.

26 January 1854
Lizzie

When I returned to London, I learned that Dante was planning to travel to the Middle East with Hunt. While I was gone, he hadn't missed me. In fact, he intended to abandon me.

"Dante, please don't go. I beg you. I need you." I wept and reached out to him, but he turned his back to me and walked away.

"Don't beg, Lizzie. It's unbecoming," he said as he sorted through papers on his desk. "Besides, Hunt seeks my company and I need to find new projects; Palestine will inspire me."

"I thought that I inspired you," I said. "Besides, where will you find the money to travel? Have you thought about that?"

He turned and looked at me with contempt. "I don't need to be reminded that I'm in debt." He paused. "Hunt will lend me the money, and I'll pay him back as soon as I sell my paintings."

"That seems foolish," I replied. "You know that you don't paint quickly, and you haven't sold any paintings."

Now, he looked at me hatefully, even though he knew that I spoke the truth. He grabbed his cloak from the coat tree. "I'm going out now. I'll be back late. I trust when I return, you'll be less peevish and quarrelsome."

After he left, as I was tidying up, I looked at the papers on his desk and found a note from his sister Christina. I was shocked that she wrote about Dante's impending journey but said that he'll never leave me because I'm some sort of sorceress. I nearly laughed aloud at this ridiculous assumption. If she met me, she would understand that I am a mere mortal, with no power over Dante. He is obviously a free man. I am the one who has unfortunately fallen under his spell. He is the sorcerer. I am not free to fully be myself. He hinders me from becoming all that I could be.

When he returned in the early morning, he crawled into our bed and whispered to me that he will forgo the journey. He will stay with me. He didn't explain why, and I didn't ask. Then in the morning light, he stroked my hair and my face, and he called me his queen. I wrapped my legs around his waist; I opened like a rose, and we made tender love.

28 January 1854
Lizzie

Once more, we have quarrelled. Mam told me it would be like this. Don't trust him, she said. Even though he sometimes treats you as his queen, deep in his heart, you are no more than a working-class woman willing to pose as any tart would. And remember that evil can reside in the most pleasant façade. Remember the greengrocer who promised to make an artist of you.

Lydie arrived at our studio unexpectedly today. She knocked on the door and asked me if she could come in. I hadn't seen her in months, and I was eager to visit with her. I replied, "Yes, just wait a minute while I tidy up." I shut the door and quickly straightened the bed clothing. When I opened the door, I saw her study the room.

"Would you care for tea?" I asked.

"No, I haven't time. I'm only here because I am concerned about you. Dante and his Brotherhood are taking advantage of you and your good nature. They have destroyed your reputation," she said.

I sat down at my easel. "No, you're wrong about him, Mr. Millais, and Mr. Hunt. These artists have noble goals, and Dante worships me. It's not their fault that some people look with disdain at artists' models." I didn't mention Dante's frequent neglect. "They do have good intentions. Look, Hunt took a common girl, Annie Miller, and is trying to transform her into a lady."

"Has he succeeded?" Lydie said icily.

"Well, no, she remains as common and uncouth as ever," I replied, as I picked up Dante's palette and started to paint. "But I'm not her; I don't need transformation. I'm already a lady with refined tastes. I write and read poetry. My friend Barbara says that my mind is poetic. I create art; I'm like them, the Brotherhood."

Lydie stood next to me but didn't look at my painting. "You're deluding yourself. You will never be part of their Brotherhood. It's a boys' club. And Dante Rossetti doesn't agree that you are a lady. And you are not *his* lady. If he believed that you are a lady with the same upbringing, tastes, and talents as himself, he would introduce you to his mother. You have been promised to him for two years, and he hasn't found a way for you to meet his "lady" Mother. Why is that?" She looked at me sceptically and then shook her head in disbelief at my seeming folly.

I tried to ignore her, but she kept pressing.

"Lizzie, look at me, why is that? Why won't he introduce you to his mother?"

I turned toward her. "Lydie, there are many reasons, and all are reasonable. She and his sister Christina were travelling. Then she wasn't well, and Christina was also poorly. His father was gravely ill too, but luckily, he has recovered."

"Surely, they can't be ill or travelling every day for the past two years. If he truly adored you, as you claim, and intended to fulfil his promise, he'd arrange a visit and then announce your engagement. But he doesn't. I always thought that you were sensible, but you're a fool, Lizzie," she said with a shrug. "He thinks that you aren't good enough for his family. I hope that you haven't allowed him liberties. If you have, he'll never marry you, and no other man will have you."

"Oh, leave me alone. I must work. I don't really need Dante anyway. I can be an independent woman. And perhaps I'm the one who doesn't wish to marry. Have you thought of that?" I said as I continued to paint my Lady of Shalott, trying to flee her tower. My Lady had begun to resemble me with her long ginger hair cascading down her back.

"You can lie to yourself all you want, but the truth will eventually prevail," she said as she turned toward the door. "As your sister, I'm just trying to protect you and your reputation, which I fear you've lost by your association with this Brotherhood. They vampirize your beauty and give nothing substantive in return."

I continued to paint, but I felt tears welling up in my eyes and the image of my Lady became blurry. I tried hard not to cry in Lydie's presence. I knew that she was right but couldn't admit it. As she opened the door to leave, she said, "Mam, Da, and I agree that you should come home before Dante Rossetti destroys you; before he kills you. You must leave him . . . to save yourself."

I didn't reply or turn toward her but kept my eyes on my painting, looking closely at my Lady who suddenly appeared to weep. And after a few seconds, I heard the door shut. Then I allowed my own tears to flow. My Lady and I wept, until we had no more tears.

30 January 1854
Lizzie

I fear once again that Dante is ashamed of me. He insists that I drop the last letter of my surname. He thinks that Siddal is more genteel than Siddall. I don't see that it makes a difference. Will my name change persuade his mother to meet me? His sister to accept me? Will this name change transform me into the woman that he is willing to take as his bride, his mate for life?

1 February 1854
Lizzie

Of late, Dante has spent more time in the pleasure gardens. I went with him last evening but the fireworks and the gaudy, painted women hanging on the coat sleeves of the gentlemen and lords deeply disturbed me.

I asked Dante if we could leave and he said, "Whatever for? Have some champagne, my dove. Let's not quarrel. Let's be joyful tonight."

"No, Dante. Please, let's leave. I feel ill. The crowd overwhelms me. I find no pleasure here."

"Do what you like," he replied. "I shall hail you a hansom, if you wish."

He grabbed a glass of champagne from a tray held by a passing waiter, drank it, and then reached for another glass. Then he turned toward Hunt, whose fiancée Annie Miller, the uncouth girl, was hanging on his shoulder. Dante grasped Annie's hand and twirled her about.

"Lizzie is leaving, Hunt. You won't mind if I dance with Annie, do you?"

"No, but we should be on our way. Annie is tired."

Annie let out a yelp and fell into Dante's arms. "Oh, 'untie, be a good chap and fetch me some champagne. I ain't the least bit tired, and besides Dante is ever so fun!"

I walked away, and Dante did not even turn to watch me find my way through the throngs of partygoers, who gawked at the fireworks that festooned the sky. I hailed a carriage by myself.

When he finally returned in the wee hours, I was waiting for him. I once again accused him of neglect and betrayal. He told me that he was only having fun; I was being overly dramatic.

"But you want me to be an actress, don't you? You always want me to bend to your will and never exercise my own."

"Oh, Lizzie, stop your ranting. You make my head ache. I'm going out again, for I can't bear to be around you when you're peevish. When I return, I hope that you've calmed yourself," he said as he grabbed his cloak and left.

6 February 1854
Lizzie

Dante and I have not discussed our future, assuming that we have a future together. He still professes that I am his destiny, but last evening, it seemed as though I was his refuse, a castoff garment, his easily dismissed mistress, who can be replaced.

I have paused in my painting of my Lady. I don't know who she really is. I cannot place her face or her true identity. I feel confused about her longings and must examine them in light of my own. Instead, I attempt to console myself daily by drawing and painting my favourite poems. My love of Wordsworth's and Keats's poetry inspires my art. Dante was surprised that I know so much poetry by heart. But I have memorised poems from the first day that I encountered Mr. Tennyson's poetry when Mr. Greenacre gave me the newspaper clipping of "The Lady of Shalott." After that, I begged my father and mother for books of poetry, and because they are lovers of the literary, they procured small volumes for me.

Wordsworth's "We Are Seven" is my subject. I have thought much about the lines, "A simple Child,/ That lightly draws its breath,/ And feels its life in every limb,/ What should it know of death?" I have endeavoured to draw a dead child, but how is it different from a sleeping one? And how does one convey voice, spirit, or soul in a painting? How can I evoke that in my Lady?

I am also working on a drawing of Keats's "St. Agnes's Eve," which is such worthy contemplation for me. Perhaps, if I had waited until St. Agnes's Eve to discover whom I should marry and practise the art of love with, I would have been better off. Alas, it is too late. I have given my heart away to an unworthy fellow, but there is no cure for this ailment, the way that he possesses me, despite his ill treatment of me. My only consolation is to become more of myself by becoming a genuine artist.

15 February 1854
Lizzie

Mr. Ruskin has heaped praise on Dante's sketch of me, his _Dante Drawing an Angel_. He visited Dante and me and, after he looked at more of Dante's paintings and sketches, he saw _Pippa Passes_ on my easel. He inquired if it was Dante's but thought that it couldn't be, since the style is far different. When he learned that I was the painter, he bestowed high praise on my work too. Just as Barbara Leigh Smith believes, Ruskin also says that I have innate genius. Unexpectedly, he purchased all my sketches, and then returned the next day and offered me his patronage. He offered to provide me £150 per annum! And he proposed to buy all my new work and act as my agent. Dante feels rather humiliated, since Ruskin does not offer to be his patron at this point, although he made it possible for the Brotherhood to exhibit at the Royal Academy.

I wonder about Mr. Ruskin's true motivation. Is he fawning over me as a woman artist because he was recently disgraced by his wife Euphemia when she sued him for divorce due to non-consummation of marriage after seven years? We learned that she left her wedding ring, keys, and account books on their parlour table and returned home to her parents. Does he wish to show that he can fully support a woman artist, after he has made disparaging comments about women artists and our supposed inability to portray truth and beauty in our creations? Or is he pandering to me to ensure that Dante will never stray from needing his support? If I accept Ruskin's patronage, will that make me a genuine artist? I don't even own my own oil paints; I must use Dante's. At least with patronage, I will be able to purchase my own paints, and perhaps I can rent my own studio. Then I will not be beholden to my lover who gives me his body, but not his soul.

20 February 1854
Lizzie

I sometimes wonder if Mr. Ruskin wishes to court me. After I accepted his patronage, he took me to meet his mother and father, who treated me with the utmost respect, even though, in the past, they had belittled Mr. Ruskin's wife Euphemia. Dante accompanied us as well, but he was virtually ignored. I was lauded. Mr. Ruskin introduced me to his parents by announcing, "This is Miss Elizabeth Siddal, the artist of whom I spoke. She is going to change the art world."

"We are genuinely pleased to meet you, Miss Siddal. John has told us of your work and your extraordinary grace and genius. Please do sit and take tea with us. Gertrude, you may bring in the tea tray now," Mrs. Ruskin said as she beckoned to the maid who had escorted Dante and me into the elder Ruskin's parlour.

"What a noble-looking woman you are, Miss Siddal. Are you sure that you are not a duchess?" Ruskin's father asked.

I thought that he was teasing me. I felt blood rush to my cheeks. "I am a humble woman, sir. My father is a cutler, even though my ancestors were said to be noble people in the North. They owned an estate called Hope Hall. I'm afraid that our fortune and history are lost for all time."

"Nonsense," Mr. Ruskin Sr. said. "Perhaps you can recover, resurrect it, and hope itself, through your art." He chuckled.

All the time, Dante just stood there. No one paid him any attention. Ruskin himself treated Dante as the invisible man. Secretly, I felt vindicated. It served him right for treating me so shabbily of late.

After a time, Dante asked to be excused, and no one begged him to stay. I sat like the queen that Dante sometimes believes me to be.

24 February 1854
Lizzie

Mr. Ruskin has visited me to see how my work proceeds. He encourages me to continue. He has started to call me "Princess Ida," after Tennyson's poem "The Princess," after I told him about my visits to Langham Place. I fear that he mocks me. Certainly, I am not Princess Ida, who needs to sequester herself from all men, but, like Barbara and Anna, I do seek complete human rights for women.

I also told him about our séance, and he said, "Now, my dear, that is sheer folly. Don't be duped into believing that nonsense."

"Mr. Ruskin," I replied, "even Mrs. Browning believes."

"But her husband Robert doesn't. He discourages his wife from this madness. Likewise, I discourage you."

I wanted to tell him, but you aren't my husband, and, even if you were, you would have no right to tell me what I may or may not do. Besides, even though Ruskin is an exceptional art critic, he seems to lack a complete spiritual centre. Has he never felt the uncanny presence of the dead as I have? Has he never experienced the sense of wholeness that comes from dreaming of and encountering the dead, who never truly die? I have. Mr. Ruskin, despite all his knowledge and aesthetic sense, does not appreciate the many layers of life in the world and the thin veil between the living and the dead. Despite his patronage, he does not control me or my destiny.

3 March 1854
Lizzie

Dante starts but fails to complete many projects; his many watercolour and oil paintings are half-finished. The one that he has completed though gives me pause. His *Found* depicts a fallen woman whose ex-lover finds and recognizes her. She is ashamed and cowers, hiding her face from him. I was not the model for this painting, but am I its true subject? I saw one of Dante's letters to his friend Allingham, where he says that I have "been degraded." What or who, pray tell, has "degraded me?"

14 March 1854
Lizzie

Dante agreed that I could visit Miss Smith at Hastings. I told him that I didn't need his approval.

"You aren't my husband, and if you were, I wouldn't need your permission; as Mr. Mill says, marriage is an unjust contract whereby a wife becomes her husband's slave, which is a total injustice."

"What do you know of Mr. Mill?"

"I've read his essays and I agree with him," I replied.

His silence was deafening. I supposed that he hadn't read Mill, and perhaps he was ashamed. At any rate, he ignored my and Mr. Mill's views on marriage and Dante proceeded to act as if he were my lord and master. He insisted that he finance the trip, even though I have my own money. To do so, he had to borrow 30 shillings from Hunt for my train fare. He also had to borrow £25 from his aunt Charlotte, and to pay our rent, he even had to sell his gold pin that his father gave him as a gift when he matriculated from Sass Academy. Luckily, I have my allowance, but, on occasion, he even spends that, as if he is my husband, which he is not.

3 April 1854
Lizzie

I spent a profitable time at Scanland's Gate in Hastings with Barbara, who is a good, patient teacher, unlike Dante. And I'm inspired by Barbara's work, for her paintings hang from ceiling to floor on the walls of every room in the house that she designed. As we paint together, (I've continued with painting My Lady), while she has begun a painting of Boadicea, she tells me of her unusual upbringing. As the love child of her father Benjamin Smith, the son of a Member of Parliament, and her mother Anne, a milliner like me, her parents defied convention. Even though she and her numerous siblings were not legitimate in the eyes of the law, her father and mother lived together, and her father provides Miss Smith with an income. When her father passes, she, like her brothers, will inherit her father's land and income. In this way, she is an independent woman and is free to be and do what she likes, so she is true to her calling; she is a painter, a benefactress of the poor, and a social reformer, as well as an apologist for women's rights.

Under her tutelage, my sketches and paintings continue to improve, as I learn more about dimension and shadow. Like Hunt, I enjoy painting outdoors and no longer paint from memory. I love the feel of the breeze on my arms and the sun shining on my face. I often doff my hat, even though the sun makes my fair skin freckle.

Barbara has introduced me to two of her friends, Emily Faithfull and Helen Codrington. Miss Faithfull plans to start a literary journal just for women, and she also advocates for women's education and professions. She is most devout, and her father is a clergyman. Mrs. Codrington is married to a naval officer, who is frequently away at sea. She and Miss Faithfull have been friends since childhood, and they are extremely close. They walk arm in arm and often act like a married couple; they finish each other's sentences; they exhibit affection, even in public. Miss Faithfull seems to take the place of Mrs. Codrington's husband and she seems glad to do so. The Langham Street group grows more intriguing, since they offer new ways of being a woman in this world.

Even though I was enjoying Hastings, I started once again to miss Dante, so I wrote to him. He arrived late one evening for a visit, and immediately I felt once more assured of his affection. For once, we refrained from arguing. He and I rambled the fells and strolled the beach. We wrote our names in the sand, as if we were young lovers. We are reconciled, at least for the time being. I have tried to forget that he thinks me degraded.

6 October 2019
Hastings

Bethany and Maggie had both grown hoarse from their reading of the journals.

"We must leave off for now. There is so much that is new here that it's hard to take it all in," Bethany said. "Of course, I knew of Dante's mistreatment of Lizzie, but I never knew of her great desire to be a painter."

"Nor did I," Maggie said.

"I had read about Miss Siddall's longing to excel in her art. She was much more than a model. And, of course, I readily knew that Dante was a cad," Agatha added.

"How did you know that?" Maggie asked.

"I've read biographies of both. I have a great interest in the mystery surrounding Lizzie's death," Agatha replied.

"As do I. Perhaps that mystery will be solved through these diaries. And I wonder what was occurring in Christina's life as Dante was mistreating

Lizzie," Maggie said. "But now that we've read quite a lot, I'm also interested in tracing Lizzie's footsteps. Agatha, do you know where Lizzie lived in Hastings? Might we go there?"

"Surely, but not now, my dears."

"No, early tomorrow then," Maggie replied. "I think we're all quite spent. Let's walk you home, Agatha. Reginald will be looking for you."

"Oh, he's had his nightcap long ago and is snoring away. But I wouldn't mind company on the walk home," Agatha said, as she took Maggie's arm. "It will bring some solace, more of a sense of sisterhood after hearing Miss Siddal's tragic tale in her own words."

7 October 2019
Hastings

Maggie, Bethany, and Agatha climbed the steep hill that continued beyond the church until they came to a red brick building at 5 High St. that had a blue plaque on it, one that said Elizabeth Siddal, the poet and painter, stayed here. The flat was occupied and so they couldn't gain entrance. Maggie recalled Dante's pencil sketch of Lizzie standing in the doorway, looking rather like the Lady of Shalott stepping out of her tower.

"Lizzie had an extraordinary view of the sea from here. I wonder if this is the place where she wrote some of her poems. She might even have painted from this prospect," Maggie said. "But, of course, she must have spent much of her time at Barbara Leigh Smith's residence. Is that residence also marked with a blue plaque, Agatha?"

"I'm afraid not, dear girl. Scanland's Gate was the name of the place where she held her artistic society; it's now called Scanland's Folly. It was on the road between Robertsbridge and Brightling."

"How sad that this women's artistic retreat is no longer extant and now it's deemed a folly," Bethany said. "I wish we could do something about that."

Maggie and Agatha agreed.

"Well, for now, we could read more of the diaries," Bethany said. "Shall we head down to the sea?"

"Yes," Maggie said as Agatha nodded.

And so, they gingerly descended to the sea with Agatha and her cane leading the way. They sat on chairs on the shingle beach as clouds covered the sun and it started to lightly drizzle. Even so, Maggie read first and then alternated with Bethany.

As she read, Maggie's mind wandered as she thought about Lizzie's great longing to fulfil her artistic destiny. Maggie struggled with how she would tell Bethany that Lizzie inspires her so much that she may take a leave from the academy and dedicate herself to art. This would be difficult and could permanently estrange her from Bethany. And since Bethany had been in Hastings, they rarely spoke, except about Lizzie and Christina, even though they slept, hardly touching, in the same bed, like two corpses in their sarcophagi. Was their love dead or was it possible to resurrect it?

Later that afternoon, she returned to the sea to paint her canvas of the women strolling on the beach. The women had definitely begun to resemble Lizzie and Christina. And, while she painted, two women wearing long gowns, one woman with dark hair and one with a red braid, descended the steps and walked out to the sea. They took off their shoes and lifted their skirts. Maggie watched as they ran out into the sea with the ebbing tide and then back again as the tide overtook them. One of them stumbled and the other lifted her friend up. They laughed and then dunked one another as if they were playfully baptising each other and then they sat nearby with their arms intertwined gazing at the sea. Then, they strolled arm-in-arm towards Maggie. They stood in front of her and smiled. They turned toward her painting and laughed when they saw themselves and then ran back toward the sea.

16 April 1854
Christina

It is Easter Sunday, the day of Resurrection and new life. Gabriel is not here; he is in Hastings with his Sid. We have tried to reach him by post because Father's health has deteriorated; Father's doctor, Mr. Horner, believes that Father has diabetes and an infection in his heart. His mind is confused. Father thinks that he sees his mother in his bedroom, and that she is scolding him as if he is a child. He believes that one of his old friends, General Pepe, is in bed with him. He calls out repeatedly, "*Ah Dio, a juatami Tu!*" God help me.

God help us all.

26 April 1854
Christina

Gabriel returned from Hastings in time to witness the death of the crocodile. The crocodile weeps no more; his crocodile tears that lure his victims to their death have dried. I have written a poem about the crocodile.

Here is one section:

His punier brethren quaked before his tail,
Broad as a rafter, potent as a flail.
So he grew lord and master of his kin:
But who shall tell the tale of their woes?
An execrable appetite arose,
He battened at them, crunched and sucked them in,
He knew no law, he feared no binding law,
But ground them with inexorable jaw.
The luscious fat distilled upon his chin,
Exuded from his nostrils and his eyes,
While still like hungry death he fed his maw;
Till every minor crocodile being dead …

The house is silent; there is no more wailing and crying out to the God that forsook him; there are no more mad rantings about Dante Alighieri and Beatrice and what Dante's love for Beatrice truly meant: not unrequited love of an ideal woman but an alchemical formula that explains the mystery of the world. The crocodile was a madman, and I am relieved that he is no more. My scars are healing.

Mother ordered that Father's book *Amor Platonica* be burned. She did not indicate the reason, and no one has asked why. She handed the manuscript to our maid Hazel, and Hazel walked it out to the garden. I watched as she fed the book to the flames in the garden fireplace. I waited until it turned to ash and embers, grateful that it will never reach the heavens.

30 April 1854
Christina

After Father's funeral, Gabriel quickly left to attend to his Miss Siddall in Hastings, where she has fallen ill; Mother and I also travelled to Hastings to recover by the sea. Even though Mother objected, I donned a swimming costume, and allowed myself to be dunked and bathed by a strong man in the ocean. I felt cleansed. I thank the gods that no crocodiles swim or demons lurk there.

Although we are in Hastings, Mother thinks it is improper to meet with Miss Siddall at this time. We are in mourning, and she has been ill and is unlikely to receive visitors. I have not seen Gabriel, who acts the nursemaid to his Dove.

8 May 1854
Christina

After we returned home, Gabriel wrote to me. He wants to arrange a time for me to visit him and his Sid. He tells me that she and I have much in common—we are both poets; she is learning to paint. She dwells too much on death, as I do. She is his muse, as I once was, when he painted me as the girl Virgin, an irony that has always troubled me.

I will meet her, but I fear that I will have little to say to such a wonder. As I've noted, I have seen her as Ophelia and recognize the deep longing within her to drift away to another world, a world of her own choosing. That longing is too much to bear because it is my own.

I dreamt that I was flying, as Eve does in *Paradise Lost*. Like her, I peered down on the green and golden land, the deserts, the mountains jutting into the heavens, and the sparkling and tortuous seas that kiss the shorelines. I saw the myriad of animals—the big cats, the tortoises, the flamingos—as they shimmered in the sun. I saw man and his puniness when viewed from the near heaven. As a new Eve, not Milton's, the trees in paradise wept for me. But, from my vantage point, I saw that Eden is this entire world, not just the original garden from which we were banished. Mr. Pusey would call me a heretic, but I no longer care. We can re-order our thinking and see as the new Eve sees, but only if we transcend our worldly and provincial limitations.

12 May 1854
Christina

I feel crestfallen. I bravely submitted six of my poems to *Blackwood's* and all were rejected. I took heart and tried again, this time submitting to *Fraser's,* but again received no offer to publish. Where does the fault lie? Are my poems unworthy? Is there no audience for them? Have I been dwelling on egotism and pride and thus will not be rewarded for my work? I must think of Milton—but must not think myself a Milton—"They also serve who only stand and wait." I must patiently wait. God will reward my patience if He so wills it.

30 September 1854
Lizzie

Dante has started to work for Mr. Ruskin at his Working Men's College; he teaches labourers how to paint canvases, not walls. He doesn't give a hoot about the men, only that he can spread the religion of art, for art is his only true religion and perhaps his only true love.

We had to vacate our flat because the Thames has grown putrid with garbage and pestilence. The stench is unbearable, even with the balcony doors closed. Dante has asked Brown if we can stay with them until the air clears. Emma is my dear friend, so I will be glad to stay with them, if they will have us. Emma is likely overwhelmed with work, so I will be eager to help Emma with Catty. I am used to taking care of children, since my younger siblings were often left in my charge. I do love children and hope that Dante and I will have a child, if and when we are finally married.

3 March 1855
Lizzie

Why do my friends and superiors always assume that I am sick. Mr. Ruskin, like my friend Miss Howitt, wanted me to return to Oxford to see his physician, Dr. Acland. I did so with reluctance because I knew how misguided this doctor's diagnosis would likely be.

Like Dr. Wilkinson, Dr. Acland believes that my mental powers have been "overly taxed" due to my creativity. He doesn't claim that my womb wanders, but he says that I need complete rest—I should not write, sketch, or paint.

When Mr. Ruskin learned this diagnosis, he insisted that I seek a "cure" by going south. He has agreed to fund my travel to Southern France and Germany. He warns me about travelling to Paris, claiming its decadence will ruin me. I do not agree with Dr. Acland's diagnosis; I will take paints and an easel with me, and I will defy Mr. Ruskin and visit Paris. It will be the only way that I can experience the "Grand Tour" and study art as male artists do.

Dante says that he will miss me, but he has arranged, through his mother, for me to be accompanied by his mother's relative, Mrs. Kincaid. I would much rather Dante accompany me, but Mr. Ruskin insists that Dante would be distracting and distracted, which is likely true. Dante must focus on his work, for Mr. Ruskin has agreed to buy Dante's current paintings and any future ones. He wants him to produce more mediaeval, Gothic paintings, to paint in a more "primitive" style that Mr. Ruskin says is the new modern.

While in Oxford, Dr. Acland introduced me to Reverend Mr. Pusey, one of the leaders of the Oxford Movement. Of course, I am not a believer in their creed, but Mr. Pusey and I had a long, rather heated discussion of the Woman Question. I took great offence when he spoke about women and their need to atone for Eve's grave sin, which led all of humankind to perdition. I do not believe such myth and think that women suffer because we are likened to Eve, as if she were a real person. This is nonsensical, and I told Mr. Pusey so. We need a new idea of the first woman, a new idea of Eve, not as the harbinger of evil but as the mother of us all.

Although Mr. Pusey is somewhat offensive, surprisingly, his daughter is a lovely person. She suggested that I spend time on the Bristol Channel at Clevedon, where I can relax and paint by the sea. I spoke with Lydie about travelling there and she agreed to accompany me.

14 March 1855
Lizzie

I met a donkey-boy today in Clevedon, who asked me if there were any lions in the parts that I came from. He seemed rather disappointed when I said "No" and then inquired if I had ever ridden an elephant. Somehow, he believed that I was some exotic creature, and when I replied, "Certainly not! I've never even seen an elephant," he commenced to tell me how he once rode an elephant at the fair and paid two pence for the ride. He was a rather talkative creature and dreadfully fond of donkeys, unlike David Copperfield's aunt, who prohibits donkeys from ambling onto her land. The young fellow explained that he had a sure-fire way to lead donkeys without beating them.

As he laughed, he said, "I tempt them with grass that I hold in front of their noses!"

My acquaintance with the donkey-boy made me feel rather light-hearted, particularly since he seemed so assured that I was not native English, but perhaps a denizen of Africa or India, although I can't understand why. Perhaps I've spent too much time in the sun or perhaps this foretells my future or proves another past life, as Dante believes.

Besides providing me with ready amusement via the donkey-boy, Clevedon has been a productive time for my painting. I created my *Ladies' Lament*, based on the ballad of Sir Patrick Spens. Lydie was happy that I was working independently of Dante.

19 March 1855
Lizzie

On my return to Oxford, Dr. Acland praised my good health! Little did he know that instead of heeding his rest cure, I improved my constitution by creating art and envisioning women mourning the loss of their men, a sorrowful topic to be sure, but one with which I feel well-acquainted.

20 March 1855
Lizzie

Lydia and I are on the train returning to London. Dante has written that on this day Millais and Euphemia, the former Mrs. Ruskin, are getting married in Scotland. Mr. Millais has loved her since he first painted her in Ruskin's presence and per Ruskin's commission. Mr. Millais was the one who first learned that she was unloved by Mr. Ruskin. I am pleased for them, but it seems that everyone is married except me. Of course, Emma married Ford Madox Brown, despite their daughter's early birth. Now Millais and his "Effie" are tying the knot.

Whenever I raise the question of when we will marry, Dante says, "Not now. I haven't the tin. Plus, Lizzie, if we marry, you'll need to forgo Ruskin's patronage. And then what will we live on?"

2 June 1855
Lizzie

The Browns have been staying with us, because of their need to find new lodgings. I'm ashamed to say that, even though Brown is Dante's good friend and Emma is mine, Dante treats them most shabbily. He is disturbed by their baby Catty's fussing and does not like the noise and chaos of having a baby in our midst. He is inconvenienced and is not subtle about letting them know. He demands that they "Keep that baby quiet! I cannot work with her howling so." He blames Catty for his failure to complete his commissions. Besides, does he not recall how we inconvenienced the Browns when we stayed with them in their tiny flat when the Thames was so putrid that we could not withstand the stench coming off the river into our studio? Where is his heart? Where are his manners? He calls himself a gentleman, but his actions and attitudes often belie that assumption.

14 June 1855
Lizzie

Even though Mr. Ruskin insisted that I spend time in Wales or in his home (which seemed to me a rather indecent proposal) to complete my "rest cure," I decided to first travel to Paris, and then on to Germany and Switzerland. Mr. Ruskin continues to finance my trip. He is still certain that Paris will "kill or ruin me," but I am certain that it will stimulate me in ways that will benefit my health and my art. Paris has always been the epitome of all things artful—from visual art, to architecture, to music, to fashion. Visiting Paris will help me continue my artistic education.

While here, I plan to indulge myself in every way that I wish. Perhaps I shall buy myself more exquisite paints and perhaps the latest bonnet or evening cape.

26 June 1855
Lizzie

Paris is extraordinary, especially for one who has only travelled to Hastings and Oxford for a rest cure. There is no rest here. The streets are full of artists, tourists, religious folk making pilgrimages, book lovers, and lovers in general. The French have little reserve, as we English do, and I am often shocked to see how openly affectionate women and men are. It would be unheard of for them to not kiss and embrace one another on the street; whereas, at home, we Brits save our loving affection for the dark and under the covers. Women are also affectionate with other women. They hold hands and embrace warmly. We Brits might learn a lot about loving one another from the French. It's unfortunate that we are often at odds with them, that they are our rivals and enemies.

When I am not gawking at the public displays of affection, I occasionally escape Mrs. Kincaid's gaze while she naps, and I walk about the City of Lights on my own. No one accosts me or harangues me. I sip burgundy in sidewalk cafes and eat baguettes and then head to the museums. My favourite is the Musée d'Orsay. I am struck by the vast number of nude paintings of women, by men of course. We women artists are not allowed to study human anatomy and paint nudes, but it would certainly benefit our art if we could do so.

I keep looking for paintings by women, but do not find any. Someday, perhaps, one of my paintings will reside in a Paris museum.

Even though Dante so often infuriates me, I do miss him. We write frequently and get on better when we are apart. He says that he will defy Ruskin's order and visit me soon. In the meantime, he is having a grand time. The Brownings, who are visiting London, have befriended him. He was ecstatic when Browning quoted lines to him from memory from Dante's "The Blessed Damozel." Dante is not only Robert Browning's ardent fan, but it appears that Mr. Browning is his; Browning finds Dante's poetry captivating. Now, Dante feels encouraged to write more and he hopes to receive a painting commission from Mr. Browning. Both Brownings viewed Dante's paintings and he says that they even saw my *Pippa Passes*. They remarked on its unique style and themes, which differ from the usual portrayal of the outcast prostitute as represented in Mr. Browning's poem. Mrs. Browning found it of particular interest, and she said that it gave her food for thought. Perhaps she will write about my sense of the outcast woman at some future date. (I like to think that I may inspire EBB, whom I have long admired). Dante felt quite honoured when Browning read from his new works, "Fra Lippo Lippi" and "One Word More," the latter poem ponders what we might give to read one of Raphael's lost sonnets or view Dante Alighieri's drawing of an angel.

Because of their interest in Dante's work, Dante has offered to paint both Robert and Elizabeth Browning. They agreed that he will paint a watercolour of Robert. Dante has even met Tennyson. I am quite envious and wonder, if I had been there, would Dante have included me in the visit, or would I have been an outcast? Would I have been neglected in the usual manner, as a secret lover is?

16 September 1855
Lizzie

The fall is glorious here in the City of Lights! Dante has defied Mr. Ruskin and has arrived along with the Brownings. He confessed that Mr. Ruskin is furious with me for "disobeying" him. I asked Dante why I need to obey Mr. Ruskin.

"He is paying our bills, Sid; we don't wish to lose his patronage," Dante replied.

I thought, we don't have Ruskin's patronage. I do. Even so, I shall do what I wish, for Ruskin is not my overlord.

Despite Ruskin's "orders," we will remain in Paris as long as we wish. Dante promises to introduce me to the Brownings. I would rather just meet Mrs. Browning because I prefer her sonnets to Robert Browning's monologues and other poems, even though I did use his "Pippa Passes" to inspire my own painting.

Dante and I visited the Exposition Universelle, France's rendition of our Great Exhibition and I was thrilled to see that Millais's *Ophelia* was exhibited. I may not have my own art exhibited, but here I am thinking my Ophelia thoughts for all of Paris to see. I am a bit of a celebrity, especially when I stand in front of the painting and am recognized as the model. People approach me and ask me to autograph their museum guidebook. And Hunt's *Light of the World* is also on display; my hair is Christ's own. I told Dante that I hope that my work is exhibited in Paris someday and he laughed.

"Lizzie, mine had best arrive before yours does." He smirked.

I felt hurt by his remark, since he has told me that I am a natural artist. Is my genius not equal to his?

When we left the exhibition, we were about to hail a carriage, but Dante saw Mr. Browning as he was about to enter a nearby café.

"Lizzie, here's your chance to meet one of the great poets. I see Browning. Come, let's join him."

"Is his wife with him?"

"I think not. Why should that matter?"

"I much prefer her poetry to his."

"Oh, don't be silly. He's a genuine genius," he said, as he tugged on my arm.

"And what is she, if not genius?"

"Never mind," he said. "Do you wish to meet him or not?"

"I'm not opposed."

"Then let's go," he said as he pulled me through the throng of people on the sidewalk.

We made our way into the crowded café, and Dante spotted Mr. Browning seated at a small table. He was talking with the waiter and then opened a book.

As we approached, Dante bowed and then said, "Good afternoon, Mr. Browning. So nice to see you again. Please allow me to introduce my model and friend, Miss Elizabeth Siddal."

As usual, I was deeply offended that he referred to me as his model and friend. Why couldn't he admit that we are engaged?

Mr. Browning did not acknowledge Dante's greeting but rose and turned towards me.

"Delighted to meet you, Miss Siddal. I see that you are the toast of Paris. Everyone is raving about Millais's extraordinary painting of you. Please join me," he said as he pulled out the chair for me and then took his seat.

"Thank you, Mr. Browning." I took the seat next to him, as Dante motioned to the garçon. "I'm pleased that you like the painting. Mr. Millais worked on it for many months."

"Well, you were a patient model, especially being submerged in a cold bath as you were. But I understand that you're an artist too. I saw some of your work, *Pippa Passes*, at Rossetti's studio. Even though your approach to the prostitute differs from mine, I found the painting most impressive. And my wife liked your work immensely."

"I'm most grateful. Do thank her for me," I replied as I felt my heart swell with pride that EBB, my idol, admires my work.

"She's quite supportive of women's art, of course."

"I love her poetry and have memorised much of it. She is an inspiration for me. A new Sappho. We read her work in my women's society."

"Oh, which society is that?" he asked as he sipped his coffee.

Dante shuffled around in his seat and raised his eyebrows, as if he wished for me to desist. I continued.

"The Langham Society. Do you know it?"

"Is that the ridiculous one where they meet to talk with the dead?"

I hesitated. "That sometimes occurs, but most of the meetings focus on women's suffrage and education, our right to be treated as full human beings."

"Well, the former activity is utter nonsense; you should stay away from it, as I've told Mrs. Browning. I proved that it's a sham when, during a séance, I grabbed a wreath that was being lowered onto a woman's head by a delicate string."

I didn't care for such paternalistic talk from one who was supposed to be a genius. "But it does no harm, sir . . . We have heard from Mary Wollstonecraft . . . She . . ."

"That harlot?" Browning asked.

"When might you sit for the painting that you promised?" Dante interrupted. "Is it possible to begin while we are still here in Paris?"

"I'm afraid that my wife's health precludes me from sitting now. We are leaving for our home in Italy, Rossetti. You are most welcome to visit us there. You and Miss Siddal, of course."

"Miss Siddal is also recovering from an illness. She can't join me," he announced. "But I am free to come to you at any time. I'm at your disposal."

I looked at Dante and tried to pipe in to contradict him.

"I'll let you know. I'm afraid that I must shove off, Rossetti." He quickly quaffed his drink and stood up. "Mrs. Browning expects me; we leave for

Florence tonight. So nice to have met you, Miss Siddal," he said with a deep bow. "Keep up your painting. I look forward to seeing it exhibited here in Paris one day. But do stay away from those spiritualists. It's all fraud and rubbish, I tell you. They feed on women's suffering."

When he left, I said to Dante, "Why did you deny me the chance to meet Mrs. Browning? You know that I admire her."

"But you don't really care for her husband. Besides, you are always ill and likely would not fare well on the journey," he replied.

"I grow ill because of you," I said under my breath.

"What did you say?"

"Nothing. You don't care to know."

14 December 1855
Lizzie

Mrs. Kincaid and I leave for Nice today. Dante remains in Paris and will return to London soon. He apologised to me for his offensive remark about my art. All is well between us at the moment, but every time I think about his remark and his denial of my chance to meet EBB, I rage. I must quiet my mind and quell my anger at that point. I must believe that he supports my art and views me as his equal.

To change the subject, Dante brought up Mr. Browning's antipathy for spiritualism. Dante told me that he himself is a believer, of course, because he has even seen the ghost of Dante Alighieri himself. He knows that the spirits remain with us often because they are troubled. On this point, at least, we seem to be on the same plane of feeling and thinking. I told him that I wished that I could go home with him, instead of spending my Christmas holiday with Mrs. Kincaid.

He told me, "Soon, Sid. We'll be together again soon."

16 December 1855
Lizzie

Mrs. Kincaid doesn't seem to care that I paint. She spends all her time immersed in her prayer book and visiting Roman Catholic churches and cathedrals, despite being a strict Anglican. She does remark about the popery, but finds the cathedrals exquisite, noting that something is missing from Anglican churches.

23 December 1855
Lizzie

It seems that I have overspent and am nearly broke. I suppose that I should not have purchased that exquisite green bonnet with the delicate lace veil, something similar to one that I created and modelled but could never have previously afforded when I was just a milliner's assistant. I have written to Dante, who promises to paint something quickly to sell to Ruskin, so that I have funds for the remainder of my trip. Dante never paints quickly, but he says that he has a plan to produce a painting based on Dante and Beatrice. This, of course, is his perennial subject.

14 February 1856
Lizzie

Along with some funds, Dante has sent me a Valentine, begging me to return to England. He says that he cannot work when I am gone:

> Come back, dear Liz, and looking wise,
> In that arm-chair, which suits your size,
> Through some fresh drawing scrape a hole,
> our Valentine and Orson's soul
> Is sad for those two friendly eyes.

He misses and needs me! I am ready to return and am eager to lie in his arms once more, but Mr. Ruskin, my keeper, insists that I remain on the Continent throughout the winter. I can return when the daffodils bloom, but not until then.

16 February 1856
Lizzie

Dante and Mr. Ruskin report that my work is on display at an exhibition on Charlotte Street. *I* should be there to meet the art patrons. Of course, I am pleased to have my work exhibited, but why would Ruskin set up an exhibition while I'm away? Would he do that to a male painter? Am I not sufficiently significant to attend my own exhibition?

5 April 1856
Lizzie

The daffodils bloomed and I recently returned to London. After I returned and seemed to have earned some success at the exhibition where my work was praised (but unfortunately not sold!), Dante was initially happy to have me home, but then he immediately cooled toward me. I suppose that my absence makes him miss me, but when I'm near, he no longer fancies me.

With Hunt away painting in the Middle East, Dante found new friends, a couple of young admirers. A painter whom he calls Ned, whose name is Edward Burne-Jones, and another painter-poet named William Morris. He spends much time with them and less with me, although he does have me play hostess when he has guests. The three of them plan to work together on some murals in Oxford at the Debating Hall; once again, the work will be mediaeval-themed, which suits Morris, who often writes of Guinevere.

I have been reading EBB's *Aurora Leigh*. I wonder if my work inspired her depiction of Marian Erle, the fallen woman. That's rather presumptive of me, but she did find my work intriguing and enjoyed the way I presented the fallen woman in *Pippa Passes.* In any case, I am fascinated by EBB's advice against writing about the past:

> [I]f there's room for poets in this world
> A little overgrown, (I think there is)
> Their sole work is to represent the age,
> Their age, not Charlemagne's—this live, throbbing age
> That brawls, cheats, maddens, calculates, aspires,
> And spends more passion, more heroic heat,
> Betwixt the mirrors of its drawing-rooms,
> Than Roland with his knights at Roncesvalles.

Perhaps Mr. Ruskin is wrong, and Mrs. Browning is right. Art should concentrate on the present, not on the distant past. Yes, the material world is troubling, but we can never truly return to what once was, and even if we did, what would that accomplish? All our attempts to recover a lost world— Eden, the Golden Age, the days of chivalry, are futile. Futile and backward leaning, which can never afford women our equal and legitimate rights as artists and writers.

My latest poem reflects the current state of my heart:

> Many a mile over land and sea
> Unsummoned my love returned to me;
> I remember not the words he said
> But only the trees moaning overhead.
>
> And he came ready to take and bear
> The cross I had carried for many a year,
> But words came slowly one by one
> From frozen lips shut still and dumb.
>
> How sounded my words so still and slow
> To the great strong heart that loved me so,
> Who came to save me from pain and wrong
> And to comfort me with his love so strong?
>
> I felt the wind strike chill and cold
> And vapours rise from the red-brown mould;
> I felt the spell that held my breath
> Bending me down to a living death.

Dante's false love buries me.

15 April 1856
Christina

I have sent a story, "The Lost Titian," to an American magazine. Here is a summary:

> Once upon a time, there were three painters. One painted outdoors in all weather and at all times of day. He wanted to capture the sunlight and moonlight on the canvas. He studied the heavens and the earth below it. He painted a red-haired Christ as the Light of the World. He travelled to Palestine and dressed as an Arab. He enjoyed much success and was lauded by art critics as pure genius. He was inspired and he promised to paint an enormous number of paintings, both religious and secular, and he fulfilled his promise to himself and others. He was happy.

The second painter didn't paint a grown-up Christ, but he did paint a childish Christ, too human for some, but lovely and playful in his earthiness. He not only painted the child Christ, but he nearly drowned a girl when he sought to replicate the fictional Ophelia's death on canvas. He too was well-received by those who were aesthetic experts. They liked the way that he posed the girl in death, and they took his painting to Paris, where hordes of people watched in awe, as the girl appeared to die repeatedly as she drifted downstream. He too was happy because he had reproduced a sensual death, a petit mort that everyone longs for.

The third painter had many ideas that floated around his head, like bubbles in clouds. He would try to reach for them, but they seemed to drift away every time he tried to grasp one. He painted and sketched his muse, his love, a ginger-haired woman he said he knew in a past life, but never found a way to replicate her heart. He had grand ambitions to be the next Titian, who also painted a red-haired woman. He promised much but fulfilled little. He thought that he was happy, but he wasn't, especially when he saw what the two other painters, his friends, his rivals, had produced in the same amount of time, the amount of time that he had spent drawing and painting the same face over and over, as if he were an automaton. In the end, he was extremely unhappy in choosing to fall into obsession. He would never be the next Titian. He would be a failure. Would he ever paint a masterpiece that would engrave his name in the annals of artistic excellence?

Unlike my poems, the story has been accepted. I intend to read it to Gabriel, but I doubt that he will see his own reflection in the story, vampire that he is.

2 May 1856
Lizzie

I finally met Dante's mother. I was ushered into tea and asked to sit next to Mrs. Rossetti. The room was cold, for no one had lit a fire. Mrs. Rossetti was as chilly as the room and Dante attempted to make small talk by talking about my art.

"Lizzie . . . Miss Siddal, is an exceptional artist, a painter, Mother. You should visit Chatham Street sometime to see her work."

"I thought that Miss Siddal is your model. Why are her paintings there?" she asked him, as if I were invisible.

"Well, she shares my studio," he replied. "Truly, she's a prodigy."

"As gifted as you?" she asked.

Just then, his brother William dashed in, and Dante stood to greet him. William was cordial and kissed my hand. We had previously met at Chatham Street, which is technically his flat.

Even though William was friendly, I felt uncomfortable and rejected. The cake Mrs. Rossetti served was tasteless and the tea was cold. I did my best to appear pleased and happy to meet her, but after a short while I confessed to feeling ill, and Dante and I made our excuses and returned home.

We did not speak about the visit, and Dante soon went out for the evening with Hunt. When he returned, we argued. While he was gone, when looking through his desk for one of my poems, I found a letter that he had written to Hunt's fiancée, Miss Miller, in which he expressed flirtatious and lustful thoughts. When I confronted him with it, he claimed that the letter was pure fantasy.

"I never sent the letter, Sid. It meant nothing. She means nothing to me," he said.

"I don't believe you. Why would you write such a letter if you did not fancy and lust after Annie Miller?"

He had no answer. He could not refute what he and I knew to be true.

Even though Dante begged me to forgive him, I immediately packed my belongings and returned to my parents' home. They said nothing to me when I came in with tears streaming down my face. All they said was "Go to bed now. We'll talk in the morning."

3 May 1856
Lizzie

On Tuesday, I received Dante's letter at my parent's home, along with a love poem that implored me to forgive his infidelity with that coarse, illiterate woman, Annie Miller. In the letter, he finally admitted the entire truth. It seems that while I was away and Hunt was in Palestine, he did more than flirt with Miss Miller. And he mentioned another indiscretion with the actress Ruth Herbert. He said he was extremely sorry and regrets his actions. I cannot reply to him because I am enraged. He tells me that these women mean nothing to him, but that he must exercise his lust. Of late, we have not practised the art of love. He argues that, if he can't have me the way that he would like, then he will have them. He tells me that for all my fiery spirit, I am cold, perhaps frigid, that I would benefit, perhaps, from seeing another doctor. That I am the epitome of my ginger hair, a miscreant, who possesses no loyalty. Miss Miller and Miss Herbert, on the other hand, are comfortable with their sexuality and are willing and able to perform acts, including illegal French ones, which I never will and have likely never imagined. His letter missed its mark. It was not an apology, but rather a rant against me.

I despise how he speaks of the acts these women perform. I am a lady, perhaps not in the peerage sense, although my father professes that we were once noble. In any case, we were of a higher social rank than his immigrant family. I am a lady who owns herself, and I do not sacrifice my body to a man who fornicates with prostitutes, who likely give him a host of venereal diseases that necessitate visits to the apothecary to obtain the mercury cure.

I grow weary of all his promises to marry me. First, he had to wait until he had sufficient income—that will never be, of course, because he is an absolute wastrel beholden not only to Hunt but his own brother Michael, who gave up his plan to become a doctor, in order to support his "genius" brother. Then his excuse was that his mother had to be comfortable with me and approve of me, but she was not even willing to meet me for the longest time, because my father is a cutler, and I once worked for a milliner. She refused to sully her hands with common workers. And when she met me, she acted as if I were a ghost, not a flesh and blood woman sitting before her.

In addition, his mother likely thinks me a tart, because of my modelling career, and believes that I am Dante's mistress, but Dante and I have not had relations ever since he began to sleep with his other "muses," and we will not have further intimacy unless, and until, he fulfils his promise to marry me.

Unfortunately, our earlier intimacy resulted in a pregnancy. Tragically, I had to dispense with the child. The abortionist was horrifying with her rusty hooks and spikes. She looked as though she would cleave me in two, just like Mr. Greenacre did his beloved. I needed to take a half of a bottle of my cordial, over 50 drops, to bear the pain and the emotional toll.

Of course, I wanted Dante's child, but he didn't. He didn't want anything to come between us. A child would be a burden and interfere with his art. He sees how a child distracts Brown from his art. I believe that a child could enhance my art, but I will not bear one, unless Dante is legally bound to me. Otherwise, I risk everything—abandonment, penury, societal condemnation, loss of patronage from Ruskin, my child labelled a bastard. I will not relent to Dante's selfish begging and his lust. He cares not for my soul. He wrecks my heart.

15 August 1856
Lizzie

As I gaze out the window of the Chatham Street flat, to which I returned after Dante's pleading, I can see the withering garden below—the one that Dante and I do not tend. Just like how we stopped tending each other.

When we first met and when he was utterly enchanted with me, he tended me well. He brought me Queen's Cake to eat with our tea. He brought me daffodils, irises, and yellow poppies, my favourite flower, from the flower seller in Regent's Park. He purchased juicy peaches, quinces, and apricots from the greengrocer, and fed them to me. He wrote me poems that posed himself as my steadfast knight and me as his fair and resolute maiden. He showed me how he mixed his vibrant colours: his ruby, his golden orange sunset, his iridescent blue, as he painted us as past lovers. Unfortunately, he painted us meeting our doppelgängers, which everyone knows begets death.

I coddled his bruised ego, bruised from his failure to achieve greatness as Millais and Hunt have. He told me that he needed to be famous to satisfy his mother's and father's ambitions for him. He needed to achieve more than his exiled, belittled, mad father had. He desired and needed to be an immortal artist. I stroked his temples that incessantly throbbed with anxiety from his failure to complete or even to begin his work. All he ever did was sketch my face and body. He created a drawer full of Lizzies. Hundreds of Lizzies. Lizzie gazing out the window. Lizzie with her eyes closed, Lizzie reclined in a soporific sleep, a living death. Lizzie curled in a ball like a child. Lizzie waiting.

I told him that he was a genius, even though I wasn't sure that he was one, and told him that one day the world would take note.

"Don't fret, Dante," I advised. "You will be known throughout time as a revolutionary painter and poet, one who captured truth and beauty. I'm certain that you will become famous for making *me* immortal."

And he replied, "Come here, my beloved immortal and turn your face toward me so that I can feast on your neck, your eyes, your magnificent hair that flows like a waterfall. You are all the truth and beauty that I need." Even though his language was pretentious and exaggerated, when he spoke in this way, my heart always fluttered. Despite all his failings and infidelities, I cannot help myself. I still love him. I cannot let him go. I willingly gave myself to him.

5 September 1856
Lizzie

After his latest infidelity, he tried to buy my affection by purchasing an exquisite Indian cloak for me to wear to the theatre. He wishes to parade me around in it to demonstrate that he loves me alone. His attention reminds me of Mr. Greenacre's display of his intended. So, like Delia, whose lover betrayed her, I now keep my bed dedicated to Diana.

My work is my true solace. I try not to focus on the past as Ruskin prefers, but because I still love Keats, I have studied his "La Belle Dame Sans Merci" and make plans to paint it. I think about this lady's enchantment and feel the irony that underlies my study of the poem, and its meaning in my life. I am accused of being an enchantress, but clearly a web of spells has been cast around me in my relationship with Dante. Perhaps his *How They Met Themselves*, which he continues to work on, has poisoned our lives.

10 September 1856
Lizzie

Ruskin finds my painting of *The Witch* far too gruesome, but I find it most appealing. If I am truly a sorceress, as they presume, let me weave my spell in my art and heal myself.

15 October 1856
Lizzie

Dante appears distraught ever since Hunt has returned, and despite the fact that I find it troubling, Dante frequently speaks of Annie Miller's beauty and charm, even though he knows that such talk injures me.

"What's charming about her?" I asked. "Her ill use of grammar. Her cackle? Her inability to act a lady after she has received training? Her ignorance?"

"Lizzie, please don't be uncharitable. She tries her best, but she lacks the grace that you were born with. I find her refreshing."

"Keep your thoughts to yourself, please. I have work to do," I said as I shut the door to the room that I've now claimed as my private studio.

I regretted my outburst, but he must see that his words sting, and his focus on Annie grieves my heart.

16 October 1856
Christina

I have finally met his "Sid," whom he also calls his "dove," and she is as extraordinary as he claims. I felt inordinately shy in her presence and barely spoke to her; instead, I conversed with Gabriel, who told me about his plans to paint murals in the Oxford Debating Halls. His "Sid" barely spoke to me either; she seemed as bashful as I, but she did gaze lovingly at Gabriel. When I returned home, I reflected on the way she looked at and listened to him and this poem surfaced.

> She listened like a cushat dove
> That listens to its mate alone;
> She listened like a cushat dove
> That loves but only one.
>
> Not fair as men would reckon fair
> Nor noble as they count the line:
> Only as graceful as a bough,
> And tendrils of the vine:
> Only as noble as sweet Eve
> Your ancestress and mine.
>
> And downcast were her dovelike eyes
> And downcast was her tender cheek
> Her pulses fluttered like a dove
> To hear him speak.

Perhaps I will share this with Miss Siddal someday; she seems a new Eve to me.

10 November 1856
Lizzie

When did he first say to me that he should have run away and married me? I don't rightly recall, but he did promise that he would rectify this failure. He was too worried about his overbearing mother, who thought that I was unworthy of her genius son Dante, who would be as famous as his literary forefather. He would perhaps supersede his mediaeval namesake. He would be England's poet, the next Milton; he would be as great a painter as Titian. I was just a painter's model and a shop girl—who sewed ribbons on hats and modelled them for ladies. But I wasn't merely that and Dante knew it. I was of noble blood, and potentially as great a poet and artist as he was. He said himself that my artistic and poetic talents were prodigious.

He broke his promise countless times. He never ran away with me, because he was like a little boy afraid of his mama. He never gave me an engagement ring, even though I gave him a lock of my ginger hair, a sure sign that I was committed to him and no other, even though others, like poor Walter Deverell, genuinely adored me and wished to marry me. He broke his promise that, when he made me an immortal, he would earn a sufficient income and tin, and then would sweep me off to the deserts of Algeria, where my health would be restored. He broke his promise that he would love me every day of my life. He broke his promise that his sister and mother would love me as he did. He broke his promise that I would become a full member of the PRB—that Hunt would accept me as their equal.

He broke his promise that he would not sleep with, flirt with, or joke with street women—that he would not bed sluts.

I wrote this poem and left it on the nightstand for Dante to read.

> Thy strong arms are around me, love
> My head is on thy breast;
> Low words of comfort come from thee
> Yet my soul has no rest.
>
> For I am but a startled thing
> Nor can I ever be
> Aught save the bird whose broken wing
> Must fly away from thee.
>
> I cannot give to thee the love
> I gave so long ago,
> The love that turned and struck me down
> Amid the blinding snow.
>
> I can but give a failing heart
> And weary eyes of pain,
> A faded mouth that cannot smile
> And may not laugh again.

Yet keep thine arms around me, love,
Until I fall asleep;
Then leave me, saying no goodbye
Lest I might wake, and weep.

I can confirm that he read it while I was sleeping. I later found it torn and crumpled in the rubbish bin.

I can't explain why I continue this farce, this relationship that never flourishes. Dante is certainly *my* only love, but he has wrecked my heart, and I can't dive into the watery depths to retrieve it. He does nothing to bring it to the surface, but instead throws an even heavier anchor that drives it deeper into the depths of the sea.

Would that he were a true lover, and not just the one who feeds on my face and acts the vampire? Would all be different if he didn't rail against me? If he genuinely supported my emotions and my art? He claims that I am jealous of his talent, that I am envious and feel inferior to the other women in his life. He playacts the lover rather than truly being my soulmate.

I wonder what it would be like to take another lover as he has done countless times. Would I find satisfaction, genuine ardour, a lover who tended my soul? Who might that be, and where can I find him? Or her?

Perhaps I will place an ad in the classifieds. Wanted dead or alive: One lover, must be loyal, not given to choleric attacks, must have a first and equal love of poetry and art, must adore and long for a woman with ginger hair.

22 November 1856
Lizzie

Once more, I packed a suitcase. Dante's promises are false. Instead, he has dreamt of me dead in his painting *Dante Dreaming of the Death of Beatrice.* Although he used another model, she looks eerily like me with my waterfall of ginger hair. I am his Beatrice, but rather than marry me, he dreams of me dying. I fear that his love is truly hatred. Why would he paint me dead?

I must flee Dante and his death wish for me. I will go to Bath with Lydie and take the waters, even though I know that the waters cannot quench my thirst or heal my ills.

23 November 1856
Lizzie

A stranger asked me to dance; he bowed to the waist and held himself as if he were royalty himself. I wanted to laugh because he seemed so awkward, but Lydie nudged me forward and coaxed, "Go ahead, Lizzie. You've nothing to lose." Although I have a lady's manners, Mam never taught us proper dancing, but Lydie and I had been practising in our room here in the Orange Grove in Bath, because we thought that the occasion might arise. We laughed heartily at our fumbling feet as we stumbled about the room. So, even though I am a poor dancer, I followed Lydie's advice and thought, Yes, I have nothing to lose, and I must get on with my life without Dante. I must begin again. I stepped forward, and Mr. Prince Charming, as he seemed to think of himself, grasped me by the waist and began to twirl me around the floor. I thought that I might get sick, but I kept my head. Like me, he was not an accomplished dancer. We must have looked a comic sight for any bystanders. He trounced repeatedly on my toes and apologised profusely, and I accidentally elbowed him when he twirled me. When the music finally stopped, we both seemed relieved. He bowed once more, nearly folding himself in half, and I was able to escape the prince, who looked around for another potential victim.

I have never been good at these social customs, but I came to Bath for a cure, and dancing seems to be one of those "cures" in which everyone participates. I would rather walk through the town to the Crescent and then look down on the valley below. That soothes my spirit somewhat; I look at the angle of the light and think about how I might paint the scene and who would populate its greenery.

I try the other cures. Two glasses of mineral water per day, even though the water literally makes me feel sicker than before I drink it. And four times a week, when ladies are allowed in the Roman Baths, I permit myself to be dunked as if the pagan Romans are "christening" me themselves.

Nothing helps. Nothing assuages my tormented spirit.

24 November 1856
Lizzie

Dante has arrived. Because my illness lingers and grows worse, I did not have the strength to refuse his affection. He begged my forgiveness once more and I relented. Even though I know it is foolish of me, it is hopeless to fight my feelings for him.

While here, he tried to amuse us. Lydie was not impressed, and I thought that his acting the "invalid" was rather troubling. He rented a wheelchair and played the sick man, while we pushed him around to the Baths. His mockery of the crippled angered me, but Dante always wishes to play the jester and be the centre of attention.

1 December 1856
Lizzie

I have returned from Bath uncured. Dante and I have tried to sort out our relationship, and are once again growing reconciled, but news from Dante's friends about a possible artists' "college" has angered me. Their idea is for all of us to live together as couples and fellow artists. At first, I thought that this would be appealing and that it would mean that Dante and I would at last be wed. But, last evening, Brown came to dinner, and he revealed that one of the couples will be Hunt and Annie Miller.

I became irate and shouted at both Dante and Brown, "This is impossible. I cannot abide this. I cannot live near Hunt and that woman. Not after what has happened!"

Brown looked confused and Dante rather sheepish.

"What do you mean, Lizzie? What's happened? Has Annie offended you in some way? I know that she's rather ill-mannered, but she has a good heart," Brown said.

"You mean you don't know? You don't know what Dante and that woman did? You don't know that they betrayed Hunt and me? That they carried on and made a love nest while we were gone?"

"Oh, but that was harmless," Dante chimed in. "It meant nothing. I was lonely. I missed you." He reached for me.

"Don't touch me, Dante," I said as I stepped away from him. "What other secrets are you keeping from me? Why didn't you tell me that Hunt and his hussy would live in the artists' colony with us?"

He looked guilty and said nothing.

For once, I grabbed *my* cloak and stormed out of the flat.

Later, after I walked around the neighbourhood for hours to cool down, I returned and Dante said, "Let's settle this." He left Chatham Street, and then returned with £10, which he borrowed from Brown; he says that he will use the money to purchase a marriage licence. Do I want to marry a man who has so little respect for me that he must be coerced into marriage?

15 December 1856
Lizzie

Dante foolishly spent the licence money in the pleasure garden. I also see that he is painting the scene from Hamlet when Hamlet reneges on his marriage proposal to Ophelia. I have had enough. I leave for Hampstead tonight. I shall not see him, no matter how much he implores forgiveness this time.

Part III

8 October 2019
Hastings

Maggie spoke frequently about how Dante Rossetti had proven himself to be a miscreant, how he had abused Lizzie's love, how he was unworthy of her. The three women were exceedingly happy that Lizzie had the courage to finally walk away and begin again. They hoped that she would stay away from him for good, but thought it unlikely, even though they knew that Lizzie and Christina set up house together. Bethany knew the truth about what Dante had done to Lizzie and she suspected that Agatha did too; still, she didn't discuss his ultimate abuse of Lizzie with her fellow sleuths for fear that they, especially Maggie, would be terribly disheartened.

As they sat in the Queen's Consort's Tearoom on High St., Bethany remarked, "Of course, I knew of her flight from him and how she took up residence in Hampstead, but I had no idea how truly wretched he was to the person he claimed was his destiny."

"It's far worse to hear Lizzie describe how he treated her. I wish I could go back in time and make him pay for what he did to her," Agatha added, as she took a bite of her scone.

"Yes, revenge or justice would be righteous. Plus, the destiny idea haunts me, as I read her words," Maggie replied. "She had to have known that he was either mad or manipulative in claiming that he knew her in another life."

Bethany said, "Well, of course, the notion of reincarnation had arrived in England during the Romantic period; Percy Shelley believed in reincarnation. And the Victorians picked up on the idea, mostly as artists abandoned attachment to the material world and sought solace in spiritualism or in days long gone. The PRB itself longed for the past. They certainly didn't dwell on the present in either their poetry or their paintings, not in the way Barrett Browning advocated."

"You mention reincarnation. It's odd and perhaps sounds utterly bizarre, but sometimes, when I'm painting, I think that I see Christina and Lizzie walking on the beach, hand in hand; they even frolic on the beach; they are quite present in this world to me, even though they have been dead for over a century. Perhaps they are reincarnated. I've started to incorporate them into my painting. I wish you'd take a look at it, Beth." Maggie didn't mention that she thought that the two artists had stopped to gaze at her painting, for she thought that Bethany would deem her quite mad.

"My dears, you won't believe what I just read apropos to our mystery," Agatha said. "According to *The Times,* there's an exhibition scheduled soon at the National Portrait Gallery. It will be entitled the Pre-Raphaelite Sisterhood. I wonder who the producers will include in the Sisterhood besides Lizzie and perhaps Christina. It's about time that their work is recognized."

"May I see?" Bethany asked as she took the paper and quickly read the article. "Of course, we must attend. First though, we must think about what to do with the diaries. I'm in favour of publishing them. We could send a few of them to the *Times w*ith a notice that there's far more to come. The diaries deserve the light of day."

"I'm not sure. I'd rather wait until we know the full contents. What if there's something that injures their reputations, like suicide? People suggest that Lizzie killed herself, but what if it's true? Remember how Mary Wollstonecraft was much maligned after her husband William Godwin revealed her suicide attempts? We don't wish for that to happen to Lizzie, do we?" Maggie asked.

"Of course not, but publishing the diaries in the *Times* near the moment of the upcoming exhibit would be brilliant, wouldn't it? That would add further notoriety to their art," Bethany argued. Maggie thought about how such publication would also likely add to Bethany's scholarly notoriety as one of the discoverers of the literary trove, but Maggie hated to think that this was Bethany's sole aim.

"There's ample time later to decide whether to publish them," Agatha piped in. "Meanwhile, I would very much enjoy seeing Maggie's painting, wouldn't you, Bethany?"

Maggie smiled broadly for the grace it took on Agatha's part to settle the issue for now. The painting was sitting next to Maggie in her portfolio, for she intended to continue to paint that afternoon.

The three headed down to the beach and Maggie readied her painting for the others to study. While waiting, Bethany let down her red hair, sat on a rock and looked out at the sea, as if she were a mermaid or selkie cast onto the shore searching for her lover.

Once the painting was on the easel, Agatha praised its use of colour, and the way Maggie had captured the sun's iridescence on the sea. In contrast, Bethany had little to say other than, "Maggie, you know I have little sense or knowledge of painting. I can't make a judgement. I can't discern what is good and what isn't. You'll have to judge the painting yourself, love."

"But don't you see these figures here? They are Lizzie and Christina walking hand in hand as I imagine them, as I've actually seen them on this beach," Maggie said. "They walk together as if they were one being. They shine brightly and gaze at one another as we used to."

"I've seen them. First, Lizzie appeared. She even added herself to the canvas. Then they both showed up. They frolicked on the beach, and they even stopped to look at the painting and seem quite pleased that I've noticed them and rendered them in art."

Agatha looked away and Bethany remarked, "Now you're scaring me, Maggie. Are you sure you aren't hallucinating?"

"Of course, I'm not. The women laughed when they saw themselves in my painting."

"I would need to see them for myself," Bethany replied. "I may be a literary sleuth, as Agatha says, but I'm not given to Blakean visions as you seem to be."

"You seem to have no truck with the supernatural, but there's a thin layer between the living and the dead; I know, for I've encountered several spirits in the church," Agatha said, as Maggie removed the painting from the easel and placed it back in its cover. "Maybe you should open your mind and heart to let the visions in as Maggie does."

Bethany didn't reply and instead turned her back to them and walked away. Her footsteps were washed away by the tide.

Later that night, Maggie plucked up her courage and told Bethany that she intended to enter the painting in a contest. That Lizzie had inspired her.

"But what about your research, the articles that you've started? A painting won't help you get promoted."

"What if I don't want help? What if I don't want to get promoted? What if I want to leave the academy and pursue art?" Maggie asked.

"You're quite mad, you know. Few can make a go of it in art. Remember what your teachers said about your work."

Maggie grimaced but refused to take the bait. "Let's not fuss, Beth, I do feel inspired. Let's read more of what Lizzie and Christina have to say. I'm eager to see what happens next, to see if they found love and happiness." She pulled the mobile from Beth's bag and began to read Lizzie's diary aloud.

18 December 1856
Lizzie

Today, I culled through the mail forwarded to my new address in Hampstead. In it, I received the following poem entitled "In an Artist's Studio."

One face looks out from all his canvases
One selfsame figure sits or walks or leans
We found her hidden just behind those screens,
That mirror gave back all her loveliness.
A queen in opal or in ruby dress,
A nameless girl in freshest summer greens,
A saint, an angel—every canvas means
The same one meaning, neither more nor less.
And she with true kind eyes looks back on him,
Fair as the moon and joyful as the light:
Not one with waiting, not with sorrow dim;
Not as she is, but was when hope shone bright;
Not as she is, but as she fills his dream.

It was signed Christina Georgiana Rossetti. No note accompanied it.

I read and re-read it countless times, as I recall the room where false replicas of me and my face adorn the walls and lie in heaps on tables, in dresser drawers, strewn across the bedstead. Here, in this sketch, I am a queen, there an angel, there a nameless girl. In every canvas, I am a different persona, but behind each mask, I am myself and, in each case, I do look out at him, the painter, my intended, with kind eyes. The poet is right; he has created his dream; the real me now lies hidden in sorrow, forever waiting for love and the soul's true affection.

I must write to Miss Rossetti to express my thanks that someone, some other Rossetti, finally knows the true me, not the dream.

20 December 1856
Lizzie

Dear Miss Rossetti,

I write with heartfelt thanks in knowing that you understand who I am behind the mask, the persona that I put on like the royal garments that Dante asks me to wear. I am not a queen or Dante Alighieri's muse, his unrequited love. I am Lizzie and I've been waiting for someone to recognize me behind my façade.

When I dream and, in my fantasies, I am not the face that Dante feeds on. I am the one who gazes at beauty and then replicates it on the canvas. In *my* dream, I succeed, and I become an artist and poet, whose talent renders beauty and truth.

I aspire not to greatness but to realisation. To developing my gift and then giving it to others. To leaving some creation behind as my artistic legacy. To have someone know that I lived and made art. To be a painter, not just the painted.

I regret that we began our acquaintance in a frosty manner. I am naturally shy and felt in awe of you and your poetic genius. You see, Dante and I have often read your poetry together in the evenings. I am most moved by your "Song," which speculates that a woman might have a secret lover beyond the one to whom she is bound.

Your indebted friend,
Miss Elizabeth Siddal

23 December 1856
Christina

Dear Miss Siddal,

I am profoundly moved by your appreciative letter. I too regret that our acquaintance began as it did. I felt shy towards you as well. You see, I attended the exhibit where *Ophelia* was unveiled, and I saw you. I thought about asking Gabriel to introduce us then, but I felt too bashful to approach you, because of your absolute beauty and grace. And then, when we finally met, I felt somewhat tongue-tied, which I know sounds odd, since my work is words, but they are words on a page, not spoken utterances. My reticence came off as snobbishness. I also lament the tone of our meeting.

I am indeed pleased that you find my poetry moving. I understand from Gabriel that you are also a poet. Perhaps you would be willing to share some of your verses with me. Perhaps in person. Please feel free to call on me at any time. I sense that we have much we could share and discuss.

Ever your humble friend,
Christina G. Rossetti

23 December 1856
Christina

I rarely think of Mr. James Collinson, and am glad that I am not his "horse in harness," but I saw in the *Times* today an announcement of his marriage to an older widow. Obviously, he didn't find the seminary appealing. No doubt he married a devout Catholic. I'm glad that I didn't marry him, but I do dislike being a solitary traveller, alone in the world with no one in whom I can confide. Such melancholy led me to write:

The door was shut, I looked between
   Its iron bars; and saw it lie,
   My garden, mine, beneath the sky,
Pied all with flowers bedewed and green:

From bough to bough the song-birds crossed,
   From flower to flower the moths and bees;
   With all its nests and stately trees
It had been mine, and I was lost.

A shadowless spirit kept the gate,
   Blank and unchanging like the grave.
   I peering through said: "Let me have
Some buds to cheer my outcast state."

He answered not. "Or give me, then,
   But one small twig from shrub or tree;
   And bid my home remember me
Until I come to it again."

The spirit was silent; but he took
   Mortar and stone to build a wall;
   He left no loophole great or small
Through which my straining eyes might look:

My hope is that someday soon I will no longer be a solitary traveller in
this life. I wish for deep friendship; I desire love.

1 January 1857
Lizzie

How odd! After all this time, Christina said to call on her anytime. What
has changed? Why am I no longer a pariah? Why am I no longer common?
Is it because she looked at all of Dante's renditions of me and found them
lacking? All the copies that do not convey my true self, my soul? If that's the
case, why didn't she look earlier and more closely? Why didn't she at least
give me a chance to show her and her darling mama that I am a woman with
a good, noble heart, that I am not a tramp, a strumpet, a tart, that I am not
like other artists' models?

I will write to her again and perhaps call on her, but I have no calling card nor carriage. I must walk once again to the Rossetti home, and then compose myself before I enter the lion's den alone. I must be a brave Daniel. But even with the facade of Daniel, I shall be myself. I will not wear the customary corset as I did last time. I will be like Barbara and once again be an unconventional woman.

3 January 1857
Christina

Of late, Mother and I have visited the women at the St. Mary Magdalene Penitentiary for Fallen Women. We counsel them and try to persuade them to rectify their ways and redeem themselves. Mother insists that I go with her, but I grow reluctant because I wonder about these women and their fallen state. Surely, the men who frequent them or lead them into perdition are just as guilty and sinful as they are, but these men are never reprimanded in the same way as the women, who find it difficult to earn a living by proper means. There are no true professions for women, other than the profession of marriage.

I once considered becoming a nurse, when Miss Nightingale tended to the men fighting in the Crimean War. Mother claimed that nursing was like prostitution though. That nurses follow men and camp near the battlefield, and then minister to them in unseemly ways. She forbade me from following Miss Nightingale to the Crimea, and so I took to my bed, feigning illness, and did the only thing that I knew how to do. I wrote my poems. Later, I read that EBB considers nursing an unworthy endeavour and a waste of women's talents and gifts. And I learned that Miss Nightingale is Barbara's cousin and Miss Nightingale refused to visit her and her siblings because their parents were unwed. Perhaps Mother and Mrs. Browning are right, and Mother's refusal allowed me to pursue my own world, to emulate EBB, and thus enter my own profession as a poet. And I think less of Miss Nightingale for lacking compassion for her relations.

15 January 1857
Christina

Miss Siddal came to call, as I had hoped. When I knew to expect her, I told Mother that I was catching a cold, so that I could decline visiting the fallen women with her and meet privately with Miss Siddal. Mother suspected nothing and I asked Gillian, our kitchen maid, to prepare a special tea with Queen Cake to serve my fellow poet.

Miss Siddal asked me to read one of my poems and I obliged.

When I finished, she said, "As I mentioned, Dante has often read your verse to me. He is quite proud of you. And I believe that you are a fine poet. On par with Mrs. Browning."

I felt myself grow crimson. "I'm pleased that my brother is finally proud of my work. But, no, Miss Siddal, I fear you exaggerate about my poems in relation to Mrs. Browning, although I would like to be as gifted as her. She truly is my poetic idol."

"As she is mine," she replied. "She should be our next poet laureate. Don't you agree?"

"Indeed, her work is so expansive, from writing about children maimed and persecuted in the factories—to writing about her greatest and deepest love—to writing now about women's artistry. Her work is quite ground-breaking. She considers the full scope of life and can see as a god." I felt a little blasphemous about saying so, but it is what I believe, and it felt good to say it out aloud rather than remain silent, as I usually do, about my true feelings and beliefs.

"She certainly disproves male theories, like Aurora Leigh's cousin Romney's, that no woman can actually be a poet or an artist," Miss Siddal replied.

I agreed with her and then changed the subject slightly and asked if she would please show me one of her poems.

She hesitated at first, but then pulled out a small notebook from her satchel and opened it. Then she said, "I'm still working on these two poems, but would be happy if you would read them and offer suggestions and insights. I wrote them in response to one of your 'Songs' that Dante read me."

> I read these lines aloud:
> Oh, grieve not with thy bitter tears
> The life that passes fast
> The gates of heaven will open wide
> And take me in at last.
> Then sit down meekly at my side
> And watch my young life flee.
> Then solemn peace of holy death
> Come quickly unto thee
> But true love seek me in the throng

Of spirits floating past
And I will take thee by the hands
And know thee mine at last.

In some ways, the poem reminded me of the content of Gabriel's "The Blessed Damozel," but with a tone of even greater longing for one's love to join them in the afterlife, and only then would the dead love belong to the speaker. I was troubled by the implication that the persona sought her own death. Suicide is against God's will and suicides are damned. I did not mention this to Miss Siddal; perhaps the implication was only in my own head.

And then I turned the page and read another and was surprised by the title, content, and tone.

"Dead Love"

Oh, never weep for love that's dead
Since love is seldom true
But changes his fashion from blue to red,
From brightest red to blue,
And love was born to an early death
And is so seldom true.

Then harbour no smile on your bonny face
To win the deepest sigh.
The fairest words on truest lips
Pass on and surely die,
And you will stand alone, my dear,
When wintry winds draw nigh.

Sweet, never weep for what cannot be,
For this God has not given.
If the merest dream of love were true
Then, sweet, we should be in heaven,
And this is only earth, my dear,
Where true love is not given.

When I finished reading it, I said, "Gabriel is correct that you and I are much alike; our poems dwell on death. But how different is the tone and message here in the first poem, where the dead beloved seeks her lover to travel to the next world with her, and thus the beloved will finally possess the lover's soul."

I saw her face turn pink and realised that I had touched a nerve. I dared not discuss her relationship with my brother, but I have sensed, ever since I saw his paintings of her, that she feels great melancholy because he likely does not give himself fully to her as she would wish. He always has been selfish and egocentric and therefore, even though obsessed with her stunning beauty, he cannot become the lover she would wish him to be.

I continued, "If you don't mind this observation, the second poem conveys more sadness than my own poetry imparts. Do you genuinely believe that one can never attain love on this earth?"

"I fear it's true," she replied, as she looked down at her hands in her lap.

I fear that my brother has severely injured her, broken her spirit and her heart.

Her poetry is exquisite, and I told her so. It does resemble mine in content; however, it does not imitate my own. Perhaps it demonstrates that we have great affinity for one another and are genuine kindred spirits, despite our differences in upbringing and life's circumstances. Perhaps we are like Aurora Leigh and her Marian Erle in EBB's epic, the fallen woman that Aurora befriends. I hesitate to call Miss Siddal a fallen woman though. I have no knowledge of her carnal experience; I must assume that, like me, she is free from taint, despite the goblins' lure.

Perhaps Miss Siddal and I can be such friends that the melancholy can lift from her soul and mine as well. When two hearts share affinity, surely sadness cannot reside therein.

After she left, I quickly scribbled these lines:

> I long for one to stir my deep—
> I have had enough of help and gift—
> I long for one to search and sift
> Myself, to take myself and keep.

At one time, Gabriel had suggested that Miss Siddal illustrate my collection of poems that I hoped to publish. Now, I am most interested in writing a poem about two sisters, me, and my sister Maria. Perhaps Miss Siddal and I can discuss the narrative poem, and she could sketch out a few ideas.

3 March 1857
Lizzie

Dear Miss Rossetti,

Thank you for your generous hospitality, and for being so kind in regard to my poems that you have read and critiqued. Of course, my verses are juvenile in comparison to yours, but I am exceedingly grateful for your praise. I try to follow Goethe's advice to write a little each day, and paint and sketch, even though two physicians have advised against doing so. They think that art makes me unhappy, that expressing myself makes me melancholy. Little do they understand how a woman needs to fulfil herself. I know that you understand this. Surely our souls themselves would wither and die if we were not allowed free expression of thoughts and feelings.

Perhaps I am overstepping bounds and seeking your friendship and companionship too soon, but I wonder if you might wish to attend a Langham Society meeting with me, where we discuss art, poetry, and women's rights. Sometimes we attempt to converse with the dead. The latter you may find alarming, since I know from Dante that you are a committed and strict Anglican, but I assure you that our conversations with spirits are real, and that the women in this society practice no witchcraft; there is nothing profane or devilish about the séances. We only seek the dead's wisdom and guidance, as we move forward with our own lives and art.

I know from Dante that you know some of the women artists who organise the Society, so I feel assured that you will feel comfortable with them and their friends. I have found their support invaluable, as I attempt to become an independent artist. One who does not depend on Dante, one who finds inspiration among my fellow female artists.

Your friend,
Miss Elizabeth Siddal

4 March 1857
Christina

Dear Miss Siddal,

Yes, I would gladly attend the Langham Women's Society with you. Although I am shy about sharing ideas, I believe that it is important for women artists and intellectuals to seek each other's companionship and support. We have laboured at our art for too long in solitary ways. Every time we pick up a pen or brush, it is as if we are starting from scratch, because we often do not know each other's work, because our work has not been published or exhibited as often as the artistry of men. Often our written work appears under the name Anonymous or under a male pen name or initials to hide our female sex. I believe that we can draw together (certain pun intended) and learn from one another, unlike the men in the Brotherhood who make their artful society a competition, rather than a means of energising their art.

You and I have considerable in common. When you mention the doctors, who have advised indolence and stagnation, I was also told to drop my pen and pick up a darning needle. This occurred when I was young; right after womanhood announced its arrival. The doctor, Queen Victoria's very own physician, supposedly the most learned doctor in all of Christendom, tried to cure my malady, what he termed "religious mania" by applying leeches to my womanly parts. I was, of course, appalled, and never told anyone after that about my monthly haemorrhaging for fear that this doctor might kill my developing poetic voice in the same way that young Keats was killed by being excessively bled. Of course, he was not killed for being feminine; at least I think not. But perhaps his soul was too womanly or androgynous for this world, and thus was not embraced by the masses.

Please advise when the next meeting is, and I shall escape my family prison and meet you there.

Yours affectionately,
Christina

5 May 1857
Christina

Gabriel is unaware that Miss Siddal and I have become acquainted, that we are becoming friends and confidants. I prefer to keep it that way, and so does she. Besides, she tells me that she still refuses to see him, even though he continues to write to her and tells her of his escapades. He says that he is translating Italian poems and hopes to publish them. He often visits the pleasure gardens. She does occasionally write back, mostly because Gabriel has arranged for her art to be shown with the PRB's, as if she is truly a member. Perhaps he thinks that she will return to him if he makes her a member of the Brotherhood. That, of course, will never happen because it is strictly a male-only club. She tells me that she will attend the exhibition, but shall try to ignore Gabriel who will, no doubt, seek her attention. Her painting *Clerk Saunders* will be displayed, and she hopes to sell it, so that she can forgo Mr. Ruskin's patronage and thus move on, away from the tentacles of the Brotherhood and my brother in particular.

6 June 1857
Christina

Last evening, I accompanied Miss Siddal to the Langham Society Meeting. I felt a little hesitant, but once I was there, I felt invigorated. It reminded me of my youthful meditations about women's art. All my hopes that women would pick up pens, pencils, and paintbrushes, not in secret or in-between caring for children or parents or minding the stew, but out in the open. That we would express our art freely without encumbrance or interference. That we would encourage one another and find a separate space in our homes, rooms of our own, where we can practise our art. That we would attend art and writing schools, that we would flourish as male artists and poets have been encouraged to do. Miss Howitt and Miss Smith have a women-only artists' colony, a permanent space for women to pursue the arts. Oh, what a dream! I have scribbled my poems in the quiet confines of my bedroom, while falsely claiming illness, but what if we could come together in good health and vigour and share our work as Miss Siddal and I have? I wouldn't need my brother or any man to praise my art's worthiness or highlight its unworthiness. I wouldn't need to pretend illness. Perhaps we could create and run our own presses, our own galleries for the visual artists among us, our own women's art colleges.

Miss Siddal also introduced me to two unusual women, Emily Faithfull and Helen Codrington, who have been friends since childhood; they seem a loving couple. Their arms are often entwined; they look at one another in a delighted way as if the other person is the most fascinating person they have ever met. They live in the same flat and, it's assumed, share the same bed. Miss Siddal told me that Miss Faithfull's father is a clergyman, and he does not disapprove this arrangement, for Miss Codrington's husband is mostly away at sea, and Miss Faithfull's father does not wish for his daughter to be alone. I first thought this scandalous but when I see them gazing at one another with utter devotion and love, I think that it would be exquisite to have such a loving partner. The Langham Ladies, as Miss Siddal has remarked, are models for the possibilities of what women can become, if we throw off the yoke of male dominance.

In their presence, I have never felt so alive. I sense that Miss Siddal feels the same. Afterwards, on our way homeward, as we walked across Battersea Bridge, I reached for her hand, and we held hands like sisters. She did look the queen, even though she wishes to be an ordinary girl. She is tall and stately, and I am a dwarf in comparison. She seemed not to care and gave my hand a squeeze and then kissed me on the cheek, as I turned toward home and she made her way to her desolate Chatham St. flat, to which she has once again returned at Gabriel's behest.

When I returned home, I thought about the need to confide in someone about my troubled past with my father and wrote these lines:

> I tell my secret? No indeed, not I:
> Perhaps some day, who knows?
> But not today; it froze, and blows, and snows,
> And you're too curious: fie!
> You want to hear it? Well:
> Only, my secret's mine, and I won't tell.
>
> Perhaps some languid summer day,
> When drowsy birds sing less and less,
> And golden fruit is ripening to excess,
> If there's not too much sun nor too much cloud,
> And the warm wind is neither still nor loud,
> Perhaps my secret I may say,
> Or you may guess.

When will the time come? When will the fruit be heavy on the bough? When will I confess my secret and to whom?

8 July 1857
Christina

We continue to attend the Langham Society. I meet Miss Siddal . . . Lizzie there. I can't get used to calling her by her Christian name, as she has requested, but I shall endeavour to speak of and to her in a more familiar, a more personal way. She thinks that we are becoming like sisters, and so must refer to each other by our first names. I don't wish to take advantage of her as Gabriel has; I intend to show her the utmost respect as a woman and fellow artist. As a sister who grows closer to me than Maria currently is.

Anna and Barbara have invited all of us Society members to Barbara's Scanland's Gate near Hastings. There she keeps a small studio where we can spend quiet time, not being bothered by domestic duties, for Anna has hired a woman and paid her well to care for our daily needs. I have told Lizzie that I wish to go, and that I hope she will accompany me.

She tells me that she has been to the house and that she painted there and found it an inspiring place, but she asks, "What shall I tell Dante? He will wonder where I'm going."

"Tell him that you need time to yourself. Tell him the truth. That you need to go to a place where your art will be rightly expressed without encumbrance or interference."

"Shall I tell him that I will go with you, Christina?"

"No, let's keep our friendship a secret for now. There is ample time for him to grow jealous of our affection."

16 July 1857
Christina

Lizzie and I spent a week at Barbara's Hastings retreat. How glorious it was! We both gazed at beauty when we were near the sea. While I wrote more poems about sisters embracing, from time to time, I broke my poetic reverie to also stare at beauty and grace, as I watched Lizzie paint. She is working on an oil painting of the Lady of Shalott walking near the sea after escaping her tower. I've told her that she is that lady and that her figure certainly resembles her. When I said that, she laughed and continued to concentrate her attention on the colour of the sea and mix her paints to mimic what she observed. *I* observed the sun shining on her ginger hair cascading down her back. I observed her painting herself free to be who she wishes to be. I felt such contentment that I wished every day could be like the days when we created art together in Hastings.

This evening I visited St. Clement's Church on the hill above the sea. I prayed that Miss Siddal, Lizzie and I, would grow close. That we would serve as each other's support and confidant. That we would eventually be like family to one another without the interference of my brother. I prayed that both Lizzie and I would find genuine, heartfelt love and happiness in this world, not the next.

Sadly, the week was over and as we returned to London, I felt melancholy and dread overtake me. And then I felt my heart ache, as Lizzie alighted from the carriage to return to Gabriel and her frigid Chatham Street flat.

4 August 1857
Lizzie

I sold my first painting to someone other than Mr. Ruskin. An American purchased my *Clerk Saunders* and has taken it to Boston. I finally feel legitimate as an artist; I've been endorsed. I now feel it appropriate and necessary to give up my allowance from my patron. Then I will be free to paint what I wish, rather than appease his aesthetic desires. I continue to paint my Lady of Shalott as she's left her tower and walks near the sea. (Mr. Ruskin tried to dissuade me from painting my Lady in this way, telling me that I know little of the Lady and should stick to Tennyson's version of her). When I paint her, I feel somewhat liberated from Dante, Mr. Ruskin, and Mr. Tennyson.

17 September 1857
Lizzie

I found several new paintings that Dante had squirrelled away in the closet. The model is a full-bodied woman. "Who is she?" I asked.

"Oh, just someone that I met in the gardens," he replied. "Her name is Fanny."

"You've painted her often. Is she your new muse?"

"Of course not. I only painted her because you were away. You're my only true inspiration," he said. His eyes were averted from me; he stared at one of the paintings, *The Bower Garden*, where her broad face and bosom fill the frame.

After I watched him gaze at his painting of this new muse, I penned my latest poem:

Opt not thy lips, thou foolish one
Nor turn to me thy face;
The blast of heaven shall strike thee down
Ere I will give thee grace.

Take thou thy shadow from my path,
Nor turn to me and pray;
The wild wild winds thy dirge may sing
Ere I will bid thee stay.

Turn thou away thy false dark eyes
Nor gaze upon my face;
Great love I bore thee: now great hate
Sits firmly in its place.

When did my love turn to hate? Why are love and hate so closely aligned? Is that always the case or only with Dante? Can love truly overcome hate when it has settled in one's heart?

While he paints Fanny, I find solace in painting my Lady of Shalott. Even though she still weeps as I do, I see that her tears are different, for hers appear to be tears of joy as she escapes her confinement.

26 October 1857
Christina

Lizzie wished to visit Keats's house in Hampstead, and so we took the train and wandered through the house that he had rented and where he wrote his poetry to his beloved, Fanny Brawne. We gazed at his death mask and lamented the loss of so bright a star in the poetry firmament. He died so young and had much more to give to the world. Lizzie and I agree that, had Keats lived, he would have been as profound a poet as Tennyson. In any case, even though his life was cut short, his poetry, sparse as it is, is among the greatest in the English language.

Afterwards, we climbed Hampstead Hill and looked down at the City of London. It was foggy, but through the mist we could see the dome of St. Paul's and the expanse of the Tower Bridge straddling the dirty Thames. In the far distance, I glimpsed the green lawns of Hyde Park and Kensington Palace. I've always said that I am of London, but seeing it from this view, made me wish to follow the road out of London and see more of my country, but only if my friend could accompany me. I felt for a moment like the Lady of Shalott who needed to break out of her tower and roam the earth.

"Lizzie, have you ever thought of going away from here? Of leaving London? I mean permanently as I have?"

"Why do you ask? Are you unsettled?" she asked as she stretched the length of her body on the green lawn and looked up at the billowing clouds.

"Of course, I'm unsettled, aren't you? Besides, if we left, who would miss us?"

She sat up and grimaced; she looked hurt but didn't say anything.

"I mean no one would miss *me*. Surely, Gabriel would feel loss if you were to leave him. Perhaps that's what he needs to wake him up from his stupor and realise that he should marry you as he promised."

"Well, where would we go? I know no one who could accommodate us except for Anna."

"Let's do what Ruskin's father told you to do. Let's go seek your golden age, your golden past. Let's travel north and find Hope Hall, your ancestral home."

9 October 2019
Hastings

"Oh, we finally arrived at the moment of their flight," Maggie excitedly said as she and Bethany sat on the floor next to their bed. "They've grown to be true sisters; they are sisters in art. Beth, they've left it all behind and are starting a new life."

"Yes, this is truly remarkable. No wonder the family doesn't wish this to be known. Women as artists, not art, is not the usual life course," Bethany replied.

"Their work has given me a new idea for my painting."

"What is it?" Bethany asked, suggesting for the first time interest in Maggie's avocation.

"You'll see; I must get back to it before the light fades," Maggie said as she gathered her wares and donned a sun hat. "When I return, let's pick up this evening where we left off."

"In the meantime, I'll begin to type the entries into my computer."

"If you must," Maggie replied as she fled out the door into the blinding sun.

20 February 1858
Christina

No one contested our residency at Hope Hall. No Eyre family member showed up and told us that we must leave. No constable came to our door and ejected us. No female ghost, no barghest, appeared in our midst. We've heard no chains clanging, doors shutting or opening when no one else was in the hall. If the ghost had been here, perhaps she fled when she saw that we're intent on reclaiming Hope Hall as our own, as a place of creativity, imagination, and aspiration, rather than despair, chaos, and death. Perhaps she gave us her blessing.

So, after six weeks of setting up house and our studios, we invited Barbara, Anna, and Bessie to join us, and they agreed. Barbara also invited other women artists, including Joanna Boyce, who has exhibited at the Royal Academy and, who, through the intercession of her father and brother who are also painters, has studied in Bruges, Amsterdam, Cologne, and Brussels. Barbara also invited Georgiana Burne-Jones, an illustrator. Joanna and Georgiana come and go for they have families, but they have sworn to keep our location secret. Now, we have a true "sisterhood in art." We shall not be like Anglican nuns, like my sister Maria and her community, who devote themselves to God, but shall be genuine sisters devoted to art who share all with one another and who encourage each other's imaginations, rather than stifling them through doctrine and self-sacrifice. We shall not give up our desires or ourselves but become ourselves; what we are meant to be—artists. We shall flourish in each other's care. This will be *our* artists' studio, our utopia, a women's world, a women's country, set apart.

4 April 1858
Christina

As Barbara did in Hastings, we hired young women from the village to perform domestic duties, so that we do not need to cease our work as artists and writers. Barbara and Anna have sufficient funds now to pay them handsomely. We have offered to provide writing and drawing lessons to Briony and Belinda, the good lasses who care for us, and they have taken us up on the offer. In a sense, we are providing an artistic education to women, as Gabriel did with men at the Workingmen's College in London. But we differ, in the fact, that we care about our workers and students, unlike Gabriel, who only cared about the tin that he earned, rather than the men he instructed.

(Briony has natural talent. She used coloured pencils and drew the sunset, what those in Yorkshire call the "day-gate." I commended her rendering and she broadly smiled, telling me that "It's nowt!" Even so, I sense her pride in creating something with her own hands and heart.)

4 May 1858
Christina

Perhaps I shouldn't have but I wrote to Gabriel to let him know that Lizzie no longer needs him. I didn't inform her of my letter but feel assured that she would approve. I wanted him to know that we are creating our own world, our own country, where men are no longer necessary. Our enterprise is brave, and we feel emboldened.

Dear Gabriel,

I suppose you all are wondering what has become of your "intended" (why did you never tell the family?) and me. And I assume that you or Mother have hired a detective to locate us. But you will never find us for I write to you from a far-off country, one that doesn't exist in your world. A country that J.S. Mill advocates on our behalf—claiming that for us to have our own literature and art, we must have our own country. We've created a woman's "country" and "Princess Ida," your Lizzie, is its monarch, and I am the mayor of its major city, the City of Ladies.

I can hear you scoff, but you can't realise how freeing it is for us to live without men, not to be judged by our beauty or lack thereof, and not to have male influence or ideas pushing against or blocking our creativity. There is no one here like Aurora Leigh's Cousin Romney arguing that "We get no Christ from you, verily, we get no poet." There is no one here calling our art and poetry trivial, naïve—there is no one here telling us to stick to drawing or painting still life (as Ruskin once told Anna Howitt when she painted our British heroine Boadicea who fought the Roman conquerors—he told her that she knew nothing about Boadicea. She should paint him a pheasant's wing) or insisting that we copy Will Shakespeare's sonnets to learn to write poetry. There is no one telling us that, as writers, we must use pseudonyms or attribute our work to "Anonymous." There is no one who stands in our way, like Milton's bogey hovering over our shoulders saying, "Tsk, tsk, you musn't write, think, or paint that. That's not lady-like, that's not seemly."

Instead, in our City of Ladies, we gather to share our work, to have it critiqued by other women artists and poets who share our passion for making ourselves fully human. We gather on our verdant lawns to hold up our accomplishments—to receive judicious and salutary advice and sometimes praise. We care not to condemn but to uphold our right to create, not to *be* art. Here we think and write about what Sappho would have said.

You should know that Lizzie is no longer an object to be gazed upon. She herself gazes. You should know that, unlike your habit of/obsession with feeding on Lizzie's face, she does not feed on yours. She doesn't draw or paint you or even think about you anymore. She is finally free of you. Instead, she paints her "Lady of Shalott," finally free from her tower.

We must keep our location secret, lest we are invaded by intruders, Peeping Toms or Gabriels. Lizzie *is* the artist Lady of Shalott who has escaped her tower and the paintings and poetry rendered by men. And I am her Guinevere, not her Lancelot.

Ever your affectionate sister,
Christina G. Rossetti

P.S. I've had a friend post this letter so that you can't locate us. I advise you to leave us alone. Do not try to find us.

4 June 1858
Lizzie

Luckily, I squirrelled away funds from the patronage that I received from Ruskin, funds that Dante couldn't touch. That will hold us over for a while, but I will need to paint and sell some more paintings, for us to continue and for our sisterhood to survive. Barbara, Bessie, Anna, Georgiana, and Joanna also provide for our welfare here in our commune. At some point though, we may wish to try to find another patron. I wonder if Mrs. Browning herself would be willing to help support our sisterhood in art. Surely, she supports women as artists. I truly wish that I had met her in Paris, but, unfortunately, she was indisposed at the time. Since I've met him, I could write to Mr. Browning and seek his counsel, asking him to intervene with her on our behalf. Sadly, EBB's assets are her husband's, even though they live in Italy. This is something that Barbara and Bessie are contesting. They seek to pass a Married Women's Property Act in parliament that would enable women to hold onto their own assets, rather than forfeit all to their husbands once they are bound to one another for life. If EBB endorsed and sponsored us, she would need to obtain approval from Robert Browning. Surely, he would also support our art since he encourages his wife's and praised my paintings.

13 July 1858
Lizzie

I spend much of my day searching for impossible light—not golden sunlight, but the clear, white light that surrounds some holy objects and perhaps emanates from all living things if you are discerning and look hard enough.

I have become my Lady and I have added Christina as my Guinevere to my painting. Both of us have escaped the crumbling tower and we walk along the sea. Christina's glow is exceedingly natural and has grown stronger the longer we have been away from our former, our past lives. If I look at her when the sun has fallen below the horizon, I see the white light that surrounds her. I try to capture that light on canvas.

We've talked about her saintliness, but she refuses to call herself a saint; she tells me that her minister tried to get her and other young girls to become saints through starvation. I confess to her that I think I nearly did the same when I was unhappy in my previous life, but I do not tell her how close I came to death whenever I was with her brother. I did not wish to become a saint through dying, but I felt starved of affection, and I literally starved myself. She still loves her brother, and I love who he was when I first met him in Walter's studio when Walter painted me as the boy-girl Cesario-Viola. Unfortunately, Dante did not remain that adoring man; I fear he has become his doppelgänger.

In any case, she's not the shadowy person that her brother is; she is a saint to me regardless, and is worthy of canonization, if there is such a thing in the Anglican Church. She is worthy because she rescued me from Dante, who tried to capture and control my light but never could, no matter how many hundreds of times he tried. She encouraged me to find my way north, here to Hope Hall, to find hope itself and reclaim it, not for my family, but for all of us, for all sisters in art. She urged me, and I her, to give up fear, self-doubt, self-loathing.

I wish that I could capture the light that emanates from her. If I could, I would bottle it and drink it every day, and then give it to other women who need to escape their troubled lives and create themselves through art.

4 November 1858
Christina

The geography of home. In our women's world, our new country, all of us artists have separate rooms of our own, and common spaces. Hope Hall overlooks the Sheaf River in Southern Yorkshire. We are set atop a hill in a vast forest. This is the greenest part of England, and well-hidden from the material world and its temptations.

My space, my studio, is adjacent to Lizzie's in the northern part of the house, where the light is the best for painting. We look out on the deer park and the living river that glides toward Sheffield. We step in and out of each other's studios frequently during the day, and we do the same with Anna, Barbara, Bessie, Georgiana, and Joanna. Our art feeds each other's creativity. We ask one another for opinion about colour, shape, and trajectory of line (if a poem), trying hard not to foist our view when it's not asked.

The geography of our world is like an island that can only be found through careful craftsmanship, good sailing, and steady winds. So far, no Yorkshire ghosts, females or otherwise, have appeared in our midst and no uninvited interlopers have found us, although we've erected no artificial barriers.

Our experiment in a Sisterhood of Art may fail, but we do not worry. We are no longer faces on which other (male) artists feed, as they did with Lizzie. We are the artists that I dreamt of who picked up pencils, charcoal, and paint to create our own visions of the world.

My sisters and I meet regularly to read together and to share our work. Of late when we read, we read aloud from EBB's masterpiece, *Aurora Leigh.* Each of us takes to heart Aurora's direction in her poem:

> [I] [w]ill write the story for my better self
> As when you paint your portrait for a friend,
> Who keeps it in a drawer and looks at it,
> Long after he has ceased to love you, just
> To hold together what [s]he was and is.

Do each of our creations tell our story of our better selves? Should we always strive for that better self, whomever that better self is on that particular day? Is each creation, whether poem or painting, a portrait of ourselves? I think that is so and so do Lizzie, Bessie, Anna, and Barbara.

17 October 2019
Hastings to London

On the train from Hastings to London, Maggie, Bethany, and Agatha shared their thoughts about the diaries and their own hopes for women as artists and how to best inform the public of the diaries. Agatha thought that they could perhaps take the diaries and write a mystery novel about them; she said that she is an expert at creating Gothic worlds of enclosure and terror. "I've written a fair number of Gothic tales myself; one is called the "The Lady's Crypt," based on the ghosts I've encountered. I do think that there's potential in these diaries for a frightening tale with Dante Rossetti as the villain that he is."

Bethany disagreed but did so gently. "Agatha, perhaps you could work on that later, but for now, we must concentrate on learning what the Pre-Raphaelite Sisterhood produced. They must have reached their apex while they lived together up North among their fellow sisters. I believe that there are a fair number of articles that I could write or even craft a full reproduction of the diaries along with cultural commentary that would make a fine scholarly book."

Maggie didn't respond immediately but gazed out the window at the trees turning scarlet. She wished that she could step off the train and continue to paint her portraits of Lizzie and Christina by the sea. In her imagination, she had begun to add the figure of Lizzie Siddal painting a portrait of Christina, and of Christina writing a poem about Lizzie; both of them creating their better selves in their portraits of one another. But even though she could see the image in her mind just as she hoped to eventually paint it, she could not work on it until she had seen the PRS exhibit. And after that she needed to convince Bethany that her longing to devote herself to art was the right path for her to follow. If it destroyed their relationship, so be it. This is what she learned that was most important from their discovery of the dairies. Women artists must paint. Women writers must write. Only then do they feel whole. She realised that she was exactly what Christina Rossetti and Lizzie Siddal envisioned for women artists. She had picked up her paintbrush and had begun to paint her better self.

18 October 2019
London

Agreeing to meet afterwards in the tearoom at the top floor of the National Portrait Gallery, the three women went their separate ways to look at the exhibit on their own once they passed through the gallery's doors and sent their bags and satchels through the metal detector. Ever since catastrophe struck New York City and terrorists had blown up a London Tube Stop, the British government remained vigilant about checking all satchels brought into precious places. Maggie had her sketching pencils and pad with her and when the female guard found these and smiled, Maggie returned the smile and then proceeded to the first room of the exhibition. She saw that the room was devoted to Christina, Lizzie, and Effie Gray Millais, who apparently painted in watercolours. Her painting of a rose arbour covering a garden path was comforting and her pencil copy of her own husband's *Foxglove* was exquisite. Maggie was surprised that Lizzie or Christina never mentioned the fact that Effie painted, for both knew Effie, at least tangentially. It was unfortunate that she hadn't been invited to their Sisterhood at the time that it existed. Maggie also wondered why Anna's, Barbara's, and Bessie's works were not included in the exhibit.

Maggie spent most of her time studying Lizzie Siddal's drawings and paintings. It is true that her figures are "boneless" as some critics say, but the emotions wrought by the paintings and drawings were powerful. *The Macbeths* shows Macbeth restraining his Lady while she holds a knife and looks as if she is in ecstasy. All the drawings and paintings are dark and foreboding, even the one of lovers listening to music. These figures appear ghostly, while two dark women at their feet play lutes. *Ladies' Lament* portrays a woman caught up in great longing for her lover, Sir Patrick Spens, who lies at the bottom of the sea. Maggie wondered how many of the drawings and paintings were related to Lizzie's sense of lost love and rage against Dante. And what became of Lizzie's self-portrait and why wasn't it exhibited and what about her *Lady of Shalott*? What became of the latter? Was it ever completed? And what about other paintings? Had someone saved them or had Lizzie or Dante purposely disposed of them?

The portion of the exhibit concerning Christina included Dante's portrait of her as the Virgin, but also Christina's delicate sketches of her mother Frances and her brother William. Christina had been wrong about her sketches. They demonstrated her keen artistic eye and showed enormous potential. In contrast, Gabriel's sketch of Christina's fury, which was also on display, made Maggie livid. He had belittled her, making her a comical figure, when she was rightfully angry about her unjust treatment and abuse.

As Maggie proceeded through the exhibition, she was most struck by the work of Joanna Boyce Wells, who had been invited to participate in the Sisterhood. Her *Elgiva,* a painting of a persecuted Anglo-Saxon queen, was astounding. Clearly, Joanna Boyce had received a stellar artistic education, and from reading the inscriptions and notes, Maggie learned that Boyce had been educated abroad but also by her father and brother who were painters and who relished her artistic gift. She herself said, "I have talents or a talent and with it the constant impulse to employ it . . . for the love of it and the longing for work." Yes, this is what artists must do, whether they inhabit a female or male body.

Maggie also observed Boyce's *Thou Bird of God*, an oil portrait of a young angel and she wondered if Lizzie had been the model for the angel's ginger hair.

Other artists and models were included in the exhibition: Georgiana MacDonald, a painter, Jane Morris, an embroiderer, Fanny Cornforth and Fanny Eaton models, and Evelyn de Morgan, a painter in the late Victorian period, whose *Queen Eleanor and Fair Rosamund* with its dragons and cherubs was exquisite.

Maggie sat on a bench and thought about the women, like Lizzie, who had little artistic education and how they would have flourished had they received the exemplary training that men had.

She returned to the room that held Lizzie's work and saw in a glass case a lock of Lizzie's ginger hair that remained intact for a century and a half. Was this the lock that she gave Dante or was it obtained by some other means? Was it perhaps shorn from her when she lay in her coffin?

Now Maggie became impatient to read the remainder of the diaries on her own; she didn't wish to wait for the others. Bethany and Agatha could do what they liked, but Maggie longed to read and hear the entire story as soon as possible so she returned to the hotel room that she shared with Bethany and read the remainder of the entries that she'd downloaded onto her computer from Beth's phone, taking notes as she proceeded. As she read, she wondered what they should do with the diaries. Which other secrets did they hold? Ultimately, what was the truth regarding Lizzie's death? Did she kill herself or die by some other means? Did a treacherous man end her life as Mr. Greenacre had ended his beloved's life?

3 December 1858
Christina

Barbara and Anna have been bathing naked in the river even on the coldest days. Some hunters spied them, but Barbara stood tall and rebuffed them, telling them to vacate our land. I do wish that I had the audacity to submerge myself as she does, to feel the flowing water on my skin, to stand firm when confronted with adversity. To stand naked in the sun.

5 January 1859
Lizzie

Our funds are running low. I will write to Mr. Browning to ask him to convey our message to his wife. Surely, she will help us.

4 February 1859
Christina

How does one dispel loneliness? Perhaps one must first recognize that one is lonely and not just merely introverted and solitary. I'd never completely realised that I was genuinely lonely until I met Lizzie, not during that first cold encounter with Gabriel sitting there trying to fabricate our friendship, but when we began to meet privately and to exchange letters and poems.

Gabriel was right about one thing at least. Lizzie and I have much in common, even though she's regal like a queen, and I'm like her dwarf vassal. Little did he know though that we both starved our bodies and hungered for true affection and love. We both love words and play with them as a way to express what lies deep within, that which we hide from superficial view. We disrobe, take off our masks, our personas when we play with words. Both of us are artists striving to be understood. Both of us seek truth and beauty, but the soul's beauty, not the physical attributes that lie on the surface.

Lizzie and I walk together nearly every evening after our work is done. We hold hands, like sisters, like would-be lovers (assuming women can love each other in this way, perhaps in the way Miss Faithfull and Miss Codrington do). We burrow into the deep woods behind Hope Hall and often seek the waterfall that we found on our first excursion into the woods. We sit on a boulder and listen to it, as it burbles and cascades down the ancient rocks. I'm reminded of my "Queen of the Ocean" poem that I wrote for Maria, where my naiad lived under the waterfall, and then swam to meet her sister every night. We sit in silence, like two mute mermaids. Here we need no words. After a time, one of us notices the first evening star through the canopy of oaks and maples, and we know that it's time to head home to Hope Hall. We have no trouble finding our way; we do not stumble, because we have become like one person. We seem to have found our other half that was lost before we began this life. Or what William Blake calls a conjugial angel. We don't talk about it, but it's clear that both of us understand that we've found our true soulmate in each other. We feel fulfilled and whole. We are home.

5 March 1859
Christina

We visited the grounds of what used to be Sheffield Castle, the castle where Mary, Queen of Scots was held captive by her cousin Elizabeth. The Parliamentarians razed the castle, but the old gate still stands. As we walked through the gate, which leads to the town market, I thought about Mary and her cousin, considering how divisive religion has been. Of course, I remain committed to Christianity, but in speaking with and knowing Lizzie, I have softened my stance. We both find considerable solace and peace in nature, which has become our cathedral. We do not need ceremony and edicts about how we must behave. We do not think about the afterlife or end times. We live in the present. We allow our consciences to be our guides and art to be our religion. I suppose that we are becoming like Gabriel in this regard. That's not a bad thing. At least I no longer suffer from religious mania. And I now realise how destructive were the fasts demanded by the Reverend Mr. Pusey, who hoped to make me and other girls invisible. Now, my appetite is good and so is Lizzie's. Like her, I now wear my hair loose. We sometimes play chess in the evenings, and I do not fret about winning. I indulge in many custard tarts that Briony makes us (as does Lizzie; they are also her favourites). I think that I have atoned long enough in my lifetime or in a thousand lifetimes.

6 April 1859
Christina

One night, before we returned to Hope Hall, Lizzie said, as we watched the waterfall, "Christina, let's bathe in its waters."

"I can't," I said. "I don't know how to swim. I never learned. But I'll watch you."

She turned her back toward me and asked me to unbutton her dress. My hands trembled as I fumbled with the buttons, and then she stepped out of her gown and walked into the water wearing only her chemise and knickers.

"The water is lovely, Christina," she said, as she ducked under the waterfall and turned around with the water flowing down her body. I sat on the rock, as I saw her dive deep, and then arise like a naiad from the dark water. I felt such contentment and peace watching Lizzie, as she frolicked without a care.

Afterwards, once home, I dried her hair with a towel, and brushed it dry until it glistened in the candlelight. After I had dried her hair, she told me that she wanted to tell me something that she had never told anyone outside her family, not even Gabriel. I sat down next to her and held her hand.

"What is it, Lizzie? What's troubling you?"

"Lately, I had recurring dreams, nightmares really. You see when I was a child, my family lived below our greengrocer, our landlord. He often gave me fruit: apples, pears, pomegranates, and he praised my juvenile sketches, telling me that I would be a renowned artist someday. He even promised to pay for art lessons for me, but then something quite awful happened . . . something too terrible to think about. He had promised himself to a young woman, a wealthy young woman, but when he discovered that she wasn't as rich as she claimed, he murdered her; he cut her into pieces; he cut out her heart and, with the help of his mistress, tossed pieces of her into the Thames."

I hesitated because I had never heard of such evil and horror. "Oh, Lizzie, how dreadful for you to learn of evil in this way, especially as a child. You must have been terrified." I squeezed her hand and moved closer to her.

"Yes, I was; I was terrified, and the worst part is I trusted him. He was like family to me. He often tempted me with the fruit and his promises to help me become an artist."

"But you have become an artist, despite his betrayal and his violence," I said as I put my arm around her. She had started to weep, and she rested her head against my shoulder.

"It's true and I don't understand why I've dreamt about him once more. After he was hanged, I often dreamt of his terrible deed and imagined that I was his next victim. There was nothing that I could do to stop him," Lizzie stated. "The only way that I felt reassured, and calm was when my sister Lydia would hold me tight when I was frightened, just as you're doing now."

"Then I shall act as your sister, for you truly are my family now. Do not fear this monster, this goblin, this man; he cannot touch you," I said as I wiped the tears from her face with my handkerchief.

After I had calmed her, we said our goodnights, and I returned to my room where I found a letter addressed to me that Briony had fetched from the post. I recognized the handwriting. It was my mother's. I didn't need to open it, for I knew what the contents were. How had she found us? Perhaps she had visited with the Siddals, and they suspected that we had journeyed to Hope Hall. Or perhaps Gabriel somehow traced the postmark or hired a detective to find his Sid. I wondered how long it would take him to arrive.

8 April 1859
Christina

I haven't informed Lizzie of the missive I received, for fear that she would be upset and then couldn't continue her work on her *Lady of Shalott* and her drawings of our serving girls as queens. Instead, we continue with our enterprises. And yesterday, I approached her with a new idea—that we publish our poems jointly, but she immediately dismissed the idea.

"My poetry pales in comparison to yours, Christina. And most of my poems are about loss and love; they would need considerable rewriting, which means that I would need to read them again. I don't wish to dwell on those dark times," she said, as she sketched our maid Briony dressed as if *she* was Queen Guinevere. Briony looked as regal as any queen, even though she is a young lass, barely come of age.

"I write about loss and love, too, Lizzie. Our poems would perhaps be in dialogue with one another. They could perhaps help other women who struggle with such sadness. Will you at least consider the idea?"

She hesitated, but then replied, "If you think that it may assist other forlorn souls, I shall read some of them again soon. And then I will sleep on the idea of publishing them."

"Do you promise?" I asked.

"Do you doubt my word?"

"Of course not. I trust you explicitly." I wanted to add that I'm growing to love you, but chose to withhold my tongue, until I knew that the feeling was reciprocated.

Lizzie showed her sketch to Briony, who was delighted, and then she handed the drawing pencil and sketchbook to Briony, who began to instinctively add shade to the drawing. When she finished, she said "Ta'rra," and headed into the kitchen to prepare our tea. Lizzie picked up the sketch and remarked that Briony's shading was brilliant. Then, she returned to her work, while I watched as the sunlight shone on her ginger hair.

20 April 1859
Christina

I heard the clock strike twelve, and then I heard the door creak open. I saw Lizzie standing in the doorway holding a candle. She was in her nightdress.

She whispered, "Christina, are you awake? I've had another wretched dream. May I come to bed with you?"

I threw back the quilt and held out my arms to her and she ran to them. "What happened? What did you dream?"

"It was horrible. It frightened me so. I dreamt that Dante came here, and he tempted me with sweet fruits and then cut me to pieces. He cut out my heart. I begged him to stop but he refused to listen. He told me that my heart belonged to him and to no one else."

"Don't fret, Lizzie, Gabriel's not here. And he can't find us. It was only a bad dream. Don't worry, love," I replied as I held her close. Secretly, I fretted that her prescience was a terrible foreboding.

I tried to comfort her. At first, she shook, but then she calmed and fell asleep. I stroked her soft red hair; it felt luxurious; I thought about how I was now seemingly taking Gabriel's place in Lizzie's life and wondered if he ever soothed her in this way when she suffered from bad dreams.

8 June 1859
Christina

Lizzie claims that I have saved her from my brother, but I tell her that she has saved me from loneliness and the goblins, like her greengrocer, who lure us with their tantalising fruits. Her nightmares and her tale about the greengrocer inspires a poem in which two sisters are first enticed by the goblins' succulent pomegranates, strawberries, and melons. One sister succumbs, eats the forbidden fruit, and falls ill, nearly dying. The other intervenes, sucks the fruit the goblins offer, and brings the juice back in her mouth. She kisses her sister. Her sister lives.

I shall write this poem and share it with Lizzie, who is *my* salvation. As we sat on our boulder near the waterfall one evening after Lizzie swam, I said, "Lizzie, I have a confession; like you, I have something to tell you that I've never told anyone, even Maria." I then bared my heart and told her my dreadful secret about my father from long ago.

When I finished, both of us were crying, but I felt relieved that the secret was out and no longer a burden on my heart.

As she placed her arm around my shoulder and pulled me closer, she said, "You called this a confession but what happened to you was not your fault; you were an innocent child." With Lizzie, I realised I had no need to confess. I felt safe.

A goblin ravaged me long ago. I have nothing for which I need to atone.

9 July 1859
Christina

Every day, Lizzie and I grow closer. I continue to wear my hair loose and I feel as free as she seemingly does. I have started to join her as she swims, and she holds my back up while I float. I trust her to save me. Afterwards, she joins me in my bed each night and we snuggle.

One warm evening, she undressed me and I her, and we lay naked skin to skin. She rubbed my back and shoulders, and I did the same for her. I felt shy because I had never been near another human in this way, nor had I touched another's skin. Briefly, I thought about the Reverend Mr. Pusey and how he would condemn this action, and tell me that I was destined for hell, but I pushed that thought from my mind, for our action was loving and natural. If we are condemned for loving one another, so be it.

After a while, we tenderly touched more of each other, and Lizzie showed me how to love her. Her bosom was soft and succulent. I touched her chest and felt her beating heart beneath her breast. The sweet spot between her legs was moist and welcoming. I did not fear this space but loved and embraced it.

Now, each night, we explore each other's bodies. When we are entwined, we are one body filled with holiness and light.

23 July 1859
Christina

This is the geography of her body. I have travelled her body and visited, sojourned, and then mapped its contours and crevices, its peaks and valleys, its oceans, and lakes. Its bushland and interior, its shores, its forests, and savannahs. I have burrowed into its caves and rafted its rivers. I have climbed its highest peak and descended into its mines filled with the most precious jewels—a diamond itself lies at the centre of her heart.

I will hide this map so that no one will find it and then travel its destinations. The geography and map are mine to traverse alone.

I feel reborn and have penned this poem:

> My heart is like a singing bird
> Whose nest is in a watered shoot;
> My heart is like an apple tree
> Whose boughs are bent with thickset fruit;
> My heart is like a rainbow shell
> That paddles in a halcyon sea;
> My heart is gladder than all these
> Because my love is come to me.
>
> Raise me a dais of silk and down;
> Hang it with vair and purple dyed;
> Carve it in doves and pomegranates,
> And peacocks with a hundred eyes;
> Work it in gold and silver grapes,
> In leaves and silver fleurs-de-lys;
> Because the birthday of my life
> Is come, my love is come to me.

Do I dare share this with Lizzie? It reveals so much about my love of her, and my unfathomable loneliness until I met her. I shall wait until a proper time to tell her that I've been reborn because of her. In the meantime, I shall work on my sisters' poem, which is now based on her, not Maria.

30 July 1859
Christina

I shared my draft of my sisters' poem with Lizzie. I shall call it "Goblin Market." These stanzas were the most appealing to her.

> "Lizzie, Lizzie, have you tasted
> For my sake the fruit forbidden?
> Must your light like mine be hidden?
> Your young life like mine be wasted,
> Undone in mine undoing
> And ruined in my ruin,
> Thirsty, cankered, goblin-ridden?"
>
> She clung about her sister [Laura],
> Kissed and kissed and kissed her:
> Tears once again
> Refreshed her shrunken eyes,
> Dropping like rain
> After long sultry drouth;
> Shaking with aguish fear, and pain,
> She kissed and kissed her with a hungry mouth.

Such images speak of our love for one another. Her approval of these stanzas lets me know that she loves me too. She need not say it. Lizzie, my sister, my love, *my* destiny.

18 October 2019
London

Maggie's heart broke as she read Christina's diary. Lizzie and Christina were lovers. They belonged together. "Goblin Market" was about them and their love, their attempt to prevent the goblins from killing them. This is why the diaries were buried. Maggie wept as she continued to read.

188 Kathleen Williams Renk

4 October 1859
Christina

I walked into Lizzie's studio and saw her beginning to sketch my poem. She draws the two sisters entwined in each other's arms, each feeling secure in each other's love and embrace. In the background, the goblins lurk, trying to tempt the sisters, but the sisters have closed their eyes and dream of other worlds.

7 January 1860
Lizzie

I continue to illustrate Christina's new poem, which she tentatively entitles "Goblin Market." It's odd to me that originally Dante tried to get Christina and me to work together on a project. I guess he knew that we were meant to have an affinity, but he did not understand how profound that connection would be. I do wish that I had found Christina earlier. We both would have experienced less heartache, less trouble, less loneliness. Neither of us would have been betrayed by those we loved and who supposedly cherished us. I know that many people, including our queen, believe that women cannot love one another in the same way that women and men love and have passion for one another. How ignorant our queen is, for the love between women is as deep as any love between a woman and a man, perhaps stronger than female-male love because we understand one another in ways that women and men cannot.

Christina approves my preliminary sketches for "Goblin Market." They are still rudimentary, but I also continue to sketch Christina's face frequently, just as Gabriel sketched me. I find her inner light though, which he failed to find in me.

And I continue to paint my Lady freed from her tower walking with her Guinevere.

5 February 1860
Lizzie

My work flourishes here in our artists' studio. Now that I am free to paint what I wish, I have decided that in addition to painting my Lady, I will complete my painting *The Witch*, even though Ruskin thought it too gruesome. Ruskin no longer dictates what my work shall entail. I contemplate the way women were maligned for being healers and labelled as witches. To that end, Christina, Barbara, Anna, Bessie, Joanna, and I travelled to Lancashire to visit a place known for its witches, Pendle Hill. In the seventeenth century, twelve women were accused of witchcraft and hanged nearby at Lancaster Castle. Some of them were healers, some had political motivations, and supposedly one of them made a wax figure to harm those who maligned and sought to harm her. I found their story fascinating, and I told Christina about it as we ascended the fell known as Pendle Hill, the hill that the supposed witches climbed to meet in their coven. I also reminded her that she had once told Dante that I was a sorceress, a witch of sorts, and she laughed at her absurdity.

But then I said, "Perhaps we're both witches in that we heal one another. I have no designs on harming or murdering anyone though, not even your devilish brother, even though he wounded and nearly killed me."

As we climbed, we could hardly keep up with our sisters, who had far more experience hiking over the fells. And then, it began to rain, and it suddenly turned into a squall with rain pelting us mercilessly. The rocks that we walked on were slippery; the ascent was steep. We sought shelter under a lone tree, and Christina said that she had never climbed the fells before because her mother forbade it; it was unladylike. I told her that she was with me now and now that I feel strong and robust, one day we will climb fells and mountains just like Barbara. Perhaps we will travel to Italy and Switzerland and climb the Alps. We resumed our climb, and when Christina slipped or needed to catch her breath, I waited for her and helped her with the ascent which took two hours. We marvelled at the men we saw who ran up the fell as if they were mountain goats. When we finally arrived at the top of the hill, we were utterly drenched and the wind nearly blew us off the plateau, but we held tight to each other and withstood the "witch's" wind. We looked for shelter but found none. Our descent was just as wet and treacherous but afterwards, we gladly took tea at our lodgings, finally meeting up with Barbara, Anna, Bessie, and Joanna, who had already taken their tea, and were about to return to their rooms. We remained at the table and Christina, and I talked about my "Witch" painting, which will include Pendle Hill as the landscape. She spoke about writing a poem about it. In the morning, we returned to Hope Hall eager to begin our new work.

3 March 1860
Lizzie

I continue to paint a companion to my Lady, my Guinevere, my sister Christina. It took some persuasion, but I have convinced Christina to slightly disrobe, baring one of her breasts. She asked me, "Is it proper?"

"Why not? Men have painted the nude female figure for centuries? Why can't a woman? Besides, you are exquisite, Christina."

She blushed when I said this and the roses in her cheeks painted an even fairer face for me to paint.

10 March 1860
Christina

Last evening, Lizzie and I shared our diaries with one another. She has been keeping hers exactly as long as I have. I was quite moved to learn on paper how alike we truly are and how both of us have been thwarted in our art, at least until now.

When I came to the entries that describe my brother's ill treatment of Lizzie, I grew furious. He emotionally abused her, kept her waiting for years to have the "honour" of marrying him. He fed on her beauty and vampirized it. He tried to possess her and jealously kept her from others who may have loved her more. I was so angry that I wrote another letter to him, telling him that he's an untrustworthy and undeserving man. I told him in the letter and later told Lizzie that he will never harm her again. I will do everything I can to keep him away from my love.

5 April 1860
Lizzie

The worst has happened. Our peace has been breached; our hope shattered. Somehow Dante has found us; he has written to me telling me that he is arriving on the evening train. Perhaps Mr. Browning gave away our hiding place, I don't know. I felt so distraught that when Christina suggested that we work on our Goblin Market project, I told her that my head hurt and that I needed to spend time alone in my room with the curtains drawn.

I don't wish to see him. I think about my nightmare, and the potential harm that he could inflict. Even if he doesn't injure me, he will, no doubt, try to tempt me to return to him, but I shall endeavour to ignore his pleas.

15 April 1860
Lizzie

He arrived and intruded on our peace. Christina bravely met him at the door and told him to go away; he was not welcome.

"What do you want, Gabriel?" Christina asked. "We live a quiet life here with our sisters in art. You don't belong here."

"I want Lizzie. *I've* grown ill without her. I need her; I can't paint; I can't write. I give into base desires without her."

"That's your problem. She doesn't want *you*. She is happy here; she's well. She paints; she writes; she creates herself without you." Christina didn't tell him that last evening I was weak and ill. That would only feed his ego and make him think that I need him to grow well.

"Let me in, Christina. I must . . . I need to see her," he said, as he tried to push past her. Although diminutive, she stood firm.

"No, go away. Go back to London. She's done with you," she said as she continued to bar the door.

"I won't go until I see her." He yelled, "Lizzie, I need you, please let me in. I beg you."

I had been waiting in the foyer and stepped into the doorway. At the moment, with Christina by my side, I felt strong and resolute.

"Begging doesn't become you, Dante. Leave us alone. We are happy here. I am happy without you," I said, as I grabbed and held Christina's hand.

His face turned ashen. His hair was dishevelled, and his eyes looked wild. "You don't mean it; you're my destiny."

I said nothing. He seemed shaken, almost at a loss for words, but then he said, "You've lost your wits and need help. What you're doing is unnatural. It's mad. You must return to London with me."

To be honest, he's the one who looked as if he had lost his wits; he looked mad. Perhaps he was becoming like his father, as Christina had surmised. I grew more fearful but said nothing. Even though I had momentarily felt strong, the longer I gazed at him, the weaker and sicker I felt.

As we were speaking, Briony suddenly stepped out of the shadows with a pitchfork in hand and aimed it at Dante. "Go away, you. Stop mitherin' my ladies! Leave them alone. They don't want or need owt from you. Their home is here."

Dante suddenly became more like himself; he laughed sardonically at her and turned toward us. "If you stay here long enough, Lizzie, you'll end up talking like this ruffian. I'll stop mitherin' you, but I'll be back with the constable, who will look into what's going on among you women at your ancestral home."

As soon as he left, we packed our satchels. We told Barbara that we were leaving for Hastings, and we told her and Briony to tell no one our location.

"Please do not reveal our destination. I can't see him. The thought of him makes me ill."

Briony nodded in assent and Anna agreed to keep our whereabouts secret, even though she and Dante remain friends. She does not know the harm that he has caused me, the way that he has wrecked my heart and spirit.

18 April 1860
Christina

We have ensconced ourselves in a small hotel along the sea in Hastings. We cannot stay at Scanland's Gate for Gabriel would know to look for us there. We keep a low profile. Lizzie has been wretched since she saw Dante. She says that she can't get him out of her mind; seeing him reminds her of all the sorrow that he caused her and continues to cause whenever he appears. I tell her that she must let go and forget about him. We are a loving couple now; I am not ashamed of our life together and our sweet, quiet times in the darkness. I won't give her up to my brother, who has always gotten his way, until now.

I took her down to the sea and for a brief time we sat on the sea wall and gazed at the sublimity, the beauty and terror of the sea. Once again, I imagined that she and I were mermaid sisters, whose hearts would be forever entwined. I imagined us diving into and swimming in the sea, saving each other in the waves. Lizzie looked sad though, and even the sight of beauty did not restore her spirit. I tried to coax her into the sea to swim, but she refused. We walked along the beach and I found a dead seahorse. I quickly buried it in the sand.

24 April 1860
Christina

We remain hidden in Hastings and try to write and paint, but Lizzie can't; she has frequent nightmares where Gabriel appears, not as her saviour, but as her gravedigger.

She awakens with a start and cries out, "How can you do this to me? You once said you loved me and now you wish to bury me . . ."

I spend a long time trying to console her, but she becomes hysterical and tells me that Gabriel is killing her.

25 April 1860
Christina

Lizzie grows weak; it is as if Gabriel is a worm that feeds on her flesh. Even though she fears him, she now tells me that she must see him; she feels as though she will die, and she wants to say "goodbye" to him; after all, she did love him once. She wants to see if there is anything left of the person who once loved her or whether, as in her nightmares, he has truly become his doppelgänger.

I tell her that I will not contact him. He will only try to manipulate her.

"Can't you see, Lizzie, that he is ruining our sisterhood? He's intruded, come between us and our art. I don't want our love and our sisterhood to end."

"Our love won't end, Christina. It can't. I will always be yours. Our love and our artistry are the only things that give me life and make me my better self. I must see him though. I fear that I'm dying."

"Oh, Lizzie, you've been ill before . . ." I do not want to appear as though I do not believe her.

"Yes, I have, but I feel my life, my vigour fading. I am not well and likely will not recover this time. Please, if you love me, send for him. I know that it doesn't make sense, but I must know if there is anything left of the old Dante. And I wish to say goodbye. Perhaps, if he sees that I am truly dying, he will reform his ways and become *his* better self."

I don't reply. I just hold her hand and try to soothe her spirit, which I see is deeply troubled. Perhaps I am not enough for her. Perhaps we have eaten forbidden fruit and now need to purge ourselves.

26 April 1860
Christina

I refused to send for Gabriel as Lizzie asked, but instead wrote to her sister Lydia, telling her that Lizzie was extremely ill and that it would be wise for her to come to Hastings. Lydia immediately arrived and sat as Lizzie's protector by our bed. She asked me to leave the room. She knew what her sister needed, she said. She needed her own kin beside her. I wanted to tell her that, even though I am not Lizzie's kin, I am her soulmate. I knew that she wouldn't understand though.

Lizzie slept peacefully with her sister nearby. I slept in the parlour on the settee. It must have been evident to Lydia that Lizzie and I share a bed, but she never remarked about my sleeping arrangement. I slept fitfully but woke suddenly when I heard Lizzie scream out Gabriel's name.

Two days later. Gabriel arrived in Hastings.

18 October 2019
London

Bethany walked in and put down her satchel. "Where were you? We waited at the tea room for you for hours. Agatha gave up and caught the train back to Hastings. She wishes us well and hopes to learn more of our artists, but after she saw the lock of Lizzie's hair on display, she wondered whether Lizzie cut it herself or if someone else cut it as a token when she was dead. She said that she's keen on writing her own mystery novel about Lizzie, Christina, and Dante. What happened to you? What did you discover at the exhibit?"

She looked at Maggie, who was wiping tears from her eyes. As Maggie read, she had felt such fullness of emotion, great sadness because of Dante's intrusion on them but also immense joy in knowing that Lizzie and Christina loved one another.

"What's wrong, love? What happened?"

"I had to continue reading the diaries to find out what happened next in Lizzie and Christina's lives after I viewed the Sisterhood's art," Maggie said. "I found out that the worst happened. Dante intruded on their sisterhood and their love. Bethany, Lizzie and Christina loved each other; "Goblin Market" is about them, and Dante came between them. Lizzie never completed her *Lady of Shalott.*"

"Oh, my, that changes everything, everything that's known about that exquisite poem about temptation and survival. But it also changes what we know about Christina and Lizzie and women artists who loved one another. We must finish reading the diaries." Bethany sat next to Maggie and pulled her close. "Read to me, my love."

Maggie continued from where she left off, stopping periodically to catch her breath and to process what happened next. As they huddled together, Bethany entwined her hand with Maggie's.

26 April 1860
Lizzie

After I implored her, Lydie reluctantly agreed to write to Dante, telling him that I was gravely ill and that I wanted to say goodbye. When he arrived, initially, Lydia stood guard, but then I told her that I needed to speak with

Dante alone. Once she left, he told me he would nurse me and bring me back to good health. As usual, he said I was his destiny. I was his former love from another life. He's lost without me. He cannot write or paint.

"But I have a new life," I said. "I only wanted to say farewell because I am ill. I think that I'm dying." My breath felt weak at that point and when Dante reached out to touch me, I pulled away and turned my head from him.

"You won't die; I won't let you," he said. Even though I tried to prevent him, he picked me up in the same way that he had when I was the drowning Ophelia. He gathered me in his arms; he cradled me like I was his child. I struggled to escape his embrace, but he was too strong.

"Put me down, Dante. I'm not a child."

He pretended as if he didn't hear me. He buried his face in my neck, whispered in my ear that he loved me, and then pulled up my nightdress.

I yelled "No," and struggled against him, telling him that he is a fiend, an outright devil. Even so, he did the unthinkable.

26 April 1860
Christina

I heard a ruckus in the bedroom. Lizzie was crying as if she were in pain. I tried the door, but it was barred. I pounded on it, but no one came to let me in.

I yelled, "Lizzie, my love, are you injured? Let me in."

I ran for Lydia but could not find her, so I fetched the hotelier, but they refused to open the door, saying whatever went on behind that door was a private affair.

I continued to pound on the door, but no one answered. An eerie feeling befell me. Where were they? What had happened in that room? Had Lizzie died? Had Gabriel murdered her as she believed he might? I tried to calm myself, believing that my brother could never murder the woman he called his destiny.

27 April 1860
Christina

In the morning, after another fitful sleep, where, in my dream, I saw Lizzie lying dead with her eyes wide open and her hands folded as if in prayer, I awoke abruptly and was relieved to see the door ajar. I rushed in the room and saw Lizzie lying on the rumpled bed. She was alive but she looked dazed.

When I asked what happened, she refused to talk. Gabriel sat quietly in the armchair.

He turned to me and dismissively said, "Thank you for taking care of Lizzie for me, but, as you see, she needs me to help her recover. She has missed me, Christina. And I her. We need one another. You can go back to London or Sheffield or wherever."

"Why should I? Lizzie and I belong together. We need one another. She doesn't need you," I replied.

I looked at Lizzie, but she had closed her eyes, and then she turned away from me toward the wall. My heart ached.

Gabriel looked at me with contempt, but I didn't say anything but returned to the parlour and wrote to Lizzie, asking her what had happened between her and Gabriel. Had he hurt her? Tempted her? I asked her to rise up and come to me. We would run away together. We would flee to Italy or France. She must escape him and return to me. We would continue to make art together. We would continue to gaze at beauty together. We would continue our sisterhood.

I waited until Gabriel had gone out and slipped in to see her. She was asleep. I wished to take her in my arms but didn't. I stroked her hair and kissed her on her forehead. I didn't rouse her. I then left the note by her bedside, closed the door, and went back to the parlour. I waited all evening for her to come to me. When she didn't, I wept and then packed my bag. I surmised that no matter what happened between her and Gabriel, she would eventually come home to me. I would be like Milton and patiently wait.

28 April 1860
Lizzie

I am furious with Dante for his treatment of me. How could he brutalise me so? Just as he appeared in my nightmares, he *has* become his doppelgänger.

I read Christina's letter, where she confessed her love once more. She begged me to flee with her. She sent me a poem:

> Love, Love, that having found a heart
> And left it, leav'st it desolate; —
> Love, Love, that art more strong than Hate,
> More lasting and more full of art; —
> O blessed Love, return, return,
> Brighten the flame that needs must burn.

I wanted to flee with her, but I felt ashamed. Dante had violated me, and I would never be the same. I didn't know what to tell her. I didn't write back and when I heard someone knock on the door later and enter the room, I feigned sleeping. I felt Christina's touch and her soft kiss, but I continued to play possum. I had to think about what I needed to do and to whom I should turn.

28 April 1860
Lizzie

Christina has left. I don't know where she's gone. Our sisterhood is dissolved. I regret that I didn't go to her; we could have become like the Brownings and fled to Italy. I shall write to her at the Rossetti home and seek her forgiveness for my betrayal of her.

I remain in Hastings to convalesce; Dante stays nearby and often attempts to see me, but I refuse.

14 May 1860
Lizzie

Weeks have passed and I've found that I missed my course. I am nauseous and my breasts ache and are swollen. I visited a midwife and found that I am with child.

15 May 1860
Lizzie

I needed to tell Dante that his mistreatment of me resulted in the creation of an innocent life. I asked Lydia to find out where Dante was staying and then I went to see him at his hotel. I was too weak to climb the stairs to his room, so I asked the hotelier to fetch him so we could meet in the private parlour on the first floor. In actuality, I didn't wish to be alone with him in his boudoir for I feared him. I asked Dante to shut the door; I told him that I had something to tell him. After I told him that I was pregnant, he said, "Are you sure? Perhaps you didn't bleed because you're ill."

"No," I replied. "Even when I'm sick, I always bleed. My breasts are tender, just like the last time."

"What last time?"

I hesitated but then replied, "I rid us of a child some years ago, when I discovered that you believed children are a burden."

"Why didn't you tell me?" he said. His face grew red and blotchy.

"I didn't think that you cared," I said with finality. "You hated it when Emma and Brown's Catty was nearby, or have you forgotten?"

He didn't argue with me about his feelings about Catty. "What are you going to do now, Lizzie?"

"What do you mean?"

"Let's think about this. You're not well; you're still recovering and have a long way to go before your good health returns. A pregnancy would gravely affect your well-being," he said with his head in his hands. Then he looked at me straight on. "Besides, a child will come between us, Sid. We're not even married. Isn't there something that you can do? Take a purgative? See someone who can help you?"

"Do you want me to rid us of this child too?" I asked as I felt the blood rush to my cheeks.

"I think that would be best. Don't you agree? We could try later, when you're more stable, when you've fully recovered." He was deadly serious, and I felt betrayed and violated once more.

I sat up straight and looked at him. He hardly seemed a man. He was still a boy who needed to have his way.

"I already rid myself of one child that you didn't want. I thought at the time that I would be cleaved in two by the abortionist. I won't do it again. Even though this child was not created through love, I want it. Perhaps Christina and I will raise it together."

"What in God's name are you talking about? You and Christina? That's absurd. Whoever heard of two women raising a child?" he said with contempt.

"It happens sometimes when women are widowed," I replied.

"You're not a widow," he said.

"I'm not even a wife," I said sarcastically. "I'm not even sure that I wish to be anyone's wife, least of all yours, especially after your brutal treatment of me."

He didn't respond at first and didn't deny what he had done, that he had forced himself on me, but then reluctantly said, "Lizzie, if you won't dispose of the child, even though your health is in danger, I will have to marry you,"

"Don't do me any favours, Dante; I don't need you and your guilty conscience to rescue me."

He sat in silence for several minutes. "Sorry, but you do. You need me. The child will be a bastard otherwise. You don't want the child to suffer, do you?"

"Of course not, but you seem not to care. You would rather that I dispose of it."

"Don't over-react, Lizzie. Let me think through this problem. You know that despite all, despite the fact that you ran away with my sister, I still care for you. You've *always* been mine; you're my destiny."

"Christina and I love each other, and she loves me more than you ever have. And I grow tired of hearing that I am your destiny, Dante. Perhaps it's not true. Perhaps we should part ways for good. Perhaps Christina is *my* destiny."

His face grew crimson, and he angrily said, "No, I'll finally do what I should have done long ago. I will marry you. I'll do what I ought to do." I recalled Christina's diary where she'd noted Dante's inability to do what he ought and I nearly laughed but I controlled myself.

As we sat staring at one another, my heart sank. He acted as though I had no say in the matter. Although I hated to admit it, I supposed that he was right. I could not allow my child to be a bastard who would likely be socially ostracised. I thought of the poor, tragic woman who jumped into the Thames, and hoped that my end would be different from her likely eventual demise. So, I bravely donned my actress face and reluctantly agreed with him. I hoped that perhaps, after some time, I could find some semblance of love for Dante, despite how he had brutalised me. I hoped that I could resurrect positive feelings for him, but it would take work, especially since my heart belonged elsewhere, with a person who actually cherished me. How would I ever recover from his cruelty toward me?

19 May 1860
Lizzie

Lydia has returned to London. I didn't tell her that Dante has purchased a marriage licence and he and I are to be wed at St. Clement's Church, here in Hastings. I feel despondent. I don't wish to marry him but will do so for the sake of the child. I wrote to Christina at her mother's home, where I suspect she has fled. I asked her to see me, to come to me so I could explain what happened; why I'm marrying her brother, but she never responded to my request.

I don't know that I can ever genuinely love him again. He has ravaged me. He is cruel. I have little room in my heart for him. Besides, his sister has taken his place in my heart.

23 May 1860
Lizzie

In my dream, I was the first to arrive at the church. I looked around. Although the chapel had been decorated with white roses, there was no one there, not even the vicar or his staff who ought to be preparing for the nuptials. Where was everyone? Perhaps I had the wrong day? Dante said 23 May, his birthday, and I had consulted the calendar. Today was the day. I felt silly and a little ill standing in the church in a white brocade gown straight out of a mediaeval painting, as if I was indeed Ophelia meeting Hamlet. Had Dante called off the wedding? Backed out of his promise? Broken his promise once again? Had Dante run off with Annie Miller or Ruth Herbert, or some other tart? Why didn't Christina stay when I needed her? She had to have known that eventually I would return to her. She promised that, unlike Dante, she would never abandon me.

I looked toward the altar and there stood Christina, who had been waiting for me. My heart beat violently, and then when I ran toward her, I dropped the yellow poppies that I carried, and then she turned her back to me and faded away into the mist. I awoke and my pillow was soaked with my tears.

25 May 1860
Lizzie

Dante and I are married. I was so ill and weak the day of the wedding that I needed to be carried into the church. I thought that I would faint, and Dante had to hold me up as I stood in front of the vicar. Even though I felt sick at heart, I pledged myself to Dante Rossetti, a man who is now a stranger to me. I kept wondering why he was marrying me after all this time, these nine long years that we have known one another (or, in his view, the lifetimes we have known each other). Does he actually care for this child? Does he assume that I will quickly die and that he will soon be rid of me and my troubles? Why did he have to interfere with and ruin our sisterhood and the love that Christina and I shared? Is he jealous of her? Had he realised that she and I had grown close and were intimate? Is that why he intruded, in order to destroy our happiness?

I told him that the only reason that I had agreed to marry him was because of the innocent child. My heart is hard towards him, and I doubt that it can be softened.

When we left the church, I saw a blonde-haired, portly woman weeping outside it. I recognized her from one of Dante's paintings. She rushed toward Dante, but he put out his hand to her to keep her from grabbing him.

"Not now, Fanny," he said.

She looked crestfallen and retreated. I wondered how long he has dabbled with her heart; perhaps she was just like me. She was his plaything, as I was. Maybe he also told her that she is his destiny.

30 May 1860
Christina

Mother says that Lizzie and Gabriel are married and have left for Paris.

My heart is shattered. I never thought that Lizzie would turn away from me and return to my brother and then marry him. Why would she do that? He is charming though; he's a Byronesque figure that women find hard to resist. Everyone loves him and they always have. Even so, if it weren't for the fact that Lizzie wrote to Robert Browning, Gabriel would never have found us and acted the interloper. Or perhaps it's my fault somehow, realising that Mother had located us and sent Gabriel to fetch us home.

I feel betrayed on all counts—by Robert and especially Elizabeth Barrett Browning, by Lizzie, by my mother, but most of all by my brother, who has severed the bond between Lizzie and me.

I dream of Lizzie each night and long to lie in her arms. It seems years since she and I embraced. I awoke tonight and penned this poem:

"Echo"

Come to me in the silence of the night;
Come in the speaking silence of a dream;
Come with soft rounded cheeks and eyes as bright
As sunlight on a stream;
Come back in tears,
O memory, hope, love of finished years.

Oh dream how sweet, too sweet, too bitter sweet,
Whose wakening should have been in Paradise,
Where souls brimful of love abide and meet;
Where thirsting longing eyes
Watch the slow door
That opening, letting in, lets out no more.

Yet come to me in dreams, that I may live
My very life again tho' cold in death:
Come back to me in dreams, that I may give
Pulse for pulse, breath for breath:
Speak low, lean low,
As long ago, my love, how long ago.

It seems so long ago that I held her in my arms and stroked her soft hair. Now, I can only pray that she will come to me in a dream.

Why doesn't she write to me?

30 May 1860
Lizzie

We travelled to Paris for our honeymoon. In truth, I am recovering; I know that I must eat so that the child can thrive; I sleep as much as I can, but Dante takes that as despondency. I ask him not to touch me, and sometimes I feign illness to keep him from lying with me. At least he doesn't further force himself on me. And I think that he would prefer that I were ill. I dream of Christina and in my dream, we embrace as we did. We hold each other close and save one another from the goblin men.

Paris was not the same as it was when we were here in 1855. Early on, I was there with Mrs. Kincaid, and I experienced freedom to go where I would like. Then Dante and I enjoyed our time together. We climbed Montmartre to Sacre Coeur; we visited the Left Bank; we saw the grand French Exhibit of new paintings. I dreamt that my paintings would one day hang in the Musée d'Orsay.

Now I feel lost; I had once longed to be Mrs. Rossetti, but now that I am, I don't know who or what I am. I feel trapped. Am I still Lizzie, the poet and painter? Am I Dante's underling? Will I ever again truly feel fulfilled as a woman artist, as a full human being? I felt most complete when Christina and I made love and art together. I was becoming my better self.

I don't wish to blame the child for the circumstances in which I now find myself. I will endeavour to love this baby. It is not her fault that I am now tethered to a man, who only married me because he felt guilty and obligated and thought that I would possibly die before I made it to the altar. I think that he counted on that and was surprised when I rallied for the sake of my child. Now he can't get rid of me; unfortunately, we are legally bound until death.

He seems happy enough though. He is painting and writing again. He worked on the painting that he started years ago of the two of us meeting our doppelgängers. I despise the painting and I told him so. He thinks it fanciful and imaginative, mystical even. I think it is a bad omen. Why would he dwell on such a theme, especially right after we finally married? He is also writing a poem called "The Bride's Chamber." In it, a woman has become pregnant and must marry her now-despised lover and seducer. Once again, he cruelly writes about us; his paintings and poems speak the truth of our lives.

I cannot paint. I cannot write. I cannot speak the truth. My muse is gone, and she won't see me. I still dream about her nightly and long to lie in her arms.

5 June 1860
Lizzie

Dante doses me with medicine even though I am recovering.

I tell him, "Dante, I don't need the cordial. I feel well."

"No, Lizzie, the tonic is good for the child. You want him to be healthy, don't you?"

"Why are you suddenly concerned for the child? Do you want it?" I ask.

He doesn't answer. He acts as if he doesn't hear me and continues to paint. He is once again painting me as Beatrice. I wish that he wouldn't. Why can't he paint me—Lizzie? Why must he see me as some mediaeval muse or some former lover?

10 July 1860
Lizzie

We have returned from Paris and now live in Hampstead. I grow rotund and am beginning to feel close to this child, as I feel her stir about in my womb. Perhaps the child will heal my heart. Perhaps the child can reconcile Dante and me again. He has become more attentive, but still insists that I take my medicine. I grow increasingly dependent on it though and to get the same effect, I always need to take more. Dante gladly purchases more of "Godfrey's Cordial" from the neighbourhood greengrocer. Dante himself never takes it. He says that he sleeps well and has no need for it. He claims that he doesn't suffer from insomnia, depression, or mental afflictions. He no longer sees or feels the presence of ghosts.

"You know, Lizzie, I should have married you long ago. This union has cured me of my maladies," he says.

I don't respond. I doubt that this is true. Perhaps the marriage just keeps his afflictions at bay. It has done nothing to relieve me of mine.

3 August 1860
Lizzie

I finally felt well enough to paint today but I cannot complete my Lady. Besides, Dante painted over Christina in my painting. So, I took as my subject "The Bride's Chamber," renamed "The Woeful Victory." The bride's true love is slain by his hated rival, his very own doppelgänger. I have painted truth and beauty, if only Dante would recognize it.

Dante is working on a new watercolour of a woman dying while her lover paints her portrait. Again, I wonder, does he wish me dead?

3 September 1860
Christina

When loneliness comes stalking, I think of my sweet and quiet times with Lizzie, but then it becomes unbearable, because I remember how soft her skin is and how her exquisite ginger hair cascades like a waterfall. I would often draw it across my own face and head, and we would hide under it to block out the world. I feel her body heat and my body alights with fire and we embrace deeply and more fully. Once I begin remembering, I tell myself that I must cease my daydream, for such loving will never happen again. I am dead to her.

I now understand why she left me for Dante. I cannot forgive her, but I hear from William that Dante has given her the child that she desired. I could not. She had always told me that she wanted to be a mother, and believed that a child would enhance her art, not prohibit it. I told her that few women have been able to be artists and mothers. It's generally not done.

"Well, Mrs. Browning is a poet, and she has her 'Pen,' her son, whom she adores. I want my Pen too."

"You think you're like Mrs. Browning?" I asked.

"Why not? I could be if I develop my art."

I thought her boastful but didn't say so. Now I regret not telling her that she is an artistic genius. I briefly forgot that sisterhood in art means supporting the aspirations of our sisters. I allowed my ego and desire to be a great poet (I once told Lizzie that I wanted to be the poet laureate) to stand in the way of believing in my love's work.

6 October 1860
Lizzie

Dante has suddenly become a prolific poet. He has finished his "The Bride's Chamber," and has written a bevy of poems, 25 in all. One called "Jenny" about a prostitute, others are "The Last Confession," "Sister Helen" (about a witch who kills her beloved), "My Sister's Sleep," and "Ave." It appears that I *am* necessary, at this point, for him to create art. I have read and commented on his poems. None are love poems. None are dedicated to me. "Sister Helen" seems to draw somewhat on my witch painting, which he studies. He asks me about Pendle Hill, and the wax figures found there. I tell him that there was never any proof that the women accused of witchcraft at Pendle Hill had murdered their enemies.

He has dedicated some poems to Jane Burden, Morris's wife. I cannot understand why he would dedicate work to her. Is she his new muse? His new love?

2 January 1861
Lizzie

Several weeks ago, my child stopped stirring in my womb. I thought she was merely asleep and so I prodded her, poked her, talked to her, sang to her, but she was fast asleep. I visited my midwife, Mrs. Jenkins, and she listened for the child's heartbeat but heard nothing. "Sadly, Mrs. Rossetti, your womb is as silent as a grave," she said mournfully. Mrs. Jenkins fears that my child has died.

"She's just asleep," I replied. "She likes it when I sing to her. She'll wake up soon I assure you. If the singing doesn't awaken her, I shall read her Wordsworth's poem about the sleeping child."

2 February 1861
Lizzie

My child was born dead. Her body was flaccid and blue. Dante said it's for the best. I believe that he wished her dead, so that I would never have love in my life again. I believe that he brought this about through his violation of me and his painting of our doppelgängers. I had told him that painting us in that way would beget death.

I held my dead child and asked Mrs. Jenkins if she was sure that the child was dead. I thought that I heard her cry when she issued forth from my body.

"No, my dear," Mrs. Jenkins said. "She was weak and struggled to live in your womb but could not. Her cord strangled her. The crying you heard was your own."

"Perhaps if we rub her, she'll come alive?" I asked, as I tried to massage her limbs that had already grown stiff.

"No, no, my dove, give me the child," Dante said, as he handed me my cordial. "Here, drink this; it will help you feel yourself and you can begin again." He tried to steal my baby from me. I slapped his hand away and the bottle of cordial shattered on the floor. I picked up a piece of glass and held it up to his face. I told him that he had killed my baby.

He told me that I'm mad, but then he walked out of the room and left my little May and me alone. I held her tightly to my chest and tried to get her to nurse, but her sweet little lips were blue and cold when I touched them.

8 February 1861
Christina

Gabriel reports that Lizzie has delivered a dead child. He tells us not to visit, because Lizzie is despondent. He says nothing about his own grief. I wonder if he grieves as she does. Oh, my love, my Lizzie, if you had stayed with me, you never would have given birth to death.

6 July 1861
Lizzie

We said we'd never speak of it. The baby that is. The baby that I lost. But how can I never speak of it, when I see her in her cradle and when I hear her cry? She wails in the night, and I arise from bed to find and console her, but she is not where I left her. Perhaps she trundled outdoors, so I walk down the steps out into the street, all the time worrying that she ran out among the clattering carts or that someone picked her up and made her their child. Their little queen. Their May.

The street is quiet though, except for the night watchman, who asks me if I need help. He is startled to see me in my nightdress and cap.

"Are you distressed, madam? Have you lost your way? Do you need a constable?"

"No, sir," I reply. "Unless the constable knows how to keep a child from crying in the night."

He looks at me peculiarly and I return to my cold bed, which lies next to the empty cradle.

26 July 1861
Lizzie

I woke up and found him gone. We hadn't quarrelled, but he had told me, "Lizzie, the child is dead; she never lived. She was a stillbirth. You must stop pretending that she lives. Stop your playacting."

I didn't say anything, but he knows that I'm not playacting. I know that she's dead, but her ghost, her barghest, inhabits this space. I've seen her with my own eyes. In truth, I think that he has too, although he would never admit it. My darling, child, my May. She cries out for me, and I must rush to her. Sometimes I rock her in her cradle and sing to her as she liked when I protected her in my womb. When Emma and Brown come calling, I must remind them to hush, because I fear they will wake her.

I do feel as though I am losing my mind. My nerves are constantly on edge, unless I take my medicine (after I broke the vial, he purchased three more), which Dante convinced me was still necessary; even so, I'm only calmed for a short while. I can't paint. I can't write. I can't sketch. I write to Christina, but I think that Dante intercepts the letters. He tells me that Christina is no good for me and that she has moved on and doesn't want to speak with me. That can't be true because I am her Lizzie. She knows me in ways that Dante does not, and cares about me more deeply than he ever did or could.

Dante warns me that if I don't get better soon, he will need to consult with a doctor, and perhaps send me away to an asylum. As my husband, he can do this. He controls my fate. He owns me. I think that he wishes that he could send me to an asylum so he can be rid of me. I never should have married him.

I tell him that I cannot go to an asylum, because then I wouldn't see my May. And I would never make art again.

30 August 1861
Lizzie

Anna, Bessie, and Barbara have returned to London. They've left Hope Hall to Briony and Belinda, who agreed to look after it. Anna has come to see me. She tells me that she has seen my child at her séances. I ask her if she will sit with me soon, so that we can communicate with my child. Anna tells me that she will visit on Friday night.

"Tell Dante to stay away," she says. "He cannot be here, because the child likely knows that he did not want her."

"Oh, how sad that makes me. Is that why she left us?" I ask.

"We will inquire to be sure," Anna says.

4 September 1861
Lizzie

I told Dante that I needed to rest and that he should spend his evening in the pleasure gardens with Hunt. I don't care if he sees Annie or his other wench, Fanny Cornforth, who replaced me, when I was at Hope Hall. Or Jane Burden. I was adamant about him leaving the flat so that Anna, Bessie, and Barbara could arrive.

"Are you well enough to sit for the session, Lizzie?" Anna inquired.

"Oh, yes, I must. I must see my May. I must learn the truth about why she left, and why she continues to haunt me."

We gathered our chairs in a circle around our dining table. I had swept it of Dante's paints and brushes and tidied the room so that there was little evidence of him. I didn't want May's spirit to be disturbed by his presence in any form.

Anna brought a candle from the mantle and placed it on the table. We held hands, as Anna called on May to manifest before us.

"Darling child, we know that you're here. Please show yourself, so that your mother can see your face. We shall not harm you. Your mother loves you and worries about you, because you remain here and have not ventured into the next plane of existence."

We felt a cool breeze and then saw, hovering over Anna's head, a sweet face, the face of my baby, my darling girl. It was only there for a second and then dissolved.

"Come back," I cried. "Oh, May, stay with us. I'm your mam."

Anna squeezed my hand. "Dear child, thank you for manifesting. We know that it takes significant effort to show yourself. Please stay close, so that your mother's heart can rest. We only want you to answer two questions. Why did you leave? And why do you remain here?"

Suddenly, Bessie started to write. She inscribed the words, "D.G.R. hated me. I stayed to protect Mother. He hurt Mother."

When Bessie read what May had written through her, I swooned, and Anna reached for the smelling salts. Suddenly, the candle blew out and we sat in darkness.

6 September 1861
Lizzie

The next morning, I set up my easel and painted what I had seen at the séance. My baby girl appeared angelic, like an intercessor, a guardian. I hadn't protected her, but now she seeks to protect me. I painted her with her arms surrounding me. She embraced me and I her. She is a real spirit and has not left our human world.

Every day I paint my darling girl, whom I see lurking in the shadows.

14 November 1862
Lizzie

Dante watches as I incessantly paint the image of our child. I paint her with light emanating from her head and hands, just the way I saw her. He stares at the image and just sits and watches me paint.

After a time, he says, "I know that you're sad and lonely. I am too."

I didn't say anything but continued to paint. For a moment I felt a brief flicker of love for him, but it was soon extinguished by my memory of his brutality towards me and of how my May knew that he despised her.

Dante and I act the roles of husband and wife, but we keep our distance. One evening after he returned from the pleasure garden, he climbed into my bed. We talked. He said that he was sorry that our child died. He wished that he could make up for her demise. He was sorry that he hadn't been ready to be a father. "I am now," he claimed.

"I wish that I could believe you."

"Lizzie, I'll do anything to make it up to you. Please, let me comfort you," Dante said. He seemed at the moment transformed. He seemed the old Dante, loving, tender. I was desperately lonely and after more coaxing, I let him comfort me. I so wanted a child to love that for once I acted as his wife and allowed him to come close. Even so, as we made love, I closed my eyes and thought of Christina.

15 December 1862
Lizzie

I carry another child, and this time I will protect her as her sister attempts to safeguard me. I feel May's presence most days, but sometimes she seems to have vanished. Perhaps she thinks that I no longer need protection. Perhaps she has found the next plane of existence. If that is what she needs, I will not begrudge her At least I have my paintings of her.

30 December 1862
Lizzie

Now that I am with child again, Dante seeks comfort elsewhere. I have tried to love him again, but I can never tell which Dante I am encountering. Is he the old Dante whom I adored or is he his shadow self, the one who injures me, neglects me, ignores me, because I wanted more than he could ever give me? Did his shadow kill the old Dante? I wanted his entire self, but I also wanted my own life and artistic career; I wanted to be as great an artist as he wished to be. And he can never replace Christina.

26 January 1862
Lizzie

Dante has purchased a songbird for me. He claims that taking care of the bird will give me purpose. He advises that I stop painting our dead child. How can he say that when he spent years painting me and trying to capture my likeness? I only saw my child's face briefly; her face still haunts my dreams, even though another child sleeps in my womb.

The songbird is lovely though. I have named her Gwen, like Guinevere. I shall try to love it and take care of it. It is an innocent thing, a holy thing, and does provide joy when my heart feels heavy.

28 January 1862
Lizzie

I have seen the lamplighter as he makes his rounds through town. He lights rows of lamps in succession, one after the other; the gas permeates the air and dispels the darkness, disclosing all the filthy secrets. The streetwalkers look gaudier than usual when the lamp's glow shines down on them. Their faces creased with lines, their makeup full of arsenic caked on and pooling in crevices around their slack mouths. Their patrons also can't hide in the alleys when the streetlamps are lit, because the light travels down the path that they've walked.

I know that Dante visits his favourite trollop. He has crept down the alley to her, but my lamplighter sees him and them as they wrap their legs about each other and become the beast with one back. I was his muse and his supposed great love, but once we were joined by law, made legitimate and sanctioned by society, he gave me up and returned to fat Fanny, his pornographic pinup, his substitute for me, but one who can never replace me as his ideal. And he denied me my true love, Christina. Then he continued to tell me that I was ill and that I needed my medicine, which he dosed me with liberally. He thought the medicine could serve as a substitute for love and genuine affection.

I have long wondered why he fell out of love with me. Was it because I would not submit? Because I wished to be his artistic equal? Because I desired to be independent of him? Because he thought me frail and ill even when my inner self glowed with light? Was it because I ended up having a greater affinity with Christina than I did with him? Or was it because I was not like the other women in our inner circle who were satisfied with being objects of art rather than creators of art? Even though he advocated for me with Ruskin and sold my work, was he threatened by my raw talent? I guess I will never know. I will leave him these questions though on this note that I will pin to my dress when the end-times come. He can grapple with all of that after he finds me lifeless and cold. His own heat and light will flow out of him, when he finally sees what he has done to me, not necessarily out of sheer malice, but out of benign neglect of my soul. I will end his life as he is ending mine.

30 January 1862
Lizzie

My debt is to memory and the scenes that they inspire. I remember when Dante first courted me. His jealousy of other painters' attentions. His delight in making me his muse. His attempts to make me laugh when Walter Deverell painted me.

I also remember the too-frequent rows, the way he believed that love is fraught with suffering, peril, and pain. I remember the reconciliations, the many times I loved him, the many times I loathed him.

What is the balance between the two? If I were to place both on a scale, which would win? Which would be heavier?

My debt is to memory. I recall how Christina reached out to me after I secretly wished to place an ad to find real love. Was that destiny? Would it have happened if I had not imagined placing the ad? I recall our eventual flight to the North, our country of women, our sisterhood, our sweeping out of the old lives fraught with pain, our rambles on and over the fells, our secret loving. I recall no rows, no jealousy, no injuries. There is nothing to weigh in these memories, for genuine love weighs nothing and does not produce a heavily burdened heart.

I will write to Christina once more and confess my undying love for her. Perhaps she will come to me and save me from my "destiny," the destiny that Dante plans for me.

2 February 1862
Lizzie

I posted my letter to Christina. I walked to the post office and handed my letter to the clerk. He asked me if I was all right.

"You look ill, madam. May I fetch you some help?"

"No, I only live around the corner. I promise that I will return to my bed as soon as I find home."

"Shall I escort you?"

"No, that's kind of you, but I have no need."

I held my head high, as I walked through the door, but, once outside, I grasped a fence railing and struggled to recall which way was home. Oh, yes, I thought, I must go back to the place where I am despised, the place that makes me ill. I know now where I stand with Dante, and there is nothing that I can do to remedy the situation. I wish that I could run away again but I haven't the strength.

4 February 1862
Lizzie

No word from Christina. I wonder if my missive was somehow intercepted.

I am alone, except for the child I carry within me.

5 February 1862
Lizzie

I pray for death, much like the woman I saw jump into the Thames. I grow weaker each day. I know that Dante has poisoned me, overdosed me over time. He gives me more laudanum each day, claiming that I need it to recover from the loss of our child and the conception of another. I am not stupid. This time he wants to rid himself of me *and* our child, so he can set up house with his Fanny. He wants to dispense with us, even after he insisted that I marry him and abandon Christina, who was far better to me than he ever was. She was my Sappho. *She* was *my* destiny.

I cannot pray for Dante, whom I will pursue even after I cease to breathe. He will never be completely rid of me. I shall visit him in his dreams, and he shall feel my presence in his bedroom as he mounts his fat Fanny. He shall be disturbed by his "Beatrice" for the remainder of his days. The heartless, selfish, self-serving man that he is. His mind and spirit will always be fraught with pain.

6 February 1862
Lizzie

It is obvious that, when I die, the doomed child that I carry, the poisoned child, Dante's child, will die with me. Unless of course Dante finds me struggling to breathe and he cuts me open with the knife that sleeps beneath his pillow to ward off intruders, gallant knight that he is. Our child would then be a Caesar. I plan to hide that knife though, because the child must go with me, for I fear dying alone and Dante cannot be trusted with the care of our child.

The other children, the one that I banished and one that Dante killed, I frequently seek now, through the help of the spiritualist Mr. D.D. Home, whom Anna introduced to me. I take the advice of Mr. Home, who has told me that when I die, I will meet my children, the one that I threw away when Dante first neglected my soul, the one that Dante killed, and the one whose hand I will hold when I leave this world.

8 February 1862
Lizzie

I found my bird, my Gwen, lifeless in her cage. I took her into the garden and dug up the hard ground and laid her to rest. She was a pretty, delicate thing, a holy thing, too good for this world.

12 February 1862
Christina

Oh, my darling Lizzie, I should have protected you as I promised and kept you from Gabriel, who never truly knew or loved you in the way that I did. I knew and loved the real Lizzie, not the myth and fabrication. I should have saved you.

Gabriel sent for William and me on the morning of 11 February. He didn't say why we were needed, but it became obvious when we arrived. I immediately saw that the mirror was turned toward the wall. My beautiful love lay inert on their bed. Just as she had in my nightmare, her eyes were still open, as if she were looking toward the heavens. The roses had left her cheeks; her chest was immobile. Her hands were folded, as if in prayer across her torso.

I screamed when I saw her and nearly collapsed. William carried me to a chair, as Gabriel looked on. He didn't rise but seemed to hang his head as if he were ashamed.

"What happened?" William queried. "How did she die? Did she kill herself? If so, we must hide the fact—"

"I returned from teaching last evening and found her unconscious," Gabriel said. "The full bottle of cordial that I purchased yesterday was empty. I had given her a dose before I left to calm her, because she was rather belligerent, accusing me of all sorts of dastardly deeds, including deliberately trying to kill her and her songbird. She had become rather unhinged, ever since the stillbirth."

"Did you seek help for her?" I cried as tears streamed down my face.

"Of course, I did, Christina. I immediately ran for help next door and Mr. Twickam, our neighbour, fetched a doctor who came and pumped her stomach. I ran for more help and found three other physicians who tried to rouse her. Lizzie vomited but never regained consciousness. And then she gasped one final time, and she was gone."

We sat in silence. I walked over to her corpse, took her hand in mine, and lifted it to my cheek. Her flesh was cold and hard; she felt like stone, and I struggled to breathe. I gently closed her eyes as I wept.

I turned toward Gabriel and shouted, "You did this to her! You should know that Lizzie had bad dreams about you, Gabriel. She dreamt that you killed her. Did you deliberately give her too much tonic?"

"God, no, Christina, why would I do that? She was my destiny, my love from ages past. Besides, she was carrying our child. How could you think that I would purposely harm my wife and child? Do you think me a fiend?"

I felt a twinge. This was the first that I had heard that Lizzie was once again pregnant. She wanted a child. She would never have killed the child and herself. She was no ordinary Ophelia. She wanted to live. She wanted to create art.

I must believe that she died of neglect. But perhaps there is more to it than that. Perhaps he wanted to rid himself of her as she feared. Even though he betrayed her and endlessly hurt her, I can't think that of my brother. If I did, it would destroy me. He may be a bit mad, but he's not a murderer, a fiend like Lizzie's childhood neighbour, who cut his beloved into tiny pieces.

I didn't answer him. I only know that I feel deep regret. I have lost my only love, and I can never bring her back. Despite what Lizzie believed, I am no saint, no Christ, with the powers of resurrection.

14 February 1862
Christina

The coroner has ruled her death an accident, which is fortunate, for she will not be buried as a suicide in unhallowed ground. And Gabriel has not been charged with murder, even though the authorities found a crumpled note in the bin that Lizzie wrote, claiming that Gabriel murdered her.

Even so, Gabriel exudes guilt. He remains in his room and cannot oversee Lizzie's burial, which falls to William and me. Gabriel does not see the irony in me having to bury my Lizzie; I saved her once from him but did not keep my promise to keep her safe.

Occasionally, he comes out of his room and cries crocodile tears, bellowing, "Lizzie, my love, where have you gone? Why have you forsaken me and left me alone? Come back to me!"

15 February 1862
Christina

We have arranged that Lizzie will be buried in the family plot at Highgate, above the father-in-law she never met. He would perhaps have liked her because she was what the men called a "stunner." I am glad though that she never had to meet the crocodile-man and *his* false tears.

I feel such grief but can't reveal my deepest feelings. Mother and William do not understand love between women, and thus I cannot talk with them about my loss. And Gabriel cannot be my confidant, even if he knows that Lizzie and I were in love.

I failed to sleep last night. All I could think of was seeing her corpse, her spirit fled. To begin to quell my pain, I wrote this poem.

> Her face was like an opening rose,
>   So bright to look upon;
> But now it is like fallen snows,
>   As cold, as dead, as wan.
> Heaven lit with stars is more like her
>   Than is this empty crust;
> Deaf, dumb and blind it cannot stir
>   But crumbles back to dust.
>
> No flower be taken from her bed
>   For me, no lock be shorn;
> I give her up, the early dead,
>   The dead, the newly born:
> If I remember her, no need
>   Of formal tokens set;
> Of hollow token lies, indeed,
>   No need if I forget.

16 February 1862
Christina

Yesterday afternoon, I approached her coffin. I touched her arm once more, which felt like petrified stone, and I thought of my poem where those who indulged in pleasure turned to stone. I was shocked to see that Gabriel had placed yellow poppies in her hands. Even though we orchestrated the service and burial, it seems that Gabriel still chooses to portray her as one of his models, not his wife. Why portray her in this way? Why reveal to all what some would believe to be her moral failure to maintain control over her health and well-being? To withstand the lure of the poppies?

I had met Lydia in Hastings but had never met Lizzie's mother. When I saw a woman with flaming red hair that cascaded to her knees, I knew that this woman was likely Lizzie's mother. She was an older replica of her. She seemed to wear her hair down in mourning for her lost daughter. Lydia and her mother had quietly slipped into the mourning room and both wept as they sat down among the bereaved. I watched Lydia stare at Gabriel, and I could see fire in her eyes. She approached the coffin and knelt before her sister. Then she reached into the coffin and grabbed the poppies from Lizzie's folded hands. She quickly walked toward Gabriel and threw the flowers in his face.

"What did you do to her? I thought that you would help her, heal her. I was right all along about you. I had warned Lizzie about you. But you made her marry you and then you killed her. Why didn't you leave her alone, you heartless bastard? She was happy without you," she proclaimed. She then looked at me and I felt myself grow red.

Gabriel didn't reply; he shut his eyes and ignored her truth-telling. I watched as Lydia took her mother's arm. They headed to the door, crushing the poppies as they walked away in silence.

17 February 1862
Christina

We are bewildered and stunned. Before the mortician closed the coffin, Gabriel walked over to it and slipped a bundle of paper under Lizzie's arm.

I ran up to him. "What are you doing? What did you put into the coffin?"

"My poems, the ones I wrote while Lizzie was ill. I have no need for these now. My heart is too shattered to ever publish my work," he replied. "They are better off buried with my dove. I wrote many of them when I should have been tending to her and her illness. Now they shall go with her to her grave. I also found her diary, full of insane scribblings. That too shall go to the grave with her, for they are foolish writings."

William too questioned Gabriel. "Are you mad? You are being rash. What good will they do Lizzie? She has no need for them. You'll regret your whimsy."

"I know what I'm doing," Gabriel retorted. "I must make some sort of atonement and sacrifice for my beloved. Unless I do, I will never be happy again."

I immediately thought of my *Maude*, which I know that Gabriel read. Was Gabriel hiding some secret in his bevy of poems? Was he burying her diary so no one would learn of our love? Was he ashamed of the lack of quality of the poems, which were about to be published? Were they better off in the grave? Would relinquishing his poems to the grave make him seem the ultimate romantic and thus bolster his reputation as a poet? His sacrifice, they will say, was so profound. He loved and worshipped her and entrusted her with his work. He was a humble, noble man, they'll say, in giving up so much for her.

I tried to remove Lizzie's diary from the casket, but Dante rushed toward me. He said that Lizzie's writings were ludicrous, the rantings of a mad woman, and that no one ought to read them. He motioned to the mortician who promptly closed and nailed the coffin shut.

19 October 2019
London

"He buried her diary," Bethany said, "so that no one would know that Christina and Lizzie were lovers and that Lizzie loved Christina more than him. I wonder how the family came upon it. How was it removed from the casket?"

"I don't see how we'll ever know, but maybe the answer is in Christina's diary. Now I'm beginning to believe that the family wished to uphold Dante's reputation, which they had carefully shaped after his death," Maggie said. "They wanted him to be known as a great painter, not as a paranoid man who buried his poems and his wife's diary in her coffin. They wanted to make sure that no one believed him to be a murderer or knew that Christina and Lizzie were in love."

"Yes, they wished to protect him, it seems. Beth, we should make a pilgrimage to Lizzie's grave. We need to see it, but before we do, we should try to find Hope Hall. It ought to be preserved for posterity," Maggie said.

They took the train home to Sheffield. Once on the train, they snuggled close to one another. They didn't speak but both thought about Lizzie and her vow to haunt Dante for the remainder of his life. Had she succeeded? They hoped so.

20 October 2019
Sheffield

Once in Sheffield, Maggie and Bethany inquired about the estate known as Hope Hall. They were surprised that no one had ever told them of it. The town historical society manager directed them to the outskirts of town but said that there was nothing to see. The place had fallen into ruins and during the war the remainder of it was bombed. Maggie thought it was as if the Nazi fascists themselves, without knowing it, wished to destroy a women's artistic community and a place where women loved one another.

Disheartened, Maggie and Bethany returned home.

"Well, love, Hope Hall may be gone, but we still have Christina's diary. Let's see what she wrote after Lizzie passed."

"After Lizzie was murdered, you mean," Maggie corrected.

4 March 1862
Christina

It's been two weeks since Lizzie passed, and Gabriel claims that Lizzie lives. He says that he sees her daily lying on their bed on which she died. He rushes to her and then she vanishes. He claims that she is playing tricks on him and plays a game of hide-n-seek. We tell him that he needs rest, but he says that he cannot sleep because he fears that, if he sleeps in their bed, he may accidentally crush her. Instead, he remains awake all night in the hopes of seeing her.

Ironically, William has procured some "Godfrey's Cordial" for Gabriel, who eagerly quaffs it.

9 March 1862
Christina

"Goblin Market," my poem about Lizzie and me and the way the goblins tempted us with their forbidden fruit, has now been published, even though Mr. Ruskin expressed distaste for it and its sensuality. I mourn the fact that Lizzie is not here to enjoy its success with me. She never completed her illustrations of it, so I reluctantly and regretfully had to turn to Gabriel, who took Lizzie's drawings and finished them. He did not remark about the sisters being wrapped in each other's arms. We never discussed the provenance of the poem or that it concerns Lizzie and me, rather than Maria, but Gabriel is smart enough to discern the truth. One sister resembles my Lizzie, and the other looks like me. I know he knows that Lizzie and I were lovers. He read her diary. I wonder if he continues to see me as his rival. He must know that I mourn more deeply than he does; I've only witnessed him crying his crocodile tears. But I don't let on about my grief in front of him. Instead, I do what I have always done. I write my poems to express the inexpressible. I travel to Highgate Cemetery daily and read my poems to my Lizzie, as I once did in person. I read the entirety of "Goblin Market" to her. I sense her presence and her pleasure. She is happy that I visit. I only wish that she had not relented to the goblin's temptation.

14 April 1862
Christina

Gabriel certainly seems to have rebounded from his supposed grief. He no longer wears widower garb, but I wear widow's weeds. He acts as though nothing has happened. He appears rather manic. He is producing many small paintings, often of his new muse, Miss Fanny Cornforth, his "housekeeper." She reminds me of Annie Miller, one of Gabriel's previous models, and is as far removed from Lizzie as she could be. She is completely unrefined, rather portly, and uncouth. She calls him "Mr. Rizetty" and Holman Hunt "Mr. 'olman 'unt." Gabriel claims that she's refreshing and amusing, and her visage has made him prosperous. He is so "prosperous" that he has somehow managed to purchase Tudor House, the former mansion of Catherine Parr, one of Henry VIII's wives, on Cheyne Walk, far west in Chelsea. He has invited Mother and me to live with him, but I have refused on the grounds of needing to be close to my church, to which I have returned. The real reason is that I feel much pain and rage whenever I'm around Gabriel. I now fear that he murdered Lizzie whether deliberately or accidentally. He gave her too much cordial and she died. And I do not wish to share a home with Miss Cornforth. Mother doesn't say it, but I think that she finds Fanny Cornforth as unappealing as I do. Mother never cared for Lizzie, but she agrees with me that Miss Cornforth lacks social grace, talent, and beauty. I wonder how Gabriel is attracted to her after having loved Lizzie, a born duchess as Ruskin's father believed. Lizzie was also a genius in several senses of the word, while Fanny Cornforth is an outright imbecile.

16 April 1862
Christina

When I collected Lizzie's belongings right after her burial, I retrieved the poems that she had written before Gabriel had a chance to dispense with them. They were hidden away in various nooks in their flat, some in dresser drawers, some in her small studio, some stuck into books, including her copy of *Aurora Leigh*. I explored every possible hiding place and then gathered them in a sheaf. I read all of them and I heard her voice sing as I read them. I intend to copy them and have them published alongside mine, just as I had hoped before she died. Our two voices will sing together. I so wish that I had fetched Lizzie's diary that Dante buried.

18 April 1862
Christina

Gabriel visited today and found me copying one of Lizzie's poems. He asked me how I came upon them, and I confessed that I had retrieved them from their flat after we buried her.

"What right do you have to them?" he asked in a huff.

"She was my sister in art; we were close."

"How close?"

"You know, Gabriel; why do you ask?"

"What you and Lizzie did was unnatural," he proclaimed.

"My love for her was as natural as your own. She loved me too, until you came along and destroyed everything."

"I saved her from you and your seduction of her. You're no longer the pious little nun you were. Now, let me see the poems, which are rightfully mine, since I was her husband, her partner in law." He grabbed the poem from my hand and quickly read it. "I remember this; it is far too sad and cannot be published."

"It's as sad as many of my own poems and you have found them to be worthy of publication. Why would you deny her voice to the public? Why would you deprive the world of knowing her genius? Are you afraid that your own genius would be found wanting? Are you worried that Lizzie is your rival in art or that the world will know how you treated her?"

He didn't reply, but instead walked toward the door. He turned towards me and said, "If you publish the poems, I will expose you and your sin. I will do this even though you are my sister. You have no right to my property;

you had no right to my love, my destiny. Besides, why should her poems get published when mine are in her coffin?"

4 May 1862
Christina

Gabriel and I have been at odds ever since that day in my study. We have not seen each other. I hear from William though that Gabriel claims that Lizzie still haunts him. He sees her everywhere in Tudor House. She sits in chairs or on the divan. He sees her painting on the veranda. She refuses to speak with him when he tries to talk with her. She looks disdainfully, he says, at Miss Cornforth, who also claims to have seen Lizzie watching them as Gabriel mounts her. Gabriel seeks a kind of exorcism of the house; he wonders why Lizzie is not at rest and why her ghost has migrated to Tudor House, why she won't leave him at peace. He has consulted with the spiritualists, the Misters Davenport who are experts at mesmerism, phrenology, and the like. They say that they can speak with the dead Mrs. Rossetti and will learn why she migrates from Highgate to Tudor House, what her aims are, and what will entice her to let go of this world and Mr. Rossetti in particular.

3 February 1863
Christina

Walking at night through solitary streets, I search for Lizzie. Gabriel thinks that she haunts his home, but I think that she haunts this place. She has left a mark and I can feel her presence and sometimes it comforts me. Often, it makes me even more melancholy, for I know that she is unhappy, and I wish that I could do something to soothe her spirit. I often wish that she would haunt me or visit me in my dreams. If only I could touch her once again, even though I'm not a saint, I could try to heal her. But that is impossible.

   I still go to Highgate daily, but I often visit the Tate Museum and gaze at her as Ophelia. I know that she thinks her own Ophelia thoughts, that she is not mad; I admire the way that Millais captured her serenity as she floats down the stream. I think about how we often talked about how our journey to Hope Hall was our attempt to find and retain our own new world or new Eden. Unfortunately, the Siddall legacy was never fully recovered by our habitation of Hope Hall. Good fortune did not last.

Even so, we should never have left that new world, that woman's world, that artist's studio, where we saved each other nightly. If we had remained, Gabriel may have left us alone and none of what followed would have happened. She wouldn't have become his victim; she wouldn't have married him; we would have remained intimate partners, sisters; she wouldn't have been ruined by his interference in our bond. She wouldn't have given birth to death. He wouldn't have killed her. She wouldn't continue to haunt him.

I sent Gabriel a letter and told him that if he holds a séance I wish to be there. I know that Lizzie believed in the supernatural and the Fourth Dimension where the spirits sometimes live. I wish to hear her voice.

He did not reply.

4 June 1863
Christina

William relays that Gabriel has started to paint Lizzie again. He says that he will memorialise her. Perhaps that will appease her restless spirit. I don't know why he thinks that when painting her never soothed her spirit when she was alive. He has saved every one of the drawings that he made of her and is glad because, even though he sees her daily, her face is now often a blur; he is beginning to forget what her countenance looks like. He confuses her with Dante's Beatrice. I find that ironic since he has always conflated her with Beatrice and himself with Dante. Even his *How They Met Themselves* does not resemble the authentic Lizzie and Gabriel, but rather mediaeval versions of themselves overlaid with a sense of the inferno. Sometimes when he paints his memorial to her, he says that he finds the painting disrupted, the paint smeared, and he must begin again. He knows that Lizzie tries to interfere with his painting, which she is trying to escape. He says that he will call the painting, *Beata Beatrix*, "Blessed Beatrice." Perhaps the completed painting will eventually satisfy her, and she will leave him alone. Or so he hopes.

Gabriel told William that he found a partially melted wax figure placed on his bed. He attempted to destroy it by burning it or trying to break it into pieces by stomping on it, but it appears invulnerable.

3 January 1864
Christina

I have returned from Tudor House after attending the spiritualist session, the séance orchestrated and supervised by the mediums, the Misters Davenport. Gabriel refused to speak to me when I entered, but he did not bar my entry. Perhaps he is softening toward me, but I feel such hatred and animosity toward him. I know that he is troubled, and I wish that I could forgive him for what he did to her. I visit Christ Church often and pray about my resentment of my brother, but so far, I have not been able to let go of my tortured feelings. I feel certain that he is as guilty as the king in the Scottish play. I'm certain that Gabriel killed Lizzie and their child; it may have been an accident, but it was clear that he felt her to be a burden and the child as well. To him, she was an invalid, and he did not want to be saddled with her for the remainder of his life. He preferred fat Fanny to lithesome Lizzie.

All of this was on my mind, as the candles were lit and we made our way to the grand dining table around which we sat; everyone who knew Lizzie was there: The Browns, Holman Hunt, Millais and Effie, Jane Burden and Morris, Burne-Jones and his Georgiana, William, Gabriel, and me. Even Miss Cornforth sat at the table with us, and we joined hands; Miss Cornforth insisted on sitting next to Gabriel, and I could see that she entwined her fingers with his.

Mr. Edwin Davenport was the medium and his brother Frederick supervised the spirit guide that was kept inside a large, locked box. Mr. Davenport asked for silence, and he started to hum as he fell into a deep trance. Suddenly, his voice changed into that of a young girl. He asked, "Are you with us, Mrs. Elizabeth Rossetti. Do you wish to come forward and appear to us?"

We heard a loud rap, and the table trembled. Miss Cornforth grabbed Gabriel's shoulder and said, "What's 'appening?"

"Be still, Fanny," he replied as he removed her hand from his shoulder.

Then the shutters rattled just as the large box shook. A white mist started pouring out of the box and hovered over our heads.

"Are you here? Can we see you? Please, if you wish to show yourself, rap once for yes, two for no."

I felt the table thump twice.

"All right. Are you unhappy with someone in this room? Is this why you remain bound to the earth?"

Suddenly, Gabriel cried out, "Lizzie, why do you torment me? Please I need to move on, to be left alone. I am painting you so that you will always be remembered as my guide on this earth, my destiny, my Beatrice! You will be immortal. Isn't that enough?"

I heard her voice. It was unmistakable. She said, "You never loved *me*. First you ravaged me and then you poisoned me with your forbidden fruit. You poisoned our child, our children. You only loved Beatrice. I am not Beatrice. I am Lizzie but if you want me to act like Beatrice, I will gladly lead you through hell."

The wind gusted; the candle blew out. Gabriel cried out and rushed from the room. Miss Cornforth collapsed.

2 February 1865
Christina

Doctors have attended to Gabriel, who rants about how Lizzie follows him everywhere. He sees her as he paints his Blessed Beatrice, and she mocks his effort. She continues to thwart his painting. She attempts to erase herself and escape from the painting. He hears her voice reciting her poems, especially the one that warned of a "living death." He says that it now refers to his own.

The doctors have prescribed rest and a change in scene. They have told William that if Gabriel doesn't recover soon, they may need to admit him to an asylum because they fear that he may harm himself or someone else. They give him inordinate amounts of laudanum, and sometimes he looks to be in a trance, a kind of living death.

William escorted Gabriel to the sea, to Hastings, but, according to William, that was a poor choice on his part. There was too much there that reminded Gabriel of Lizzie and when they visited St. Clement's Church to bestow on the vicar one of Gabriel's paintings, his painting of me as the Virgin in the *Annunciation* to commemorate the time we all spent in Hastings, and particularly his marriage to Lizzie in the church. I wonder why he gave the church his painting of me as the Virgin and not one of Lizzie as his Beatrice, which seems more fitting, since in marrying Lizzie he seemed to have wanted to join himself to Beatrice and not Lizzie.

Gabriel said that he saw Lizzie sneaking around in the sacristy, hiding behind the sarcophagus of a noble woman. Clearly, Lizzie is keeping her promise to never leave him at peace. Unlike him, she keeps her word.

3 March 1865
Christina

Because of his continuing mental affliction, the physicians have prescribed a rest cure at a private asylum; ironically, he's not allowed to write poetry or paint. Luckily, he will not be housed in Bedlam. I went to see him at the asylum and was appalled by the conditions; the place may be private, but the conditions are no better than those experienced by the afflicted at Bedlam. As at Bedlam, there are men and women in chains; many cry out continuously. Some are even in cages. I feared that I would find Gabriel in one, but luckily, he is housed in a separate cell. He sits and does nothing. He cannot talk. The doctors say he's in a state of catatonia. I sat with him in silence. He acted as though he didn't know who I was. Perhaps the medicine that they give him makes him forget all, even his relatives. Perhaps it will make him forget Lizzie, so even if she continues to haunt him, he will not recognize her.

7 June 1866
Christina

After lengthy treatment, Gabriel has been released and the doctors proclaim him cured. He has gone to stay with Morris and Jane Burden. who say that they will watch over him at Kelmscott Manor in Oxfordshire. I saw him briefly before he travelled, and he did seem his old self. He was animated and jovial. I didn't speak to him of his troubles or of Lizzie. As a Christian, I'm trying to forgive him, but it seems an impossible task.

9 August 1866
Christina

William has just returned from Kelmscott, where he says that Gabriel and Morris are designing furniture and home décor in a mediaeval style. William reports that Gabriel continues to experience good health. No one speaks to him about Lizzie, but recently Gabriel began speaking of her again, when he discussed writing poetry once more. He says that Lizzie no longer haunts him. William overheard Gabriel talking with Morris, lamenting the fact that he had buried his poetry with Lizzie and wondered if there was any way to retrieve it.

Morris said to Gabriel, "Are you mad? Sorry, but it seems ill advised to disturb the dead. Is that really a good idea? Is that even legal?"

"They are my poems," Gabriel said. "Not hers. Of course, if I do fetch them, no one must know."

William fears that once again Gabriel exhibits signs of madness, of mania, of wild thinking and feeling. Would he dare profane and rob her grave, disinter her? The entire thing is absurd, and William assures me that he will not allow Gabriel to disturb Lizzie now that she seems to have finally settled peacefully into death.

2 March 1867
Christina

Gabriel refused to listen to William. He has done the unimaginable, the unthinkable, an unholy act. He has once again violated her. He has robbed her grave, as if she were a criminal, a thief who stole his beloved poems. Now he is a thief; he has defiled a sacred space. I must go to him and express my outrage. He will pay a price for this. I don't know what that price is, but it will manifest itself.

3 March 1867
Christina

Gabriel once again resides at Tudor House, from which I have returned. I confronted Gabriel in his studio. He was working on a painting of Janey Morris, his new muse. He is painting *her* as Guinevere. He became quite defensive as soon as I asked him about his grave-robbing.

He said, "*I* didn't rob the grave. Don't be ridiculous, Christina. I merely had some workmen retrieve my poems. They are mine and I need them. I made a mistake in giving the poems to the dead Lizzie."

"What you did was wrong! How dare you disturb her grave, dig her up. She was at peace."

"But I wasn't, Christina. I needed those poems. They were my only copies. I have a use for them. I intend to publish them as I should have years ago. Besides, they had nothing to do with Lizzie. None were dedicated to nor written about her. And, knowing her in ways that you never could, I know that art was the only thing for which she felt and took seriously. Had it been possible for her after she was buried, I should have found the poems on my pillow. She would have opened her grave herself."

I looked at him in disbelief. "You are mad, Gabriel. Lizzie would not have defiled her own grave for you. That's ludicrous. And after she died, you said that your poetry writing led to your neglect of Lizzie. Don't you think that's still true?"

"No, I don't. She was ill and there was nothing that I could do for her but give her the cordial. It calmed her madness. It made her better."

"Gabriel, it killed her, and you know it. You gave her too much."

"Indeed not, I ladled out just the amount the doctor prescribed. She's the one who imbibed the entire bottle."

He barely looked up from his rendering of Jane, which he was painting from a photograph. He seemed to want to move on and tried to change the subject.

"How do you like my painting? Janey is quite the stunner, don't you think?"

"Don't avoid the subject. Did you seek anyone's permission?"

"Permission for what?"

"To dig her up!"

"Oh, you mean fetching my poems. Yes, of course I did, a solicitor who oversees Highgate gave permission with the express understanding that I would not disturb Lizzie, only retrieve the poems. I watched as the workmen dug her up. You'll be pleased to know that after all these years, she looked the same. As stunning as always. Her hair filled her coffin. She looked perfect and had not decomposed in the least; she looked rather like a saint really. She did not seem in the least distressed by the exhumation."

"You are quite mad, Gabriel. Of course, she was disturbed. She will likely let you know in due course what you have done to her. She was finally at peace, and you disturbed her sleep," I replied.

"When will you let go of her, Christina? I have. I have moved on. She has too. Perhaps she will haunt someone else, not me."

"Gabriel, you are selfish and amoral, but I guess that you always have been; I guess that I should have realised that you were just like Father," I said as I fled his studio. He didn't even look up but continued to paint his new stunner.

William reports that the poems were putrid. They needed to be disinfected and even then, they reeked of death. Gabriel's favourite poem, "Jenny," had a worm hole eaten right through the middle. Gabriel must have lied about the condition that the graverobbers found Lizzie in, if the poems had been eaten. Even in death, Gabriel feeds on Lizzie.

I was surprised when William handed me Lizzie's diary, which one of the graverobbers fetched from the grave per William's order without Dante knowing. "I think she would want you to have this."

"Have you read it?" I asked.

"Yes, it's as if you two were sisters, but more than that. I know that you loved her."

"How did you know?" I asked.

"I saw the tender way you looked at her and she at you," he replied.

I gladly accepted Lizzie's diary. I read the remainder when she wrote about her life with my brother, her rape (she had not willingly given herself to him!), her dead child . . . his poisoning of her. I placed it in my own dusty chest, where I keep my own diary and all of my writing. I collated and arranged our diaries, so they are chronologically continuous. I no longer wish for my writing, our writing, to be buried. I wish for our love and our art, the beauty that we gazed on together, to be known. I wish for our joint musings to be published along with our poems.

8 September 1868
Christina

Gabriel has published his poems, dedicated to his new love, Janey Morris. But he has not achieved the acclaim that he hoped for. The critics find them wanting. Robert Buchanan wrote that they are examples of "the fleshly school of poetry." Gabriel is despondent. Now he regrets exhuming the poems and believes that Lizzie seeks revenge and that his destiny bodes ill. He told me that he, like Feste singing to Orsino in *Twelfth Night*, is "slain by a fair, cruel maid."

She does not slay him, but she does not leave him at peace. As I predicted, Lizzie has returned to haunt Tudor House. Because of the constant torment and the return of her nightly visitations, he once again seeks the help of spiritualists and has even tried an exorcism, but the priest who spoke the incantations said that the spirit is angry and intransigent. She refuses to depart.

Gabriel says that he will seek another priest, one more expert at exorcisms. How odd that Gabriel the disbeliever now seeks help from God. I do believe that he is beyond help. Gabriel himself needs to be exorcised, not the house in which he resides. I doubt that even Christ Jesus himself could cast out the devil that took possession of his soul long ago. Gabriel is truly mad once again. Just like his dear papa.

8 July 1869
Christina

Gabriel now claims that he hears the voices of his dead children. When he paints his *Blessed Beatrice* to placate Lizzie, he hears children whimpering, crying in another room. He goes to investigate but finds no one. William relates that Fanny Cornforth tries to comfort Gabriel, but he pushes her away.

"Leave me alone, Fanny. I must make it up to Lizzie, then perhaps the children will be consoled." He told William that he will complete his painting, and it will be his masterpiece. "She will know that I forgive her for haunting me and that I still care for her. I will transform her from sinner to saint. I've put all of myself into this painting. I give myself to her in this painting. I share my soul with her, as I truly make her Beatrice."

10 February 1870
Christina

Gabriel has completed *Blessed Beatrice*; he has finally painted his masterpiece on the anniversary of Lizzie's death. At the moment that he brushed his last stroke, he heard her voice, "What has thou done to me?"

1 November 2019
London, Highgate Cemetery

Maggie and Bethany joined the tour group that visited the "celebrity" graves in Highgate Cemetery. Karl Marx, George Eliot, and Michael Faraday were among those "celebrities," but most visitors wanted to learn about Elizabeth Siddal, who was now known in Britain, as Agatha had earlier remarked, as the first supermodel.

Maggie and Bethany listened to the inane questions that some of the visitors asked. "Is it true that Dante Rossetti propped her up after she died and painted her as his Blessed Beatrice?" one man asked. "I would have liked to have seen that."

"Certainly not; Mr. Rossetti would never have abused her in that way," the tour guide replied as she shook her head in disbelief.

"Well, I read that he dug her up himself," a woman said. "Just so's he could fetch some poems that he wrote. He even said that he thought Miss Siddal would've opened her grave herself and given him the poems, if she had the ability. While fetching the poems, he cut her long red hair, which filled the coffin, and kept it in a pillow that he slept on. I heard that pillow lays under his head in his coffin. Part of her went with him to his grave."

Maggie and Bethany stopped listening to all of the outlandish rumours and they waited for the group to move along. They stood over the Rossetti family plot and read the names: Gabriele 1783-1854; Frances 1800-1886; William 1829-1919; Christina 1830-1894; Elizabeth Siddal 1829-1862.

Someone had recently placed poppies on Elizabeth's grave. The "supermodel," who was really an artist, still had fans.

"What, no Dante?" Maggie asked.

"He wanted to be cremated but he's buried at All Saints Church in Birchington-on-Sea; I wonder why," Bethany replied. "Perhaps, after he disinterred Lizzie, the family thought it unjust for him to be buried next to her and the rest of the family?"

"Or maybe he came to realise that she would never forgive him for what he had done to her," Maggie said mournfully. "He must have because she exacted her vengeance. Maybe he didn't wish to be close to her in death."

"Agatha would be happy to know that Lizzie haunted Dante for the remainder of his life. She *was* Beatrice leading Dante through hell. Good for her. I'm quite glad that Dante is not sleeping next to Lizzie. And it is wonderful to see that Christina and Lizzie are finally eternally lying together. And that we know that Christina wants the world to read their diaries and their poems. We must carry out her desires."

"Of course, we'll publish them just as Christina wanted. And, yes, what matters most is that Christina and Lizzie are together," Bethany said, as she took Maggie's hand, "as I hope we will be one day." She paused. "Maggie, Christina and Lizzie have taught me much. I learned that you should follow your bliss. This is what I've learned from our fellow sister artists. Women artists must make art. Besides writing my scholarship, I may even return to writing poems, odes to my love. And perhaps Agatha is already busy writing her mystery novel. I hope she makes Dante the villain that he was."

"There's no doubt about that," Maggie replied. Then, acting more like a Frenchwoman than an English one, Maggie gathered Bethany into her arms and held her tightly, realising that they still had an affinity for one another. Hope and love had been restored just as Lizzie and Christina wished for all women artists.

Then, the two women artists sat on Lizzie's grave and read Christina's final entry.

10 February 1871
Christina

Lizzie does not haunt me, although I wish she did, so that I could see her once more, but I can never forget her, as Gabriel has tried but failed to do. As I've expressed, she was my destiny and her life, our life, was cut short by my brother, who tried to break the bond that we had forged. I continue to wear widow's weeds, while Dante wears gaudy colours that Fanny, his housekeeper, procures for him. He looks like the clown in Deverell's painting.

I still hold tight to Lizzie, as I think about her daily, and consider how much more she had to give the world, both in her art and her poetry. Her gifts were profound, and we will never know the full extent of her talents. What she left behind though is testament to the way women artists courageously pick up their pens and their brushes and create themselves, their better selves.

Recently, I returned to Hastings and buried Lizzie's portrait of her Lady and me, her Guinevere, in the crypt of the church where she and Gabriel were married and where I first prayed and dreamed of loving her. After Gabriel blotted me out of Lizzie's painting, I painted myself back in. I also compiled my diaries along with Lizzie's and have directed William to see that they are published after my death. We read each other's diaries each night until Gabriel took her away from me. We knew each other's intimate thoughts, our struggle and longing to make art and to make ourselves through our art. Because of this and because of our sisterhood and love, we did not go mad as our society intended for us.

Afterwards, I returned to Hope Hall. I intend to make it my home. Perhaps my own hope can be revived here in this place where my sisters and I made our art. Perhaps I will convince Anna, Bessie, and Barbara to return to this, our spiritual home. Perhaps Briony and Belinda will once again be our students and we will, at last, found a women's art school.

I was shaken when I saw Hope Hall though, for it had now fallen into complete ruin with windows broken and the exterior crumbling, as if it were about to collapse into itself. Once more, the vines covered the doorway. I looked through the window to the hearth where we often sat in the evening. Now, I saw mice scurrying across the floor. I turned around and watched as deer vanished into the wood and I followed behind them, hurrying to the rock where Lizzie and I sat near the waterfall. I expected to find Lizzie there, but the rock was barren. I climbed onto it and sat where we last gazed at beauty together. While perched on the rock, I wrote my final poem about her. Unfortunately, once again, my subject is death, but this time the death of my Beloved. I hope that someday I will join her, and we shall once more gaze together at beauty.

"Gone Before"

She was most like a rose, when it flushes rarest;
  She was most like a lily, when it blows fairest;
She was most like a violet, sweetest on the bank:
Now she's only like the snow cold and blank
        After the sun sank.

She left us in the early days, she would not linger
For orange blossoms in her hair, or ring on finger:
  Did she deem windy grass more good than these?
Now the turf that's between us and the hedging trees
        Might as well be seas.

  I had trained a branch she shelters not under,
  I had reared a flower she snapped asunder:
  In the bush and on the stately bough
Birds sing: she who watched them track the plough
        Cannot hear them now.

  Every bird has a nest hidden somewhere
  For itself and its mate and joys that come there,
  Tho' it soar to the clouds, finding there its rest:
You sang in the height, but no more with eager breast
        Stoop to your own nest.

  If I could win you back from heaven-gate lofty,
  Perhaps you would but grieve returning softly:
Surely they would miss you in the blessed throng,
  Miss your sweet voice in their sweetest song,
        Reckon time too long.

Earth is not good enough for you, my sweet, my sweetest;
Life on earth seemed long to you tho' to me fleetest.
I would not wish you back if a wish would do:
  Only love I long for heaven with you
        Heart-pierced thro' and thro'.

After I wrote the poem, I went back to the house and pulled down the vines. I yanked open the door and entered. Then I thought I heard an interior door creak open. I glimpsed Lizzie standing in her nightgown with candle in hand. I walked toward her, closing the door and the world behind me.

Author's Postscript

In 2006, I had the pleasure of teaching in a study abroad program in Oxford and while there I traveled to Hastings to visit the 1066 battlefield and to spend time at the sea. Standing on the beach, I spotted an old church on a hill and decided to visit it. At the door, I met a woman who told me that she had just locked the church, but, if I cared to visit briefly, she would let me in. Once inside, I was thrilled to see a Dante Rossetti painting on the wall, and I asked why the church exhibited one of his paintings. To my surprise, the caretaker told me that Lizzie Siddal and Dante Rossetti had been married in this church, St. Clements, in 1860. Thus, began my fascination with their marriage and what I would soon learn was a torrid relationship.

As a scholar and teacher, I was fascinated by the Pre-Raphaelite Brotherhood and their exquisite work, but then also became intrigued by the extraordinary work of what is now termed the Pre-Raphaelite Sisterhood and Lizzie Siddal's and Christina Rossetti's parallel lives and longings. While writing *Women Writing the Neo-Victorian Novel: "Erotic" Victorians* (Palgrave Macmillan 2020), I researched this Sisterhood, especially in terms of the ways in which Victorian women artists were prevented from fully developing themselves as artists. And as a professor teaching a course called "The Victorian Age," my students and I were also always struck by the erotic nature of Christina Rossetti's "Goblin Market," and I began to imagine Lizzie as the subject of that tantalizing poem. Thus, this novel was conceived and eventually born. Overall, it is dedicated to women artists everywhere who pick up their pens and paints and create their better selves through art.

Acknowledgements

Writing is a solitary activity, but it takes many people to bring a book to print. First, I must sincerely thank Bedazzled Ink Publishing, especially Elizabeth Gibson and CA Casey, who made it possible for me to share this novel with you. Bedazzled Ink publishes work by women about women, so this is the perfect press for this novel. I also express sincere and heartfelt thanks to my Iowa City friends who read and commented on numerous drafts of this work: Mary Helen Stefaniak, Mary Vermillion, Anne Zerkel, Kris Vervaecke, Eileen Bartos, Marjorie Carlson Davis, Marianne Jones, and David Duer. All of them helped guide the development of the novel while offering generous encouragement.

I read and consulted many sources, including several scholarly books by Jan Marsh: *Christina Rossetti: A Writer's Life, Dante Rossetti: Painter and Poet, The Legend of Elizabeth Siddal, Pre-Raphaelite Sisterhood,* and *Pre-Raphaelite Sisters*. I also read and consulted Christina Rossetti's *Complete Poems,* Dinah Roe's *The Rossettis in Wonderland: A Victorian Family History,* Jeremy Green's play *Lizzie Siddal,* Elizabeth Eleanor Siddal's *My Lady's Soul: The Poems of Elizabeth Eleanor Siddal,* and Lucinda Hawksley's *Lizzie Siddal: The Tragedy of a Pre-Raphaelite Supermodel*.

It is my hope that the reader's interest will be piqued and that they will investigate and marvel at the extraordinary artistry of the Pre-Raphaelite Sisterhood as well as that of the Brotherhood.

Kathleen Williams Renk taught British and Women's literature for nearly three decades in the U.S. and abroad. Her scholarly books include *Caribbean Shadows and Victorian Ghosts: Women's Writing and Decolonization* (Univ. Press of Virginia, 1999), *Magic, Science, and Empire in Postcolonial Literature: The Alchemical Literary Imagination* (Routledge, 2012), and *Women Writing the Neo-Victorian Novel: Erotic "Victorians"* (Palgrave Macmillan, 2020). While earning her Ph.D. in English at the University of Iowa, Williams Renk studied fiction writing with James Alan MacPherson. Her short fiction, creative nonfiction, and poetry have appeared in *Iowa City Magazine, Literary Yard, Page and Spine, CC & D Magazine*, and *the Scarlet Review*. In November 2020, Cuidono Press (Brooklyn) published her debut novel, *Vindicated: A Life of Mary Shelley*. *Vindicated* won Story Circle Network's 2021 May Sarton Award in Historical Fiction; it was also a finalist for the CIBA Goethe Award and was longlisted for the Chautauqua Literary Prize.

In her spare time, Williams Renk plays violin and guitar. She also loves to hike on the Front Range in Colorado where she lives.

Visit Kathleen's website: http://www.kathleenrenk.com

Printed in the USA
CPSIA information can be obtained
at www.ICGtesting.com
JSHW020219141123
52003JS00004B/15